SE7EN DEADLY SEALS

SEASON 1

ALANA ALBERTSON

Se7en Deadly SEALs
Season One
Copyright © 2017 by Alana Albertson
Cover Designer: Regina Wamba of Mae I Design
(https://www.facebook.com/MaeIDesignandPhotography)
Cover Models: Callan Newton and Dani Cooper
Interior design and formatting by JT Formatting (http://www.facebook.com/JTFormatting)

"EVERY JUDGEMENT OF
CONSCIENCE, BE IT RIGHT
OR WRONG, BE IT ABOUT
THINGS EVIL IN THEMSELVES
OR MORALLY INDIFFERENT,
IS OBLIGATORY, IN SUCH WISE
THAT HE WHO ACTS AGAINST
HIS CONSCIENCE ALWAYS SINS."

— THOMAS AQUINAS

PART I

CONCEIT

SE7EN DEADLY SEALS EPISODE 1

"IT WAS PRIDE THAT CHANGED
ANGELS INTO DEVILS;
IT IS HUMILITY THAT MAKES
MEN AS ANGELS.".

— SAINT AUGUSTINE

1

MIA

THE PRISON GUARD LED ME down the hall to the waiting room. A pregnant girl cowered in the corner, an older couple embraced each other, and a pale, skinny woman bit her nails as a young boy fidgeted in her lap. The rancid smell of vomit loosely masked with bleach made me gag. This scene was so pathetic. We were all here to see our loved ones incarcerated in this hellhole.

"Your boyfriend will be out in ten minutes," the guard sneered, his eyes undressing me.

"He's not my boyfriend. He's my brother. And he's innocent."

The guard laughed and wiped the beads of sweat from his forehead. "Sure, he is, sweetheart. Never met a guilty one."

Jerk. That guard wasn't fit to polish Joaquín's boots.

After an agonizing wait, the prisoners stumbled out into their partitioned section of the room. My brother came last. All my girlfriends were in love with Joaquín—who could blame them? Even in this pit of despair, he still looked like the ultimate alpha male. His muscles bulged in his orange prison jumpsuit, the elbow-length sleeves barely covering his tattoos.

At least I didn't have to worry about anyone screwing with him in jail; he was trained to kill a man with his bare hands. Joaquín had everything going for him. Until he was charged with a crime he didn't commit. I knew my brother, and he simply couldn't be guilty of what he was accused of doing.

Joaquín was an easy target—a poor Mexican-American orphan with no trust fund, no senator endorsements, and no college education. But my brother had integrity, loyalty, and honor. He would never disgrace his Teammates, betray his country, or destroy his brotherhood. And he could never hurt a woman.

He tapped on the glass, and we both reached for the phone. "Thanks for flying down, Mia. Are you okay?"

I threw my free hand in the air. "Yeah, I'm okay. I'm not the one in jail facing the death penalty for murder. I took the first flight I could get. What the hell happened?"

The man on the other side of the glass wasn't the brother I'd grown to respect and adore. He was still strong, still resolute, and seemingly impenetrable. But his eyes ... I looked right into his eyes. Though his long dark lashes covered his pain, I knew him too well. To anyone else, he would seem formidable, but to his baby sister he looked broken, torn.

"I didn't kill her. I can't talk about what happened in here." His eyebrows motioned toward the cameras in the corner of the room. "But you have to believe me."

I swallowed. I'd watched the incessant news coverage. It didn't look good. Two weeks ago, one of Joaquín's commanding officers, Paul Thompson, had thrown a huge party for his SEAL Team at his in-laws' oceanfront home in Encinitas. Witnesses interviewed by the police said they heard loud music and saw women coming in and out of the place. Guess the neighbors weren't exactly going to call the cops on a group of SEALs.

In the early hours of the morning after the party, Joaquín had discovered a lifeless stripper named Tiffany in his bed. He called 911, and the paramedics determined that she'd been dead for hours. Joaquín told detectives that he'd slept with her the night before, but that she had been fine when he fell asleep. The police didn't charge him immediately and waited for the autopsy results. Two days ago, the coroner ruled that she'd died from asphyxiation and had the date rape drug Rohypnol in her system. Since Joaquín had admitted to having sex with her, he had been arrested and charged with her murder.

He already said he didn't kill her. He would never lie to me, and we kept no secrets from each other. Well … we never used to. I held my own deep secret close, never wanting to add any burden to Joaquín's intense life.

"Can't anyone clear you? Are the other guys in the Team trying to help or did they desert you? What about Grant …" My voice trailed off.

My ex-boyfriend Grant Carrion, Joaquín's swim buddy in BUD/S, had been there that night. And I knew the rest of the guys on their Team pretty well. After our parents had died, Joaquín had become my legal guardian, and I'd moved to San Diego to finish my senior year in high school. I met Grant right before I graduated, and we started dating at the beginning of my freshman year at San Diego State. I'd transferred to San Francisco State as a junior two years ago because it had the best drama department. Well, that was the official excuse for me fleeing—I could've finished school in San Diego. The reality was much more painful. Too painful for me to think about, let alone deal with.

Joaquín pursed his lips; his eyes leveled me. "Leave Grant out of this. I'm not going to ruin his career, too. I slept with Tiffany, but I didn't drug her. None of the guys are talking to me right now, probably under orders from the command. Our Team doesn't need this publicity, especially with all the rumors going around about Pat saving Annie from that brothel. My brothers don't have a choice but to obey. My lawyer thinks I should take a plea. If it's the best for the Team, then I will."

I seethed. The public should still be happy that Joaquín's Team just saved a group of USO cheerleaders who had been taken as hostages in Afghanistan. I didn't even know what to say about the Pat and Annie mess, except that I wasn't buying the Team's cover story. "Take a plea? Have you lost your mind? You're gonna confess to murder because that's best for your Team? Who cares about your damn Team—can't you be selfish for once in your life?" I knew the bonds of these SEALs ran deep; they'd kill for each other; they'd die for each other. I couldn't fathom the pain Joaquín had to be going through, but pleading guilty to a murder he didn't commit was insane.

He blinked hard, too hard, as if he was trying to stop tears from escaping. "You don't understand. You never could. I'm not going to ruin the rest of the guys' lives and tarnish our Team's reputation further. It's complicated, and I really can't talk about it."

I didn't want to hear about his Team loyalty. "Who's your lawyer? Is he any good?"

"Daniel Reed. He's a former Team guy."

Sure he was—the world's most exclusive fraternity. Even when these guys left the service, they only hired their own. "What did he say about bail? I'll find a way to raise money."

"We won't know until the arraignment, but he thinks the judge will probably make an example of me. No bail."

"But you're a SEAL."

"Exactly. No playing favorites."

From his posture, the edge in his voice, I knew I was treading on his patience. I needed to garner any information I could before he cut me off. "What's the last thing you remember? The girl, did she pass out?"

His nostrils flared, and he bared his teeth. "Knock it off, Mia."

Whoa. He never raised his voice to me. There was no use arguing with him. Joaquín was a stubborn Taurus—I'd never win. I bit my lip and tried another approach. "You can't tell me anything about that night? Who was the dead girl? Were you dating her?"

"No. I'd never met her before." Joaquín shrugged. He wasn't really a relationship guy. A complete player, he claimed no one could ever be faithful to a SEAL, which was bullshit. I'd never even looked at another man when I was with Grant. I still hadn't, even though we'd been broken up for what felt like forever.

"Who invited her?"

His tone became more agitated. "One of the Team guys invited a bunch of strippers."

Yeah, I'll bet. Strippers and SEALs went together like rum and cola. At least Joaquín wasn't a cheater. I couldn't count the number of times wasted SEALs had called Grant to be picked up from Panthers, the local sleazy strip club. Grant would drag me along, and then his buddies would beg him to act as an alibi to give to their wives. We used to fight about him covering for the philanderers all the time. I had to make small talk with their wives at the family barbecues, knowing that their husbands had their dicks sucked by strippers the night before. Grant always told me to stay out of it—it was their marriages and not our place to get involved. I argued that we were involved because covering for them made Grant an accessory to their infidelities. At least Grant never went to the strip clubs; he swore it wasn't his thing.

I tried to stop myself, but I had to know. "Which guy asked the strippers to the party? Mitch?"

He let out a growl. "One more word, and I'll drop this phone and walk back into my cell."

My gaze darted around the room. I was grateful that this crime had been committed off the naval base so at least he wasn't stuck in the brig. Under a civilian justice system, I could find him the best lawyers. I'd do whatever it took. "I'll get you out of here. I'll find out the truth."

He laughed, and although it was nice to see him smile, I knew he didn't have a shred of faith that I could help him. "How are you going to do that, Mia? You're a theater student. We're talking about a bunch of Team guys."

I preferred the term "highly trained actor," but I wasn't about to correct him. Plus, who was he trying to protect anyway? Did he suspect one of his Teammates? Did he know who killed the girl? "I know. I'm just trying to help." But my mind started racing. Why *not* me? Joaquín was my brother—the same blood ran through our veins, the same dedication, the same stubbornness. Just because I lacked testosterone didn't mean I was any less capable than he was.

He studied me. "I know that look. Don't get involved, Mia. That's a fucking order. I didn't drug or kill Tiffany, which means someone else did. I don't have a clue who, and I can't protect you from in here."

I cringed when I noticed that his hands were shaking. This was real, not some fucked-up nightmare. "I can protect myself." He'd always protected me, been my savior. It would kill him if he knew what had happened to me years ago. But it wasn't his fault. He and Grant had both been deployed, and there was nothing either of them could've done to save me that night. Telling them the truth would accomplish nothing.

"No, I need you to trust me on this." His voice firmed. "I'll be fine. Don't worry about me." He was proud, pigheaded, and I knew he didn't want me to see him defenseless. Just like Grant. These macho SEALs never allowed themselves to be truly vulnerable, not to their families, and most certainly not to their women. Though I completely understood—I was too proud to admit my own weaknesses.

He focused on me. "Mia, I can't take care of you anymore. This is important. I need you to hear me. You have to be strong for me. Remember that place in Marin we used to hike to?"

How could I forget? On the top of Mt. Tamalpais, on a ridge overlooking the fog, was a group of rocks. Joaquín and I used to go up there and spend hours playing make-believe.

"Of course I do. Why?"

"If you need to feel my presence, go there."

What on earth was Joaquín talking about? He hated what he called my "New Age bullshit" about vortexes and spirit guides. But my spirituality guided everything I did. I didn't care if he didn't understand it. "I won't need to. I'm going to take a leave of absence from school, move down here, and visit you every week until you're free."

"Don't you dare. You only have one semester left. Don't ruin your life, too. Listen to me. I don't want you to visit me again. Promise me you won't come back to San Diego."

I bit my nails, and my stomach clenched. He was the only person I had in my life since I'd ended things with Grant. Without Joaquín, I couldn't breathe. I didn't exist. He would never ask me to abandon him. It was then that I knew in my heart something was gravely wrong. Not just the murder of Tiffany and the charges against Joaquín, but something else. Something hidden deep in the secret realm of the SEAL brotherhood. "I promise."

I nodded and placed my hand on the thick plexiglass. He did the same. Would this be the closest I ever came to touching him again? "I love you, Joaquín."

"I love you too, *Angelita Mia*."

My little angel. He hadn't called me that since we were kids. That name had always meant so much to me. I wanted to be that angel for my brother. No, I *needed* to be that angel. And I would. I would live up to my birth name and become Joaquín's angel.

We only had a few minutes left, so I tried my best to cheer him up. My hands trembled, my body froze. He'd worked so hard to be a SEAL. It was all he ever wanted. The possibility of his career being destroyed was almost worse than him being accused of a crime he didn't commit.

The bell rang, and the guard came and escorted Joaquín out of the room. I stared at him walking away, praying that this nightmare would end soon. This couldn't be goodbye.

I walked out of the San Diego County Jail. Determined. Dedicated. Definite.

I would clear my brother's name. For my entire life, he had protected me, lifted me up when I had fallen. It was my turn to rescue him.

I took off in Joaquín's truck, a brand new Ford Raptor. The scent of the fresh leather tickled my nostrils. For a second, I actually questioned his innocence. How could he afford this new truck? He'd told me he'd saved up during deployment, but I knew he spent most of his money on my tuition and housing. Even though I worked part-time as a makeup artist, living in San Francisco was not cheap. Paul was a second-generation Navy SEAL officer and came from old money—was Joaquín involved in something shady that had resulted in him being framed for murder?

I pushed the thought of his guilt out of my head. My gut wrenched for even questioning his honor.

Speeding on Harbor Drive, I rolled down the window and allowed the crisp San Diego breeze to blow all doubt away. Though it was January, the sun was still bright in the sky. As Joaquín's words replayed in my head and the look on his face haunted my thoughts, I choked back tears.

The Raptor seemed to have a mind of its own, and I found myself driving toward Grant's place. I had to see him. I had no choice. He was my only hope. I needed to ask for his help. I prayed that he would be able to fix everything like he once had. He'd been with Joaquín at the party that night. He must've seen something.

My insides twisted. The intersection of excitement, desperation, and guilt left me unable to focus. Grant was the one man who rivaled my brother in his steadfast character. He'd been my first love, my only lover, and I'd shoved him away. Like every great thing in my life.

I pulled up to his tiny apartment in Point Loma, praying he wasn't off somewhere training. The sight of fresh mud on the door of his lifted truck alleviated that fear.

My fingers traced the doorbell. His dog Hero let out a friendly bark. There was no turning back. I pressed the button.

"Hello?" Grant's deep, sexy voice sounded groggy through the intercom.

He must've been asleep even though it was three in the afternoon. Probably another balls-to-dawn training rotation. Back when we were together, I'd make sure to have his place clean, his favorite meals cooked, Hero walked and fed when he came home from those all-nighters. It was some of the only times he allowed me to take care of him. "Hey, it's me."

His tone turned bitter, dark. "What do you want, Mia?"

I couldn't help but smile that he still recognized my voice immediately, even though we'd been broken up for two years and hadn't seen each other in six months. I knew what I had done to him—abandoned him in his hour of need, secretly blaming him for being gone when I needed him the most. I had been unwilling to allow him to see me at my lowest point, and unable to open up to him and confess my secret. My fatal flaw had ruined our love. My conceit.

Joaquín would never turn his back on someone he loved. He would embrace his anxiety. Shake hands with fear.

Somehow I would have to learn to do the same.

"I need to talk about Joaquín."

Grant opened the door, and I gasped at the sight of him standing in front of me wearing only pajama bottoms. I'd forgotten how incredible his body was; his broad shoulders and V-shaped torso displayed no body fat, just a perfect eight-pack of abs. His skin glowed in the afternoon sun, highlighting his sculpted arms, which were covered with ink. My eyes focused on his huge hands, remembering how they had explored every inch of my body. He ran his fingers through his golden hair, and I imagined those fingers deep inside me, sending spikes of pleasure to my core. The scruff of his beard hid the deep scar on his neck. His green eyes seemed to shoot beams of kryptonite at me, exposing my soul.

Right, I came here for my brother.

"Let me in, Grant." I pushed my way inside the door, scanning the place for signs of another woman. All clear. Hero, his black lab/pug mix, gave me a lick on my face and lay by my feet.

The last time I saw Grant was at an awkward run-in at my brother's apartment last summer before they deployed. Grant had ignored me the entire time. No matter how hard I'd tried, he refused to engage with me.

Today, he had no choice.

2

———

GRANT

T HE VIXEN STANDING IN FRONT of me barely resembled my beautiful ex-girlfriend Mia. Her waist length brown hair that had once carried the scent of coconut milk and vanilla beans was now tinted fuchsia and chopped off into a long, angled bob with spiky bangs. Her freckled skin was painted up like a streetwalker's. Her soft curves were hard, skinny, angular. Her nails, which had always been kept short and pale, were filed into sharp points and polished black, like daggers. I fucking hated her full look. Like some bullshit revenge breakup make under meant to ensure that I wasn't attracted to her anymore.

It didn't work—I still wanted her.

My eyes lingered on her small breasts and fell down to her wide hips. "There's nothing I can do. No one remembers anything—and if they do, they aren't talking. I'm sorry. For what it's worth, I don't think he's guilty."

"Of course he's not guilty. But you can help him, right. You know the men on your Team. You were at the party. We can find out who killed that girl. I'll do whatever it takes."

"Whatever it takes? What the hell are you talking about?"

She inhaled deeply through her nose and then exhaled through her mouth. "I don't know. I haven't figured it out."

I laughed. "Well, let me know when you do. Until then, you can get the fuck out of my place." I urged her toward my door.

Her eyes darted around my place, but she held her body firm, refusing to budge. "I know we can figure out something if we put our heads together. We can do this."

I sneered at her. "We? There is no 'we.' You made sure of that."

A flash of guilt must have caused her to avert my gaze, as she looked down at her feet and bit her nails.

"Maybe I could go undercover? I'm a chameleon. An actress, a makeup artist. I've reinvented myself so many times even you wouldn't be able to recognize me."

This bitch was crazy. "You can't be serious. You're five-feet-four inches tall, one hundred thirty pounds. I used to have to open spaghetti jars for you. You think you can defend yourself against a SEAL? No way can you outsmart my Team. Sorry, Mia. It will never work. You're delusional. I could recognize you no matter how you changed." I had memorized every inch of her body, the sound of her voice when she whispered my name, the way her lips parted when she was embarrassed, the glint in her hazel eyes when she wanted her way, and the flush on her cheeks when she came.

I loved you.

Picturing her smile had gotten me through those long muddy nights freezing my balls off in the frigid water during BUD/S. Her faith, her love, her belief in me had kept me from quitting, from ringing that bell.

Too bad it was all complete bullshit.

She touched my face, tracing the beard that hid the scar on my neck. "I just need one of them to talk."

I pushed her hand away. My stomach churned, I couldn't stand the sight of her anymore. Couldn't she see the hurt in my eyes? I'd once looked at her with warmth, love, devotion. Now only her betrayal lingered in the air. "SEALs don't talk."

She let out a laugh. "You did. You used to tell me everything."

Smartass. My fist clenched. "Yeah, I did. Only because you were my girl. What are you going to do—fuck them all?"

A wicked smile graced her lips. "Why the hell not? I'm single, remember? You made it clear you never wanted anything to do with me again."

My chest tightened. She was taunting me. The thought of her, my girl, being screwed senseless by my friends made my palms sweat. She was mine —only mine. She'd lost her virginity to me, and I'd always found comfort knowing that no other man had ever touched her. Images flashed through my head of another man kissing her, fucking her, making her come, her screaming out his name.

I swallowed hard and steadied my breath. "Stop, Mia. We both know damn well you were the one who fucked things up. Even if you were that much of a bitch and wanted to fuck me over more than you already have, none of them would touch another Team guy's woman. Especially since you're also Joaquín's sister. I only got away with sleeping with you because we started dating before Joaquín and I became SEALs. And no matter what you think, in their eyes, you will always be mine."

She cringed, and I noted the look of shame on her face. Had she cheated on me back then? I would never believe that. Like a wild animal, I was confident that I could've sensed another man's scent on my woman. Even so, Mia was hiding something from me. There was more to her leaving me than being too young for a serious relationship. Unfortunately, I didn't have a fucking clue what her secret was. She never even gave me the chance to fix it.

She leveled her gaze at me. "Yeah? Yet you are sure quick to abandon Joaquín at the first sign of trouble. So much for leaving no man behind. You know if the situation were reversed, Joaquín would do anything possible to set you free."

Dammit, I shouldn't have let her in the door. This was already too intense, too emotional. "It's not that simple, and you know it. I'm under orders not to talk to him. I don't have a choice."

"Fine. I understand that you are forbidden to talk to him. But I can. You need to help me help him. This isn't about us; this is about Joaquín. Can you tell me about the girl who died? Who invited her? Was Joaquín dating her?"

I clenched my teeth. Some people thought that since I was a SEAL, I'd have a wicked temper, but I had complete control of my emotions at all times. That composure allowed me the mental strength to point a loaded gun at my enemy and still be able to make a conscious decision not to pull the trigger. I'd never raised my voice to Mia, ever. Even so, she knew when I was pissed off.

"What the fuck? Do you think you can just walk in here like you didn't rip my heart out and I'm just going to comfort you and fix this mess? I already fucking told you there's nothing I can do. And I don't owe you anything."

Her chin dipped to her chest, her shoulders slumping. "I know you don't believe me, and I don't expect you to, but I had to leave. I didn't have a choice."

"There's always a choice." I looked back at the rumpled covers on my bed. I remembered watching Mia sleep, the way she always curled up in a ball, with Hero at her feet. I never told her, but she used to talk in her sleep, sometimes even said my name. "And we aren't in this together. My world started and stopped with you. All my friends told me that we wouldn't work, that we didn't have a chance because we were so young and because of my job, but I told them you were different. That you would have my back no matter what."

Her voice cracked. "For what it's worth, I've never even looked at another guy. I want you to know that."

My eyes bore into her. "That's supposed to make it better? That I'm the only man you've ever been with, but you still don't want to be with me? Well, I wish I could say it was that easy for me. Since you left, I've fucked a bunch of girls, trying to get you out of my head." But she was still fucking there every night when I closed my eyes. I prayed her face would soon fade from my mind.

Her mouth tightened. She wasn't stupid—she had to know from her brother that I'd been with other women since her. But she only had herself to blame. "Please, Grant, if what we had meant anything to you, please help me exonerate Joaquín."

My eyes met hers, and I cupped her face, fighting the urge to kiss her. "You meant everything to me. You know that."

She pulled away from me, her bottom lip quivering. "I came back."

"You left me. Period. You can never come back." As much as I loved Mia, I could never give her another chance. I refused to let myself rely on any woman after she had abandoned me. I didn't need that type of stress. My job was consuming—my personal life had to provide me stability and comfort. Or at the very least, simple release.

"But—I need you."

I'd needed her once also. Now, I needed her to leave. "I can't help you. I'll do anything I can to clear Joaquín; you know that. But my hands are tied. You need to leave." I pushed her out of the entryway and slammed the door behind her, never looking back. I wished I could say it was easy, shutting her out of my life again, but her scent still lingered in the air, and my heart remained with it.

I hoped I never had to see her again, which was now a realistic option since her brother was in jail.

Still, my heart ached for her, and for my swim buddy. There was no way Joaquín could've intentionally killed that stripper. Maybe he'd just gotten too rough in bed. Regardless, the reputation of our Team was now tarnished. The public was supposed to see us as heroes who rescued hostages from ISIS, freed boat captains from pirates, and assassinated leaders of terrorist regimes. Not as a bunch of sex-crazed, hard-partying hooligans with no morals. The average American citizens would be blown away if they learned the truth about our lifestyle—just last month we had rescued some kidnapped USO cheerleaders from insurgents and my boy Pat had saved his wife Annie from a sex-ring in Aruba. We worked hard, but we partied harder. And no way would I ever apologize for what any of us had to do to relieve our stress. The intensity of our lives was unfathomable to most.

Even so, Mia had been it for me. I'd once found enough comfort in her touch to forget my daily burdens. But no more. I would never allow another woman to distract me from being a warrior. Plenty of girls wanted to be fucked by a Navy SEAL, some real-life hero to step off the pages of their favorite romance novel. I was now more than happy to use them the way they used me. Mia was the only woman I'd ever loved, and when she left, I'd closed my heart to anyone else.

3

MIA

I SPENT TWO DAYS SCOURING every inch of Joaquín's apartment, but came up empty-handed. I found nothing—no shady receipts, no weird email messages. Everything was clean. Too clean, as if someone had already scrubbed any evidence from the place.

I wanted to crash Tiffany's funeral to search for clues, but I definitely didn't want to affront her family, who would no doubt kick out the sister of the man they thought had murdered their beloved daughter. I skipped the service, uncertain what to do next.

Any day now, the remaining men on Joaquín's Team could be deployed, and after that, who knew when I'd be able to see them again. I'd lost my inside connections, no Grant, no Joaquín. I had only one way to see them all.

Today I was going to head to the Pickled Frog. The bar was a dive where all the SEALs went any time one of their men had passed. The looming death toll never seemed to wane—a training accident, a downed helicopter, an embassy upheaval. I'd been to enough SEAL funerals during the two years I dated Grant to know the drill. One by one, each man would pound down his trident, the SEAL insignia, on the deceased man's coffin. Then they'd get wasted. Even though Joaquín was still technically alive, I was pretty sure they'd be mourning the loss of their Teammate.

The Pickled Frog was more than a watering hole; it was a safe haven for heroes. Men who needed to drown their sorrows in hard liquor, men who wanted to forget the faces of the terrorists they killed, men whose wives had cheated when they'd been deployed, men whose kids didn't even recognize their own fathers. I shuddered, imagining all the times two years ago Grant might have sat in the seedy bar, getting hammered, trying to get over me.

I needed strength before I saw Grant again. Time to meditate. I sat on a chair in Joaquín's apartment and straightened my spine, my feet placed firmly on the ground. Resting my hands, I turned my palms upward and prayed. I alternated my breath, from tense inhales to relaxed exhales. Focusing my attention on my spiritual eye, I uttered a quick chant and closed my practice. I needed to remain calm and centered, today more than ever.

I locked up Joaquín's place, jumped in his truck, drove along the coast, eventually parking in an alley behind the bar. A deep sigh escaped my lips. I was sure I was the last person these men wanted to see.

When I pushed back the front door, the acidic stench of whiskey and sweat overtook me. It was two in the afternoon on a random Saturday, and the place was mostly empty. Despite being in the heart of Ocean Beach, no college coeds or surfers hung out here. This was a SEAL bar; SEALs and frog hogs were its only customers, though the occasional SEAL wife or girl-friend would make an appearance. But on this day, even the frog hogs must've taken the day off from their groupie duties. I was the only woman in this dump.

My feminine scent gave me away. No sooner had my heels touched the Technicolor, puke-stained, carpet than the heads of seven men turned toward me: Grant, Paul, Mitch, Joe, Vic, Pat, and Kyle. The seven other men on Joaquín's eight-man SEAL squad. Had they all been at the party that night?

I avoided Grant's suspicious glance and stared at the walls, studying the pictures of fallen SEALs. So many gorgeous men. Bearded, tatted, ripped.

Gone. Dead.

Never to kiss their wives again, never to cradle their babies in their strong arms. I might as well put Joaquín's picture on the wall. Man, this place was depressing, but it was a thousand times better than jail. Now I was the one who needed a drink.

I sat on the bar stool closest to the only friendly face, Kyle, who was tending bar. The gummy pleather seat clung to my thighs as he gave me a welcoming smile.

Kyle Lawson was a SEAL and former NFL linebacker; he was also the new owner of the Pickled Frog. He was gorgeous—smooth mahogany-colored skin, trimmed dark beard, warm chocolate eyes. At six foot five, his body seemed sculpted by Michelangelo himself. Kyle was like a celebrity in the Teams. After he'd given up a multimillion-dollar football contract to become a SEAL, the media had hailed him a hero, even before he rescued a group of cheerleaders who were kidnapped on a USO tour. But he'd refused all interviews to the press and was as humble as any of the Team guys. "Hey, beautiful. Sorry to hear about your brother. What can I get you?"

His buddies, Pat and Vic, both gave me forced nods. Their loyalty must've been torn between their hatred of the woman who broke Grant's heart and their protectiveness of Joaquín's sister.

"Malibu and Coke."

"Coming right up."

I glanced down the bar at the other SEALs. It was like a buffet of rock-hard men. My eyes watered; I was high on the testosterone levels in this place.

Kyle placed the drink in front of me. "How's your brother?"

"I saw him after he was arrested, and he looked horrible. Now he's refusing my visits." I took a sip, the warm rum coating my throat. "Were you at that party?"

"Look, honey, I wish I could help, but Joe, Pat, Vic and I left before the strippers arrived. I'm sure you're trying to help Joaquín, but no one is going to talk to you about that night." He glanced at Pat and Vic. "We keep each other's secrets to our grave."

Kyle wasn't kidding. Pat was married to Annie Hamilton, a famous missing American who had vanished on spring break in the Caribbean. Initially, the public was fed a story that she'd just run away, become a missionary, had a kid, then decided to return to the States. I never bought that tall tale for a second. I'd interrogated Joaquín about what he knew, but he just played dumb, until a recent news story broke. Apparently, Annie and another missing American girl, Nicole, had both been kidnapped and forced into sex slavery. A Marine who recognized Nicole recently discovered her in Venezuela. She had amnesia and didn't know who she was or what had happened to her. And a former SEAL named Dave supposedly saved Annie, though I think Pat was involved in her rescue.

As much as I had a window into these SEALs' worlds, as both a girl-friend and a sister, I knew that I wasn't privy to their world of secrets.

I adored Pat though; he was such an amazing guy. He adopted Annie's son, and Annie was now expecting his child. My own womb ached—had I stayed with Grant, I was sure we'd be married, and we'd probably have started a family by now. But instead of celebrating a new life with my soul mate, I was trying to salvage my brother's future.

I bit my lower lip and threw back my drink. I didn't have a plan. I didn't have a strategy. I didn't have a clue what I was doing.

Here goes nothing. I pushed myself off the seat and squeezed between Paul and Mitch, to at least try to see if I could get them to admit some details about the night of the party.

Paul resembled a young Tom Cruise—brown hair, blue eyes, dimples. He had even more arrogance than the rest of the men. As one of only a handful of second-generation SEALs, he'd been bred for this life. "Mia, I'm sorry about Joaquín, but the brass has forbidden us to talk about that night."

"I know. Grant told me the other night."

Grant, who was sitting on the other side of Mitch, didn't even look at me. "Why are you here exactly?" he demanded, his voice cold. "You should leave. You're not welcome."

"Yeah, well, you don't own the bar now, do you? Kyle doesn't seem to have a problem with me being here. It's a free country." Grant's short-sleeved blue T-shirt teased me with glimpses of his tattoos. I gulped when I noticed he'd covered up my name with some sort of vine. At least I hadn't tattooed his name on my ass, though I'd strongly considered it. My lack of ink didn't matter; Grant's name was permanently embedded in my heart.

He turned toward me, his green eyes digging deep into my soul. "What do you want from us? We aren't going to talk about that night, none of us are. We've all given statements to the police and to our commands. When this goes to trial, we will be forced to testify, and it will ruin our careers." He stood up and came over to me, placing his hand on my thigh. An electric shock pulsed up my leg. I was addicted to his touch, longed for him, dreamt of him at night. "Why don't you just go back to your 'I hate the United States military' city and leave me the fuck alone?"

How could he be such an asshole to me? He knew how much I loved Joaquín—our love for my brother was probably one of the only things we still shared. I turned to Mitch, my eyes pleading for some mercy.

Mitch's long dark hair skimmed his shoulders; his full sleeves of tattoos decorated his huge arms. He put his strong hand on my back and gave me an icy stare. "Sorry, Mia. I was passed out and woke up with some bitch sitting on my face. I don't remember anything."

"Dammit, Mitch. Why do you have to be so disgusting?" I hopped up from my chair. Grant was right; this was pointless.

But the stakes were too high to just give up. I couldn't imagine my brother spending the rest of his life caged like an animal.

As I turned back toward Paul, the doors flew open. Paul's wife, Dara, and Mitch's wife, April, came bouncing in, laughing as if they were about to meet their hubbies for date night at a five-star restaurant instead of a drink in this hellhole.

Dara gave me an insincere hug. "Oh Mia, honey. So sorry to hear about Joaquín. But who knew he was into fucking strippers?"

"Fuck you, Dara. Where were you that night? The party was at your parents' house, right? Maybe it was your husband fucking strippers." I hated her and her perfectly blow-dried hair, her designer purse, her lime skinny jeans, probably in a size twenty-six. Typical SEAL officer's wife; thought she was better than anyone else. She was a few years older than I was, and never forgot to mention her Ivy League education and her vacation home in Lake Tahoe. I didn't need her pity.

Dara shoved the hair out of her eyes and shot a bitter glare toward Paul. Without a word, he clutched her wrist and led her away from me. Paul went to great lengths to hide his other women from her. Dara loved him, unconditionally, and I knew that no matter what bullshit he pulled she would never be able to leave him.

April put her arm around me. "I am sorry, Mia. Joaquín is a good guy. I hope he's exonerated. Call me if you ever need to talk."

I thanked her. April and I had been good friends—once. A long-suffering SEAL wife, she was painfully aware of Mitch's philandering. I never understood their relationship. Grant's theory had always been that they got off on making each other jealous, but to me, it just seemed deeply dysfunctional.

I glanced at Grant, but when he turned his back on me, I decided I couldn't take any more. My heels touched the gravel outside, and the bar door slammed behind me. I felt the clang inside my heart as well. He was done with me. I was alone. Again. No Grant. No Joaquín. No parents. Alone.

This was not the Grant I knew. He was cold, aloof, distant. Something was off. Wasn't he outraged about Joaquín's false imprisonment? Could he be hiding something? Grant said he didn't think Joaquín killed Tiffany. Had Grant witnessed the murder? What in the hell was going on?

Stop, Mia. Just stop. I was clearly stressed out and not thinking rationally. I'd dated Grant for two years; he was a good guy, a hero. He wouldn't hesitate to give his own life to protect the ones he loved. Like he'd said, he was under strict orders not to talk about the case. I didn't want him to sacrifice his career. His Team needed him, especially without Joaquín. Hell, our country needed him. Grant was the best of the best.

Unfortunately, I needed him, too.

But that ship had sailed. *He'll never be mine again.*

I wasn't going to give up on Joaquín that easily. With or without Grant's help, I would clear Joaquín's name. My brother was innocent. He'd sacrificed everything for me since our parents died, and it was time for me to repay his loyalty.

There had to be a way to free my brother. And nothing would stop me until I found it.

Grant had been right. SEALs wouldn't talk.

I had only one clue left.

Time to make strippers sing.

4

MIA

PANTHERS, SAN DIEGO'S PREMIER STRIP JOINT, was located in an industrial area, tucked between used-car dealerships and noodle shops. I never understood the allure of strippers; paying women to pretend that they were interested in you seemed pathetic, not flattering.

I sat in the parking lot, staring at the entrance. I didn't want to go into the building. What was my plan? Ask the women if they'd been at the party where Tiffany was murdered? These ladies were her friends. I'd get the door slammed in my face.

I hugged my shoulders, tucking my chin into my chest. I didn't have a clue what I was doing.

My window rattled. I looked up and saw a busty redhead in a tight sweat suit standing by the window of Joaquín's truck.

I opened the door.

"Honey, you okay? Is your boyfriend inside?"

I swallowed. Here I was judging these women, yet this stripper was showing me compassion. "No. I don't have a boyfriend. My brother used to come here."

Her eyes narrowed, her gaze intent. "Hey, wait. You're Mia, aren't you? Joaquín's sister? I knew I recognized this truck. Oh, honey, I'm so sorry. Your brother is the nicest guy. Not like his friends, especially that jackass Mitch. None of us think Joaquín killed Tiffy."

I jumped down from the seat, my breath bottled in my chest. "You know my brother? Were you at the party? I know he didn't do it. Can you help me exonerate him?"

She gave me a warm smile. "I was at that party. But nothing was out of the ordinary. It was just some Team guys and some girls from here. The police interviewed us all. I've racked my brain trying to think of something, anything that stood out. Maybe it was an accident? I'm so sorry, honey. I wish I could help."

My mind raced. There had to be something she could tell me. Some clues to give me hope. "Which guy invited you?"

"Grant. Tall, amazing body, tattoos, blond hair, green eyes."

I gasped and almost tripped on the cracked asphalt. "Grant Carrion? You must be mistaken. He hates strip clubs. I know—he's my ex-boyfriend."

She let out a laugh. "So, you're the girl who fucked him up? Sorry to be the one to tell you honey, but Grant's a regular. Comes in here every Tuesday night when he's in town. He has a thing for bleached blondes with huge tits and fake lips. We call him Ken because he's always scouting for his newest Barbie. Shows them a good time when he's around, deploys, then moves on to the latest model when he returns." She gave me a sad smile. "Look, I have to go to work. My name is Emma, but my stage name is Pepper. If you have any more questions, don't hesitate to stop in and find me. I'd be happy to help any way I can. Best of luck with your brother."

"Thanks, Emma." I hugged her, and she waved goodbye to me.

I got back into the truck and drove out of the parking lot.

Heat rose in my body. Could she be right? Had Grant become addicted to the strip clubs since I'd left him? Spending his free time here, drinking himself into oblivion, finding comfort with women who had no expectations, women who could never disappoint him the way I had?

I winced, pushing away the image of Grant getting a lap dance from some troubled woman with ragged extensions and fake tits.

But Emma had given me what I needed, what I craved. Hope.

I now had a clue. *Grant* had invited the girls. This man, who I thought I knew everything about, was nothing more than a stranger to me. Maybe he was hiding something.

Seven Deadly SEALs—Seven Achilles' heels. I would smoke out their secrets and figure out what happened that night.

5

MIA

I'D BEEN BACK IN SAN FRANCISCO for two weeks. I attempted to honor Joaquín's wish and stay in school, but I couldn't focus. Even attending guided meditations and kirtan chanting hadn't helped. My mind raced in class. I hadn't slept well since I'd returned.

I glanced around my room in the tiny North Beach apartment I shared with two other San Francisco State students. Scripts lay across my desk, with stacks of books huddled against the wall. Just a little over a month ago my life had been so simple, so easy. One focus, one goal. To be the best actress possible. How stupid and trivial my dreams seemed now.

I swiped through my iPhone to the San Diego News app, scanning for headlines about Joaquín. I didn't have to even scroll down the page. There it was at the top. *Bail denied for U.S. Navy SEAL accused of murdering a stripper.*

Fuck.

My ears pounded and my vision blurred. I couldn't even read the article. No hope. This was it—the realization finally sank in that he might get convicted of this crime.

I called Joaquín's lawyer, but the secretary told me that my brother had given instructions not to talk to me anymore. The secretary had only one thing to say: Joaquín had transferred the title of his truck to me. I knew Joaquín too well—this was his way of ensuring I went on with my life. But what he didn't realize was that I would never be able to enjoy my life unless I fought for his.

I needed to clear my head, meditate, try to find some peace. Find a way to connect to Joaquín.

Despite being desperate for sleep, I climbed into his truck—my truck now—and headed over the Golden Gate Bridge toward Mt. Tamalpais. It was a clear day; San Francisco's famous fog seemed to have cleared the way for this mission. The winding hills through Mill Valley reminded me of the weekend adventures Joaquín and I had gone on with our parents.

Mt. Tam was more than a mountain to me—it was a sacred place, a vortex of energy. Grant and Joaquín never missed an opportunity to tease me about my spiritual beliefs. I was raised Catholic, but after my parents died, I'd become deeply spiritual. I practiced yoga, became a vegan, attended kirtan chants, and meditated. My dedication only grew stronger after I'd left Grant. For me, my spirituality was a way to center myself, develop a personal relationship with God, and feel closer to my parents.

As the Raptor approached our favorite trailhead, my breathing slowed, and a memory took hold of me.

"Let's do a time capsule!"

Joaquín, a skinny boy around age twelve with a devilish grin, led me down the trail. Our parents slowly lagged in the distance. Always the Boy Scout, Joaquín took a Swiss army knife from his pocket and notched a hole at the base of a tree.

"Give me your bracelets."

I shoved the candy-colored beaded bracelets off my wrist and handed them to him without a second thought. A big deal, considering at age eleven, those tacky things were my prized possessions.

Joaquín's eyes twinkled. He loved going on adventures, and I was always his right-hand girl. Most brothers and sisters fight, but we were truly best friends.

He took a small leather pouch out of his back pocket. "This was made by the Miwok Indians." He slipped his Swiss army knife inside, wrapped in my bracelets, reached deep between the roots of the tree, and dropped the pouch inside.

"One day, when we're older, we'll come back here and find our treasures."

I thought it was stupid, but I would never tell him that. I just hugged him, and we ran off toward the voices of our parents.

Centering myself back in present day, I touched the damp soil. I closed my eyes, and I could hear my parents' voices calling us. *"Mia, Joaquín. Where are you two?"*

The voices became quieter in my head, and I found the tree. Eleven years later, the old oak had seen better days, but it still stood, leaves gathered at the base.

I knelt beside the trunk, my hand wrestling with the soil, which was surprisingly loose like it had been disturbed not long ago. Digging faster, furious. *It has to be in here.* I'd all about given up when my fingers touched something smooth. I reached down and grabbed ... the pouch!

I tore it open, now weathered with dirt and rain. My bracelets flew out, but instead of Joaquín's knife, I found a small wooden box.

He's been back here?

The box was new. When had he come up here? He hadn't visited me in at least a year.

I flipped the box open, and inside was a small key and a dog tag. I pulled the dog tag to me and squinted at the etched numbers. WF #1459.

WF—Wells Fargo? I examined the plain key. It looked like the safe deposit box key from our bank. Joaquín and I had opened this box for my mom's jewelry once I turned eighteen, but I'd forgotten all about it. I had my own key somewhere back at my place, but I would've never thought to look in the box.

My jaw dropped. I knew he hadn't killed Tiffany. He must've known something was going down. Joaquín was so smart he had planned to send me on this chase. He believed in me and knew I could save him.

My watch read four thirteen. The bank was open until six. I stuffed the dirty pouch into my pocket, raced back to the truck, and sped down the hill.

After stewing for twenty-five minutes in traffic, I reached the bank. I handed the teller the key, she asked for my ID and gave me the signature card.

Joaquín's name was signed above mine; the date entered was a week after the murder.

Holy shit! He'd come up here just the other week and not told me?

I scribbled my name on the card, and she led me to the safe deposit boxes. When she placed the bank key in the lock with mine, it clicked open, and she handed me the box. My heart fluttered.

I took the box to the room, anticipated what I would find. A note? Instructions?

I slowly opened the lid. There was a certified check made out to me for seventy-five thousand dollars. Also dated a week after the murder.

Where did he get this money? Was this money dirty? Related to Tiffany's death?

A note floated out of the box. *Mia, here's the rest of Mom and Dad's life insurance. Please spend it wisely. I love you.*

Please spend it wisely. He knew. He knew he'd be arrested. But why? How could he possibly have known? It was a testimony to our close relationship that he knew he could provide the one hint that would send me here. It was also testimony to how much he loved me that he wanted to provide for me, look after me. Just as he had always done.

The only thing I could conclude was that he was in over his head in something…I didn't know what. His last gesture, which didn't surprise me, was to make sure I was taken care of. It brought tears to my eyes. My heart ached.

I emptied the safe deposit box, desperate for another clue. But it was completely barren.

But I had other plans. I would take this money and find out the truth. I'd clear his name.

I slammed the box shut and walked out to the teller. "I'd like to deposit this check."

6

MIA

THE FAINT SMELL OF CURRY, chickpeas, and fried pastry from the Afghan restaurant below wafted through my tiny apartment. A potato sambosa sounded amazing, especially washed down by a cherry blossom iced tea, but I was running late again. I'd taken leave from my college, moved out of my place, and quit my part-time job applying makeup at the MAC counter at Nordstrom, styling the drag queens in the city.

Now, four months after Joaquín had been arrested, I was living in San Rafael, across the San Francisco Bay. I hated isolating myself, but I couldn't afford to make any mistakes. If Grant came looking for me, any connection to my former life had to be erased. That meant no catching the latest indie band at Bimbo's 365 Club with my girlfriends, no hikes to Mount Tam with my old friends from high school, and no spring auditions for Marin Shakespeare Company's summer season with my drama cohorts. Whenever I thought of my passion for theater, my chest ached. For so long that had been my dream. Sometimes your dreams would simply remain that: a dream. It was hard not to feel sad, bereft.

Still, I actually loved being back in my hometown of Marin—the cool, creative vibe, being among the musicians and artists who flocked here. But I wasn't here to make friends, and this time I wasn't running away from my problems. This was my BUD/S. Joaquín had undergone six months of rigorous training to become a SEAL. I was training just as rigorously to make sure he could keep being one.

I threw some gel into my hair, pulled on a vintage Mötley Crüe T-shirt and some faded jeans. It was a relief to be back home, away from the flock of picture-perfect *Baywatch* bitches who inhabited San Diego. I never fit in there. Not that I was doing an excellent job of blending in here, especially with my new looks, though I was doing a better job after trading Joaquín's monstrous Ford Raptor for a Honda Accord Hybrid. The Raptor was too conspicuous among the eco-friendly Teslas, Toyota Prii, Nissan Leafs and Chevy Volts of Marin.

Saying goodbye to Joaquín's truck gutted me. Every time I drove it, I'd thought how it should be him behind the wheel, free from shackles, and my resolve to clear his name grew. But I had to erase any connection I had to my old life, to Joaquín, in order to go undercover and save him.

I locked up my place, filled up a bottle of water, and hopped into my car. Today I had a long day of training in San Francisco: a Russian lesson in the Richmond District, kung fu in Chinatown, pole dancing at a studio on the unfortunately named Bush Street. Tomorrow was equally packed with weapons training, CrossFit, an acting workshop, and computer classes. I was so exhausted and sore every night I would usually stumble back to my place, soak in a warm bath filled with Epsom salts, and crash.

The lessons and training were actually fun, but I had done something drastic. Something I swore I would never do, something that was completely against my belief system.

I'd gone through an extreme makeover.

As a rule, I was fundamentally against plastic surgery. I loved my body, my unique looks, my distinct features. I was half Latina—I had flat breasts, wide hips, almond-shaped eyes, a weak chin, and a cute bump on my nose. At first, I didn't even consider surgery as part of my plan,

After Joaquín was denied bail, I'd gone to San Diego one more time and, as promised, my brother had refused my visit. But I refused to give up on him—I drove like a madwoman across the Coronado Bay Bridge. I was no longer a military dependent, so I didn't have an ID to gain access to base. I parked at the Del and headed toward the beach that borders the SEAL compound.

I hoped one of Joaquín's friends would see me, take pity, and offer me some help or guidance. As luck would have it, Grant and his buddies were helping to train the BUD/S recruits. Grant's face flashed a notice of recognition toward me, but he ignored me. I might as well have been a stranger.

Then a wicked idea crossed my head. What if I *was* a stranger? To not just him, but to his entire Team. Could I find out what really happened that night? Go undercover with the strippers at the club and discover the SEALs' secret sins? Learn about them with their masks off, from the vantage point of a fantasy temptress instead of the good girl they wanted to protect.

It was the only way. I drove back to San Francisco that night and booked an appointment with a surgeon.

Having to go under the knife last month was excruciating, especially without anyone to take care of me. The nurse I'd hired to help me recover kept lamenting that such a pretty young girl would ruin her face and body. I agreed with her completely, but she didn't have a clue what was at stake.

I was trying to go undercover with Navy SEALs, men who were impossible to fool, and I couldn't take any chances, especially with Grant. He knew every inch of my body. So I'd had breast implants, a nose job, a chin implant, fillers in my lips and cheeks, lipo on my neck, lasers to remove my freckles, and Botox on my eyebrows. I looked like a plastic freak, but the doctor swore my features would get less tight and I might someday resemble a human again.

Still waiting.

My entire body throbbed, the chin implant burned through my skin, my nose was still swollen. Blinking was a daily struggle. These silicone balloons on my chest strained my back.

I forced myself to stare in the mirror, not recognizing my own reflection. The rest of my body had transformed also. As soon as the doctor cleared me, I'd started weight training. Squats to give me a nice butt, weights to make my skinny body toned and lean. Was this the type of woman Grant really desired? A stereotypical plastic blonde bombshell with perfect features devoid of any uniqueness?

I reminded myself I hadn't changed my appearance to win Grant back. I'd altered my looks to lure Grant to me so I could go undercover and clear Joaquín's name. After all I'd done, this had better work. Failure was not an option. I wasn't sure I could survive the heartache if I didn't complete this mission.

I was used to being alone, but I missed my brother. And I missed Grant. What was he doing now? I had always kept tabs on him through Joaquín—

but for the first time since I'd met Grant, I didn't have any clue where he was. Was he deployed? With another girl? Training somewhere? Bastard didn't even have a Facebook account I could stalk. His Scorpio ass had become even more elusive since we broke up.

When we were together, I never doubted his fidelity or love; he was honest and open with me. But I also felt that I could never penetrate his core. Even after dating him for two years, he always held a part of himself back. Like he was afraid to let me see his true self. Joaquín and I shared so much with each other that Grant's exclusion had sometimes made me wonder if he really wanted me in his life. But I was far from innocent—I kept my secrets too.

I crossed the Golden Gate Bridge, and my heart raced when I viewed the city skyline. This was my hometown, the last place where my life had made sense. The Transamerica Pyramid, where my father had worked nights cleaning, glowed in the distance. My dad had been so proud, so principled. In a way, I was glad he never lived to see his only son accused of murder.

I turned off Geary Boulevard and pulled the car in front of Blue Danube Coffee, grateful to the parking fairy for finding me a spot. I dashed out of the car but paused before opening the front door of the coffee shop. The *San Francisco Chronicle* stand held a paper with the headline—*U.S. Navy SEAL Joaquín Cruz Murder Trial set for August.*

I pushed four quarters into the metal slot and grabbed a paper from the top. My muscles quivered, and I ground my teeth. I hated not being there for him, showing him support and unconditional love every step of this mess. I had to make this work. I was his only hope.

My instructor, Roman, was waiting for me at a back table. I ordered myself an almond milk Mexican Mocha and slid into the chair across from him. This gorgeous man was the polar opposite of Grant. Roman's jet-black hair skimmed his eyebrows, highlighting his almost black eyes. His lips were full, his skin was pale, his body was lean. His accent was so alluring; every time he pronounced the word *pleasure* "plea-shure" my knees went weak. In another life, another time, I could fall madly in love with the man sitting across from me sipping a single black espresso. But I was focused on Joaquín, and unfortunately for me, Grant had a permanent hold on my heart.

He slowly eye fucked me. "You're late."

"I'm sorry, it won't happen again, Roman. Traffic."

"Call me Roma." His eyes focused on my swollen breasts. "Why it is that you want to learn Russian? You never told to me."

Of course I didn't. I found you on Craigslist.

"It's a sensual language. Always wanted to learn. I'm an actress. I would love to perform Chekhov in his native tongue."

He smirked, clearly not buying my story. I now started to doubt my acting skills. "You will tell to me when you are ready. *Davai. Kak vas zovut?*"

Let's go. What's your name?

I took a sip of my mocha, the warm liquid coating my throat, helping me slip into my character. *"Menya zovut Ksenya."*

Ksenya, derived from the Greek word *xenia,* which meant stranger. My eyes perked when I found it on a list of Russian names. I was a stranger now, a stranger to Joaquín, to Grant, to myself. Grant had been right. Mia couldn't help Joaquín. Mia couldn't break the SEAL code. Mia couldn't get anyone to talk.

But none of those SEALs stood a chance of resisting Ksenya.

7

KSENYA

A S I REINVENTED MY LIFE, Joaquín rotted in a jail cell for five months. Per his request, I made no further contact. Just one final call to his lawyer, telling him that I'd been accepted into a theater program in England and that I'd check in when I could.

I missed Joaquín so much, every day, but I couldn't focus on that pain. Today was game day.

I pulled my car into the parking lot at Panthers. Was I really going to do this? The thought of taking my clothes off for a bunch of leering men made my throat burn.

Roma had helped me secure a new driver's license, social security number, and birth certificate. He'd even found me a place to live—a tiny room in an elderly Russian lady's apartment in El Cajon. The place reeked of pierogies and tea, but it didn't matter. I was pretty sure Roma had Mafia ties, but we'd both adopted an unspoken rule about not asking about each other's activities.

One final glance in the dashboard mirror and I was ready to go. My hair was now bleached and blended with platinum blond extensions, my hazel eyes were masked with brown contacts, accented with heavy dark eye shadow and false eyelashes, and my lips were painted pale pink and frosted. And thanks to the combination of my depression and my physical training, my skinny frame now looked like it could grace the cover of a Victoria's Secret catalog.

And I hated to admit it, but I loved the way I looked. Conceit. Vanity. Pride. My lack of humility saddened me. Though I would've never gone under the knife in any other circumstance, this dilemma forced me to fix every one of my physical insecurities. As a woman, it was almost empowering, no longer having to worry about my thin lips or crooked nose. I did realize through the recovery that my previously low self-image didn't matter, that my soul and dedication was what was important. I just wish I could've understood this new truth without having to change myself.

I'd transformed myself from cute girl next door to, according to Emma the stripper, Grant's ultimate fantasy. It was still hard for me to believe her; I would have to see it with my own eyes. But if Grant dreamt about blonde bombshells, I would become the woman of his nightmares. I was unstoppable. I was in control.

I pushed by some guys in the parking lot, made my way to the entrance, and spoke to the bouncer. "I have meeting together with Jim," I said in my affected Russian accent. Roma kept telling me no one would be able to distinguish me from any other Russian speaker. I'd studied not only the language but also the grammar mistakes the recent immigrants often made when they spoke in English.

The bouncer eye-fucked me. "Ka-sen-e-ya? Jim is expecting you. In his office."

I nodded and made my way toward the back of the club, watching the girls on stage out of the corner of my eye. Smoke filled the place from the adjoining private hookah lounge. The sweet, musky smell made my eyes water. Better get used to it.

Jim greeted me at the door. Bald, fat, hairy, pretty much what I expected the owner of a strip club to look like. "Welcome, Ksenya. Wow. You're a little minx, aren't you?"

Gross. I'd made a strict pact with myself—I'd go rogue, but under no circumstances would I sleep with a man who disgusted me. "Good to meet together with you." I hated using improper English, but it was a necessity now.

"Come into my office and relax. Tell me about yourself. Where are you from?"

His office consisted of a squalid cum-stained couch, a desk with papers piled all over it, and walls of framed pictures of him mugging with celebrities who had come to this joint.

I perched on the edge of the sofa. "I'm from Kharkov, in Ukraine. I was ballroom dancer. I come here with my baba, my grandmother, who was engineer. But she is dead and so I must work. I do not disappoint you. I hear you are the best, and me, I always want to be the best."

He motioned me to stand up and twirl around, and I obliged, wiggling my hips.

"Let's see what you've got. We have striking girls come in here every day, but I need to know you're the real deal. You can give me a dance in the VIP lounge."

He led me to the room, which was painted electric purple. The pole in the middle glowed from the bright lights.

"Undress."

I slowly took off my sweat suit, fighting the urge to flee. Now stripped down to my matching pink bra and panties, my cheeks burned, and I hid my blush behind my hair. I'd always been modest; the only man to ever see me naked was Grant. The music started, almost as if it sensed my presence. The hypnotic rhythm of the R&B song seemingly overtook my body. Centered, calming, crafted. Seducing this dirty old man with my moves would be easy —tricking Grant would be the true test.

My eyes focused on Jim, but I didn't see him. I wasn't dancing for Jim. I wasn't even dancing to save my brother. I was dancing for Grant—I saw Grant's face, his lips, his eyes trace my movements. Slow and seductive rather than fast and frenzied. How many times had he sat in this room, watching a broken girl dance for him? What had these women given him that I hadn't been able to? Did he open up to them? Truly let them in instead of how he always tried to be tough and resilient for me?

As I made love to the pole, my heart pounded, my stomach fluttered. This was where I was meant to be. After seeing Grant again and having him shut me out, literally and figuratively, I realized I wasn't done with him. As much as I didn't want to admit it, I missed him, despite the fact that he had been an asshole to me. I'd hurt him, but behind his vicious words to me, I wondered if he still loved me no matter how much he tried to fight it.

A loud clap sprang me from my haze. "Bravo. Ksenya, you are enchanting. Can you start tonight? We have a huge party booked. VIPs, extravagant spenders. They love seeing a new gem. Are you game?"

I wasn't sure if this transformation would work, that I could even get close enough to any of the Team guys, but I had to try. My plan was to strip here until I saw Joaquín's Teammates. I'd focus on the first one who paid me any attention, entertain them at a similar party, and try to figure out what happened to Tiffany.

"*Da.* Thank you, Jim. I won't let you down."

I put my clothes back on, and Jim gave me a bunch of forms to fill out. Surprisingly, he actually ended up being quite nice and went out of his way to make me feel comfortable.

VIPs. It was Thursday night. I'd done my research—driven by the houses of my brother's Teammates, seen their cars in the driveway, the "Welcome Home Daddy" banners in the windows. They must've just returned from a training exercise or a deployment. Which meant they were due to make their appearance here any day.

When Grant walked through these doors, I'd be on that stage. And I would be able to dance for my man. In the shadows.

8

KSENYA

UNFORTUNATELY, JIM'S BIG SPENDERS THAT first night didn't include Grant. Or the night after that. Or the next. Days turned into weeks. It seemed as if I'd been stuck in this hellhole forever, and there was still no sign of my former lover, or any of his Teammates. I'd gone from star of the SFSU drama department with a promising future, living my dreams, moonlighting with the best thespians at American Conservatory Theater, to a lowly stripper with limited hope, stuck in a nightmare, dancing—if you could call it that—for lonely men.

I hated it—the baby talk, the lap dances, the inappropriate touches, the lewd remarks, the constant propositions. I kept telling myself—*You can do this, Mia. You're preparing for the role of a lifetime.*

The other strippers were nice at least. I was surprised that they weren't as messed up as I'd assumed they'd be. Emma was long gone though. From what I could glean, this place had a high turnover rate.

It was Taco Tuesday—carne asada, salsa bar, Coronas, churros. I'd decided to have a little bit of fun with the crowd and dressed up in a sexy border patrol costume, enjoying the irony since I was an undercover Latina. I was dancing to a Latin pop song when the doors flew open. The loud laughter of deep male voices perked my ears.

Then I saw him—my man was standing right in front of the stage.

Jolts of electricity coursed through my veins. The sweat on my back moistened my costume; the heat from the dazzling lights burned my skin. Could I really pull this off? Would Grant take one look at me and call my bluff? My mouth became dry and my heart palpitated.

We were in the same room, breathing the same smoky air. Dreaming of his face every night for months made him seem like my own mirage. But this time he was very real.

"Blurred Lines" started playing. Well, at least the song was appropriate. I glided to the pole, my partner in this urgent dance, a dance that could help me enter into this new world I so desperately sought to infiltrate.

My hips swayed, I licked my lips. Climbing to the top of the pole, I spread my legs, determined to get Grant to notice me. I had to remind myself to stay the course, not blow my dance or run over to him.

I made eye contact and he winked. I knew that wink, that look of desire. The first time he'd winked at me, sitting across from me at a coffee shop, I'd completely melted. Back then the giddiness of first love consumed me. Now, I had to hold back tears, since I was pretty positive that he had no idea I was Mia. Just some sexy stripper he hoped to see naked.

I pranced up and down the catwalk, narrowing my gaze on him. Dancing for him, willing him to connect with me. His eyes turned hungry as he followed my every movement. Soon I could barely see him through the bright lights and smoke. My hair whipped in the air, my body seduced the pole. The song ended, the smoke waned, the lights dimmed. And Grant was relaxed in a chair, motioning me to come toward him.

The plan. Stick to the plan, Mia. Watch which girls go over to his group. Don't approach him immediately, take your time. You have dreamt of this moment, planned, prepared—now it's showtime.

I gave him a coy smile, blew a kiss, and walked off the stage. I headed to the bar to get a better vantage point and some liquid courage. A quick shot of vodka calmed my nerves. Grant's skin looked darker, perhaps he'd just returned from the Middle East. His massive biceps bulged out of his black T-shirt, looking bigger than when I'd last seen them. His hair was longer, his beard fuller. And he was looking right at me.

I waved and he moistened his lips. If I avoided him, he might suspect something. I was just another dancer, and if a customer was staring at me, it was my job to flirt back.

Shoulders back, tits up. I reapplied my red lipstick, locking my gaze on his. I'd turned myself into his dream girl, his personal fantasy pinup. But I was real—well, mostly. And he was still the only man who had ever sent ripples of pleasure pulsating throughout my body.

A casual flaunt of my blond locks, a batting of my false eyelashes, and I made my way over to him. "Hi, handsome. My name, it is Ksenya. How are you doing tonight?" My accent was crisp, I rolled my *r*'s, my tongue touching the top of my mouth.

"Much better now that I saw you, sexy. I'm Grant. Where you from?" He pulled me onto his lap. I ran my fingers through his hair. He smelled the same as I remembered—pine, lemon, and vodka, as if he had just chopped down a Christmas tree and drunk a spiked lemonade to refresh. Did I smell the same to him? Could he recognize my scent despite me switching to new brands of lotion and shampoo?

"Kharkov, Ukraine." I figured my recent-immigrant ruse would explain my terse conversation. Reduce the chances for him to find me out.

His eyes zeroed in on my chest. I arched my back to give him a better view. My mind flashed to him sucking on my nipples, cradling my small breasts. He'd always seemed so pleased with me, with my body—did he really want a girl with fake tits and silicone lips?

"I've been around the world twice, but never to Ukraine. Maybe you could show me around some time." His words were slurred.

I've been around the world twice? Really—he was actually quoting the Navy SEAL "Ballad of the Frogman"? His bloodshot eyes told me he'd been wasted before he ever set foot in here.

I focused my energy on controlling my facial movements, ensuring that my eyes didn't shift or my nose didn't twitch as I spewed out my lines. "I'd love to show to you whatever it is you like to see, handsome." Had he gone to strip clubs behind my back when we were together? My heart wrenched, thinking of those nights I'd spent practicing lines from a script for class in his apartment, waiting for him to come home from boys' night, supposedly at bars and steakhouses. He'd always sworn to me he was the designated driver, that the older Team guys had forced him to join them, since he was merely a SEAL pup.

By now, every Team guy was talking to a girl. My gaze scanned to the other present members of Joaquín's Team—Paul and Mitch. Had one of them murdered Tiffany and framed my brother?

I turned back to Grant. Rules for keeping a SEAL's interest: #1 always make him the center of attention, #2 never let him see you checking out his

Teammates, no matter how insanely gorgeous. "Can I dance for you?" Talking too long would arouse suspicion. He thought I was a stripper. I needed to earn my tips.

"Sure, sexy. Follow me."

Follow me? Even now, even in here, he was taking charge. I usually led my customers—emasculated husbands, inebriated frat boys, insecure businessmen, even conceited rock stars—back to the VIP room. But no, Grant was in control. He was a regular. He knew the drill.

He grabbed my hand, and instead of recoiling at his touch and being disgusted about his ease in this place, I couldn't fight my arousal toward him. What the hell was wrong with me for still wanting him? Especially in here, when I looked like a porn star. When would this pain end? The combination of disgust, sadness, and guilt crashed through my mind. Had my abandonment driven him to seek comfort with these women? Or had he been seeing them all along?

But I didn't have a moment to reflect. I needed to give the performance of a lifetime.

9

GRANT

I LED KSENYA—HOWEVER THE fuck you pronounced it—to the back room. After months on a mission, I couldn't wait to see her peel off her clothes. Alone with me, without a group of guys also getting off on her.

She was so fucking hot. Physically, she was exactly my childhood fantasy pinup, as if she had been designed for me. Long platinum-blond hair. Full, round breasts which busted out of her black negligée. Plump, pouty lips. Definitely not the girl-next-door type, like my ex Mia, the only woman I'd ever loved.

But I could tell something was off with this chick. I was a regular here, and she didn't seem the type to take her clothes off for money. She was too stunning, almost too sexy. Why was she stripping?

Strippers were the best; I didn't care what anyone else thought. They were fucking hot, listened to your problems, loved sex, didn't nag you, didn't expect anything in return. Sure, they danced practically naked for money, but men paid for women no matter how you looked at it. Whether it was nice dinners, designer clothes, expensive jewelry—nothing was for free. At least with strippers, you got what you paid for. I hadn't been this callous, cynical man when dating Mia. This was who I was now.

Fuck it, I didn't care. I wanted to see her naked. That was the problem with these titty bars—rules, cameras, bouncers.

I sat on the blue velvet sofa. "Dance for me, baby."

Her mouth turned up into a smile, and her long hair brushed against my face. That sweet, citrusy scent of her skin—smelled like Mia, even though she had always masked it with coconut products. I pictured Mia naked, rubbing lotion all over her thighs, an image I could recall to my head anytime, anywhere, day or night—a useful skill when I was stuck in a dirt hole in Afghanistan. I wondered if Ksenya tasted like Mia, too?

Fuck. I couldn't think of Mia now. I had a sexy woman in front of me and refused to think about my ex. All those nights when I was alone in the hospital, missing her, hoping she would come back to me. She had made it clear she didn't want me. I had moved on.

A slow melodic beat started playing, not the upbeat dance crap the strippers usually chose. I recognized the song, a power ballad by a hair metal band. Interesting choice. Why had she picked that song? Doubtful she was even born when it came out. Whatever—Eastern European chicks were live wires.

I relaxed, took a swig of my beer. Ksenya's chocolate-brown eyes locked onto mine. Though the color was different, something about the shape of her eyes reminded me of Mia. Dammit, what was wrong with me?

Without prompting, Ksenya turned around, her fingernails, filed short and painted red, dug into my jeans, her tits rubbed my chest. A coy glance, a warm touch. She was totally into me. Not in the normal stripper bilking her client way, or off in her own mind dancing and thinking about her problems. This chick seemed one hundred percent present and focused on me. I loved it.

I needed her to come home with me. "Baby, how long've you worked here?"

She turned away from me. My only way to connect with her was through my voice—I wasn't allowed to touch her, which was so hard since her juicy ass was only inches from my tongue.

She shot me a glance over her shoulders. "Few months. It is job."

Her broken English was charming. The only foreign girls I had met were overseas. Some of the Team guys liked going to brothels, but I refused to pay for sex, especially after what happened to my buddy Pat. He'd hired a hooker in an Aruban brothel, and she turned out to be a sex-trafficked American. I couldn't help thinking that all those women overseas in those places were forced into the sex industry, victimized, abused. I refused to be a part of their nightmares.

Besides, I could get plenty of women right here. I was used to San Diego coeds, no challenge at all once they found out I was a SEAL. Ksenya hadn't even asked me what I did for a living. "Yeah? You're too gorgeous for this place. I've seen some other Eastern European women here, but most of them seemed harder. You seem fresh. What's your deal?"

She bit her bottom lip; her eyes glanced down at her clear stripper heels. I paused for a second to catch my breath, Mia always used to bite her lip when she was nervous. "I have no story. I need it, the money, and my English is not so good. I have no family. Dancing it is what I am good at."

"Do you have many regular clients?" Strippers lied, would tell you whatever you wanted to hear. But I was pretty talented at detecting bullshit.

"Few. But I don't do extras." She squeezed my thighs. "Not even for you, handsome. I just dance."

Fuck, I hadn't gotten laid in months. I didn't want to get blue balls or waste my time trying to meet a girl in a bar. I didn't do the fuck-buddy thing either. Way too much drama, and if I was fucking a girl, she better not be foolish enough to cheat on me. At least Mia never screwed around with other men. And my dumb ass had been faithful to her too. "Hey, when's your shift over? I'd like to see you out of here. I know this great little sushi place downtown."

"I have plans tonight." Her eyelashes lifted. "I'm not hooker. Only dancer."

"Hookers hold no interest for me. All I want is to grab a bite to eat." I wanted her to know I didn't see her as just a stripper. She had an angelic face, and I needed to get to know her, carnally.

She nuzzled my neck, cupped my face in her hands. "Tomorrow? I get off at eight."

"It's a date." I took out a hundred dollars and handed it to her. She started dancing again, but I stopped her. She could give me a private dance tomorrow night. And fuck if that couldn't come a moment too soon.

10

KSENYA

S USHI? HAD GRANT SERIOUSLY ASKED a stripper out to dinner? He couldn't possibly know I'm Ksenya. Emma must've been right when she said he wooed the girls at Panthers, taking one out whenever he was in town. I knew he was single—no steady girlfriend since me—but when had this stripper fetish started? What if he'd cheated on me when we were together? Bile rose in my throat. Was I simply naïve expecting him to have been faithful to me?

Dinner with Grant was not the plan. I wanted to observe him with the strippers. See who else talked to the guys, try to figure out which girls were at Paul's place the night of the murder.

But I couldn't say no to Grant. I was in character. I was Ksenya, and she wanted someone to save her.

I seethed inwardly. I didn't need a man to save me. The only good thing that had resulted out of this nightmare was that for the first time in my life I had proved I could take care of myself. Without my parents, Joaquín, or Grant to pick me up when I fell. Yes, Joaquín had left me the money in the safe deposit box, but every red cent had gone toward this plan. Once my brother was free, I refused to ever rely on anyone but myself again.

What was I going to wear? I'd just finished my shift twenty minutes ago. I rummaged through my duffel bag in the dressing room—stripper costumes, Victoria's Secret PINK sweats, and a skintight black dress I'd worn last week for VIP night. Mia would've worn sweats, but Ksenya would choose the dress. And heels, earrings, and makeup. Playing Ukrainian Barbie was hard. I just hoped she was hot enough to get her Ken doll to talk.

What I would give to go home to my room in El Cajon, shower, scrub off this makeup, crawl into my pajamas, and binge-watch *Dancing under the Stars*. The arches in my feet were cramped from those ridiculous stripper shoes, my empty stomach was craving a heaping plate of pesto pasta, not sushi, and my eyes were heavy from lack of sleep. Not to mention these humongous tits were killing my back. But I wasn't going to blow my big chance.

I waited by the back entrance for Grant. My goal for the night was to get him to open up to me, even just a little. Then maybe he'd invite me to the next stripper party he and his buddies had. But I had no intention of sleeping with him—not now, not ever again. I was confident in my acting ability, but I couldn't control the way my body would respond to his touch. If we made love, he would know I was Mia. I closed my eyes, imagined the warmth of his chest pressing on my skin, the stubble from his beard tickling the nape of my neck, the tender way he used to hold me.

I stared down Convoy Street, scanning for Grant's truck. Our club was next to used-car dealerships and Korean barbecues, and the scent of burning animal flesh and kimchee made my skin crawl. A few customers catcalled me, and I resisted the urge to flip them off.

The roar of a motorcycle shook the air. Grant had bought a bike? I was so pissed at him. He'd always wanted one when we were together, but I refused to let him get one. It was one thing for him to risk his life overseas defending our freedom; it was another to end up as road kill for a drunk driver and die the way my parents had.

I wanted to go off on him, but I highly doubted Ksenya would nag him. I took a deep breath and centered myself, slipping back into Ksenya's world.

His windblown hair framed his face. I loved his masculine jaw line, his beard, his intensity. The deep scar on his neck beckoned me to reach out and caress it. I had clearly underestimated the hold this man still had over me.

"Hey, gorgeous. Hop on." He handed me a helmet.

"You drive motorcycle? Is dangerous, no?" Screw it, I figured Grant would like a little bit of sass from Ksenya.

"Nothing's dangerous when you're with me. Let's go."

Cocky son of a bitch. In the past six months, I'd never once considered how hard it would be to shut my mouth and not call Grant out on his bull-shit. I pulled the tight helmet over my head, wrapped my arms around his waist, and held on.

The wind chilled my legs as we entered the freeway, my skintight dress riding up around my thighs. I'd never been on a motorcycle, fundamentally refused to ever ride one after my parents died. But gliding through traffic, I had to admit, for the first time since Joaquín had been arrested, that my pulse steadied, my heartbeat calmed. For our brief ride I vanquished memories of my parents, Joaquín's troubles, my heartache—this overwhelming sense of urgency. I was truly enjoying living in the moment.

We pulled up to some hole-in-the-wall sushi joint. We weren't in the ritzy part of downtown. No, we were on Broadway, a few blocks from the county jail where Joaquín was being housed.

I'm here, Joaquín. I haven't abandoned you.

It was hard being so close to him and not being able to reach out to him, but I had faith I was on the right path.

I removed my helmet and crinkled my nose. The stench of urine and tar churned my stomach. Grant would never have taken me to a restaurant like this. This was a place where a guy took a girl to hide her, not to show her off. Was he shrouding me because I was a stripper? Or did he have a girl-friend somewhere who he was cheating on?

Last night, I almost felt guilty for using him to find the truth after having dumped him in the past. But he chose to date a stripper, who on the surface was clearly not the type of woman to get serious with. So if he wanted a fling, at least he would be spending time with a woman who actually cared about him.

Grant studied my face. "This place is great, I promise. I know it doesn't look like much, but the food is incredible."

Great, he could still read me even as Ksenya. "I'm sure it is wonderful. I'm excited for good meal."

His eyebrows lifted. "It's refreshing to meet someone who looks beyond outward appearances."

I bit my lip. "Compared to where it is I am from, this place is like palace." Grant had a point. This could be the best sushi in the city, but I would've never agreed to go here when we were dating.

I'd never considered myself to be pretentious, but I admit I'd been a tad judgmental. I wondered if Grant had held himself back with me, afraid to push me to try new experiences. Why hadn't I just been more open when I was with him?

The waitress sat us at a cramped table, stuck between the sushi bar and the restroom. Grant ordered a bunch of rolls, Asahi beer for himself, and sake for me.

He held my hand across the table. "So, how long have you been in San Diego?"

"Few months. I lived together in San Francisco with my baba. She died, and it was too much money for me there to live. I have friend here who was dancer and made good money, so I come down. The clubs in San Francisco are good, but houses are not so cheap." My story was solid—I'd gone over it a thousand times—but gazing across at a man who regularly interrogated terrorists caused my palms to sweat.

The waitress brought us the first batch of rolls. Grant swirled a neon green mound of wasabi in the soy sauce with such concentration I shuddered from his intensity. "So you live with your friend?" he asked.

"No. She got boyfriend and quit the club. I live with older woman. She gives to me room in home, and I help with cleaning and cooking." I tasted a piece of sushi—the Motion in the Ocean roll. The spicy jalapeño sauce lit my lips on fire while the sweet citrus put out the flame. I swallowed the tuna, the slithery fish sliding down my throat. *Dear God, please don't let me gag.* I had been a vegan for years. But I knew there was no chance I could remain one in front of Grant.

"You could clean and cook for me."

"Very funny."

He popped a crunchy soft-shell crab roll into his mouth. "I'm serious, I travel all the time for my job. I could use some help."

Was he kidding me? He had to be joking—he did not invite a stripper he had just met to move in with him. I dated this jackass for two years and we hadn't even lived together.

"No, thank you. I do not know you."

His eyebrow lifted, and his mouth widened into a sly smile. "Well, get to know me."

My head pounded and it wasn't from the cheap saké. Who was this man who sat across from me? Was it possible to change that much or did every man reinvent himself when dating someone new? I fought the desire to kick Grant in the balls, hightail it out of there, and get back to my life.

"What is it you do for living?"

"I sell pharmaceuticals." His nose didn't even twitch; he'd become an expert at hiding his lies. Though this fib didn't bother me. SEALs never told civilians what they did for a living. Joaquín told everyone he met that he drove an ice cream truck. That guy you met in a bar boasting about being a SEAL? He was a liar.

"Let's get out of here. I want to take you somewhere." He signaled to the waitress and paid the bill in cash.

We slid onto the back of his bike, and I placed my arms around him. I wanted to vanish into this moment, go back to the way we were when we had first fallen in love. Before he deployed that first time. Before I'd done something stupid. Before I didn't have the guts to confide in him.

Grant headed down to the pier, in front of the *USS Midway*, a retired Naval carrier turned maritime museum. The millions of lights from the ship illuminated the ocean, as the view of Coronado's Hotel Del beckoned in the distance. Grant might be lying to his date about his job, but he was also sharing his love of the Navy. Maybe he didn't see Ksenya as just a conquest.

We stood under the world-famous *Unconditional Surrender* statue, which portrayed a sailor kissing a nurse at the end of World War II.

Grant took me into his arms, and I was sure he was going to kiss me under the moonlight. "You're so incredibly hot. Let's go to a hotel."

"Nyet."

"Come on, babe. We'll have a great time. If you feel uncomfortable, I'll take you home. I just want to spend some time with you."

My first instinct was to slap him. But my panties became damp as I imagined what this new Grant would do to me. Which way should I go— sweet, shy, good girl forced into stripping? Or nasty, freaky, bad girl who owned her sexuality?

I had vowed when this deception started—hell, when this date started— to never sleep with him again, fearful that he would discover my identity. Now I decided I wasn't going to make any rules. I'd fooled him so far— maybe I could fool him in bed as well. I'd spent every night for the past two and a half years imagining making love to him. As Mia, I'd been the girl next door, a young inexperienced virgin, petrified to ask him to act out my deepest fantasies. But I had always harbored a secret desire to play the temptress.

If Grant wanted to party, I'd be ecstatic to rock his world. This time, I wouldn't hold back. I couldn't. Ksenya would have to be a wildcat in bed for me to pull off this deception.

Sleeping with Grant might be the only way to truly have him let down his guard and open up to me. But this time, sex would be on my terms, on my timeline—and for once in my life, I'd be in control.

11

GRANT

I WASN'T BUYING KSENYA'S GOOD-girl act, but I was game to play along. Her eyes had dilated at my request, but she still agreed to go to the hotel with me. She was, in fact, a stripper, not that I cared. It was about time I dated a girl who loved sex.

I'd worshipped Mia—we'd been each other's firsts, and I would've never made it through BUD/S without her support. But whenever I wanted to ask her to try something new in bed, I'd chickened out, afraid of how she would react. I didn't want to lose or disrespect her, so I'd repressed my desires. She was a "good girl," and I'd figured that making love to her should only be about tenderness.

Since we'd been apart, I'd had mostly one-night stands with chicks in bars and flings with messed-up strippers. I wanted to be with a girl who could fulfill my every fantasy. I wanted to *fuck* this girl, not marry her.

I sent a quick text to my buddy to reserve the Bachelor Pad Suite at the Coronado Bay Hotel. Equipped with its very own stripper pole and a huge mirror over the bed, I couldn't think of a better place to watch Ksenya ride me. The trip over on my motorcycle was sexy as all hell. Her tight little body wrapped around mine, her huge tits pressed into my back.

The regular girls who worked at Panthers didn't seem to have any light inside them. Their eyes were cold, their hearts dead. Fuck, I felt dead when I dated them. But not with Ksenya. This chick was different. There'd been other damn sexy strippers from there, but this girl seemed almost innocent. Her immigrant-orphan hardship story was way more compelling than the typical stripper drama. She awoke something inside me.

Even so, I wasn't going to chase her. I had enough willing women ready to drop their panties and suck a SEAL's cock.

I'd only pursued one woman in my life. And frankly, I didn't have the time to put into getting to know someone when I was deployed nine months out of the year. How could I ever build a relationship with a sweet girl who'd always be there for me if I didn't have any time to spend with her? I'd done that with Mia and failed.

I pulled up to the hotel entrance with Ksenya and tossed the valet my keys. I pressed her against the building. My lips met hers, and her fiery mouth tasted as sweet as freedom.

She let out a slow, sweet moan. My cock hardened in my jeans—only a fine layer of denim between it and her wet panties. Navy SEALs rarely wore underwear.

I checked in at the front desk, the key already waiting for me. One of my Team guys knew the concierge; whenever one of the suites was vacant, he was happy to let one of us use it.

Ksenya's mouth dropped when I opened the door to the suite. The pad was pure decadence: a black leather sofa faced the gold stripper pole, a mirror overhead. A full bar beckoned to me.

"Oh, Grant. This place it is very beautiful. It must be very expensive. Do you come to here many times?"

I studied her face; she looked almost dazed.

"Don't worry about it, baby. I have a friend who hooks me up. Would you like a drink?"

She smiled in agreement, so I poured her a glass of wine, myself a shot of whiskey. She studied the pole. "You want me to dance for you now?"

Hell yeah, I did. But I didn't want her to feel cheap. "Let's just relax for a bit."

"Can I look around?"

"Sure. Make yourself at home." She walked around the suite, examining the pole, the gaudy painting of a naked woman to the right of the bar.

I downed my shot, and poured another, then another. My head buzzed from my earlier beer.

She sat on one of the barstools, slowly sipping her wine.

Then I saw it. Her lips. Big and pouty, but the left edge of her mouth curled when she smiled. Just like Mia's used to.

Fuck. I was still so hung up on that girl that even sitting here with a beautiful woman, all I could think about was my ex.

I studied Ksenya's face. It was perfect. Completely symmetrical, as if an artist had sculpted it. No imperfections, like the small bump Mia had on her nose. Still, I'd loved Mia's face; she was unique. She had been all mine. I was still not sure why I was never enough for her. But that was history. This was my present.

Ksenya bounced her knees, fidgeting in her swivel chair. I turned the satellite stereo on in the room. "Undressed" by Kim Cesarion was playing. Perfect.

"Dance for me." I relaxed on my sofa, the bottle of whiskey in my hand, waiting for my private show.

Her skin flushed, and her fingers brushed down her side. My every nerve tingled.

A wicked smile slowly built on her lips, and she pranced up to the pole. She teased me with glimpses of her tan thighs, the round curve of her back. She was baiting me, fondling her chest.

"Take off your dress."

She obliged and it slid onto the carpet. Man, she was incredible. Easily the finest woman I'd ever laid my eyes on. Including actresses, porn stars, and every stripper I'd ever fucked. She was too good to be true.

"Now your bra." I set the bottle down.

With one hand, she unhooked her red lace bra. I motioned her to the sofa, and she rubbed her breasts in my face. My tongue lashed at them, but she slapped me away and backed to the other end of the cushions. The friction from my jeans reminded me how much I wanted her, and my breath hitched. Fine, I'd play—for now. I couldn't wait to have my way with her.

"Show me your pussy."

Her fingers traced down her stomach, and she pushed off her panties. Her skin looked soft and warm, a thin landing strip begging me to devour it.

I lowered my voice, touched my tongue to my upper lip. "Come here."

Naked except for her heels, she crawled over to me. She pushed herself on top of me and straddled my lap. I closed my eyes for a second, just to feel her sensational body pressing down on mine. I lived for this moment, the moment of anticipation before I hit my target. I leaned in for a kiss.

"I told you, I don't do extras," she hissed before my mouth found hers.

"Don't tease me, baby."

"I gave you the dance you paid for yesterday. If you want to see me again, you can come by club. Tomorrow."

She kissed my neck, my face, her warm tongue tracing my ear, and I imagined her tongue dancing around my cock. Her lips pulled away from me, and she quickly gathered her clothes, dressed, and slammed the door behind her.

Fuck.

My balls burned. I could've easily stopped her, but I knew I was being an asshole. After having my heart ripped to shreds by Mia, I just couldn't allow myself to see women as good for anything other than sex. Women treated me like this too—none of the San Diego coeds wanted to get to know Grant, they just wanted to be fucked by a Navy SEAL, something to brag about to their sorority sisters. I figured after getting fucked over by Mia, these types of emotionless hookups with no future were the only way for me.

Maybe I was wrong and Ksenya was just a typical stripper playing me—after money, fame, or power—getting me all worked up so I would give into whatever she demanded. But I had to have her. I was ready to play her game.

12

KSENYA

I RACED OUT OF THAT hotel suite and headed to the elevator— pressing those stupid buttons and begging those doors to take me away from this nightmare. I reached into my purse to grab my cell phone and call for a cab.

Had I just squandered my best chance to find out the truth and save Joaquín? After everything I'd gone through to get here, how could I be so careless?

I flicked off those ridiculous heels and threw them in my purse. I was wrong—I didn't have what it took to accomplish this. I couldn't handle being treated like a whore. Not by the love of my life. I fantasized about unbridled passion with Grant, nothing off-limits. But I had to feel like he saw me as more than a random stripper to get off with. I'd just wanted to tease him, bait him, but I panicked when I couldn't control my emotions. I needed to regroup.

The blue light on the elevator button taunted me. *Open!*

Thump, thump, thump.

I didn't need to look back. The rhythm of Grant's gait gave him away.

I shuffled back a step. He'd always been protective of me as Mia, but I was impressed that he'd come back to retrieve a stripper.

He placed his hand on my shoulder, and I shuddered. "Ksenya, I'm sorry.

You're so fucking sexy, and I can be a prick when I'm drunk. I can call you a taxi or you can stay here with me. I won't touch you."

The elevator door opened. My resolve forced my feet to stay put and not hightail it inside. I had to see this through, stay with him tonight. His false bravado masked his loneliness. I knew the real Grant. Deep down, I wanted to comfort him, hold him, make love to him, be the woman he needed, and apologize for abandoning him.

But my only goal now was to get him to trust me. "I forgive you."

His arms extended to me, and he pulled me into his chest. For a second, I tried to resist, retreat into my shell, but I found comfort in his embrace. His bulging arms seemed almost twice the size they had when I saw him at his apartment in January—how was that even possible? Sure, he was twenty-three now, not the same lean nineteen-year-old boy I'd fallen in love with. But his biceps were massive, like one of those slicked-up bodybuilding guys you saw on television. Was Grant using steroids? I'd seen him only six months ago, and he hadn't been this ripped.

I couldn't dismiss this thought, especially now. I had to find out what had happened to Tiffany, and I refused to allow myself to let my feelings for Grant get in the way of my mission.

What was the link, where were the clues? Drugs, sex, money? Maybe that saké and wine were too potent, because not a thing about Grant, or this night, made any sense to me. This man standing in front of me, who could easily be Thor's stunt double, was nothing like the man he'd once been, the man I'd given my heart to.

"Let's go inside. I'll sleep on the couch."

I nodded, and we walked back into the hotel room. He poured me a glass of water, and we snuggled up on the sofa. This was more like it. He stroked my hair, and I nuzzled his chest. I had so many questions, but I couldn't decide which ones to start with.

My throat burned. "Why did you take me to here? Do you have girlfriend at your home?" My heart thumped. I didn't want to know the answer to this question, not that I had any reason to believe he would tell me the truth.

He swallowed and his voice softened. "Nah, babe. I just thought you'd like this place. I just wanted to take you somewhere nice, figured you weren't used to a place like this. I had a girl once, a few years ago. She left me when I was in an accident."

This time he wasn't lying. I blinked back tears; my brown contacts itched. After my parents died, I couldn't imagine loving someone so deeply and losing them. Being the sister of a SEAL was bad enough; I couldn't fathom being the widow of one.

"I am sorry, Grant. I don't understand how she could leave you when you were not well."

But I did know. I had left Grant, but it wasn't because I didn't love him. I loved him more than anything—even more than my own brother, though I'd never admitted that to anyone. But seeing Grant laid up in a hospital bed, a deep scar under his neck, his chiseled face bandaged, I couldn't…I wouldn't go through that agony again. I'd watched my parents cling to this earth hooked to respirators, and I'd had to help make the agonizing decision to turn off their life support. When Joaquín called and told me Grant had been trapped in a vehicle that had been destroyed by a roadside bomb, I knew I couldn't go through the pain of losing someone I loved so deeply again. I was too young, too fragile after losing my parents, too scared to trust again. So I'd walked away from him, from us, and had regretted it ever since.

And that wasn't the only reason. Something had happened to me while Grant was deployed. I'd done something stupid and paid the consequences. My shame for my lack of judgment bore at me, and I didn't want to explain myself to Grant. So I took the easy way out and ran, like a coward.

He lifted my chin with his hand. "Look, I'm sorry. You're different than the other strippers I've met, and I thought you were into me. One of my buddies is having a rager tomorrow at this townhouse he's housesitting in Pacific Beach. Would you like to come with me?"

Hooyah! There it was. The golden ticket. The invite I'd been waiting for. This was actually working. Old Grant never invited me to the beach parties —I'd been relegated to family days with four-year-olds running around with melting Popsicle sticks. I remembered the rules—no wives, no girlfriends. Men only. But I wasn't dense—I knew their bashes had no shortage of willing women thrilled to be in the presence of sexy SEALs. These women were peripheral ghosts to every SEAL wife and girlfriend.

I knew I was in.

"I would love to go to beach." I wrapped my arms around his neck, nuzzled his ear. He attempted to kiss me, but I turned away. The sharp stubble from his beard grazed my cheek. I wanted him to pin me down and ravage me, but it was completely out of the question.

"I'll pick you up at the club at seven. Feel free to invite any of your hotty friends."

You got it, buddy!

I clenched my hands to contain my joy, fearful that Grant would somehow realize my true intentions. "Oh, I will. They will love to come. I not want you to think I go home with all man I meet at strip club. You are first, I promise this to you."

He leaned into me and made firm eye contact. "I believe you."

I already knew Grant would never forgive me for deserting him when he was injured. But once he found out I'd completely deceived him, I would be dead to him forever. There would be no coming back from this second betrayal—ever.

As a SEAL, he had to trust his partner implicitly, know she would be faithful during his never-ending deployments, confident she would be by his side and support him when he was silently suffering from witnessing the horrors of war. We could never be together again. If anything, being with him tonight confirmed that belief.

It's okay, Mia. This is about Joaquín. Freeing Joaquín. Your sacrifice for him.

I'd made my choice. I chose exonerating Joaquín over getting Grant to trust me. And as long as I could free Joaquín, I vowed never to regret my path.

13

GRANT

L AST NIGHT COMPLETELY SUCKED. I couldn't even score with a
stripper. But I wasn't about to blame myself. Call me a conceited
prick, but I didn't usually have a problem with the ladies. Ever. Maybe I
should've told her what I did for a living. Like the magical phrase "open
sesame" opened the cave's mouth for Ali Baba, the words "I'm a mother-
fucking Navy SEAL" usually opened a women's mouth to my cock.

But who knew? This chick wasn't American—the SEAL line probably
wouldn't work with her anyway. Her ignorance about SEALs suited me fine.
I didn't want to deal with another Frog Hog, begging to start a relationship
or bragging to her girlfriends she fucked a SEAL, only to cheat on me once
she got what she wanted. I wanted one woman I could fuck whenever I
desired, no talk about our futures or our pasts. Ksenya was perfect.

I'd sacrificed so much for Mia, hadn't tried out for any East Coast Teams
so I could stay close to her, spend weekends with her instead of bonding
with my guys. What she didn't know was that I'd planned on proposing to
her, had even asked Joaquín for his blessing. Then she'd left me while I was
clinging to life in a hospital bed, her engagement ring tucked in the bottom
of my seabag.

But being injured was the best thing that ever happened to me. Otherwise, I'd have married that bitch, and she would've divorced me the second
we had any problems, which was inevitable being married to a Team guy.

Last weekend we had the big welcome-home family day, though this homecoming had been bittersweet. No Joaquín, no Mia. For a while they had both been like family. All the Team guys loved Mia then. Despite my anger toward her, I wondered how she was doing without Joaquín. She was completely alone now—no parents, no brother. I was almost surprised she hadn't tried to contact me again. I couldn't blame her for giving up after the way I'd shut her down after Joaquín's arrest.

Our last homecoming rager ended with a dead stripper and my best buddy getting accused of her murder. My Team needed this party for morale, since we were struggling to get back to normalcy. And rebuild our trust.

I believed Joaquín was innocent. I hoped that I would see something tonight, a trigger, and could figure out what the fuck went wrong that night. Even on deployment, none of the guys remembered anything. Kyle, Vic, Joe, and Pat had left earlier that evening; the rest of us had all been in rooms with strippers. No one remembered anyone else being at the party, but I had to admit we were all pretty fucked up. I'd actually vowed to stop frequenting strip clubs after that girl's death, but I went back to the club to see if I could find any clues. Ksenya hadn't been at the party that night, but maybe she'd heard some girls talk.

My truck pulled up at the strip club. Ksenya stood out front, wearing a thigh-skimming black-and-pink skirt, with a tight black tank top. I could see her nipple buds begging me to suck on them. Tonight. I had to have her tonight.

She leaned into my window and kissed me on the cheek. "Hi, Grant. These are my friends Brenna, Eden, and Kristi."

Another bottle-blonde, a redhead with tacky lipstick, and a brunette with sparkly nails. My friends would love these women. But unfortunately none of them had been at the party that night. "Nice to meet you, ladies." I nodded, and they piled into my truck. The scent of cheap perfume and self-tanner filled the air.

I headed to Pacific Beach. The girls chatted in the back, but I could only focus on Ksenya's hand rubbing up my thigh. The closeness of an exquisite woman who had not once peppered me with questions was comforting. She hadn't interrogated me about my job, mentioned my family, or asked me what I wanted from her. It was probably the language barrier.

"You look beautiful tonight."

"Thank you. You look to me very handsome."

I laughed. Her accent was cute. I'd never understood the obsession some men had with foreign women. I was a diehard patriot—I bled red, white, and blue. It had never crossed my mind to date someone who hadn't been born in the United States. But maybe I had been too closed-minded. I allowed myself to entertain the thought of dating a woman who would be there for me even if I lost a leg, who would nurse me back to health. Someone who would never betray me. Like Mia had.

Fuck. It had been so long since I'd given so much thought to Mia. Yes, I had missed her dreadfully, but that pain had soon turned into anger. Why was I thinking so much about her now? I had been with dozens of women since we split, and none had ever caused me to scrutinize our relationship so much. Was it Ksenya? Was it because I felt connected to her? Her manner-isms? *Why now?*

Stop. Don't even think about it.

I'd enjoy the attention she was giving me while I was in town. Then I'd deploy again and I was sure she'd move on to her next client.

But this woman's voice, the sound of her laughter, the way she looked at me, there was comfort in her presence. I couldn't explain this unshakeable feeling that no matter how hard I tried, she was more than a one-night stand.

14

KSENYA

G RANT BARELY SAID A WORD on the car ride. I couldn't tell if he was beginning to figure me out, if he had something on his mind, or if he was losing interest in me after only one date. Despite my protests, I didn't know how long I could play the full virginal stripper act. If Grant grew sick of my games, he could toss me aside, and I'd lose my only shot at exonerating Joaquín. I really needed to pull myself together and solidify my plan.

Grant parked his truck a few blocks from the beach. A crush of tourists swarmed the streets. A young couple headed toward the water, basking in the glow of the sunset. I paused and watched them, a stolen glimpse into what had to be first love. The man gazed at the woman, their movements in sync, walking quickly, as if to erase the distance between them.

Grant had looked at me like that once—as if he thought I could do no wrong, that we would be together forever. Now he looked at Ksenya with a combination of hunger and suspicion. His skin was flushed, yet his eyes were narrowed. Was he suspicious of me? I was pretty confident that I had him fooled. Even so, I knew Grant would never look at me with such tenderness again.

Focus, woman.

I was so pathetic, thinking about my relationship with my ex-boyfriend instead of clearing my brother's name. No more. From here on out, Grant was nothing more than a job to me.

He draped his strong arm around my waist. I pursed my lips.

We approached the door of the townhouse, and my fists tightened. I had to be on my game tonight. This was my big chance to find a clue. The last time Joaquín had been free was at a party like this. I said a silent prayer, closed my eyes, and hoped our parents were watching over me, guiding me toward the right path.

The door opened. Damn, guess I wasn't the only one who'd brought friends. It was like bring-your-own-stripper night, with a proper threesome ratio of two women for every SEAL. At least twenty women in various stages of undress were cuddling the men, limbs draped over each other, bodies entwined. I counted thirteen men besides Grant, but I only cared about Mitch and Paul for now—SEALs on Joaquín's squad. I needed to either eliminate them as suspects or focus my investigation on their actions the night of the murder.

My friends from Panthers dispersed and were quickly introducing themselves to the other guys. I'd chosen the girls at random, the ones who had been nicest to me, but these ladies clearly knew how to work the room. And as any girl in her twenties who partied hard in San Diego knew, these men—no matter what they claimed they did for a living—were clearly Navy SEALs.

Once you'd been to Coronado a few times, SEALs were easy to identify. Longer hair, fuller beards, massive muscles sculpted from carrying Zodiac boats, tan skin, weathered hands, cocky attitudes that oozed through the air. Basically a gang of hard bodies who could easily star in the latest summer blockbuster.

Grant seemed distracted, his gaze focused on something or someone. "Ksenya, can I get you a drink?"

I glanced in the direction of his gaze and saw a young woman with short blond hair standing near the refrigerator. "Yes, please. I want vodka and the cranberry juice."

Grant headed to the kitchen. My eyes followed his movements.

Mitch eyed me from across the room. He could be the one who killed Tiffany. I recalled his vile comments to me at the Pickled Frog. April, his longsuffering wife, was probably sitting at home, doing his laundry and putting their kids to bed, while he was out getting lap dances from strippers.

Mitch walked over and sat down next to me. "So you're Grant's latest piece of ass? Nice to meet you. I'm Mitch."

I studied his face—something was off about him. His massive dilated pupils crowded out the pigment of his brown eyes, and his nose was shaded red. "Nice to meet with you also. You sell the drugs, too?" I contained a laugh, delighted at my pharmaceutical pun.

His eyebrows lifted, but his calm face didn't react. These men were used to covering for each other. "Nah, I'm a tattoo artist. My brother has a shop." He leaned into me; his alcohol-spiked breath blew hot on my neck. "Man, you're a knockout. Have I seen you somewhere before?"

I scanned the room, but Grant had vanished. And so had the girl I'd seen earlier. Did he know her? "I work at Panthers. I saw you other night when you came in together with Grant."

He laughed and placed his hand on my upper thigh, squeezing my skin so tight I was sure he had left a mark. "No, baby. Not then. You're a porn star, aren't you?"

I pressed my hands against my stomach. Where was Grant? Why was he taking so long? In all the time I dated him as Mia, not one of his Teammates ever so much as winked at me. They knew the rules—a Team guy's woman was off-limits—no exceptions. But I wasn't Grant's woman anymore. I was a stripper. Not an equal partner, a mere possession. Did he intend to pass me around to his friends?

"No, I am not in those type of the movies. Sorry, you are wrong."

His grip tightened on my jean skirt. "I'm never mistaken, bitch. I've fucking seen you somewhere before. Maybe I've even fucked you." His finger moved up my thigh and hooked the lace trim on my panties. "Quit the virgin act. Go dance for me or something." His words shot off like rapid fire, and he forced my hand against his cock.

I considered screaming, but the blaring music would've drowned out my voice. What was wrong with this man? With all these arrogant sons of bitches? I was in some alternate bizarro reality, where these men I'd always looked up to as honorable, steadfast heroes of character were exposing themselves to be misogynistic pricks.

But I knew this asshole from all of April's tearful late-night phone calls. Mitch loved a challenge; I was just shocked at how disrespectful he was toward me. I squeezed him hard, his cock already rock solid in his jeans.

"Ah, you are right. We did fuck. But you did not last. Better luck to you next time."

His mouth raped mine, and I was too blindsided to resist. My lips numbed; a bitter, metallic taste filled my mouth.

Holy shit! Mitch was high as a hot air balloon. Was it cocaine? I'd heard about some SEALs in Aruba who were arrested for smuggling kilos of coke. Was this connected to Tiffany and Joaquín?

I shoved his hands off me, recoiling from his touch. The last time I'd felt this disgusted had been that night years ago, when I'd been young and careless—the night that I had ruined my relationship with Grant forever.

He laughed and knocked back his beer. "I like you. You're a feisty bitch. Most of the strippers here don't put up a fight. You're a wildcat. Tell you what, when Grant gets sick of you in a few weeks, which he will, you can come suck me off. Let me get your number." He took out his phone.

I steadied my nerves, desperate not to screw this chance up. "Let me put it in your phone."

He didn't hesitate to hand it to me. He scanned the room for Grant, and I knew I had to be quick. I stroked my long hair while his eyes were averted and I popped the tracking chip, which Roma had given me, from my hair clip. As I typed my contact info into Mitch's phone, I pressed the chip into the back under the leather case, praying it would work.

I handed him back the phone, and he winked at me. What a creeper. I wanted to shove my fist up his coke-filled nose, but before I could do anything Grant appeared, holding my drink, a jealous scowl on his face. I fought the desire to dump vodka and cranberry juice over Mitch's head. For all I knew, that chip could lead to texts, phone numbers, some type of clue about what had happened that night. Maybe he'd come on to Tiffany after Joaquín had slept with her, and she had rejected him. He could've become pissed off and choked her.

"Everything okay here?" Grant studied my lips, then glared at the lipstick stain on Mitch's face.

"Never better. Hey, man"—Mitch sniffled—"I'm pretty fucked up. You guys gonna fuck upstairs? Can I watch?"

I expected Grant to just laugh it off. But he shoved Mitch against the wall using a chokehold.

"You have ten seconds to unfuck yourself, Mitch. If you ever talk to her like that again, I'll slit your throat. Got it?"

The rancor alerted some of the other guys, but none of them approached.

"Relax, man. She's a fucking stripper."

Grant removed his hand from Mitch's neck. "Get the fuck out of here."

Mitch let out a laugh and walked away.

"Sorry about that, babe. He's a jerk. You okay?"

I blinked back fake tears. "Yes. Thank you. Is there a bathroom?"

He pointed upstairs. "First door on the left."

"I come right back."

Away from Grant, I let out a deep, gratifying sigh. This was actually working. No one knew who I was.

I pushed back the door to the bathroom and saw the girl Grant was looking at earlier. She seemed younger than me, maybe not even twenty. A crisp blond bob framed her round cheeks as she reapplied pink lipstick.

"Oh sorry, I can come back." I turned away.

"Hey, hon. It's okay. So you're Grant's new girl? I'm Autumn. I used to work at Panthers. Grant's a good guy."

My eyes widened. "I'm Ksenya. You know Grant?"

"Yeah." She paused, glanced toward the window. "We hung out once at another party. But things got crazy. There was this murder. I'm sure you read about it in the papers."

My breath stopped. *She was there.* "I'm new to area."

"A SEAL killed one of the girls there. I was so scared. Grant and I were in the next room when this guy Joaquín found the girl dead. So tragic. Grant hasn't told you about it?"

"No. We do not know each other so well."

"I get it. Well, good luck with him."

"Thank you." My mind raced. I needed to grill this girl, find out every detail about that night. But I had to get her away from this party—away from Grant. "What do you do now for work?"

Her mouth twisted. "I work at this new club downtown, Diamond. It's very high-end, very classy. We don't even go topless. Guys respect you way more. I'm sure the owner would love to have you. You're a knockout."

I couldn't tell if she was just super friendly or she was hitting on me. Either way, I didn't care. I couldn't let her go. "So are you. Can I get it your number and I can go to see it the place?" I reached inside my purse.

She snatched my phone, didn't say a word, and tapped in her number. "Call me anytime. Nice to meet you, Ksenya."

She shut the door. Holy shit. This was huge. I bet some of the other strippers who were at the party that night worked at Diamond. Maybe even Emma? I was getting closer to the truth, to Tiffany's real killer.

I scrubbed Mitch's touch off of me and met Grant back downstairs.

"Babe, come to the rooftop deck with me. I want to show you something."

I kissed Grant on the cheek, grateful to him for inviting me to this party. His sharp stubble burned my lips. A warm flush ran through my body, imagining that stubble grazing my thighs.

I followed him upstairs—a light giggle, a deep moan, and a passionate scream pierced my ears. Was he taking me up to one of these hidden rooms? My palms were sweaty, my hands trembled.

We passed the bedrooms, and he led me out to a small deck.

My heart stopped. I knew what he wanted to show me.

"Sit, babe. Make a wish."

A wish. Grant had brought me up here to watch the sunset. To see the Green Flash.

The Green Flash wasn't a myth, or even an optical illusion. If you ever sat on a San Diego beach at sunset and noticed a group of people staring silently in the same direction, they were looking for the Green Flash. That moment when the sun set and emitted that last glimpse of light, a flash the color of the Emerald City in Oz.

Grant pulled me to him, and I sat in his lap. His arms wrapped around me. "Babe, study the sky. Legend has it if you see a flash of green light, your wish will come true."

Was he feeling a real connection with me or did he share this with all of his dates? It took every ounce of training I had not to question him. I wanted to know how many other women he'd taken to see the flash. He'd taken me to a restaurant on this same beach on our first date, but I'd been unable to spot the flash. My eyes had been clouded by my love for him, the sadness for my parents' death still fresh in my heart. We'd planned to go back and see it together for our second anniversary, but we broke up a week before. Tonight I vowed I would finally see it.

I made my unspoken wish. My throat felt thick, my pulse quickened. I wished for Joaquín to be free, as a good sister should. But another brief wish passed through my head for Grant to forgive me and for us to fall in love again.

His arms tightened around me and I studied the fogless sky, determined to experience this phenomena with my true love. The hues from the sunset hung over the horizon; the sun dipped toward the water. Every nerve ending tingled and stirred inside me. My eyes focused; the final ray of light beamed right at me. My heart beat strongly in my chest. This glorious green spark filled my soul.

Grant whispered into my ear. "That was it, babe. This writer Jules Verne described it as 'the true green of hope.'"

Oh my God. He was quoting Jules Verne now? "You are so romantic to me."

His shoulders fell. "You just seem to have so much on your mind. I've gone through some rough shit too. When I'm really down, I look at the sunset and the flash pulls me through."

A chill pulsed through my body. Grant had told me that during BUD/S looking for the flash had kept his determination not to quit strong. I remembered nursing him back to health afterward, so proud of him and my brother for finishing. Surviving five and a half days of extreme training on less than four hours of sleep was still unfathomable to me, though I had gone through my own version of Hell Week to get here.

After taking care of him then, I'm sure he was baffled why I left him when he had been injured. But I could never tell him the truth.

My resistance to Grant was weakening, despite my disgust for this new version of him. I loved the real Grant, knew now I always would. He was the only man I ever wanted to be with—if I couldn't find my way back to him, I'd rather be alone.

I relaxed into his embrace. Having his warm mouth claim mine would be even better than finally seeing the flash. We'd kissed at the hotel, but I'd pulled away, worried, a deep longing kiss would be too intimate, too risky. But now...

He held my hand. "You want to get out of here?"

"Yes. I want to go together with you."

I texted the girls I had brought, and they all told me they could find rides home. Grant and I would be alone tonight.

15

KSENYA

THE ENTIRE DRIVE BACK TO his apartment, I bit my nails and fidgeted in my seat. There was no going back now. The natural progression of our relationship beckoned for us to become intimate. I wanted him to act out all the fantasies I'd ever had about him. Only the thought of him discovering my identity held me back.

Images rushed my head of our tame sex life. Warm, gentle, loving, definitely not hot. He'd been my first, my only. I'd never allowed myself to relax, exhale, let pleasure guide me.

Tonight would be different. I was no longer a shy eighteen-year-old virgin—I was now a twenty-two-year-old woman who feared nothing but failing her brother.

He parked, and I hopped out of his truck, chasing after him in the moonlight. He went ahead, opened the door to his apartment, let Hero out in the small yard, and then invited me in. I remembered the first time he took me back to his place. He'd been so nervous, shy even. We'd sat on the sofa, just talking all night until he finally worked up the courage to kiss me.

He wasn't shy anymore. His strong hand grabbed the back of my head, pulling me toward his mouth. I offered my neck, refusing my lips. I had something else planned for them.

My hand reached to unbutton his jeans, making its way down his chest. I knelt before him, and a deep breath escaped me. I'd never done what I was about to do. Grant had never asked, though I could recall many times that he placed his hand on the back of my neck, gently urging me to go south. Not that I hadn't loved him, not that I didn't think he was beautiful, not that I wasn't curious. I couldn't even explain my resistance. It had been just as much about fear as it had been about shyness. Despite his desire, I was afraid I'd disappoint him. I was frightened that the fantasy of me taking him in my mouth would be better than the real thing.

I popped his jeans open, his huge cock freed, standing at full attention. He still never wore underwear, it seemed. That at least hadn't changed. My hand grasped his beautiful cock, harder, thicker, and longer than I remembered, but then again, I'd never seen it from this viewpoint.

"Suck me."

I obeyed, responding to his orders. But despite his words, his dominance, I was in control. I wrapped my palm around his base, and swirled my tongue along his length. He groaned, his eyes hooded.

"Harder, babe."

My mouth clamped down on his cock, sucking as strongly as I could. He tasted spicy and a tad sweet—like chili and chocolate. I wanted to drink him up, please him, make him need me again.

A groan left his lips, his back arched. "Deeper, Ksenya. Fuck."

He didn't know I was Mia. I was Ksenya to him. It almost made me cry, knowing he wasn't in any way thinking of me. He was simply using yet another woman to give him pleasure. My heart ached.

Despite that, I also felt a measure of pride. He liked what I was doing. My confidence rose. The power over him caused a flutter in my stomach. My panties were soaked, wanting more, wanting to feel this same strong cock inside me, filling up any space between us.

He was pulsing inside my mouth. I gripped his thighs, pulling him deeper into my throat.

His hand pressed on the back of my head. "Ksenya, stop, I…"

I had no intention of stopping. He was mine. My man. Forever. I wanted to be the only woman to make him feel this way.

He exploded into my mouth, and I lapped his salty cum up, wanting to taste every last drop of him. A lazy grin spread across his face.

"You're incredible." He pulled me up from the floor, placed his arms around the swell of my back. "Your turn."

No. No way. I needed to remain in control. I'd won the first round, no reason to give in now. I fought the desire to feel his tongue devour me like I was his last meal. "Tonight it was for you."

He didn't fight me, gave me a kiss on the forehead. "Stay with me?"

I nodded, wrapped myself in his arms. This was the only way I could spend time with him, so I would treasure it and lock it away.

16

GRANT

I GAZED AT THE GIRL in my arms, purring beside me. She'd just given me an amazing blowjob, though I could tell she wasn't that experienced. She seemed nervous at first, almost shy. And she asked for nothing in return.

I wiped the sleep out of my eyes, restless but afraid to move and wake her. What was her deal? She wasn't a typical stripper. She wasn't asking for anything—money, a commitment, not even love. I didn't have a fucking clue what she wanted from me. There had to be a catch.

Her body flipped over, and I escaped from the bed. I glanced around my bedroom, typical bachelor pad; any trace of a woman had been erased. My eyes focused on a picture of Joaquín. We'd survived Hell Week together, vowed to hold each other up, never let each other quit. Then he'd slept with a stripper and she'd wound up dead. How could I be dumb enough to tempt fate and allow a stripper in my bed too?

A pain grew in the back of my throat. I hated myself for not being there for him in his hour of need.

Just a few years ago, my life had been filled with such purpose. My inner circle was tight, and I'd been secure in my path.

Now I knew that nobody was who he or she appeared to be. Not my fellow SEALs or this stripper slumbering in my bed. I trusted no one. Not even myself.

I opened the sliding glass door, prepared to prevent Hero from barking at Ksenya and jumping all over the bed—the way he always greeted a stranger.

Hero bounced in the door, his nose sniffing Ksenya's scent. But he didn't jump. A friendly bark, and he lay at the end of the bed, Ksenya curled in a ball on the mattress above him. He'd never done that with any girl I'd brought home.

Except for Mia.

I studied the chick in front of me. She and Mia were the same height, but any resemblance ended there. Mia was soft and round, with tiny breasts and a perky butt; Ksenya was lean and sculpted, with tig ol' bitties and a plump ass. Mia had hazel eyes with flecks of gold, and Ksenya had chocolate brown eyes.

But I'd noticed the outline of her contacts in the moonlight earlier. Ksenya bit her lips when she was nervous. When she smiled, her mouth curled at the edge. On the left side. Like Mia.

A crazy thought flashed through my head—what if Mia hadn't been fucking kidding about transforming herself to exonerate Joaquín? The words Mia spoke last time I saw her rang in my head. *"I'll do whatever it takes. Maybe I could go undercover? I'm a chameleon. An actress, a makeup artist. I've reinvented myself so many times even you wouldn't be able to recognize me."*

Could she possibly be that insane to get plastic surgery to fool me? Mia had been in school for acting. I'd never seen her onstage since I'd always been too busy training. It was impossible for her to be that great of an actress, wasn't it?

She had vanished—I'd even called her roommates, and they said they didn't have a clue where she went. But I knew she would never abandon her brother, ever. Even though she had turned her back on me.

No way. No fucking way.

But it was hard to ignore Hero's reaction to her. He almost seemed to...*know* her. Surely it couldn't be? Was this a game?

From the outset, Ksenya had targeted me. But why? Did she suspect me of killing Tiffany? Did she want to use me to find out who did? She wasn't in it to fuck me. Otherwise the deed would have been done already.

You're crazy, Grant. Not everything is a conspiracy. After BUD/S, it took me months to walk down the street and not look at everyone as a potential threat. I was clearly paranoid.

There was only one way to know for sure.

I have to fuck her.

TO BE CONTINUED

PART II

CHRONIC

SE7EN DEADLY SEALS EPISODE 2

"MODERATION IS THE FEEBLENESS
AND SLOTH OF THE SOUL,
WHEREAS AMBITION IS THE WARMTH
AND ACTIVITY OF IT."

— FRANÇOIS DE LA ROCHEFOUCAULD

17

GRANT

I THREW A STEAK IN the pan, the scent of grease wafting through my apartment. My ex-girlfriend Mia refused to eat meat, fucking hippie. A vegan, she'd freak when I sautéed her veggies in butter. Last night, I'd been so angry that there was even the possibility that Mia thought she could trick me. But I channeled my energy. I had a plan to test Ksenya, the girl asleep in my bed. Try to figure out if she was really Mia in disguise. My fingers tingled—this would be fun. Epic, even. If my hunch was correct, I couldn't wait for the chance to see how far Mia was willing to go to try to fool me. Did she really think I wouldn't figure out who she was?

I grabbed my cell phone. The girl on the other end answered, her voice breathy and sensual. "Hello? Grant?"

"Yeah. It's me." I said, careful to keep my voice low in case Ksenya awoke. "Hey—you were right. Something's up."

The girl rattled on about her theories and offered up a suggestion. I wasn't thrilled by it, but at this point I'd agree to anything that would get me one step closer to the truth.

"Yeah. Sounds good. I'm on it. Later."

I hung up the phone. Everything was falling into place.

First order of business was to get Ksenya to quit working at Panthers and find a job somewhere I could keep an eye on her, make sure she was safe. I didn't care that we were broken up; if there was even the slightest chance this girl was Mia, I didn't want a bunch of jackasses watching her strip. She had lost her virginity to me for fuck's sake. I mean, she had even told me when I last saw her at my place that I still was the only man she'd ever slept with. Joaquín would kill someone if he knew his sister was moonlighting as a stripper. Hell, I would too. I had to put an end to this bullshit today.

Before Joaquín was arrested, he made me promise that I would look out for his sister. I gave him my word, with every intention of honoring it. But when Mia came to me after Joaquín was arrested, begging for help, I broke my vow. Too consumed by my anger, by my rage toward her betrayal, I wanted nothing to do with her. How could she have left me when I needed her most? I was such a stubborn jackass. Maybe if I had listened to her, helped her—fuck it, helped Joaquín—instead of hiding behind my pride, things would be different. Maybe Mia and I could've worked together to exonerate Joaquín, find out who really killed Tiffany. Maybe Mia could've finally told me the truth about why she really left me, and maybe we could've started fresh. The time for second chances had passed though. It was clearly way too late.

I'd kept my own secrets from Mia, too. Secrets about how far I'd fallen without her. How I couldn't live without her. How no matter how much success I had in the Teams, it meant nothing without her by my side.

I closed my eyes, for a moment, remembering the last time she had been mine, truly mine. She'd kept a vigil at my bedside, night after night. She'd dressed my wounds, given me my meds, even read to me. She had seen me at my worst, at my weakest. I'd let down my guard, allowed her to take care of me, the way she'd always wanted to. After I could take care of myself, finally independent of the machines that were keeping me alive, when I actually felt like a man again, we'd made love one last time. And it had been different than any other time we'd had sex before. Our bodies melted into one, our kisses were passionate, our lovemaking completely connected.

I'd made a decision that night—that I didn't want to live one more day of my life without her by my side. I'd even asked Joaquín for permission to marry her, had him go to the jeweler and pick up the engagement ring I'd purchased for her online.

But then, Mia had left me. Visited me one last time in the hospital, gave me some pathetic excuse about how she wanted to study acting in San Francisco and needed her space.

Here I was, years later, conflicted about the identity of this empty woman I'd allowed in my home. My heart questioned if she was my girl, my head convinced that the only woman I'd ever loved could not possibly be crazy enough to transform her body. For my hypothesis to be correct, Mia would've destroyed her life to save her brother's—and used me in the process. I'd rather believe that I was being irrational.

I headed into my bedroom and bent over the bed, watched the rise and fall of Ksenya's chest, swollen with implants, as my mind made a mental checklist of their similarities. Ksenya smelled like citrus, she bit her lip when nervous, her smile curled on the left side. Though a different color, Ksenya and Mia both had the same almond-shaped eyes and I could clearly see the outline of Ksenya's contacts. Ksenya had to be Mia. *Had* to be. Why else would Hero react to her presence the way he had? Why did I hunger to inhale her intoxicating scent? Why did my body crave her touch? When she touched me, my pulse quickened, my heart raced. I almost felt at peace.

I wasn't a hundred percent sure yet; there were just as many differences between these two women as there were similarities. I met Ksenya at a strip club where she was writhing against a pole, spreading her legs for everyone to see. Mia was modest—she never even wore bikinis at the beach. Man, it couldn't be her.

I was still at war with myself. Were the parallels really there, or were they just what I wanted to see? As a SEAL, we never conducted any operations without the intelligence to back our actions up. And fuck this chick, whoever she was, for making me doubt my abilities. Yes, they had similar features. They smelled exactly the same. Their skin felt identical when I ran my fingers over it.

But this was pretty fucking crazy. Was my Mia capable of such an insane plan? Undergo fucking plastic surgery? Mia, who used to pale at the sight of blood, cringed when we would watch gory movies. And why?

No question she did love Joaquín. They'd both do anything for each other. Anything. Maybe Mia was just as determined as her brother. There's a saying in BUD/S training—*The pain of failure MUST be greater than the pain of succeeding, otherwise you're destined to be defeated by your goal.* And I was certain that for Mia, the pain of losing Joaquín would be worse than enduring any life without him.

But I wasn't ready to accept my suspicions as truth just yet.

I was sure of this; if this stripper was Mia, my Mia, I'd never forgive her. First for abandoning me when I needed her most, second for destroying her beautiful body with plastic surgery, and finally for this deception. There would be no room for her excuses when we arrived at the end of this road—wherever it was about to lead us.

If this girl was really a Ukrainian immigrant, desperate for a new life in America, the country I risked my life to defend, then I was a completely delusional asshole. And I needed to spend some serious time confessing my sins on a sofa to a shrink.

Nah, fuck that, I was always right.

I felt it in my bones. My instincts had never deceived me. I needed to draw her out—fool her into admitting the truth. Just as she was beginning to trust me. I felt my muscles tighten in anticipation as they did out in the field. This might even be a little fun.

Let the games begin.

18

KSENYA

I WOKE IN THE MORNING groggy from sleep. For a few seconds, I almost forgot who I'd become, my heart remembering a time when I slept in this bed almost nightly, when Grant had been mine. Back then I had been loved, whole, beautiful. Last night, though I enjoyed pleasuring him, being in control, taking him in my mouth, afterward I felt cheap. I wanted to make love to Grant. No…I wanted Grant to fuck me. Raw, hard, rough. But I wanted him to fuck Mia, not Ksenya. No matter what I did with Grant as Ksenya, I still loved him. But he was probably just having fun playing house with his newest Barbie doll.

I slipped into the T-shirt he'd left out for me, the scent of steak and eggs permeating the air.

I peered around the corner, watching my ex-boyfriend pouring coffee. Hero greeted me, licking my face. I rubbed his ear like he always liked, and he let out a groan.

I noticed Grant watching my interaction with Hero. Uh-oh. I'd seen Hero with new people. He was fiercely protective of Grant, and would lunge at anyone for getting near his master. Hopefully Hero wouldn't give me away.

"Morning, beautiful. Have a seat. I made you breakfast." Grant motioned over to the reclaimed wood table that occupied his eat-in kitchen area; a warm smile graced his beautiful face. The mere sight of him made my chest tighten.

A steak topped with a fried egg awaited me, a glass of orange juice standing next to the plate. He placed the mug of steaming coffee next to me and poured in hazelnut-flavored creamer. Dammit—I was a vegan. I'd had sushi on our date and still felt sick. But avoiding this food could raise suspicion. I wasn't going to take any chances.

Grant used to make me breakfast every morning, no matter what time he had to go to work. Back in the day, he would always make me a special meal —tofu scramble with soyrizo. At the time, I didn't realize how thoughtful that small act was, but now my gut wrenched, thinking about how stupid I'd been to throw this wonderful man away. Maybe everything would be different if I'd told him the truth about why I left him; maybe he would've forgiven me.

The problem was I didn't really know the truth myself. Yes, I knew what had happened, but since I didn't know who was to blame, I could never fully heal. I couldn't move on. I was incapacitated with the daily reminder of the looming shame that had become my existence.

I halted that train of thought right in its tracks because I could feel myself retreating. I straightened out my posture and fought to meet Grant's scrutinizing gaze.

"Thank you. You did not have to cook for me this. It is sweet." My knife sliced into the meat, blood squirting into the yolk of the egg. I took a deep breath, shoved a bite into my mouth, and prayed I wouldn't gag.

Grant watched me intently. Was he testing me? A huge meat-centric breakfast for a stripper he'd known less than a week? Maybe this had become his *modus operandi* for all the women who spent the night in his bed. I was clearly being paranoid. He was probably just infatuated with the submissive character I was playing.

My face didn't flinch as I chewed the gummy flesh. Perhaps I should've forced myself to eat meat for the past six months to prepare my stomach. "It tastes very good to me."

He winked and that devilish smile crossed his lips. "Glad you like it, babe. I know this great steakhouse downtown. Maybe we can go sometime."

I gave him a big, wide-eyed nod, batting my eyelash extensions, like this was the best date suggestion ever. "I'd love to go to there." It would be a blast—I could don a cow costume and pour a bucket of red paint over my head to protest the slaughter of those magnificent animals. That would definitely be preferable than attempting to have a romantic dinner there. *I prob-*

ably wouldn't make it in the door without yakking all over the place. I focused my energy on remembering not to bite my lip when I lied. Lord, Grant was already driving me crazy. With my luck, for our next date, he would suggest we go hunting.

He leaned back in his chair and crossed his arms over his chest. "So I've decided," he said, and moved to scratch his jaw over the sexy morning growth he hadn't yet bothered to trim this morning. My eyes dropped to his fingers and I momentarily remembered peppering that jaw with butterfly kisses in the mornings to get him to wake up. "It's time for you to quit Panthers."

My eyes jumped back up to where they belonged because *what the fuck did he say?*

"Quit? No, it may not be dream job, but it is job. What do I do to get the money if I quit? I am not hooker. I will not take it, your money." Why was he taking such a personal interest in a stripper? I needed this job to exonerate my brother. This ruse wasn't about pleasing Grant; it was about gathering information. I had to keep reminding myself that. He'd never take me back anyway. He was too proud; I'd hurt him too deeply. He deserved better than me—someone who would never deceive him like I had.

He reached across the table and took my hand. "I don't want you working there anymore. That place is trashy. You're better than that."

My eyes scanned his face. Something was off. It was one thing to take a stripper back to his place, but wanting her to quit her job after two dates and a blowjob—not to mention no sex yet—didn't seem natural. "It is very kind that you to want to make me better person, but I am not broken bird for you to fix it."

His face didn't register any anger. "Ksenya, I like you. You intrigue me. We could have something here. But you have to quit stripping." His brow furrowed as he gave me his *I'm going to kill you* stare that was normally reserved for the SEAL recruits he trained. "I need to come clean. I've been lying to you. I don't work in pharmaceutical sales. I'm a Navy SEAL. Do you know what that is?"

Orange juice dribbled down my chin. My heartbeat raced. He'd just told Kseyna the truth. Did he really want to let his guard down, let this foreign girl into his heart? A flash of anger took control of my mind. I'd purposely modeled Ksenya to be my opposite. Mia had been principled, ambitious, self-sufficient, and compassionate. Ksenya was none of those things. She took her clothes off for men, didn't seem to have any real goals besides making money, was barely able to provide for herself financially, and was ice-cold. And physically Mia was soft and feminine, but certainly not a bombshell. After all these years, knowing that my soul mate could possibly find love with a woman with so many characteristics that I lacked gutted me. Maybe everything I thought was true was nothing more than a figment of my imagination. Maybe Grant never really loved me, he only thought he did, but in the years since I'd left, he'd come to discover the kind of woman he truly wanted. A woman who was nothing like me.

Could it be possible that he was on to me? If he thought I was Mia, there was no way he would want me to get naked and entertain a bunch of men. A rolling heat loomed in my belly—I couldn't read him at all. "I have heard of the Navy SEALs. You kill people, it is true? You are dangerous man." My voice felt rushed and it should. I was beginning to feel nauseous and wanted nothing more than to get the hell out of there so I could think.

He laughed, his eyes drilling into me like a laser beam directed at my soul. "We protect America. We save people, by whatever means necessary." He formed his hands into a steeple, and I could see the muscles on his arms tighten. "I'm not dangerous to you. But I'm not going to get involved with a stripper and have other men checking out my girl. I don't want you taking off your clothes for anyone. Only me. So that's the offer. You quit stripping and I can help you find another job, or you can forget you ever met me. What's it gonna be?"

My stomach rumbled more by the goddamned second, maybe from the meat or maybe from my nerves. That, and I was lying to Grant and felt like I was a second from getting caught. He didn't deserve this. I hadn't thought this whole asinine plan out fully. Would he fall for another girl who would leave him, who would lie to him? I couldn't do that to him again. I wanted to scream at him, hit him upside the head for wanting to get involved with a fucking stripper he'd just met, but I couldn't reveal myself yet.

I refused to lose focus; allow the guilt to make me become slothful in my pursuit. I was having a leisurely breakfast, nursing my coffee, while my brother remained incarcerated.

"No. I will not quit job if I do not get the new one. If you want to forget me, you do it—forget."

His eyebrow rose as he gave me a glassy stare.

Checkmate.

He paused, that mind of his clearly plotting. "Fine. There's this bar in Ocean Beach. I know the owner. I can get you a job as a bartender. You're over twenty-one, right? As long as you're legal to work in this country, I can get you hired."

The Pickled Frog? Kyle's bar? *Hell, yes!* I wanted to break out in song to celebrate, but I refused to count my chickens before they hatched—or as my Russian instructor Roman used to say, "Don't divide the pelt of the bear not yet killed."

I took a long sip of coffee, steadying my breath. I needed a moment to sit and reflect. I had already achieved my goals for working at Panthers: I'd investigated the strippers from when Tiffany worked there and found that the ones working there now barely knew her or the SEALs. The former strippers had vanished. Autumn, the girl I'd met last night at the party, had told me that she used to work at Panthers, but had since started working at an upscale club called Diamond downtown. She was with Grant the night of the murder. She'd given me her number and told me she thought I'd get hired. I needed to investigate Diamond.

My other goal for working at Panthers was to gain access to the SEALs. And I had done that; I was sitting in Grant's place after spending the night. But Grant could cut me out at any second. No way was I going to quit my job unless I had another access point to the SEALs.

Time to switch strategies. "Very well. I will go. If I get job, then I do quit Panthers."

"Deal." He got up and knelt beside me, moving his hand up my thigh. "That wasn't too hard, was it?"

Oh God. Not physical contact. I was barely hanging on by a thread as it was. If Grant started touching me, I would surely blow this whole plan.

His eyes ran the length of my body slowly before they settled on my mouth. I fought every instinct in my body to stay still. "I haven't been able to stop thinking about how good it felt to have your mouth on my cock," he breathed, running his fingers over my lips.

Before I could react, he threw me over his back and carried me into the bedroom.

After I'd given him head last night, I'd squelched any opportunity for him to go further, even though I had wanted to. I was dying to get truly intimate with him, but it was too risky.

Once he'd positioned me on the bed, he continued running his hands all over my body, exploring me. He started to undress me slowly, kissing all my skin that was revealed. He spent a lot of time at my breasts until it was almost torture. I'd been worried that my nipples would lose sensation with the implants—thank God that wasn't the case. I closed my eyes and tried to fight the battling emotions inside of me. His touch felt like coming home and I wanted to bask in the sensations that I had gone too long without. At the same time, I wanted to rip his hands away from me and curl up into a ball because I didn't deserve it. He pulled my panties down with his free hand, slipping his fingers inside of me. His body pressed into mine, his lips hovering over my own.

I closed my eyes, savoring this moment. Last night, I hadn't allowed him to kiss me deeply, afraid he would find my mouth too familiar. All in order to dissuade him from thinking I was Mia. But this time, this kiss, I didn't think—not about how to kiss him back, not about how to position my mouth, not about how to use my tongue. This time, I allowed myself to feel and lose myself in the moment. I let my love for him guide my movements, my connection with him guide my heart.

I couldn't get enough of his lips, his stubble grazing my chin. And for those few sweet minutes, there was no Joaquín, there was no Ksenya. Just Grant and Mia, back together again.

But the battle waged through my mind once again as his kisses made their way down my body—my brain wanted to slap him, my core ached, imagining him fucking me senseless. Oh, this man made me so mad yet so turned on at the same time.

A rush of pleasure swept over me, and I knew if I didn't escape from him, I'd be unable to resist him in another minute.

I caught my breath and playfully pushed his hand away, wiggled out of the bed, separating myself from him. My breathing was labored; my skin was flushed. There was no way to hide how impossibly turned on he had made me. "We can play later. If you want me to quit, I need to go to a new job."

He sat up, his hard cock visibly straining against his pajama bottoms. "Fine, I need to shower. Want to join me?" He stripped off his pants and stood there buck-ass naked.

The man was trying to fucking kill me. I wanted him more than air, but if I remained near his hard, naked, ripped body for another second, surely I would cave. I needed to focus, to think. "Um…" I had to stop to find my voice before trying again. "I will shower later. You be alone."

"Okay, babe." He gave me a quick, playful nod and a sexy wink. A fucking *wink.* "I'll be out in a few. Make yourself at home."

He walked into the bathroom and shut the door. I closed my eyes and let out the deepest, most cleansing breath, releasing all the tension that Grant had built up in my body. *How the hell did I survive that?*

I rummaged for my phone in my purse, hating that I was forced to act like one of those paranoid women who wouldn't let it out of my sight, fearful to leave it out in the open where my secrets could be discovered. There was a time when we trusted each other and hid nothing. Sadly, this wasn't the first time I'd kept a secret from Grant.

My phone flashed. *1 message—Mitch.*

I felt my pulse quicken in excitement.

Mitch: *When can we fuck?*

Ah, Mitch, the sexy jackass SEAL. Always the gentleman. I had placed a tracking device on his phone at the party the other night. I needed to wait to get back to my crappy apartment to check the data.

My fingers danced along my phone.

Me: *Never. I'm together with Grant.*

If there was one thing I knew about Mitch, it was that he was all about the chase. The second I showed him a hint of interest, he'd be gone—and if he disappeared, I'd lose any hope I had of investigating him. And I knew Mitch had secrets—lots of them. I had to find out what his deal was.

I heard the water turn on in the bathroom. I took another second to relax, pet Hero, and to give myself props for surviving this hellish morning. I'd already come so far in such a short time. But the real question was, how far was I willing to go?

19

KSENYA

W HEN GRANT'S BIKE EXITED IN Ocean Beach, the sight of the neon green sign filled my heart with joy.

A sigh of relief escaped. Returning to one of Joaquín's old haunts gave me a strong sense of comfort. Grant and I had shared some good times here too. Memories flashed back—Grant holding my hair back in the parking lot after I puked from drinking one too many rum and Cokes, Grant telling me he loved me for the first time when I picked him up smashed after one of the SEAL funerals, sitting between my two favorite men, celebrating the day they finally earned their tridents. That day I'd been filled with hope for my future. Today, I was filled with dread for Joaquín's.

We pulled up behind the dive and climbed off Grant's bike. I quickly collected myself and remembered to pretend not to know where I was.

"Where are we?"

"This is my buddy Kyle's bar."

I nodded.

A second job working at the unofficial SEAL hangout was just what I needed.

Grant pushed back the doors and my jaw dropped—the place had been completely redone. Hardwood floors had replaced the multicolored shag carpet, and the thick oak slabs erased my memory of the tacky laminate countertops. No more whisky mixed with puke stench. This place was almost respectable.

A little less than six months ago, I'd come here desperate for help. Confused, lost, alone. Without any plan. Now, I was transformed into a new woman and was making progress every day on securing my brother's freedom. I'd gained access to the SEALs, the strippers, and had placed a tracking device on Mitch's phone. It wasn't much, but it was a start.

Kyle gave Grant a bro hug.

"Kyle, this beautiful woman is Ksenya."

Kyle kissed my hand.

"Hi, Kyle." I looked up to meet his eyes. He was massive in every way, towering over his SEAL buddies, his muscles double the size of theirs, which was just ridiculous. How was that even possible?

"Your man here tells me you're looking for a job. I'm sure the boys would love to have your banging body filling their drinks."

"I am hard worker. Thank you for meeting together with me."

"Of course, beautiful. Tell me about yourself." He leaned into me, his soulful eyes studying my face. As if he knew me.

My heart fluttered and I resisted the urge to flee. "I was born in the Ukraine. My baba and me, we came to your country. She died, and now I am alone. There is nothing else to tell."

"Well, sugar, I treat my employees like family. Have you ever tended bar?"

Even though Grant was my ex-boyfriend, in a way I feared Kyle would be the one to discover my identity. He was older than the other men and had lived a full life before joining the Teams. And he was one of those rare men who actually listened.

"No, I have not. But I am the quick learner."

"Okay, then." He opened up the side door to the bar. "Hop on it and give it a try. You can start by taking Grant's order."

Grant reached across the bar and held my hand, as if to reassure me. "You got this, babe. Just give me a whisky on the rocks."

Kyle gave me a quick layout of the bar, where the different liquors were stored, different types of glasses for various drinks. My head was spinning, but every time I glanced at Grant his smile gave me confidence.

After an hour or so, I needed a break. A blinding light flashed in my head, and I feared a migraine coming on.

"Kyle, I thank to you for giving me this opportunity. When do you need me to start?"

"How about Tuesday night? Weekends are the busiest so during the week I'll have more time to train you."

I couldn't hold in my excitement. I flung my arms around Kyle's neck and squeezed him. He gave me a long hug. "Thank you, Mr. Kyle. I will not be the disappointment to you."

Kyle reached across the bar and placed his hand on Grant's shoulder. "Don't worry, man. I'll keep an eye on her."

Grant's gaze ping-ponged between Kyle and me. His hand squeezed his glass, his nostrils flared. I'd known Grant for so long that I could tell he was annoyed. I didn't think he suspected me of being Mia but maybe he just didn't want me to work with his friends. But then why would he bring me here for the interview? Something was wrong; I had to trust my gut and not dismiss my instinct.

But I couldn't allow his reaction to matter at the moment.

Grant stormed out of the bar. I thanked Kyle and raced after Grant, my high heels slipping into the gravel outside of the bar. Like quicksand, my feet sank into the earth, and for a moment, I wondered what it would be like to disappear.

But unfortunately, I recovered and caught up to Grant. He was already sitting on his bike, his tight jeans showing off that perfect ass of his. His head was turned toward the beach, and I followed his gaze to the ocean. I couldn't help myself—my desire to soothe him, alleviate any pain I was causing him, overtook my resolve to remain emotionally distant in order to guard my secrets. I climbed on the bike, wrapped my arms around him, and nuzzled his neck. No words were exchanged, just enjoyment of the silence in this moment, comforting him the only way I could. I tried to radiate warmth toward him and project with my body how much I truly loved him.

My nails lightly scraped against his beard, and I traced the scar on his neck. His green eyes gave me a wounded stare, and a guilty shiver flashed through my body, remembering how I'd left him when he'd been injured.

I turned his face toward me. "Thank you for taking me to here. Okay. I quit Panthers."

His cold glare softened and his mouth widened into a slight smile. He licked his lips and nodded. I knew that look—smug, sexy, satisfied. He loved to get his way, so I was happy to give him this false sense of victory.

I let him drive me back to my place, wondering for a second if it was a mistake for him to see where I lived. But I felt it would be odder if I refused. I had to have faith in my blessings, and believe that I was finally being granted some good luck.

We arrived at my apartment. My mind prepared some excuses to give to prevent him from coming upstairs. But to my surprise, he didn't even ask.

At the door, he pressed his body against mine, his hard cock teasing me through my pants. "Can I see you tomorrow?"

I ran my fingers through his hair. "Yes. Where do we go?"

He smirked. "I'll take you to Panthers to quit and get your car."

Shit, I'd forgotten I'd left my car parked overnight. "Okay. You can take me to there."

He pushed me up against the wall, his lips claiming mine. I let out a moan as his tongue explored my mouth. God, I wanted him. I wanted to scream *I'm Mia, I'm yours, always and forever.* Playing this sex kitten role, being this close to the man I loved, had renewed in me my deepest desires for him. I wanted to lose myself in him—in us—in pleasure. Have him fuck me until I could forget about how much I screwed my life up.

Instead, he let out a maniacal laugh. Like he'd recognized my desire, like he'd caught on to my game. "I'll pick you up at eleven."

I watched Grant walk back toward his bike, looking like some buff blond movie star sex god. Even from afar, I could see his wicked smirk in my direction. He pulled his helmet down and he took off, barreling down the road. I could feel a knot forming in my belly. I didn't know what to make of the peculiar way Grant was behaving. All this time, I thought I was the one trying to play a part, but maybe I was the one truly being deceived.

20

GRANT

ONE. MY FIRST PLAN OF attack went off without any setbacks. I sat on my bike outside Panthers in the middle of the day, watching Ksenya's fine ass as she walked inside, her blond hair covering her shoulders. A man whistled at her from his car—bastard was probably jerking off. I had to admit this scene was pathetic. After getting to know some strippers over the years, I'd learned some hard truths. Most of the women were either drug addicts, victims of abuse, or plain down on their luck. They were not the sexually empowered temptresses I'd deluded myself to believe they were. I'd always justified coming here by considering strip clubs to be places to bond with my brothers for boys' nights out. At least I'd convinced Ksenya to quit so she wouldn't be flashing her tits to the construction workers devouring their free lunch buffets.

Getting her the job yesterday at the bar gutted me. I knew Kyle and my buddies would keep her safe but it made me nauseous to think that this full mind fuck could actually be happening. Had Mia worked her ass off to be an actress only to now use her talents to be nothing more than eye candy? She'd be serving drinks to a bunch of fucked-up alcoholic frogmen while they ogled her. I prayed I was wrong about Ksenya being Mia in disguise.

I couldn't allow myself to think about the implausibility of this situation. I had to concentrate on the task at hand. I needed to get some sort of proof, something tangible that convinced me, without a doubt, that Ksenya was Mia.

If I was correct I might let her keep her ruse up to the outside world, especially if we could glean any information that could save her brother. But that was it. No feelings, nothing beyond this operation. I wasn't even sure if I should sleep with her. Sure, I'd love to fuck her sweet pussy again, make her scream my name, but I couldn't risk getting addicted to her. She was toxic to me, like heroin. I'd quit her once. I wasn't sure I could do it again.

She walked out of Panthers, her high heels making her gait lack the casualness Mia's once had. Even so, from the distance all I saw was my dream girl. I couldn't stop staring—it was almost as if Dr. 90210 had created her just for me. I had to remember that if my theory was correct, nothing about this girl was real, not her face, not her tits, not her hair. I wouldn't say she was a sociopath because she clearly had ruined her life to try to save Joaquín's. Even so, she had no problem using me to get what she wanted. If she could be this callous and treat me as little more than a stepping-stone, what we had must've been bullshit all along.

She stood next to my bike, her elbows pressed to the side of her body, making her look even more petite than usual.

I stepped on the gas and handed her the helmet. "How did it go, babe?"

Her lips were trembling. "It was fine. He understood. Said thank you to me for the hard work. I will take my car home now."

Not so fast. Time to up the game. "I'll bring you back here later. Come with me to my bro's place—his wife just had a baby."

Her brow furrowed, and she hesitated for a second. I was actually worried that she would decline. "Okay. I go." Her expression went slack, her bright eyes turned dull, and were those tears?

I handed her the helmet. I didn't know what to think—her body language conflicted with her words. No way would she turn down an opportunity to hang out with my friends if she was Mia. But why did she look so sad? I fought the urge to comfort her.

She pushed the helmet over her head and gave me an empty stare. "And who it is that I say I am to you?"

She had a point. Though Ksenya had met my buddies, and would be working for Kyle, we never brought strippers to family functions. But Annie was cool and would probably feel bad for Ksenya. "Just tell them you're my girlfriend."

Her chin dropped and she gave a weak nod.

I squeezed her hand, and she climbed on the back of my bike, wrapping her tight body against me.

What just happened? I suspected that she would be nervous to be around people who knew Mia, but I didn't understand why she seemed to be wincing. Mia loved babies, and she had to know I was talking about Pat and Annie's newborn. I was still suspicious Ksenya was Mia, but something was off. Either way, I needed to take her to this party, see how she acted around my friends. She had to slip up soon.

I took off on the bike, the road rumbling under me, Ksenya's head nestled against my back. Though the sounds of the traffic and the roar of the engine vibrated loudly in my helmet, I could almost swear I heard sobs, her tears blown away by the wind.

21

KSENYA

M Y MIND RACED AS WE drove toward Pat and Annie's place. What was today? Christmas? I was being invited to another SEAL gathering. This was too easy—way too easy. But my nerves and skin felt raw and exposed.

I'd only met Annie once briefly at the sendoff when Joaquín deployed last summer. She seemed shy, withdrawn, overwhelmed and spent most of the day latched on to Pat. Ever since this nightmare started with my brother, whenever I felt sorry for myself I would think of Annie being kidnapped, forced into sex slavery, and still finding the will to live. Learning about her survival strengthened my faith and gave me perspective about my own predicament. Unfortunately, today I would be meeting her as Grant's stripper sidepiece, a reminder of the sex industry she'd fought so hard to escape.

Grant parked his bike and I hopped off. He stored our helmets, took my hand and walked me through the door. Why was he bringing a stripper to this family function? I still couldn't shake the feeling that he was on to me.

Pat opened the door, his son Gabriel tugging at his leg.

"Are you here to see my baby sister?"

Grant knelt before Gabriel. "Yes, we are, little man."

Gabriel's dark skin and chocolate-colored curls were a sharp contrast to Pat's fair complexion and blond hair. Despite the fact that Gabriel wasn't Pat's biological son, I could tell that Pat adored him. I glanced up at Grant, my throat thick, my stomach churning. Would Grant have done the same for me? Love my child by another man? No matter how that child had been conceived? I pushed the thought out of my head. I had to focus on this party, the people here, and stay the course.

"Congrats, bro." Grant shook Pat's hand. "This is Ksenya. Ksenya, this is my buddy Pat." Grant winked at Pat.

Pat raised an eyebrow toward Grant and shook my hand. "Nice to meet you, Ksenya. The ladies are fawning over the baby in the nursery. First door on the right."

Dammit, I had to go in there by myself? Face a bunch of SEAL wives and girlfriends as Grant's stripper flame? I'd rather face a firing squad.

But Team wives were bound by their own secret code. I'd take what I could get. At this point, anything would help.

Grant followed Pat and Gabriel out to the backyard where the men were drinking and barbequing. I spotted the usual suspects through the glass doors —Kyle, Vic, Paul, and Joe. Rounding out the group was a guy with a Marine Corps high and tight cut, a blond surfer-looking dude with a mop of hair...and Mitch.

My pulse quickened. I was so thankful Grant brought me here, despite my awkwardness. I surveyed my clothes: a flowy pink blouse paired with fitted white pants, nude pumps, and a designer handbag. I was going for nouveau Russki chic, a far cry from Mia's uniform of vintage T-shirts, distressed jeans, and rhinestone flip-flops. At least I wasn't dressed like I just shimmied down the pole. I walked down the hallway and stood in the doorway of the nursery, waiting for an invite to join the ladies.

Annie was holding her baby, wrapped tightly in a pink blanket. Five other women were in the room. I saw two Team wives who knew Mia. Another woman had dark curly hair and sat directly next to Annie. The remaining two included a stunning blonde with a dancer's body, and a gorgeous African-American woman wearing a white sundress.

I waved hesitantly at Annie, struck by the glow of new motherhood. Already a natural beauty, her skin was translucent, her hair dark and shiny. She motioned me into the room. I didn't know what to say, conscious of my fake accent, my lies. "Hi. My name, it is Ksenya. I'm here together with Grant."

Paul's wife, Dara, gave me a dirty look and Joe's wife, Tori, didn't even glance at me. I was sure they suspected exactly where Grant had met me. I expected to be scorned at by Dara but Tori's dismissal shocked me. I never thought she'd be so openly rude. Tori had been my idol once, the dream Team wife. Totally committed to her husband since high school, faithful, great mom.

But more notable than who was there was who wasn't. Where was April, Mitch's wife? I'd last seen her at the Pickled Frog right after Joaquín was arrested. April always went to SEAL family events with their two kids in tow. In fact, she did her best never to let Mitch out of her sight, which was clearly a hard task.

Annie looked up from her newborn. "Nice to meet you, Ksenya. Thanks for coming." Her voice was soothing and warm.

Tori didn't acknowledge my existence. "Annie, I'm gonna go check on the boys." Dara followed Tori closely, as if they were bound together by a leash.

The other ladies gave me polite nods, but no one offered an introduction. I tiptoed into the room, placed my purse on the floor, and stared at this tiny baby in her arms, doing my best to blink back tears.

"Her name is Cherie Esperanza. Do you want to hold her?" Annie's kind eyes focused on me, as if she understood me. Or maybe the emotions in the room were causing me to read way more into this situation.

Esperanza—hope in Spanish. Could meeting this little baby be a sign for me not to lose hope? I didn't want to hold Cherie, not because I felt cold and emotionally dead inside, though that was part of it. I didn't want to cradle her, see her cute little button nose, lips the shape of a bow. One coo and I'd have a breakdown. Not here, not now. Not when I'd come so far to forget.

Before I could object, Annie placed the precious baby in my arms. I held in a breath as the fresh new baby smell wafted through my nostrils. One lone tear escaped from my eye before I could stop it. This beautiful baby forced me to savor living in the moment. A lump grew in the back of my throat and for the first time since I'd transformed, I was angry. Angry at the man who ruined my life and destroyed my relationship with Grant. Angry at the drunk driver who killed my parents. Angry at whoever killed Tiffany. And, frankly, angry that Joaquín was stupid enough to put himself in a situation like that. I had to believe this life detour was part of my path and that one day I'd be lucky enough to have my own family. Joaquín would be free, he would rebuild his life, and so would I.

Cherie started squirming—I held her so tight. I didn't want to let her go and reluctantly handed her back to her mother.

"I'm gonna try to put her down," she said in a whisper. "I'll join you all out in the backyard when I'm done."

The blonde with the dancer's body left the room with me, while the other two women stayed behind with Annie. Once outside the house, the blonde approached me. "Sorry I didn't introduce myself back there. I'm Sara. How long have you known Grant?"

I studied her face; she looked familiar. "Only a short time. He is good man. Who are you together with?"

She laughed. "Kyle."

Whoa. I'd known Kyle for over four years. He'd never had a girlfriend, ever. Such a player. I was intrigued that he possibly could've found whatever he was looking for.

Outside, Sara joined Tori and Dara at the patio table. Pat was grilling while that surfer dude and the Marine helped him out.

I made my way over to Grant and his buddies—Kyle, Pat, Joe, Vic, and Paul. Grant put his arm around me. "Ksenya, this is my buddy Joe."

"Nice to meet together with you." I offered my hand. Joe looked the same—hulking arms, long brown hair, brown eyes. But he almost seemed too good to be true.

Kyle winked at me. "I have an announcement. This beautiful doll has just been hired as the new bartender at the Pickled Frog. I know you'll all miss Vic's ass moping around, but I'll just keep him in the kitchen since no one wants to look at him."

Vic's lips widened into a grin. "That's not what Sara said last night."

All the men just laughed. I held back my own giggle, a tinge of sadness creeping over me. I used to love listening to Joaquín and his buddies razz each other.

Vic was sexy as all hell, dark skin, glinting eyes, dimples for days, full-sleeved tattoos. Since his divorce a few years ago, I'd never seen him with another woman. He didn't seem like the stripper-loving type. Then again neither had Joaquín or Grant.

My attention turned to Paul. Totally stood out from the rest of the men— short brown hair, no tattoos. If you ignored his cut body, he could easily pass as a Wall Street banker. He had money, was educated at Annapolis, a classy officer type. The party Tiffany died at was held at his in-laws' home.

Maybe an unknown person had been at the party? I couldn't imagine any of these men killing Tiffany. There had to be another explanation.

But I had to remember that no matter how these men acted, they were all Navy SEALs. They all had a dark side. And I was determined to find out what each one's vice was.

Grant narrowed his eyes, squinting at me. "Can I get you a drink, babe?"

Before I could answer, I noticed Mitch inside the kitchen. I needed to talk to him. Alone.

"I go to get it myself. I left my purse inside. Do you want one another beer?" I'd purposely left my purse in the nursery just in case I needed an excuse to snoop around.

His lips gave me a sly smile, which made me wonder what he was thinking. Then, he answered, "Always."

Yeah, that's what I thought. SEALs drank and swam like fish.

I walked back into the house and strolled slowly down the hallway, perusing the photos on the wall: Pat and Annie's wedding photo, a beaming Gabriel by their side, a picture of Pat kissing Annie at last homecoming. Hell, there were even pictures of them doing one of those cheesy maternity photo shoots with Pat rubbing her belly. Man, he must be whipped. I reached the doorway. Before I knocked, I held my breath, hoping to overhear something.

Luck was on my side.

Annie spoke in a low tone. "But, Grace, I just can't believe Joaquín murdered someone. God knows all the SEALs have serious issues—fuck, I met Pat because he hired me in a brothel. But murder? Yes, they are trained killers, but they have this code. I don't buy it, since Pat said Joaquín was such a great guy. There just has to be another explanation. Maybe something in Tiffany's past. It's still so fucking tragic, especially the way the media acts like it was her fault. Like her life has no value because of her job. After what I went through, it pisses me off. You're FBI...can't you investigate?"

Grace didn't immediately respond. The conversation lulled, and I didn't want to look suspicious. I knocked on the door, and Annie let me in. Apologizing, I grabbed my purse and headed back toward the kitchen with a new spring in my step.

I had read everything I could about Tiffany, but the information I'd found had been scarce. I needed to launch a new investigation. Find out more about the victim and maybe then I could find her killer.

I poured some cranberry juice and vodka into a red Solo cup for myself, grabbed another beer for Grant, and waited for Mitch to approach.

I didn't have to wait long.

He slapped my ass, his whisky-spiked breath hot on my ear. "I knew you'd sneak away from him. Couldn't stop thinking about me?"

What a conceited prick. Grant was sexy as fuck and even if he didn't just happen to be the love of my life, any woman would be thrilled to be with him. There was definitely no need to be fantasizing about Mitch when I had Grant.

But, although I would never admit it aloud, I did get Mitch's appeal—he was a true bad boy. A sexy, ripped, dirty-talking, arrogant, no-fucks-given asshole. Sex seeped out of his pores. Luckily, I was able to resist his charms.

Time to play him.

I traced his chest with my fingernails. "No, handsome. I could not. But I worry. Grant made me quit it—my job at Panthers. I do not have the money anymore." I batted my eyelashes. Seemed cliché but it always worked on the customers at Panthers. I needed to hear his response; if there was shady prostitution activity going on in this town involving these strippers, Mitch would be the first to know about it.

My eyes focused on his ring finger—his wedding ring was absent. Married SEALs never wore their rings at work, but they usually wore them at parties like this. Had April finally took their kids and left Mitch? He was acting even slimier than usual. Maybe I'd be able to find some clues when I analyzed the data on his phone from the tracking device.

He knocked back his beer, his other hand rubbing my left thigh. "This is your lucky day, baby doll. Meet me downtown tonight. There's this club, Diamond, on Market Street. Without Grant. I'll make sure he's called into work. You can thank me by giving me a private dance. I'd love to have those gorgeous titties rubbing all over my face. Maybe if you're lucky, I'll come all over them."

I tried to give him a coy smile while I fought the bile that was building up into my throat. "Diamond? I heard it is good club. My friend Autumn told to me about it."

His tongue darted out to lick his lips. "You know Autumn? I didn't know Grant let his girls party together. Maybe you, Autumn and I can have some fun later—you can lick her pussy while I fuck you from behind. Would you like that, baby doll?"

What the fuck? God, this man was so vile. He didn't even care that I was with his friend, a man who would die for him. Or then again, maybe these SEALs always shared their strippers. I prayed Grant didn't treat any woman like this, no matter what her occupation was.

"I do not like women the way I like men."

His smile looked even sleazier than I'd seen it look before. "Have you ever been with a woman?"

"No. Women to me, they are beautiful. But I like men," I replied, shaking my head.

I wanted to flee. But he had invited me to Diamond. And Autumn had mentioned that club to me the other night. This couldn't be a coincidence—I now had solid proof that SEALs on Joaquín's Team partied at Diamond.

"I'll meet you there at seven. Don't be late."

I glanced toward Grant to make sure he wasn't watching us. Then I steadied my nerves, and whispered into Mitch's ear, "I will be there. Thank you."

He held my gaze for a moment, looking grossly satisfied with himself, before shoving me against a cabinet, his huge cock pressing into me. I gasped and recoiled at his touch—then remembered my purpose and playfully slapped him. He let out a devilish laugh before releasing me.

I headed to the backyard, holding my drink and Grant's beer. Though my flesh crawled and I had a bitter taste in my mouth, hope beamed inside of me. I was confident there would be a clue at Diamond.

22

KSENYA

A S HE HAD PROMISED, MITCH roped Grant into some kind of work emergency. Luckily for me, being a Navy SEAL BUD/S instructor was a twenty-four hours a day, seven days a week job.

I turned my key into the doorknob of my apartment; the place I lived in was a dump. My elderly roommate, Olga, didn't say a word to me as she eyed me from her permanent place in front of the television. But a quick, disgusted snort told me exactly what she thought of me. I wanted to move out, I wished I could live with Grant. Even in my current incarnation, I only truly felt safe when he was by my side. But at the moment that was out of the question—I needed a refuge to do some of my own intel, away from his glaring eye.

Perfect example was the tracking device I'd put on Mitch's phone. I grabbed my small laptop and logged in to the private portal Roman had sent up for me. A few key swipes, and I was in. Data filled the screen. I poured myself a glass of rosé and settled in to read.

At first glance, nothing stood out. A bunch of messages to his command, his friends. Hell, he even checked in with his mom. As I went back further, I saw some messages to his wife, April. Yup, they weren't together anymore. I didn't know if they were divorced or what, but their messages were terse. She was living back home in Seattle, and it looked like most of her texts to him had gone unanswered. I definitely had to investigate that further. I can't believe she finally left him. Sure, he was a jerk. But when I'd first met them, they had been so in love. Guess they were on the 90% side of that SEAL divorce rate after all.

Marriage drama aside, another message stood out to me. To a Rafael. No text, no emoticons, just a smiley face.

Why was he sending a guy a smiley face? I was certain Rafael wasn't a SEAL. I'd never met him, and though he could be new, the established frogmen never really hung out with the tadpoles.

Maybe I was reading something into nothing. But there were no records of any other texts or calls to this number going thirty days back. I didn't have enough information now to draw a conclusion, but I stored my suspicion for later use.

I showered, changed, and got ready to meet Mitch. I dressed in a long silver evening gown; appropriate attire that I thought Ksenya would wear for an interview at a high-end strip club. Was Mitch setting me up? I just hoped Grant wouldn't find out where I was or whom I was with.

I applied blood-red lipstick and stared again at this stranger in the mirror. Would I ever get used to looking like this? Once this was over, I wished I could go back to looking like me but sadly that wasn't possible.

A short time later, I arrived at Diamond, set in the heart of San Diego. The view of the Coronado Bridge in the background still took my breath away every time I looked at it. That bridge had once represented everything I'd loved about San Diego—Grant, Joaquín, the Navy SEALs, the Hotel Del. Now, my eyes just filled with tears at the mere sight of the lights in the distance.

My sparkly gown glowed in the moonlight. A few men catcalled me, but I kept my gaze ahead until I heard my phone beep. I glanced down and my heart sank when I saw the text.

Grant: *Hey Babe. I miss you.*

It was simple. Sweet. Not a sexual innuendo in sight. It was almost like the way he'd been back when we were dating.

But I didn't have time to respond. Behind the shiny glass doors, Mitch awaited. And hopefully a clue to Tiffany's killer.

The doors swung open and before I could figure out where to go, Mitch appeared in front of me dressed in a tailored suit, his hair slicked back, his beard freshly trimmed.

I wanted to hate this man though I had this unmistakable gut feeling that

Mitch wasn't evil. He didn't strike me as one of those rare Navy SEALs who joined for the sole reason that he could become a legalized serial killer. Had he always been the cocky jerk I'd known over the years? Maybe his bravado was just an act he'd adopted to get through BUD/S, a shell to make him better able to perform on the job without allowing himself to feel the immense pain, physical and emotional, that being a SEAL required.

Right now, he smelled incredible, like those chocolate after-dinner mints I loved sucking on.

"You're so beautiful." His hand brushed a lock of my hair out of my face. "Relax, I'll take care of you."

I squeezed his hand and he placed his arm around my shoulder. For once, he wasn't abrasive; he seemed almost comforting, warm, and dare I say, like a gentleman. I allowed myself to see him with fresh eyes, tonight only. Find out why his wife had fallen in love with him.

Mitch led me down the red-carpeted hallway. I felt as if I was at a movie premiere rather than a strip club. But this place was unlike any strip club I'd visited in preparation for going undercover. I thought San Francisco had some classy joints—this place looked like a restaurant. There was no public stage for women to dance on while men gawked at them. Girls who could've been mistaken for models milled around the men, who were seated in private booths or at the bar. Male waiters carried plates of expensive-looking food and bottles of vintage wine. Definitely a step up from Panthers.

Mitch pulled me into a private booth. "Wait here, I'll be right back."

My lips spread into a forced smile as he turned to walk away. I scanned the club, eyeing the girls. A redhead in the corner I recognized as Emma, another stripper who'd worked at Panthers but had vanished. Last winter, she'd given me the first clue to this case—that Grant had invited the strippers to the party. A clue that broke my heart. If I'd only known then that her words would lead me to this new life.

Across the room, I saw a blonde with a crisp bob who had to be Autumn. She hadn't seen me yet but I would make sure to connect with her.

Yes, this was the place to be. Had Grant ever come here? Had Joaquín?

Mitch came back to my table accompanied by a short, stocky guy, late thirties, sporting a full beard. Looked like he could be a former SEAL, but I didn't recognize him.

"Ksenya, this is Jack. He owns the club."

"Nice to meet together with you, Jack." I held up my hand and he kissed it.

"Pleasure is mine. Mitch wasn't lying. You're a knockout—you look like a young Pamela Anderson. Tell me, doll, why do you want to work here?"

I used my best breathy sex kitten voice, hinged with my fake accent. "I love men. I love to make them happy."

Jack and Mitch lapped up my words. God, men were so easy.

Jack stared at my chest, and I arched my back to give him a better view. "Well, baby doll, you can make me happy anytime. Maybe, I'll adopt you as my personal pet. Let me show you around and introduce you to the girls. You can audition on Monday."

Audition? What was tonight—just a meet-and-greet? And what the fuck did he mean about being his pet? I'd drawn my lines into the sand early—no sex with anyone except Grant and I'd even managed to resist him so far. I deserved a medal for that feat. Once I'd crossed that boundary with a man other than Grant, I would never be able to respect myself again. But this new opportunity was good, I still had a chance here. A breakthrough in the case felt so close—I was in this swanky club where at least two of the strippers who knew Tiffany worked and might be able to provide me with much-needed clues.

Mitch squeezed my arm. "You owe me a dance. I'll be here on Monday."

"Thank you, Mitch. I will save the dance for you." Mitch settled into the booth as Jack led me away.

Jack lowered his hand to my waist, his fingers tapping my ass. "We have some rules. I'm telling you now so you can choose if you want to still work here. Number one—no boyfriends. If you have one, he better not step foot in here. Your job is to entertain our clients, make small talk, dance, laugh at their jokes. We don't want any trouble at all."

I swallowed. Grant. I had to tell him about this job. Otherwise he would find out for sure. I didn't trust Mitch to keep my secret.

Or maybe...I could wait a bit. Tell him I was taking an English class, stall until I got the information I needed and then quit before he ever found out. I had to keep Grant close as an informant, a spy in the house of SEALs. I'd royally piss him off when he found out I asked Mitch to help me get a job. Mitch was still on my radar, though at the moment, I felt deep down like he was just a jackass, not a murderer. But I couldn't be certain.

Jack took me into the dancers' lounge in the back of the club. Instead of secondhand lumpy couches like at Panthers, this club was filled with velvet chaises, lighted mirrors, and walls adorned with art. But I didn't care about the ambiance. I scanned the roomful of girls. Autumn was applying lipstick, and Emma was chatting on her cell phone.

Remember, Mia, you don't know Emma.

I didn't approach either one yet. I was sitting in the room with two women who were at the party the night Tiffany was killed. Two women who knew her. Two women who knew the men of SEAL Team Seven. And unlike the SEALs, these women loved to talk.

Jack didn't even bother to introduce me to anyone. He just gave me a pat on my bottom and left to go back to the main club.

Autumn now glanced my way. "Ksenya! I didn't know you were coming by. You didn't text me or nothing." She squealed like a schoolgirl and wrapped me in a big hug. "Are you going to work here? I told you this place was way classy. Let me introduce you to everyone."

Score! I had to control my feet from dancing.

Autumn linked her hand around mine and took me over to Emma.

"Emma, this is that Russian girl I told you about."

"Nice to meet with you, Emma. My name it is Ksenya. I am actually from the Ukraine."

Emma just gave me a distracted wave and went back to chatting on her phone. When I'd met Emma in the parking lot of Panthers, she'd been so kind and welcoming—this time, not so much. Now I was a threat, competition, rather than some pathetic girl sobbing over her wayward ex-boyfriend and despondent over the loss of her brother.

Autumn continued to show me around. I didn't get this girl; she was so sweet to me, and I didn't feel like it was an act. She was young, not jaded, and perhaps really wanted a friend. She seemed lonely, and I couldn't help but wonder how much longer she would be so bubbly before the realities of life as a stripper broke her spirit.

She took me aside and led me into the bathroom. "Um, can I ask you something?"

I nodded my head.

She bit her fingernails, the crimson polish chipping at the ends. "Are you still seeing Grant? I mean that's cool if you are and everything, I'm just curious and all."

I swallowed. I was standing next to a girl who had been with my man on the night Tiffany was murdered, on the night that ruined my brother's life.

"Yes, I am. But he do not know that I am here."

She blinked rapidly. "That's cool." She paused and her shoulders slumped. "Hey, what are you doing tomorrow? I wanted to head out to Temecula to visit Tiffy's family."

Tiffany's family—people who no doubt wanted to crucify my brother. But no way in hell would I squander the opportunity to meet them.

Autumn rattled on. "The girls won't go with me. They're all weirded-out by it, like they can't deal with her death. I mean everyone's just forgotten about her. It could've been me, you know? So…I just wanted to do something nice for her family. I know I don't know you, and you don't know me, but I just really don't want to go alone. And you seem nice and all."

God, I wanted to hug this girl. She was the first to tell me exactly where Grant was that night, eliminating him as a suspect, first to tell me about Diamond, and now she was going to bring me to meet Tiffany's family? She was too good to be true.

"I'd love to go together with you. You have it, my number, yes?"

"Oh, thank you. Have you been to Temecula? It's beautiful and all too! Like they have wineries and all the super-hot motocross guys live up there."

Autumn rattled on about some wine-tasting event but all I could focus on was that tomorrow I'd be meeting the family of the girl who my brother was accused of murdering.

23

KSENYA

A UTUMN PICKED ME UP IN the morning to drive to Temecula—a small town an hour north of San Diego. My hands trembled as she handed over a coffee she'd picked up for me at Starbucks.

Tiffany. After all this time, I would get a glimpse into the life of the woman my brother was accused of murdering.

Autumn's car sped north on the freeway. "Thanks for coming with. Most of the other Russian girls I've met were like super stuck up, but you're not. I feel like I know you."

"You are very welcome. I'm from the Ukraine, not Russia."

She tapped her fingernails on the steering wheel. "Right, I know. Eastern Europe I mean. So why did you start dancing?"

God, this girl needed a friend. She oozed loneliness. "I live with my grandmother. She died, and I pay the bills. My English, it is not so good. I am ballroom dancer. Now, I dance for men. Why are you dancer for men?"

She let out a sigh. "Wow. Your story is way cooler than mine. I was a fuckup in high school, dropped out. I started dating this guy Jeff—real jerk, loser, used to hit me." She looked away from me, the color draining from her face.

Poor girl. I used to always lecture Grant that most strippers were abuse survivors. Or plain bat shit crazy—I clearly fell into the latter category.

Some mornings I woke up completely shocked that I'd actually gone through with this crazy plan.

"Anyway, he told me I could make good money at Panthers so I tried it out. Him and me broke up and all. One day, I want to go to beauty school. But for now, I like dancing. I mean I meet super interesting people. Like you…and Grant. You know he's a SEAL, right?"

Yup. Painfully aware. I was the girl who'd given him massages, prepared Epsom salt baths for him, and bandaged his feet every night for six months during BUD/S. "He told to me." I paused, an ache growing in my throat. This girl was clearly still hung up on Grant, and here I was mind-fucking him, no hope of being serious again because I was lying about who I was. Using him for information. But I didn't have a choice anymore—I was in too deep. I needed him now.

"Don't worry. I'm not like in love with him or anything," she said playfully like she could read my mind. "I just think he's super-hot, and it's so cool that he's a SEAL. I'd love to be with a guy who could protect me, you know? Maybe you can hook me up with one of his friends?"

"Sure. I invite you to next party." I really liked her. I had learned since I started this experiment that I needed to be less judgmental. Autumn was a sweet girl. She deserved love.

We exited the freeway and took the back roads. The view of the mountains and the vineyards calmed my nerves. For this ride, I felt connected to life. Even Autumn's chatter didn't seem to disturb my peace. I was happy to live in this moment, no thought of my past or future.

We pulled up to a small tract house just outside of Temecula, in Winchester. The neighborhood sported matching homes, uniform lawns, and wide sidewalks. Just a few years ago, this town had been wrecked with foreclosures. It was nice to see that it was beginning to recover.

An older woman, silver hair streaked with black, a saddened glaze in her eyes, opened the door, a small boy clutching her leg. When the toddler's face came into focus, I gasped.

His eyes—deep hazel eyes with mile-long lashes. Eyes that were so familiar…I was certain I'd looked into them my whole life.

The heat in my body rose. No. It couldn't be. A horrible thought flashed through my head, like this boy was a ghost or a zombie.

Fuck, Mia, you're losing it.

I took a deep breath and said a prayer, trying to calm myself down. Who was this little boy? Was he Tiffany's son? There was no mention of a child in her obituary. This boy was around two years old—when he was conceived Joaquín would've just returned from deployment. And my brother had told me he'd never met Tiffany before that night.

Had he been lying to me?

This boy's eyes looked exactly like my dad's—almond shaped, long lashes, a slight slant on the left eyelid.

My mouth became dry. This couldn't just be some random coincidence.

The boy walked forward, his gaze focused on me. Autumn embraced Tiffany's mother.

I steadied my nerves, crouched down near the boy. "What is your name?"

The little boy didn't speak. He reached his hand out to me, pointing at my purse.

His grandmother grabbed him by his hand. "Julián, don't be so rude."

I rose from my position.

Tiffany's grandmother turned to me. "Sorry about that. Come inside. Would you girls like some iced tea?"

Iced tea? Tequila sounded better.

We walked in and sat on the sofa. The house was clean for having such a young boy. Pictures of Tiffany and Julián were everywhere—yet there wasn't a single picture of any guy with them. She had to be his mom. Had she hid this kid from the police? That was impossible. If Autumn knew about the mother, then the police would also. Why was he not mentioned in a single police report, or news article? I studied one of Tiffany's pictures, so unlike the stripper headshot the media had been running in the papers. In this one, her hair was a natural light brown, her green eyes weren't sad, and she wasn't wearing any makeup. She looked fresh-faced, almost innocent. No painted-on eyebrows, self-tanner, or jet-black hair. What happened to her? What was her story?

The grandmother handed us two glasses of iced tea. "So did you know my daughter?"

"No, I did not. But Autumn has told to me about her." My mind was racing, trying to find a way to confirm that Tiffany was Julián's mother.

"She was a troubled girl. She was definitely mixed up in some heavy shit —but the best thing she ever did was let me raise Julián when he was born. And I thank God every day she stayed clean while she was pregnant. Well the truth is, I didn't even know she was pregnant! Her own mother? Imagine that! She had vanished for a year and shown up with this baby one day asking me to take care of him. She did her best to visit when she could, but she made sure to keep Julián sheltered from her life down in San Diego."

My hands started shaking, and I choked back tears.

It couldn't be, Mia. No way. Stop. This boy is not your son.

Fuck. I needed to get away from here. I was having a psychotic break.

Focus Mia, back to the case. Tiffany had been an addict? I'd always suspected that but had no proof, just a gut feeling. Drugs. This murder had to be linked to drugs. The pieces of the puzzle were falling into place. But I had to know who Julián's father was. Maybe I was just losing my mind, but I'd bet Joaquín's life that this boy was my nephew. Had my brother kept a secret from me? The same secret I kept from him? That would be too coincidental. I needed to be rational.

I decided to make an emotional plea. "My parents, they are dead. It must be so sad to you and to her boy. Is his father still in picture?"

I waited on her words. "No. Tiffany wouldn't even tell me who he was, but I have my suspicions. I'm pretty sure he was her high school boyfriend, real loser, definitely not good enough for my Tiffy or Julián. I figure if Tiffy didn't want the dad to know, then it isn't my place to go against her wishes, you know?"

I nodded my head but was saddened by her flawed thinking. The father had the right to know about his child unless that knowledge would put the child's life in danger. Just like I had the right to know if this little boy was my nephew. But then again, I more than anyone understood Tiffany's rationale. But my situation had been complicated. And I'd handled it the only way I knew how.

Autumn tapped her fingernails on the coffee table. "Any updates on the case?"

"No. That rat-bastard should fry. They should use a firing squad on his ass and save the taxpayers' money."

My stomach ached. This woman seemed utterly convinced that Joaquín killed her daughter, not that I blamed her.

The grandmother spent the next hour reveling in Autumn's every story about Tiffany. I could completely relate to Tiffany's mom—now that I had no family left, I clung to every memory I could involving my parents and Joaquín.

After our visit came to a close, we started saying our goodbyes. Autumn promised to come by again, and try to bring Tiffany's other friends. But I knew that was a long shot because the other girls seemed to have already washed their hands of the situation. Tiffany had been forgotten.

I knelt down on the carpet to say goodbye to Julián.

The little boy stood there, assessing me, arms crossed over his chest, before a reluctant little smile eased over his face and he threw his tiny body at me in a hug. Still silent. His small frame wrapped around me, and I couldn't resist. I knelt down and hugged him back—so hard, I never wanted to let go. It was as if I was hugging Joaquín again.

As if I was hugging my own son.

This boy smelt familiar, like home, *mi familia*. But I wasn't going to miss my chance to get confirmation of my suspicions. I tugged on his head and plucked a few strands of his hair out of his scalp, shoving them into my pocket.

Julián seemed to startle but didn't cry. Just gave me a sad face, and Autumn and I left.

Once inside Autumn's car, she placed her hand on my knee. "Thanks, Ksenya, for coming with."

"Of course. I had good time."

She smiled and pulled away from the curb. Autumn didn't have a clue that she had just given me a huge break in this case. That she, a woman who'd spent the night with the love of my life, might have led me to the one clue that could unravel this mystery.

After a long drive, Autumn dropped me off at home. Once safely inside, I took the hairs out of my pocket and stuffed them into a plastic bag, along with strands of Joaquín's hair that I had collected from his apartment when I decided to go undercover. I would mail them to Roman, who would be able to send them to a DNA lab. By next week, I would know if Julián was my brother's son.

24

GRANT

L AST NIGHT I HAD AN overnight rotation training the BUD/S candidates. Joaquín was supposed to be standing by my side, yelling at these trainees, making sure they had what it took to save our brothers' asses. One time during surf torture in our BUD/S class, Joaquín and I held on to each other all night, ensuring that we wouldn't die from hypothermia. I wasn't gay, but I never felt as close to another man as I had that night. We were more than friends, more than Teammates, more than brothers—we were swim buddies. Now I couldn't help but feel further apart from him than ever. I was relaxing in my favorite chair, my dog by my side, while he was in a cold cell, alone, away from his loved ones.

But I might still have his loved one in my grasp.

Today I had a plan—a plan that would rattle Ksenya.

I asked her to meet me downtown in front of the sushi place where she and I had gone on our first date last week. She showed up, dressed casually. Jeans, white tank top, hair in a ponytail, flip flops, light makeup. She looked pretty. Normal, in fact.

Her head tilted and she pulled me toward her for a kiss. I kissed her back. Her lips tasted sweet, fragrant. Like Mia used to taste. And in this moment, I wanted to just take her away, torture her until she confessed the truth, and try to get my old girlfriend back.

"Grant, you want to eat it, the sushi again? Maybe we try something new?"

Her eyes were hidden behind huge sunglasses. I wanted to see them react to what I was about to tell her.

I squeezed her shoulders. "I'm not that hungry actually. How 'bout we grab a cup of coffee instead?"

She smiled and we went inside a seedy donut shop. I ordered two old-fashioned glazed donuts and two hot coffees. We sat at the table by the window. She took off her sunglasses, and I stared into her eyes.

"Actually, I tricked you." I studied her face, hoping she would squirm under my words.

She tapped her fingers on the plastic table, but her poker face showed no fear. "You did?"

"I wanted to see if you'd come with me. My buddy, he's in the jail down the street."

The coffee cup was halfway to her mouth when she froze.

Her face turned ashen, the tiny hairs on her arms lifted.

Bingo. I got her.

"In jail? What is the crime?" she said, her voice shaking.

I cocked my head. "Murder," I said, flatly.

Her hands wrapped around her Styrofoam coffee cup again and this time she took a sip. "Yes, of course, Grant. I go together with you."

She ate the rest of her donut in silence. When we finished, we stood up and I grabbed her hand. It was clammy.

I'd called Joaquín's lawyer last night, under the guise of seeing if there were any breaks in the case. He'd said unfortunately no. I asked him to see if Joaquín would accept a visit from me. The lawyer called me a few hours ago to let me know the Joaquín had agreed. I then requested and received permission from my command, and here I was. With Ksenya, aka Joaquín's sister.

We walked into the county jail and handed over our driver's licenses. Ksenya had a valid one that rang up in the computer. Who had provided her with her documents? I knew some guys back home in Chicago who could get people papers, but dealing with them was not for amateurs. I didn't have a clue what type of shady characters she was surrounding herself with.

We milled around the waiting room with some other hapless souls. This place reeked of desperation. The entire time we waited, Ksenya didn't utter a word, just gave me a dazed smile.

Finally, a guard led us to a room where we sat at a small partition. After yet another wait, Joaquín and some other inmates walked through the door.

Ksenya gasped when he came into focus. My jaw gaped as well. It had been seven months since I'd seen him. His body was still massive, but his face was now bloated, his eyes were tired, his skin was yellow. A single tear escaped Ksenya's eye and she quickly wiped it.

Joaquín picked up the phone. "Thanks for coming, bro." He nodded his chin in Ksenya's direction. "Guess you're finally over my sis. Who's the fox?"

I laughed. If he only knew what the fuck he was saying. "This is Ksenya, a stripper from the Ukraine. How you been, man?"

"Be careful with those strippers, man, or you'll end up in here with me. I'm fine, all things considered." Joaquín eye-fucked Ksenya some more. I understood he probably hadn't seen a woman in months but still. Talk about awkward.

Ksenya hunched her shoulders, covered her chest. I wondered if she was beginning to feel as nauseous as I was by this little visit. Served her fucking right.

"Lawyer says I have a good shot of getting off." Joaquín was still staring at Ksenya. "Have you heard from Mia? I heard she's vanished."

"Naw, dude. She's gone. She came to visit me after you were arrested but I kicked her out. Sorry, bro, but I couldn't deal with her bullshit. But I didn't expect her to drop off the face of the earth."

He looked at his feet and I took the opportunity to glance over my shoulder at Ksenya. Her eyes were locked on Joaquín, but I recognized her look. She was plotting something.

I wanted to milk this visit for as long as I possibly could—not just to see my buddy, but also to fuck with Mia a bit more. And I wasn't that much of an asshole that I couldn't admit that a small part of me also wanted to give this gift to her. Allow her to connect with her brother. God only knew when she would have the chance to again.

I gave Joaquín a quick update on the guys from the Team. Joaquín's eyes kept darting to Ksenya. I was beginning to think maybe he wasn't just checking her out. Maybe he sensed something was off with her too.

The guard gave us the two-minute warning. "Well, I appreciate you visiting me. Extra props for giving me some eye candy." He tapped on the glass toward Ksenya. "Nice to meet you."

She took the phone out of my hand, clutching the receiver like it was her lifeline, pressing her wrist to the glass. "Nice to meet together with you, too." She spoke slowly and drew out every word, as if she was hanging on to their fleeting moment together.

And that's when I caught it. Something triggered Joaquín. His jaw fell open and his eyes did a double take. Before he could say a word, the guard opened the door back up, and Joaquín was led away.

A lump grew in my throat at seeing his retreating form. I loved that guy, and I prayed that one day we'd once again be swimming in the open ocean together.

I turned my attention back on Ksenya, who had with a dazed look on her face, her eyes glassy. I studied her. What the fuck did I miss? I'd been watching her the entire time. She didn't have a chance to whisper anything to him, reveal her identity. But even if she had, I'm not sure she would be stupid enough to say something when I was present.

I held her hand. "Thanks for coming with me."

"Of course." I wrapped my arm around her shoulders as we walked out of the jail.

Once outside, I dropped her hand. But that's when I saw it. She was wearing a bracelet. It was bright and beaded and rainbow-colored—one of those ugly pieces of jewelry that had been popular when we were kids. Definitely not something a grown woman would wear, even if she were from a different country. And I knew for a fucking fact that she hadn't been wearing it earlier in the day.

I'd never seen that bracelet before. Not in all the years I dated her. Not during all the times that I hung out at her place.

Joaquín had apparently seen it though. Joaquín knew what it meant.

And I knew that the cracks in Ksenya's game were beginning to show.

It was only a matter of time before I broke her. Before I called her out on her bullshit. Before I made her beg for my forgiveness. Before I got rid of her once and forever.

I definitely wasn't ready to call her bluff. Oh no, we were just getting started. But for tonight, I had probably fucked with her enough. Joaquín was her limit. "You okay?"

"Yes," she offered, her voice breaking. "I feel bad for your friend. It must be hard to be in jail. He is innocent, yes?"

I suppressed my emotions—anger, shock, hurt, and victory—all bottled inside. I held Mia in my arms, the way I once had, years ago. "Yeah, he is. He's a great guy. He's like my brother. In fact, he almost was my brother. That girl I told you about, who left me—she was his sister. I'd never told her, but I'd planned on asking her to marry me. Had even asked for Joaquín's permission. But she's vanished from the face of the earth. And now, I'm all he has left."

She winced—her shoulders slumping—and dropped my gaze. She seemed to ponder this information for a beat and I hoped to hell she might crack, but instead she buried her head in my chest. Now my fucking heart ached. I wanted to interrogate her, demand answers. But instead, I pushed a lock of hair from her forehead, taking special notice of her dark roots that were becoming visible.

"That girl…" I could barely hear her muffled voice. "I'm sure she knows it, what a mistake she made."

25

KSENYA

A S WE SPED AWAY FROM the jail, my body chilled. The world seemed to be spinning around me, like I was stuck on some lazy Susan and I couldn't jump off.

Joaquín. I'd been inches away from my brother, close enough to breathe the same air. Yet he hadn't had a clue who I was. His own flesh and blood. Even worse, I could swear he was checking me out!

In his defense, I didn't resemble his beloved sister. Fucking joke was on me, I guess. He knew me only as Grant's chick; scratch that, Grant's *stripper*.

But I'd taken a chance, a risk. When Grant was signing in at the jail, I placed that bracelet on my wrist. *Our* bracelet. The one I'd found at the top of the mountain.

I flashed it at my brother the second I had an opportunity. Hoping Joaquín would see it. Hoping he would realize I was here for him, even though he'd tried to convince me to abandon him. A signal.

Joaquín had seen it—a treasure only Mia could possess. But I had no idea if he even understood what it meant—that I was either Mia transformed or, if that was too farfetched, that I had sent someone to see him. Either way, I was sure he was sitting in his cell, racking his brain trying to come up with an explanation.

Dammit. Now that I thought about my actions, I realized I could've put my plan in danger. Not by Grant recognizing a bracelet he'd never seen, but by Joaquín possibly contacting his lawyer, demanding an answer. Joaquín could even think that Grant was in on my deception.

Grant was smart. Could he have picked up on my exchange with Joaquín? He had never seen the bracelet before so I didn't think he'd notice it. And if Grant had noticed the bracelet, at least he would have no way of connecting it to my true identity.

As long as this random visit hadn't been some sort of test. I couldn't push that thought away. Going to visit a friend in jail didn't seem like a very normal outing choice for a fledging relationship. And it was something Grant could do anytime, on his own, with the jail being across the bridge from where he worked. Why did he want to take me with him? I hoped the reason he'd invited me had been more of an afterthought instead of a calculated plan.

I forced those thoughts out of my head as we cruised down the freeway. I clung on to Grant, needing to feel him closer to me, wanting so much to put an end to this farce. I shuddered and it wasn't from the cold wind. Grant's words had gutted me.

Marry him. Grant had wanted me to marry him back then? Unbelievable. I mean, I'd always hoped we were headed in that direction, but Grant had always fed me some bullshit about how hard it was to be married to a Team guy and that we were too young. This knowledge changed everything. If I'd only known, I would've told him the truth about that night. I would've fought for us. I would've fought for him, instead of running away. But back then, I'd felt completely alone for the first time in my life. I hadn't even told Joaquín what had happened to me.

But there was no time to dream about what could have been. Seeing Joaquín so clearly just a day after I met Julián rattled me. I was more certain than ever that Julián was Joaquín's son. Julián had to be my nephew. Apparently, that would be one of the only mysteries in my life that I would be able to resolve quickly—Roman had texted me that the results of the DNA test would be in by the end of the week.

I told Grant that I was feeling ill, and I was surprised when he agreed to drop me back at my place. I wanted to spend the night crying in Grant's arms, confessing my sins, secrets, and suspicions to him, but there wasn't any time for that.

Ksenya planned to make it up to him later, show up at his place, make him dinner. But now Joaquín's sister had to go to work.

I decided against taking my car downtown in case I was pressured to drink, so I hailed a taxi. The driver dropped me off at Diamond. After a quick elevator ride, I arrived at the club.

I was about to text Mitch to let him know I was here, but as I reached into my purse for my phone I felt a hand grasp my wrist.

"You owe me a dance," the deep voice whispered. I didn't need to look up. Mitch's presence loomed behind me.

"Of course, Mitch. I will save for you the dance."

Another voice spoke. "No, you don't understand. You don't have the job yet. We need to know you can party. Our customers don't hold back."

I looked up, and it was Jack. Damn—I knew the interview had been too easy. "Party?" I genuinely didn't have a clue what he meant, but my skin crawled at the possibilities. Did he mean would I sleep with men? Get wasted? I shivered wondering what these two had planned for me.

Jack's eyes danced around my body. "Why don't I take you to the lounge and I'll show you."

Jack headed toward the back of the club. I leaned into Mitch as he put his arms around me, and we followed Jack.

Two shiny gold doors opened up to another room. And there it was. The golden stripper pole.

My hands shook. It didn't matter if the pole was made out of gold or tin to me, I was still expected to dance and degrade the fuck out of myself on it for them.

Fuck.

Jack leaned against a booth, his eyes focusing on me.

"Let's see what you got, baby doll." Mitch slid into a black leather lounge chair, facing the front of the pole.

I hesitated and a scowl crossed Jack's face. "Look, sweetie, dance for us now, or get the fuck out of here. We have girls coming in here all the time. I don't have time for your bullshit."

What an asshole. "Okay. I'm sorry. I am little nervous."

I took to the stage, waiting for the music to start. Jack played a melodic tune, which suited me fine. I climbed the pole, did a couple of aerial moves, then decided to do an old-school strip tease, more Rita Hayworth in *Gilda* than Nomi in *Showgirls*. I slowly moved the shoulder straps of my gown off my shoulders, exposing my black lace corset, my full breasts spilling over the top. A shimmy of my hips and my gown fell to the floor, revealing my garter belt and stockings. Mitch's lips parted, his eyes hungry. I worked the pole, making sure not to volunteer a lap dance.

My song ended not a moment too soon. I stared at my rumpled dress. What would come next? I wanted to go home.

I went to gather my clothes, but Mitch stopped me. "That was good. But you're not off the hook. You still owe me a private dance."

I figured. Well, one degrading step at a time.

Jack turned to me. "Time to party, baby."

"I don't know what it is you mean. I'm not hooker."

Mitch pulled me into him, which made my mind flash with scenarios of being gang raped since I was practically naked. "I got you, babe. Let's have a drink."

A waitress came to our table and I ordered a cocktail. I felt dizzy and a sense of dread filled my body. My eyes scanned this room, staring at the exit door, trying to plan an escape route.

"Let me show you." Jack pulled a mirror and a small bag out of his back pocket. My eyes fluttered, focusing on the moonlight through the windows. There was about two ounces of white powder in the bag.

Mitch's eyes dilated.

I jerked my head back, unable to control my reaction.

It was cocaine.

Cocaine! I knew the SEALs were drug tested all the time so clearly something was amiss here. Was this the key? Had they been involved with some type of drug deal and Joaquín found out? Was Mitch involved in framing him?

Holy shit.

"Relax, baby." Mitch pulled me to him. "You've never done it? It's an incredible high."

Jack laid down a mirror and poured a thin line of coke. He took out a credit card and smooshed the powder down. Mitch handed him a dollar bill, and Jack snorted a line. Then Mitch followed. My eyes dazed and my skin tingled.

Mitch pushed the mirror into my hands and handed me a razor blade. "Here, your turn. This will help you loosen up, then we can have some fun."

Was this some type of test? This had to be a trap. Was Grant here somewhere? Or maybe he was going to take pictures of me and show Grant. What was I doing? Was this getting me any closer to Joaquín?

But I couldn't say no. I'd never even smoked a cigarette—I was an actress and didn't want to fuck up my voice. But my gut wrenched and I felt almost certain that if I didn't pass this test—the hard-partying-up-for-anything-stripper test—my game would be over.

I closed my eyes. I could do this. The drugs running through this place could be linked to the murder. I'd made too many sacrifices to get here; what was one more?

I took a deep breath, stared at Mitch who nodded at me expectantly, and inhaled a line.

My gums numbed, a bitter, metallic taste dripped in my throat. I tried not to gag. My insides were quivering but it wasn't from the blow. I was in a strange place, with men I didn't trust. Grant wasn't with me. Through this entire time, since I'd transformed, I'd convinced myself I'd always at least maintain control. But I was anything but in control of this situation. I finally realized how vulnerable I truly was.

Mitch rubbed my back, and I fought the sudden overwhelming desire to get close to him. His fingers made me tingle, and I imagined him touching me. Hell, I wanted him to touch me! I wanted to lose myself in pleasure, forget about my fucked-up life and indulge. Pulses of euphoria streamed through my body.

Mitch leaned in and kissed my neck. His now-potent scent startled me. A flash reminded me of the only other time in my life that I'd lost control. A time that ruined my life.

But I didn't have time to focus on Mitch. Because not even a minute later, the heavy doors swung open and Grant was standing there in front of me, a look of disgust marring his beautiful face.

26

GRANT

SURE, I FUCKING FOLLOWED HER, Ksenya, Mia, whoever the fuck she was. If she were Ksenya, then maybe she was a typical dancer who saw me as nothing more than another client. Did she think I was dumb and wouldn't know she was going to party with another guy? My fellow Team-mate at that? Guys have been killed for lesser reasons.

She squirmed out of Mitch's arms. "Grant!" She bit her nails, trying to cover her cleavage with her arms. She was wearing a corset and a fucking garter belt. But if she were Mia, it would make sense for her to be here to investigate the dead stripper. Though Tiffany never worked here, Diamond was the hottest new gentlemen's club, and many of the former Panthers' girls had made their ways here. I wanted to call Ksenya out right now. All I knew was that this full bullshit scenario was giving me a headache. I didn't know whether to beat Mitch up or to thank him.

Mitch pushed her off him, got up and shook my hand. "Sorry, man, I told you she was just a stripper." His nose was runny.

Fuck. He was doing blow again. He better not have given that shit to Ksenya.

Before I could respond to Mitch, the waitress brought a tray of drinks. Two whiskeys and a rum and Coke.

A rum and Coke—Mia's drink. Since I met Ksenya, she'd only drunk vodka.

I fucking knew it. If I didn't see it clear-as-fucking-day earlier today, when faced with her brother, I saw it then. How the fuck had she pulled this shit off? The Russian accent, the body, the face, the goddamned stripping! This chick was insane. My stomach wrenched—I didn't know if I should be pissed off or impressed.

I shook Mitch's sweaty palm, my mind plotting my next plan of attack. My turn to play games. "It's cool. I didn't come here for her. Is Autumn around?"

My eyes darted toward Ksenya, who was struggling to pull on her dress. Her chin dipped to her chest, her posture slumped. Too bad, I was done falling for her bullshit.

"Yeah, I'll get her." Mitch slapped me on the shoulder before heading back into the main area of the club.

Jack put his slimy hand on Ksenya. "You're hired, sweetie. Come by next weekend and you can start."

"Thank you, Mr. Jack."

Mr. Jack? Hearing her call him that in her obnoxious accent-laced baby voice put me over the edge.

Jack left the room.

Leaving Ksenya and me alone.

I stood my ground. She took her walk of shame and placed her hand on my shoulder. I shoved it off.

The cute, wounded little look she gave me did nothing whatsoever to help her case. "Grant, I'm sorry. It is not what it looks like to be. Mitch told to me at party that he could get me job here. I know you got me job at bar, but I need more money. I was afraid to ask it to you, because I know you do not want it for me to strip."

She was lying, about what I didn't know yet. I steadied my breath—I would see this through until I outed her for who she really was, though I would continue to hide her identity from my Teammates. I'd work with her to exonerate Joaquín, and then send her the fuck out of my life forever. Either way, getting rid of this chick couldn't come a moment too soon.

"I don't care what you do. I was trying to help you but if you want to do blow and get naked with a bunch of my friends, be my guest. I don't have time for a cock tease."

I raised my head and glared into her eyes. Yup, her pupils were dilated.

Man, I'll fucking kill Mitch when this is over.

Her fingers brushed up against me again and I recoiled. "Take me home together with you. I promise I will not tease you."

Don't fall for it, Grant. She's an actress. She's playing you.

I pushed her off of me. "I don't fuck junkies."

She gave me a blank stare, and I turned away from her.

Mitch returned with Autumn. She smiled when she saw me, and I gave her a big hug. Blond bob, tight clothes, perky ass. I had been about to fuck her the night of the murder, but we'd both partied so hard, we passed out. She was a nice, sexy girl, but I hadn't been able to find an emotional connection with her.

Autumn and I chatted in the booth while Ksenya stared at us. After about five minutes, I was about to walk away with Autumn, get wasted. Maybe if I fucked her tonight, I could take my mind off Ksenya.

But I couldn't resist—I took one final glance back. Ksenya's hair hung in her face like a spider web, and her lip was trembling.

Exactly like Mia's used to.

Fuck, what was wrong with me?

I kissed Autumn on the cheek, told her it was great to see her. I was a goddamned idiot not to make a night of it with her but I still needed some answers. Maybe Ksenya would break down and confess everything to me after I fucked her brains out.

I grabbed Ksenya by the wrist until she yelped.

"Fine. You want to play games, little girl? Make me jealous by fucking around with my friend?"

Her eyes widened, almost doe-like. "I made mistake. Please, you must forgive me."

"Stop talking. You want this night to continue? You will obey my orders. What I say goes. Let's get the hell out of here."

She nodded quickly, her skin flushed.

I was a Navy SEAL, the ultimate alpha male. When I'd dated Mia, I'd never let her see my whole self. I'd never brought that shit home with me. I'd treated her like the little fucking princess I'd always thought she deserved to be. I'd been the nice guy—tender, loving and attentive. I had aimed to please her, rather than myself.

Tonight, she hadn't earned that right. I'd be selfish and fuck her how I'd always wanted to.

I was done minding my fucking manners.

27

KSENYA

I DIDN'T WANT THIS HIGH to come crashing down. Because I knew that when it did, I would realize what a really horrible idea this was. Tingles ran through my body. The thought of Grant dominating me made me excited. I wanted to please him, fulfill all of his desires.

I thought for sure it was over just moments ago; that Grant was going to tell me to fuck right off for good. Clearly he was jealous. For a minute it looked like Autumn was going to be the lucky recipient of all that pent-up rage and lust, and fuck this whole thing if I was going to let *that* happen. I couldn't help it. I wanted it to be me.

We arrived at his place and without a single word, he shoved me in the front door.

Grant ran his hands over my body, stopping over my nipples, rubbing them through my dress. "So you like playing games with me? Does that turn you on?"

I reached for his cock. "Yes. It did tonight." And it did. I liked how he squirmed for me, how much he wanted me. It was a welcome reprieve in the middle of all the chaos.

He pulled up the side of my dress and snapped my garter belt. The fabric stung but the shock of pain excited me. "Do you want me, Ksenya? You are free to leave at any time. All you have to do is say no."

"Yes, I want you. I need you. Let me please you." I moved my hand to undo his belt, but he pushed me away.

"Don't speak. You are here to please me. Got it? On your knees."

I obeyed, a breath escaping me. I wanted to submit to him. I also wanted to ask him who the hell he was and where was this behavior coming from. But right now, I couldn't bring myself to care. My head was a lust-filled haze.

He dropped his pants.

"Take my cock out."

I did. I grasped his big beautiful cock.

"See how hard I am for you, Ksenya?"

"Yes—you are—"

He grabbed me by the nape of the neck. "I told you not to fucking speak."

Whoa. I nodded shakily. My pussy throbbed. I couldn't believe how much I loved this.

"Open your mouth wide, wrap your lips around my cock. And suck."

Finally, he was treating me like the stripper slut he thought I was. And I wanted it. His filthy commands, his anger, his passion. I wanted all of him. And with the mask I was wearing, I would finally be able to explore his deepest fantasies. He thrust deep into the back of my throat, my lips clamped tightly around him. My tongue circled the head, sucking, teasing.

He growled. "Good job, baby. You're a dirty little cocksucker, aren't you? Take me deeper."

I took him as deep as I could, his cock tickling the back of my throat.

His eyes closed for a few seconds. Then he placed his hand on the back of my head, guiding my movement.

I couldn't get enough of him. I never wanted to stop, but after another moment, he pulled himself out. The silence of the night filled the air.

I dared a look up at his face. "What, did I not please you?"

"You pleased me fine, but I want to taste you."

A shiver ran through my body.

He carried me into his bedroom and positioned me on his bed. His capable hands slowly unhooked my bra. His fervent kisses showered my neck, his hot mouth probing mine. But these weren't sweet and loving kisses like I'd known with him; these were animalistic and raw. My hands moved to touch his massive chest but he pinned my arms above my head.

"Spread your legs," he barked, his deep, throaty voice sexier than ever. He pulled a belt from the side of the bed and tied my wrists up to the headboard. I tried to hold on to what little composure remained. I had never seen Grant like this. But one look up at his face showed a man who was totally in control. Taking what he wanted. I was nervous, but even now, Grant had a way of making me feel safe.

Once I was restrained, his mouth made its way down my body. His tongue lashed at my nipples until they turned a bright shade of red. I ached to feel him inside me, for him to have his way with me. Luckily for me, it didn't seem like I'd have to wait long.

"You're so fucking perfect. Like someone sculpted you just for me."

Despite this hell-in-a-handbasket night, I held back a laugh.

He pushed my panties aside, his tongue just a centimeter away from my lips. But then he stopped, the vein in his neck bulging.

He sat up, his breath hitched.

It was as if time had frozen, just our labored breaths filled the room.

His eyes widened, and he placed his head in his hands, sighing heavily. "I think you need to leave. Now."

What the— "Why? What is wrong? Did I not be pleasing to you?"

His jaw dropped, and he squeezed his eyes shut.

He untied my wrists. "Get out of my house. And lose my number. Don't ever call me again."

"What did I do wrong?"

His nostrils flared, his lips pulled back, teeth bared. "Get. The. Fuck. Out."

I stumbled out of bed, covering my body with my hands. I awkwardly dressed, grabbed my purse, and dashed out of there—leaving Grant naked on his bed.

What was I missing?

My body shivered despite the warm San Diego breeze. I called a taxi, and it whisked me back to the only place I had left. I'd fucked up everything in my life. For now—the only thing that remained was this quest. I still owed Mitch a private dance. A dance that would bring me one step closer to solving this mystery.

28

GRANT

A BABY? MIA HAD A fucking baby. Where was this baby? Was I a father? I had to assume this was connected to her leaving me years ago, while I was laid up in the hospital. We'd made love when I returned from deployment, and then she'd vanished. Completely. No trace—I mean this bitch was psycho. Like that chick from *Gone Girl*.

I hadn't noticed the scar before, not when she stripped for me or had spent the night at my place. I'd been too focused on fucking her. But I was a goddamn Navy SEAL corpsman—I knew what a C-section scar looked like.

Done. I was so fucking done with her mind games. She could waste the rest of her life trying to help Joaquín but I would no longer be her pawn.

I wouldn't even consider that I was wrong—Ksenya was Mia! She was. I was surer about that than I was about the sky being fucking blue.

I had to find out if her kid was alive, if *my* kid was alive. If she had my child and had kept him or her from me, I'd fucking lose my mind.

Maybe she had cheated on me. Although I never saw any signs of that, I can't assume anything about this chick to be true anymore.

Where was this fucking baby? I wouldn't rest until I found out what happened to him or her.

Fuck. I couldn't believe it. She was my Achilles' heel. But now I was free—free forever from her.

Time to live by our motto. A Navy SEAL never makes the same mistake twice.

29

KSENYA

M
Y MIND COULDN'T STOP REPLAYING every second of my interaction with Grant. The only thing I could come up with was that he had seen my C-section scar.

But why would that bother him so much? Ksenya could've had a child before she met him. It would only bother him if he knew…and if he knew, I was well and truly fucked.

I dismissed that thought.

Mitch greeted me at the door of Diamond after I sent him a text message. The cocky son of a bitch crossed his arms and thrust out his chest. "See? I knew he'd get bored with you." Mitch rubbed his hand on my back. Fuck. I didn't want this. Especially after leaving Grant like I had. But I didn't have a choice. I felt in my soul that I was supposed to be here.

Mitch led me to another room.

This room had no pole—just a plush bed. Fuck.

"I thought you wanted a dance. We could go to other room and I can give to you, on the pole?" my voice squeaked.

Mitch took my hand and let out a grunt. "You know what you came here for. You want my cock just as badly as I want to give it to you."

I had to think fast and get the hell out of here. But before I could plot, his hand tugged down his shorts, exposing his huge cock. I attempted to look away, but something besides his massive dick caught my eye.

A scar.

A deep mark, almost like a divot dug into his waist, like someone had jabbed him with something sharp. Almost like they might've been trying to get away from him. Something like a stiletto hee—

Holy Fuck. It had been Mitch!

I gasped.

I stumbled, dizzy, disorientated.

It couldn't have been him. After all these years, wondering who had fucked up my life, ruined my relationship with Grant.

My mind flashed back to that night. Grant and Joaquín had been deployed. I'd been young and stupid. It was just a regular party on campus, right? Nothing could go wrong. Didn't I deserve to have some fun? Tori begged us not to go, but Dara, April, and I wanted to have a girls' night before our men came home. The night started out great—music, beer, dancing, typical frat party. But it quickly went downhill. I became nauseous, as if I'd been drugged. I went into a room to lie down and passed out.

I'd woken up a few hours later. The room was dark and I was unable to focus, a massive man on top of me, my panties pulled down to my feet. Powerless to scream, I made a quick decision. I grabbed my heel and pierced it into his flesh.

Left one lasting scar of his attack, something that one day would hopefully help me identify him, something that he would have to explain for the rest of his life, every time he had sex, a reminder that I would never go away.

But no matter how hard I tried, I couldn't forget about him. Especially when he'd left me with a tragic reminder of his violence. A reminder that I had loved, that I had even felt grateful for. A reminder that had given me a purpose in my life, a will to go on even without Grant. But after that reminder was taken from me, in a cruel twist of fate, I'd become consumed with bitterness. I'd shed everything that was left of my life, except for my brother.

Now, I wanted revenge.

Mitch would not get away with what he'd done to me. I hadn't reinvented myself to seek revenge. My goal was to exonerate my brother. I would spend my last breath working for his freedom.

But first, I would get mine. I had yet another mission. Mitch must pay. Especially now that I'd lost Grant.

Again.

I'd lost control, I'd snapped.

I was crazed.

PART III

CRAZED

SE7EN DEADLY SEALS EPISODE 3

FAIREST AND DEAREST,
YOUR WRATH AND ANGER ARE
MORE HEAVY THAN I CAN BEAR;
BUT LEARN THAT I CANNOT TELL
WHAT YOU WISH ME TO SAY
WITHOUT SINNING AGAINST
MY HONOUR TOO GRIEVOUSLY.

— MARIE DE FRANCE

30

KSENYA

Dangerous, diabolical, and drop-dead sexy Mitch stood above me, stroking his huge, hard cock. Millions of women would kill to be in my position right now, pinned down on this red velvet bed, the object of lust by a fine-ass Navy SEAL.

But not me, and not *this* SEAL. My heart belonged to another man, Mitch's Teammate, Grant.

Bile built in my throat. I couldn't stop staring at the scar near Mitch's hipbone. The deep, dark divot—a mark I was certain I'd been the one to inflict. Every cell in my body screamed at me that he had been the one who'd attacked me years ago.

I'd vowed this would not happen to me again, training for six months to be able to defend myself from any type of attack. But bringing down a Navy SEAL? Even the most well-oiled warriors were no match for these frogmen.

I steadied my breath and my eyes darted around the dimly lit room. The green neon exit sign beckoned me toward it, but running out of this club wasn't an option. And Grant wasn't going to swoop in and save me this time. The way I figured it, I had two options: gouge Mitch's eyes out—not simply poke them, but blind the motherfucker by ripping his pupils from the sockets—or somehow use the only weapon I had, my brain.

"Mitch, handsome devil, what it is the rush? We have together all night. I tell to you what—let me dance for you, let me turn you on, let me be pleasing to you."

His eyes narrowed, and his hand reached around my neck. I wasn't sure if he was going kiss me or choke me.

"I've already seen you dance." He pulled me to him, and fisted my hair. "Now get on your knees and suck my cock."

Fuck. I had to think fast. I'd rather take a bullet in my brain than give Mitch head. "I—I have to go to bathroom."

He released my hair. "Fine. Hurry up."

I stumbled to the bathroom, and rummaged through my purse. Cell phone, wallet, tissues, gum, switchblade. Switchblade? Stabbing Mitch was out of the question—every SEAL knew three hundred ways to kill an enemy. He'd disarm me in a second. I released the blade from the case, the shiny metal beckoning me. I could end my pain tonight—the sorrow from losing everyone who'd ever mattered to me: my parents, my baby, my brother, Grant. But I would see this through—or die trying.

But I couldn't resist the call of the knife. I needed to feel, I needed to punish myself for my mistakes, for hurting Grant. I plunged the tip of the blade into my index finger, the blood oozing out. I took my finger and tasted a droplet. Coppery, warm, slightly sweet.

Blood. Bingo.

I squeezed some more droplets out of my finger like I was Seymour in *Little Shop of Horrors*. After smearing the blood on the inside of my panties, I sucked on my finger until the bleeding stopped, and then rinsed it in cold water. I walked back out to break the bad news to Mitch.

Mitch was sitting up on the bed. I took a moment to stare at him—he looked absolutely beautiful. So masculine, so ripped. But to me, he was the most revolting man in the world.

I knelt before him, glanced up and batted my eyelashes. "I cannot wait to be together with you. But tonight is no good. It is time of month and I want to be sexy for you."

He shook his head. "Don't care, baby doll. Your mouth still works. Besides, you've probably figured out that I'm a goddamn Navy SEAL, just like your fuck buddy, Grant. I'd love to get your war paint all over my face."

Oh my god! Did he just say that? No guy is actually into that, right? What a freak!

I gently caressed his face, and kissed his lips. A slow, sweet kiss, pretending he was Grant. "Mitch. I want it to be special. I only want to be together with you." Okay, here goes the Hail Mary pass. "Grant and me, we never have been together, with the sex. I have only been together with one man." I laid it on thick. Men loved being told they were the chosen ones. Suckers.

His eyes lit up. "Really, baby doll? Don't play me. You're a stripper."

I swallowed, even dug up some tears. Method acting. My drama teacher had told me to think about personal sadness; there was no lack of material in that department. "Yes, I am stripper. I have no skill, no money. My baba, she die, and I have no family. But I swear it to you, I have been with no man for years. You can ask it to Grant if you do not believe me."

Mitch's face softened and his demeanor warmed. "I believe you." Short, simple. He placed his cock back into his pants. Wrapping his huge arm around my shoulders, he pulled me in and kissed me on the head. We relaxed on the plush, velvety bed. "I like you, Ksenya, I do. I have no one close either. My wife, she left me. She even took my kids, not that I saw them much anyway. I've been deployed so much." He sighed deep and shook his head "April was the only one I could ever really talk to."

I gulped. Was this bad boy SEAL opening up? Did he actually have feelings toward me? This was insane. He confessed to me about his divorce. I'd always had a theory that SEALs yearned to have that one person in their lives who they could fully open up to, let down their guard around. More so than other men. These warriors had to be so tough, so invincible; any sign of weakness was inexcusable in their world. Yet, those same skills that they needed to have to be successful in the Teams were the same qualities that made these men struggle in their personal lives. SEALs yearned to find balance. And the only way these men could do it was through the women they loved. Too bad so many Team guys fucked up their relationships by cheating.

"I am sorry, Mitch. Do you miss her?"

"No. I just miss my kids." He glanced up at me, and his eyes were red. I wondered if it was because he was drunk or sad. Most likely both. "I fucked up with her, and I own it. We were so young when we met—only got married because I knocked her up. We barely saw each other once I became a SEAL, and we became toxic together. She loved making me jealous and I couldn't handle it. It doesn't matter anymore. But there's something about you…I think I can trust you."

For the first time, I could almost relate to Mitch. I missed my baby, too.

"You can." My fingernails traced his beard, and I kissed him on the lips, knowing I needed to do whatever it took to get him to truly trust me so I could pump him for information. I still had a tracking device on his phone, and I wanted to figure out who Rafael was, the recipient of Mitch's weird textless text. Why would a SEAL send another man a smiley face? Grant had cut me out; Mitch was all I had left, the only connection I had left to my brother. Mitch was the only one who could help me now.

His lips took me hard and rough and his hands traveled down my body. Dominant, rugged, intoxicating. I hated myself for liking this kiss, my traitorous pussy responding to his masterful touch. This guy raped me for God's sake! What the fuck was wrong with me?

"I'm gonna make our first night together real special, you just wait. I can't wait to fuck your tight pussy. But before we move forward, I need to know that you are done with Grant."

I choked back tears, genuine ones this time. Done with Grant. More like Grant was done with me. Forever. Mia and Grant would never be together again, in any incarnation. "Yes, we are done."

Mitch pushed back a lock of my hair, his piercing brown eyes looked at me like I was a juicy steak. "Good, you're mine. It's better for you this way. Look, Grant is still hung up on his ex. He'll never love anyone else."

My heart leapt inside my chest. Hearing these words from Grant's brother-in-arms was bittersweet. Grant might be hung up on Mia, but Mia no longer existed. I doubted that Grant would ever be able to find love with Ksenya, and when he finally learned what I had done, I was pretty positive that he would never speak to me again.

"He's a good guy and I love the dude but he's not like you and me. We're different, we're scarred."

I pursed my lips and gave him an understanding nod, relaxing into his embrace. Inwardly, I seethed, thinking about his goddam literal scar. That night had ruined my life. It was more than being drugged and assaulted. It was a loss of control. Guilt, shame. It enveloped me. I had been too afraid to tell Grant what had happened to me. Would he have blamed me for drinking that night, putting myself in that situation? For a week I tiptoed around him, keeping my secret to myself. Even though he was injured, we made love one last time. Once I found out I was pregnant, I tortured myself, not knowing if my baby's father was Grant or my attacker. My baby's daddy could've been

Mitch—that thought alone made my skin crawl, reproducing with this Neanderthal. But ultimately it didn't matter, I never found out who my baby's daddy was. I loved my baby more than anything in the world, regardless of his paternity.

It had to have been Mitch who had ruined my life. There was no other explanation. I would hate him until the day I died. And I would seek revenge. I would make him pay, make him beg for mercy, make him suffer at my hands.

Even so, I refused to allow my desire for revenge to get in the way of my one goal—freeing my brother.

I had successfully portrayed the wounded-bird stripper. Men loved to save women, especially men like Mitch. Little did he know he was caught in my web. He might have fallen for Ksenya, but my soul was still Mia's.

31

GRANT

I woke with a wicked hangover, not just from the copious amounts of whiskey I'd imbibed, but from Mia's intoxicating scent. But the sharp rage that pulsed through my body quelled any desire to see her.

That lying bitch. Not only did she think I was stupid enough not to figure out her identity, but she felt that it was okay to lie to me about why she left me. I'd spent most of last night trying to figure out the timeline. The only time I hadn't seen Mia for nine months was after she'd left me, which means that had to be when she had the baby. Even though we'd broken up, because of Joaquín I'd always seen her around at least every five months. She was petite, and there was a slight possibility that she had been barely showing and I had missed it, but that was unlikely, since every time I'd been in the same room with her, my eyes were helplessly drawn to her curves. I needed to know where her baby was, and if I was the father.

I picked up the phone and dialed. "Hey, I need to see you."

The voice on the other line quickly agreed, and we arranged to meet at a coffeehouse.

An hour later, I sat at an outdoor table impatiently waiting with Hero curled by my feet.

I'd almost given up and headed back home, when I saw her walk through the door. I barely recognized her.

Gone were the fake eyelashes, the caked-on makeup, and the ridiculously high heels. She wore white short-shorts, a loose-fitting T-shirt, and flip-flops.

I stood up to greet her. "Hey, Autumn."

"Hi, Grant. Sorry I'm late, the traffic was just crazy, you know? All the tourists just flock to the beach here in the summer. I totally hate it. Oh my God! Is this your dog? He's gorgeous."

I smiled and kissed her on the cheek. She knelt down to pet Hero, rubbing his ears until he groaned. This girl was refreshing. I'd liked her since the moment I'd met her at the party where Tiffany died. And when I'd run into her at the party I took Ksenya to last week, she'd approached me and offered to help Joaquín any way she could. She'd confided in me that she thought Tiffany was involved in something dark. At the time, I was hoping she could find some clue about who had actually killed Tiffany—now I hoped she could help me find Mia's baby.

We waited in line at this beachy coffeehouse. Surfers with sand still on their wetsuits strolled in, and some hot girls in yoga pants crowded the bar. A young mom walked in, clutching her toddler's hand, and I couldn't help but stare.

After we were served our drinks, Autumn and I sat at a small table outside, a view of Moonlight Beach in the background. She squinted from the sunlight and then put on her oversized sunglasses. "So, what's up? You said it was urgent."

I had rehearsed exactly what to say in my head. Autumn was overly naïve and friendly. Anything I said could potentially be relayed to Mia. "I visited Joaquín in jail yesterday. Dude looks like shit. Bloated, depressed. A shell of the man he once was. He's desperate. I was wondering if you heard anything else about Tiffany—you said you were going to visit her family?"

"Oh, yeah, I did. Did Ksenya tell you I took her?"

Mia went? Fuck. That must've been where she took off to on Sunday. "No. She didn't. I'm done with her."

"Really? You seemed super into her last night at Diamond."

Ouch. I deserved that.

"Sorry, I shouldn't have said that," Autumn continued. "She's nice, but kind of closed off, you know? Like she's hiding something."

Ha! Tell me about it.

"Well, yeah. So we drove up to Temecula. Have you ever been there? It's super cool—has all these awesome vineyards. Ksenya seemed to like it.

Anyway, we met Tiff's mom, she's super nice. Oh, did you know Tiff had a son, Julián? He's so adorable."

I gagged on my coffee. What the fuck? "No, I didn't. It wasn't mentioned in any of the papers."

"Yeah, I mean she rarely talked about him and he lived with her mom. Isn't that super weird. I would never want to be away from my baby. Want to see a picture?"

"Sure."

Autumn took out her phone, and scrolled through some pics. The second I saw the boy's face, my heart raced. He had almond-shaped eyes, long eyelashes and his mouth curled at the edge, just like Mia's.

There was also a cleft on his chin.

Just like mine.

I squeezed my fist and grabbed Autumn's arm. "Autumn, tell me everything you know about this boy. It's important. Did Tiffany ever mention his father?"

Her eyes widened and I quickly released her. I couldn't tell her my real suspicions. "Sorry, I just—I mean he looks like Joaquín. He'd told me he had never met Tiffany. I'm just trying to help him."

"Wow, you mean you think he could be Joaquín's son? That would be crazy. She said she barely knew the dad, said he was some psychopath drug dealer. She had him before I started working at Panthers. But yeah, even her mom mentioned the other day that she didn't even know her own daughter was pregnant! I mean can you believe that? My parents suck but even I'd tell them if I was pregnant."

No. No way. This couldn't be. I needed to see this boy with my own eyes. Yes, there was a possibility that he could be Joaquín's and Tiffany's— maybe they had had a one-night stand years ago, but that would mean that Joaquín had been lying to me, and worse yet, he would have a motive for murder.

But there was also a chance this boy could be my son.

"You know what's funny? Ksenya started acting all weird too when she met Julián. Asking all sorts of questions."

My palms began to sweat. What did Mia know about Tiffany's son? Had she given our child away to be raised by some random stripper's mom? If there was any possibility that was true, I'd fucking kill her.

Fuck.

"Where is he? I need to see him with my own eyes. For Joaquín."

Autumn tapped her nails on the table. "Well, I would offer to go with you but it would be weird for me to go back up because I was just there on Sunday. But I guess I could give you the address? Maybe you can see him in the neighborhood."

"That would be great. Thank you."

She shrugged. "You're welcome." She finished her coffee, then put her hand on my thigh. I pushed it off me.

"Look, Autumn. You're a gorgeous girl and I really like you. But I'm not looking for anything serious right now, and you deserve to be taken seriously."

Her eyes cast down. "It's okay. I just really like you, Grant. Things could've been different between us. I wish, I mean for so many reasons, but I wish Tiffany hadn't died that night."

So do I.

She entered the address into my phone. We made a few more minutes of small talk, I gave her a hug, and then I got into my truck with Hero and headed to Temecula.

32

KSENYA

Today was Tuesday, the first day of my new job bartending at the Pickled Frog.

I smoothed my jean skirt and pulled on the tight white T-shirt over my body. Kyle would be training me all day. My end goal was to do a good job, get Kyle to trust me enough to keep me on staff, and to hopefully find another clue.

Driving to the bar, I struggled to focus with so much on my mind. I was still in shock that Mitch ended up behaving like a gentleman. He had even driven me home, walked me to my door and given me a goodnight kiss as if he were some eager schoolboy. His cocky demeanor had seemed to shed when I'd become real with him. I knew he had that scar, but was he really the man who had raped me?

Grant hadn't called or texted. I still couldn't figure out why he had kicked me out the other night just before we were finally going to have sex. What had I done that night that had spooked Grant? I would find a way to weasel myself back into Grant's life.

Was Joaquín Julían's father? What had Joaquín thought about after he saw me wearing Mia's bracelet at the jail? Did he realize I was his sister in disguise? Was there anything else I couldn't see? At this point, I had more questions than answers.

Kyle greeted me, pulling me out of my thoughts, and I was immediately disarmed by his smile. "Hey, sweetheart. How've you been?"

"Good." I stopped and made a calculated decision. "I want to tell to you, Kyle—Grant and me, we are no longer together. I understand if you do not want me to work here no more."

Kyle's brow furrowed at me. "No worries. Grant's not why I hired you. In fact, dating a Team guy is only a complication. As long as you work hard, we will have no problems, and if you ever need anything, just give me a call and I got your back. But let me give you a tip: it would be wise for you not to get involved with another frogman. We're nothing but trouble."

The sympathy card worked like a charm. I gave a forced nod, but wondered at his motivation for giving me the warning. My non-paranoid guess would be that he would prefer his bargirl wasn't dating the customers, which made perfect sense. One Team guy hitting on another Team guy's woman usually ended in bloodshed, if not death. Or maybe Kyle's comment meant that he suspected I was Mia, even though that was unlikely. Either way, Kyle had it all wrong. Grant wasn't trouble—I was.

Kyle led me into the bar and proceeded to give me a detailed tour of the photos on the wall.

I paused over the pictures of the beautiful men: one was a former SEAL who had been killed protecting an ambassador in a terrorist attack overseas, another featured an entire Team whose helicopter was shot down in Afghanistan. I hoped to find a picture of Joaquín and his Team, but I knew better. No active duty SEAL would ever agree to have his identity exposed, and Kyle, an active SEAL himself, would never put his men in harm's way. In fact, the reason he'd purchased this bar was to create a safe haven for his men. He helped out when he wasn't on deployment, but left most of the day-to-day operations of the bar to his hired staff.

The lunch crowd slowly trickled in. Mostly older guys, probably former SEALs. A few took their place at the bar, ordering their usual spirits. I noticed the majority of them did not have wedding rings. My heart ached for these broken warriors. Many of them retired and then spent the rest of their lives chasing the adrenaline highs they experienced in the Teams, unable to find pleasure in the mundane details of everyday life. Their loved ones were never able to understand the secret burdens these men carried to their graves.

Bartending wasn't as simple as I'd thought. I had to cut lemons and limes, learn how to use the cash register, keep track of client tabs, take inventory of the liquor, and memorize cocktail recipes. Stripping had been way easier.

As my shift dragged on, I made small talk with the patrons, lied about my life back in the Ukraine, and laughed at their silly jokes.

Near closing time, a man walked in and sat down at the bar. He was clean-shaven—a rarity among these men—in his mid-forties, dark hair, piercing green eyes, and broad shoulders. "I'll have a jack and coke."

I prepared his drink, and though I turned away from him, his eyes remained fixed on me. More so than the general eye fuck the other men gave me. "Here you go, handsome. Do you have tab?"

"No." The man's eyes burned into my face. I could see his pupils trace my lips, my nose, my eyes, my chest. I instinctively covered my body with my arms.

"Where you from?" he asked, his voice deep and slow.

"Kharkov, in the Ukraine."

"Sure you are."

I let out a nervous laugh. Who was this man, and what did he think he knew?

He knocked back his drink, then slid a folded twenty across the bar. Without saying a word, he vanished.

I unfolded the bill and a small piece of paper floated out.

I'm on to you.

My hand shook as I shoved the paper into my apron pocket. I scanned the bar but he was gone. No one knew about my identity except Roman. Had I made a fatal error?

Well, my dumb ass had shown Joaquín my bracelet at the jail yesterday, but only Joaquín would know what that bracelet meant. Maybe Joaquín had sent someone to check me out? Weren't jails run like some sort of underground mafia? Like maybe he could've bribed a guard? A sudden coldness hit my core. I couldn't even begin to imagine what Joaquín's day-to-day life was like in the jail. He'd gone from being hailed as a hero to being caged like an animal. I closed my eyes and tried to push the image of my brother pounding license plates and eating a sandwich made of stale bread and slimy bologna out of my mind.

I focused on Kyle, who was cleaning glasses by the bar.

"Who that man is I serve?"

Kyle scanned the bar and gazed out the door. "The guy who just bolted?

Never seen him. I doubt he's a former Team guy—I've met most of them in these parts. Why? He hassle you?"

I shook my head. I had to keep this under wraps. "No. He look familiar to me, maybe I see him at club."

My stomach churned and beads of sweat dripped down my forehead. If someone were on to me, I would be discovered. A ticking time bomb rang loudly in my ears. If I were smart, I would drive to Grant's house, confess my sins, and beg for mercy.

But I had lost any sense of reason. Without Joaquín, without Grant, without my baby, without my parents, I had no ties to anyone. I yearned to feel something, to connect, to be reminded my own life had a purpose independent of saving Joaquín. That someone, somewhere, loved me. But for now, the most important task was to protect my identity.

At the end of my shift, I had made a little over two hundred dollars in tips. Nothing like what I made a night stripping, but definitely a decent sum nonetheless. Maybe I should've worked here when I was Mia, to pay my way through college; not that Grant, nor Joaquín for that matter, would have been thrilled with the idea of me serving a bunch of Team guys.

I said goodbye to Kyle and walked out the door, preparing to drive home and try to shake this unsettling experience. Candy-colored clouds loomed in the sunset. A gust of wind blew into my face and I became disoriented. In my haze, a heavy feeling arose in my gut. Something wasn't right.

That man. Where was he? Was he following me? What did he think he knew?

Maybe I should've asked Kyle to drive me home. Or I could've called Grant. Hell, maybe I should've called Mitch.

No. I could handle this. That man, whoever he was, couldn't possibly know my real identity. I'd crossed my t's and dotted my i's. Even Grant didn't suspect who I was.

I ignored my paranoia and hurried into my car. As I drove down the freeway, my hands shook on the steering wheel. My fingers pressed on the volume, trying to drown my anxiety in a sea of heavy metal music. The blaring instruments pulsed through my body. The bass anchored my soul. I took a deep breath, hoping to calm my nerves.

After a few miles, I noticed a blue late-model Cadillac a few cars behind me. At first I hoped it was only heading the same direction as me. So I slowed my car, and it slowed behind me. I changed lanes, it changed lanes also. Dread filled my body.

Hell, no. Was I being paranoid? I sped up, the car sped up too.

Fuck. I was being followed.

I would lose the car.

I swerved around another car and then pressed on the gas. My eyes kept glancing at the rearview mirror. The car was still on my tail. Dammit.

The freeway twisted up ahead. I refused to exit, not wanting to isolate myself. But the traffic was thin and the moon was dim. I raced along the highway, hugging the curves. Another glance in the mirror, and I knew I was screwed.

A loud boom that sounded like a gunshot rang out behind me, followed by the crinkling of metal and the popping of an air bag. Before I knew what was happening, my car barreled down an embankment and a sharp pain blasted through my body. The honking of horns and whizzing of cars added to my confusion as my face was crunched up against the air bag, stifling my screams. There was a gash on my forehead, and blood trickled down my face, pooling in my seat, making me wet and sticky. I arched my back, attempting to turn my throbbing neck to see what had happened, when glass flew by my face, followed by an angry man's voice.

"Get the fuck out of the car."

33

GRANT

I arrived at the address Autumn had given me. The neighborhood contained a bunch of tract homes, uniform manicured lawns, and proud American flags. Julián's house seemed less vibrant than the rest on the street: the paint was chipped and faded, the grass was patchy, and there was a crack in the sidewalk. There was no vehicle in the driveway, and the lights were out in the house, so I assumed no one was at home.

The sun was still bright, and I didn't want to be conspicuous, so I drove slowly around the neighborhood, grabbed a real estate flyer, and took Hero down to a local park that had a view of the house. And waited.

After a few hours of playing with Hero, running through one of those stupid park exercise obstacle courses, and screwing around on my phone, I finally saw a car pull into the driveway.

I walked Hero up the street, pacing myself, praying I would get there in time to see Julián before his grandma hustled him into the house.

The lady was holding a few plastic grocery bags and attempting to get the young boy out of his car seat.

I commanded Hero to sit, and approached her. "Can I help you with those, ma'am?"

She turned and looked at me, her skin wrinkled, her brow furrowed. "I'm fine, thank you."

I wasn't going to give up that easily. "It's no problem really. I'm Grant, my fiancée and I are looking to purchase a home in this neighborhood. Do you like living here?"

She let out a huff, and shoved a plastic bag in my hand. "Yeah, it's a nice community. Very safe, perfect for raising my grandson."

I grabbed the rest of her bags, and she wriggled Julián out of the car. My eyes fell on this little boy, cutest kid I'd ever seen. Thick, dark hair, almond-shaped hazel eyes, tanned skin.

He looked like a perfect blend of Mia and me.

My hands shook, and my heart pounded. I wanted to rip him out of her hands and take him away from her. But I had no proof, only a haunting suspicion. Kidnapping a kid, even if he could potentially be mine, was definitely out of the question.

I took the bags to her doorstep. She fumbled behind me, clutching Julián's hand. The little boy looked up at me, blinking rapidly, and all I could focus on was his long eyelashes, Mia's eyelashes.

Did Joaquín know? Is this why he killed Tiffany? Had she kidnapped my child? What the fuck was going on?

The lady didn't open the front door. She probably thought I was some rapist. I was glad she was safety conscious, considering she could be raising my child.

"Well, thanks for helping. I think there is one for sale down the street. And now that you mention it, I may put our home on the market. I'm thinking of moving out of the state. I have no family here anymore and it's too expensive."

No! Fuck. That adrenaline rush flooded through my blood, like I was on a time-sensitive mission with my Team. I had to act fast, or the opportunity to see if Julián was mine—and if he was, to gain custody—would vanish.

I scanned Julián, taking a mental picture of his face. I focused on the cleft in his chin, and touched my own.

"Doggie?" Julián pointed at Hero.

"Yes." I knelt down to the boy. "He's friendly, you can pet him."

The lady eyed me suspiciously, but motioned that it was okay. Julián slowly tapped the top of Hero's head, as if he were dribbling a basketball.

Julián dropped his apple juice box on the ground.

"Julián. Pick that up and throw it in the trash."

I swooped in and retrieved it from the ground. "It's okay, ma'am. I'm leaving now. I'll just take it with me. It was nice to meet you."

I turned away, a lump in my throat. I clutched onto that juice box like it was incredibly sensitive and urgent intel, which it was. When I returned to my truck, I placed the box in a plastic bag I had in my car. Luckily, the straw was chewed, which would increase my chances of finding DNA. I picked up my phone and called a friend of mine in forensics. He agreed to meet me, and I raced out of the town. Leaving Julián behind.

34

KSENYA

The barrel of a gun pressed against my back, its cold steel marking my flesh. *Fuck, why didn't I listen to my instincts?* If my training had taught me anything, it was to trust my gut. I was cracking under pressure.

The man from the bar clasped his hands around my wrists as his breath blew hot on my face. He grabbed my purse from the floor and pulled me out of the car. I'd scream, but no one would hear me. Had anyone seen the accident?

We climbed up the hill and he shoved me into his car. With the mask of night, I was unsure if there had been any witnesses. The traffic was constant but not thick, and not one other car stopped to see if I was okay.

My luck had officially run out.

Every muscle in my body throbbed. "I do not know why it is you are taking me. I am just girl from Ukraine. You must have it, the wrong girl."

His only response was a deep laugh.

Despite the blinding pain in my head, I formulated a plan. I could attempt an escape when he pulled off the freeway, risking my life. But since my goal was to exonerate Joaquín, it made more sense to see this through, see where he took me, find out who he was, and learn what he wanted.

If he'd followed me from the parking lot, then maybe Kyle or another SEAL saw him. Dammit. If only Grant hadn't freaked out the other night, he surely would've picked me up at the Pickled Frog and I'd be safe with him. Or I could've lowered myself and called Mitch. But I was on my own.

I memorized the details of the car. It was a late-model Cadillac, blue with black interior. It blended in perfectly, like it could've been a rental car. The leather was pungent with smoke and sweat.

Thirty minutes passed before he exited off the freeway. We were in El Cajon. Was he taking me to my place? Did he know where I lived?

I breathed a sigh of relief when I saw that we were heading toward Mount Helix. Years ago, I'd discovered that this place was a calming retreat where I could meditate. The wooded setting reminded me of my hometown in Marin.

We parked on a dirt road near a street of older homes. The man pushed me out of the car, his hand on my neck. "Don't try anything funny or you'll be sorry." Well, that wasn't reassuring, considering he had a gun and no one in the world knew where I was. After a tightly guided walk, we ended up near a barren dirt path with some unsettled earth in a pile. Great, maybe they had already dug my grave.

The dark sky assured me that I was out of view from anyone.

I had nothing. Not my purse, not my phone. All left in his car.

A car pulled up and another man exited. I recognized him immediately from pictures on his website. Daniel Reed, Joaquín's lawyer.

He was tall, blond, slightly balding, and fairly muscular for being in his late forties.

"Mia Cruz. I'm sorry to bring you out here like this, but I couldn't risk any of the Team guys finding out your true identity."

Hearing him call me by my real name rendered me speechless. A sense of failure washed over me, knowing now that this man had found out my secret, it was only a matter of time for everyone else to figure out my identity.

"You look incredible. I have to admit I thought Joaquín had lost it the other day when he swore you'd visited him. I even looked at the security footage from the jail, convinced there was no way that Ksenya could be you. But I did some digging, and here you are. Congratulations on outsmarting a bunch of SEALs."

Despite the warm summer breeze, the hair on my arms stood on end. If Daniel thought by flattering me I would trust him, he was dead wrong.

Though his excuse for bringing me out here made sense, my gut told me this guy was dangerous.

This was my own fault. I was the dumbass who'd showed my bracelet to Joaquín in the jail. A hasty, irrational decision. I'd assumed he would keep his suspicions to himself, not go running his mouth to his lawyer. Apparently, Joaquín trusted Daniel.

I trusted no one.

Knowing the jig was up, I dropped the accent. "You got me. I told Joaquín I'd do anything to exonerate him. And last I heard, you advised him to plead guilty to a crime he didn't commit, so I think I made a good decision. Was it necessary for you to total my car in order to talk to me? What the fuck do you want? You're ruining my investigation." Despite my anger, speaking normally made my tongue very happy.

Daniel and his henchman simultaneously broke out into laughter. I was a joke to them. These jackasses must've figured that I'd ruined my life just to play a game. But this was no game. I was dead serious.

"Investigation? What have you turned up? Oh wait, let me guess, SEALs drink, occasionally get high, and fuck strippers. Real groundbreaking stuff, Miss Cruz. Maybe you can apply for a career with NCIS."

Asshat.

I bit my lip. "Why did you bring me out here? Just to let me know you were on to me? That Joaquín figured me out? Congratulations, super sleuths. I basically told him I was Ksenya. Now do something useful and tell me about the trial. What's your defense?"

Daniel signaled to his buddy to leave us alone. The other man walked back to the Cadillac.

"Defense? I'm still trying to convince him to plead guilty, but he refuses. Being a stubborn asshole must run in the family." Daniel put his arm on my shoulder. I flinched away. "Sweetheart, he did do it."

My heart sank. Were Grant and I the only people who believed in Joaquín's innocence? "Why on earth would he plead guilty? He's innocent. He swore to me."

"Despite what he told you, told me, told your lover Grant, or told the cops, your brother is guilty. The sooner he admits to it, the sooner we can get him a reduced sentence. We could make it seem like an accident, manslaughter. He'd be out in five and we could all move on. Well, maybe not you, you look like a porn star now. But I'm sure you could make sex tapes and find yourself a reality show."

That was the point, asshole—I looked like this to get close to these men. Joaquín was not guilty. Why was this guy just volunteering all this information to me, anyway? What about attorney-client privilege? How could he be so dismissive, treating me like I was a joke? My stomach churned and my feet crinkled the leaves below. My gut told me something was gravely wrong. "You are supposed to be protecting him. Be his advocate. Believe in him."

"Look, honey, I don't care about your ideas on the matter. Joaquín is losing it in jail. I think the current conditions are causing him to have mental health issues. He's downright delusional. Fortunately, his breakdowns are good for me because I might be able to show at trial that the stress of being a SEAL, having PTSD, and losing his parents made him snap. In any case, Joaquín desperately wants to see you again and I promised him I'd make it happen. I'll call Grant and arrange it."

"Grant doesn't know I'm Mia. And he told Ksenya never to call him again."

Daniel gritted his teeth. "If he says no, let me know and I'll handle it. He knows how to obey orders for the good of the Team. And don't worry, I'll keep your little secret for now. Mainly because I find it amusing and want to see how far you will go. Who knows? Maybe you will uncover some deep, dark secret."

Something about the way he said "deep, dark secret" rattled me. As if he knew there was a secret waiting to be unearthed.

"Maybe I already have."

My comment barely registered on Daniel's face. A cool smirk and he grabbed his phone.

My eyes widened, and mania captured my brain. Despite all my acting abilities, I was unable to slow my dancing mind, contain my anxiety, and relax my twitching body.

"I'll arrange to get you some cash for your troubles. I've taken the liberty of programming my number into your phone. As for the car, we had it towed and we're going to fix it up and deliver it to you later."

Note to self: get a new phone. He probably put some tracking device on it like I had with Mitch's. "I don't need your cash. I can take care of myself."

The other man walked over and handed me my purse and phone. I quickly rummaged through it to see if all the contents were still there.

"Nice to meet you, Mia. Tell Grant you were involved in a hit and run."

"Look, Joaquín may trust you, but I think you're a slimy prick. If you were doing your job, I wouldn't have had to ruin my life."

The men ignored my words and left the scene.

This entire event made no sense at all. Daniel was a lawyer, but the way he approached and treated me was more like the actions of a criminal. And what really bothered me was that he wasn't being honest with Joaquín.

I was fairly close to my apartment. I could easily have called a cab, Autumn, or even Mitch to get me. But I needed to play the damsel in distress, at least one last time. Grant had shut me out; this accident was my golden ticket, especially because I needed him to go see my brother. As a SEAL, Grant would never turn his back on a girl in need.

I grabbed my cell.

"Hello?"

"Grant, I'm sorry that I call to you. I have but no one else. I was in accident and the men gave me ride but I do not trust them so they drop me near to my house. Can you come get me?"

He paused and let out a long sigh. "Where are you?"

35

GRANT

I raced down the freeway to get to Mia. Her voice sounded weak and edgy. And I was even more pissed off at her than ever, just entertaining the possibility that she had hidden our kid somewhere. Yes, I knew she was an actress and still playing me. Either way, something didn't seem right.

An accident? Men giving her a ride? Yeah, I'll bet. Yet another scheme, another group of shady people she associated with. I understood her goal, but I still thought she was bat-shit crazy.

After stewing over the whole situation with Mia and the baby, I decided I couldn't let it go. This baby, her baby, possibly my baby. It was even worse now because I had convinced myself that Julián was my son, even though I had no proof yet. I had to fucking know what had happened to her baby. And the only way I could do that was to keep Mia close.

My plan was simple: get her to open up to me, no matter what the cost. First as Ksenya, then I'd call her bluff. I would do whatever it fucking took until I found out the truth.

I would seduce her, not just sexually, but emotionally. The second I had her right where I wanted her, I'd call her out, demand answers, demand respect.

But I had to tread lightly, there was no way she could know I was on to her. No more trapping her into eating meat. I would treat her like a real girl-friend, disarm her, and she wouldn't know what hit her.

I pulled around the corner to find her sitting on a bench, hands in her lap, shoulders slumped. For the first time since I'd met her as Ksenya, she looked disheveled.

My stomach knotted. Had she been assaulted? Until I could get her to admit to what she was up to, I had to stay close. To protect her. I had no fucking clue what or who she was involved with.

I stopped the truck, and she jumped inside. Her skin was dirty, her hair was tangled, and I noticed her dark roots and extensions. Mascara was smeared down her face. Dried spots of blood were on her neck and face.

Fuck me. "What the fuck happened to you? Tell me the truth."

She bit her lip. "It is nothing. My car, it crash on freeway. These men pick me up and take me to here. I am okay. Thank you for getting me."

Lying again. Fuck this bitch. I needed to step up my game and figure out what was going on. "Fine, whatever. You're staying with me tonight."

"But you said to me last night to get the fuck out."

"I changed my mind."

She nodded and didn't speak, which was probably for the best. I considered giving her an excuse for kicking her out the other night, but I saw no reason to lie. I never made excuses for my actions and I wasn't going to start now.

I drove back to my place, stopping at a drive-thru. I asked Mia what she wanted to eat, and even though she said she wasn't hungry, I ordered her a salad.

Back at my place, I took her into the bathroom to clean her up and examine her wounds.

"Take off your clothes."

She flinched back, but I didn't have time for her games. Not today. "Now, woman."

She pulled the tight white tank top over her neck and my eyes zeroed in on her huge tits. Her nipples were barely covered by the black bra she was wearing. I gritted my teeth thinking about all the guys at the bar today who had been eye-fucking her.

She wiggled out of her tight jean skirt, revealing a see-thru mesh black thong. My cock rose to attention. I wanted to bend her over, slap her ass, and take her from behind.

But instead I took out my first aid kit.

Her hair was tinged red and stuck to the gash on her forehead. I cleaned it up with hydrogen peroxide, but the wound wasn't too deep. My hands made their way down her incredible body, exploring her curves, looking for any more injuries, but besides superficial scratches, she was fine. My hand grasped her around the neck, pulling her body toward me, and I pressed the tip of my cock on her panties, so she could feel how much I wanted her. She gasped, leaned in to kiss me, and I pushed her away.

I left her in the bathroom and threw her one of my old T-shirts and some sweats.

I ate my meal at the table and Mia picked at her salad on the sofa. This was a fucking nightmare. I had the hottest woman—who happened to be the love of my life—alone in my place, yet I refused to fuck her. I couldn't stand to be in the same house as her. I had to treat this as a mission—a mission to find out what happened to her baby.

"Where's your car?"

"I had it towed to shop. I get it fixed and get it back soon."

She had an answer for everything. I studied her face, which now seemed less angelic and slightly sinister, her blond hair wild and sexy.

From here on out, I would step up my game. Finding out what had happened to Mia's child was my first priority, then I'd get to the bottom of Joaquín's stripper's murder case, though if Julián was Mia's kid, or even possibly Joaquín and Tiffany's kid, then the man definitely had a motive. And I didn't have any other leads. I'd laid low, listening, trying to cull some intelligence. So far I had nothing, other than a few rumors Joaquín was involved in some underground drug ring. But I'd never seen him touch drugs, not once. Mitch dabbled, a few of the other guys got high, but not Joaquín.

I was scarfing down my burger when my cell phone rang. I glanced down, assuming it was one of my Team guys calling me into work, but the number was unknown.

I picked up the phone. "Hello?"

A woman's voice played on a recording. "You are receiving a call from—"

"Joaquín Cruz," my buddy's voice said.

"—an inmate at the San Diego County Jail. Press one to accept this call and two to decline."

My finger scrambled to press one. "Hey man, you okay?"

"Yup." Joaquín's voice seemed weak. "Hey, I need you to come visit me this week. It's urgent. I'll have my lawyer set it up."

Had I been right about him noticing Mia's bracelet? "Of course, bro. I'll give him a call tomorrow."

"One more thing. Can you bring that fox you were with? I need some eye candy."

I glanced over at Mia, curled in a ball with Hero on the sofa. "You bet."

No matter how hard I'd fought to stay away from her, somehow we always wound up back together.

36

KSENYA

I barely slept all night, worrying that now that Daniel had found out who I was, Grant would be next.

I'd spent the night alone again, but in his bed. Wrapped in his covers, dreaming of cuddling next to him. I'd even slept naked, hoping he would climb into the bed in the middle of the night and make love to me. But Grant remained on the sofa all night; his only companion was Hero. I figured he was still pissed at me from the other night, though he wouldn't tell me why. He still came to my rescue, but that wasn't actually that shocking considering rescuing people was his profession. I wished I knew what was going through his mind. Our distance grew further apart. Now, more than at any other point since I started this game, I realized the chances of us getting back together were fading. Too many lies, too many secrets. Even so, I cherished every second of sleeping in his bed where we first made love, the sheets fragrant with his scent.

When I walked out of the bedroom, Grant was cooking breakfast. But this time there was no steak to make me gag—just black coffee, steel-cut oats, and strawberries.

Everything was vegan. Did he know?

"Sorry about breakfast, I haven't gone shopping in a while."

That made sense. "It is good, thank you."

"Are you sure you don't mind coming with me to see my friend?"

"It is fine. I am happy to go."

"Thanks." He sat across the table from me, sipping his coffee. "So, how was work yesterday?"

"Good. Kyle is nice to me. Money, it is good." I couldn't help staring at his biceps. He was just wearing a T-shirt and gray sweats. His beard was full, and I begin to fantasize about him. It had been so long since I'd felt his skilled tongue between my legs, just the thought alone was enough to get me wet. How had I fucked up so badly with him? Not only as Mia but also as Ksenya?

Now wasn't the time. I was going to see my brother again. And this time, he knew who I was.

We finished breakfast and then left in Grant's truck.

Daniel hadn't wasted any time setting the meeting up. And I'd come up with a plan.

I had to admit, it wasn't my best plan. There was no way I could distract Grant and try to talk to Joaquín alone. My interactions would be video and audio taped. Good thing I had some tricks up my sleeve.

We parked on the street in front of the prison and Grant fed the meter. I gazed up at the jail from below and stared at the tiny windows that faced the ocean. I choked back a tear, imagining Joaquín wasting away up in his tower, with only a sliver of a glimpse to the outside world. Grant took my hand and led me into the building.

The guard seemed to recognize me from our last visit on Monday, just two days prior. I gave him a polite nod and sat next to Grant on an orange plastic chair. The floor smelled like bleach and desperation, and the toxic environment in the room made my stomach queasy.

I squeezed Grant's hand. "Why did he want to see you so very soon?"

Grant smirked, pushing his blond hair off his chiseled face. "No clue. Said it was urgent."

I forced a smile. Grant was lying to me. He knew something was up with Joaquín. Or worse, me. Fuck.

Joaquín appeared in his jumpsuit, but mercifully this time I was prepared for his disheveled appearance. Even so, my heart wept when his frame came into view.

He picked up the phone. "Hey, thanks for coming." He waved to me and I resisted the urge to shatter the glass to hug him.

"What's up, man? You okay?"

"Yeah. I'm good. I've made a decision." He looked right at me. "I'm not going to plea."

Yes! Best news I'd heard since this nightmare started.

Grant's face beamed. "Great news. Is there anything I can do? Do you remember anything else about that night? I wish I were more helpful. Sorry, I was too fucked up and busy with Autumn to remember much of anything."

Fuck you, Grant. Even though he'd told me he was done with me two nights ago, he had picked me up from the park and brought me to visit his friend in jail. Why was he talking about Autumn? To make Ksenya jealous? Or was he just being honest with Joaquín?

"It's okay. Look, I need you to do something for me. I'm worried about Mia. I think something has happened to her. There was this man, Julián, who she dated after you. I didn't like the guy."

Holy fuck! Did he say *Julián*? I stifled a gasp and my muscles stiffened, almost falling off my chair. A sudden coldness filled my core. Joaquín was lying to Grant...but why? I'd never dated a man named Julián. He was clearly saying this to let me know that he *knew* about little Julián, who I now assumed to be his kid. But none of this made sense. If Julián was my nephew, then Joaquín had lied to me about never having met Tiffany before. And if he'd had a one-night stand with Tiffany years ago and discovered she kept a son from him...that would be a motive for murder.

Alternatively, if he knew about his son, then he'd been lying to me for years. Granted, I'd lied to him about the birth of my baby, but he'd died and Joaquín had been deployed. This was too much. Our lives couldn't be that parallel. We both couldn't have had secret babies conceived and born around the same time and both hid said babies from each other. That was ridiculous.

Grant's teeth clenched and the color drained from his face. I thought a vein in his neck was going to pop. Was he reacting this strongly to thinking about me with another man?

"I never knew about any guys after me, which was a good thing because I'd probably be the one in jail for murder. But I'll find her for you. I love you, bro, but that sister of yours is one fucked-up bitch."

Thanks, asshole.

Joaquín clenched his fist and slammed it on the counter. The guard glared at him. "Fuck you, man. No, she's not. Listen to me. I know she left you, but you don't know the real story and it's not my place to tell you. That's a conversation you need to have with her. It's really not what you think. And if I ever hear you calling Mia a bitch again, I'll fuck you up once I get out of here."

I loved my brother. Even in here, under the worst circumstances, he was my biggest defender. His reaction reaffirmed that all my sacrifices had been worth it. Joaquín would always have my back. Even so, I didn't have a clue what the fuck my brother was talking about. He didn't know why I had left Grant. Nobody knew. I hadn't told a soul. It took every ounce of self-control to hold back my voice. I wanted to demand that Joaquín explain himself.

"Whatever, man, relax. I'll make sure she's safe, but then I'm done with her. But I'll always be here for you. If you need me to testify, I'll be there."

I ran my hands through my hair, the fluorescent lights causing me to sweat. I'd abandoned my plan, which was to ask some stupid questions, say something in Spanish, flash mama's ring. My brain was too cloudy. Desperation and confusion flooded my consciousness.

Joaquín stood up, gave me a smirk and an intense glare as my world crashed down around me.

Grant seemed pissed off too. He didn't speak, and I could swear he sneered in my general direction.

We walked out of the jail without speaking a word. I needed to be alone, to call Roman about the DNA sample, to reconnect with Mitch, and to get away from Grant's intensity and bitterness.

I asked him to drop me off at home. "Do you know where she is, his sister?"

He shook his head, without taking his eyes off the road. "Not a goddam clue. And I don't give a fuck."

I choked back a sob. I didn't have a clue where Mia was either.

37

KSENYA

After Grant dropped me off, I knew I had to do something to alleviate my anxiety. The lady I lived with had left to visit her family for a week, so I was alone. I drew myself a hot bath, squeezed a few drops of lavender essence into the tub, and released my body from my clothes.

My body.

I still marveled at my transformation. Poor Grant's wheels were probably spinning trying to find Mia for my brother. Did he have a clue I was already in his grasp?

My toes slipped into the bubbles, and I settled into the tub. The aromatic scent filled the steam and I relaxed into the bliss. No magazine, no music, just the calm chords of beautiful silence. I forced my mind to be still, to enjoy this moment, live in the present and not focus on the future or the past.

When the water lost its heat, I toweled off and dressed comfortably in sweats and a tank top. I did a few yoga poses to relax and prayed that I could come up with some cold hard evidence that would exonerate Joaquín.

But all my usual calming techniques didn't work. I couldn't quiet my mind, too much information. My visit with my brother had completely rattled me. I needed some answers.

I called Roman.

"Allo."

"Privet. It's me. Did you get the DNA back?"

He let out a long sigh. *"Ksyushen'ka,* I'm glad it is you."

I loved his pet name for me. The comfort in his voice soothed my nerves. "What? Did you get a match for the hair? Is Julián Joaquín's son?"

"No, I am afraid he is not."

I choked back tears.

"What? Are you sure? Because I'm pretty positive…"

"It was not match, I am sorry."

No. It had to be. I saw him. The boy looked just like my father. "Maybe Joaquín's sample was bad? It was old. I can get another one? Or, I'm his sister. Can't you check mine?"

He hesitated, the tone of his voice sounded edgy, but maybe it was just his accent. "You are his biological sister, *da*?"

"Yes. Of course I am."

"Well, brother and sister share DNA. I will see. But my guy, he is very good."

"Just try it again, please. I'll send it today. Please call me when you get the results. Thanks."

"Khorosho. Poka."

"Poka."

My understanding of genetics wasn't my strong suit but brothers and sisters shared DNA so I was sure this would work. The sample I'd collected from Joaquín's apartment had probably been damaged anyway. I'd gathered hairs from his brush. Maybe it wasn't even his hair. I needed to wait for the new results—I couldn't stress about it now. I had bigger fish to fry.

Mitch.

I sat down again to my computer to check any updates to Mitch's trace. Again nothing jumped out, except another message to Rafael. Again with no text.

Okay. Now I had two weird messages to Rafael. Was he a drug dealer? If my plan worked, I would find out tonight.

I texted Mitch.

Ksenya: *Handsome. My time of month is no more. When can I see you?*

Mitch: *Tonight. I can't wait for you to sit on my face. I'll pick you up @ 8.*

Ah, Mitch. Such a gentleman.

I texted him my address. And plotted my revenge.

My mind unhinged, I raced into the kitchen to begin cooking my feast. Roman's grandmother had graciously taught me how to cook classic Ukrainian recipes. As my hands kneaded the ground meat, I imagined that I was squeezing the life out of Mitch. When I chopped the onions, I fantasized about slitting his throat. As I boiled the cabbage, I imagined burning his flesh.

It was official. I was completely homicidal.

I rummaged through my stripper clothes and found the trashiest outfit I owned. A white Lycra tank top attached with a silver hoop to a skin-tight turquoise mini skirt. I zipped up some thigh high vinyl boots and applied my war paint. Heavy foundation, black eyeliner, gobs of mascara, and bright red lipstick.

I frantically ran around my apartment, gathering my tools into a corner of my room. My gun, handcuffs, and Rohypnol—the drug that both Tiffany and I had been given. Mitch, it had to be Mitch. I knew now that he'd been at the party where I'd been attacked, and at the party where Tiffany had died. This motherfucker would confess to me tonight, and I could free Joaquín and get my life back.

I couldn't wait to torture him. My depraved fantasies involved humiliation, him begging me for forgiveness, ruining his career and life. But he was a SEAL; I needed to plan out every little detail.

One thing was certain—Mitch had fucked with the wrong woman. He didn't have a clue what I was capable of. And honestly, neither did I.

38

KSENYA

At exactly eight Mitch knocked at my door. His massive arms and chest bulged out of his black T-shirt, and his green cargo shorts hugged his muscular thighs. His brown eyes softened when he saw me. "Hey, sexy." He kissed me on the lips, and I fought the urge to kick him in the balls.

But I remembered my plan. It was go time.

I kissed him back, a deep open mouthed kiss that until now had been reserved for Grant. I ran my fingers through his hair, pressing my body against his, feeling his cock poke at my skirt. He reacted swiftly, shoving my ass against the door, wrapping my legs around his waist.

"Take me inside," I said between kisses.

"Fuck yeah, baby."

Once inside my place, after a few more minutes of groping, I pulled away. I rubbed my hands down my body. "I have surprise for you, Mr. Mitch."

He growled. "Yeah, baby? Did you bring Autumn?"

God, I didn't think I could possibly detest this man any more. "No, but I want to give you the pleasure. Let me take care of my man. First, I made for you the dinner."

"Kickass. I always knew you Eastern European women were good for something. Really know how to treat a man. I'm starving. And I plan on eating you for dessert."

I forced myself to giggle and then set the table, presenting my slaved-over meal. But the food wasn't the important part of my menu. For the beverage, I served vodka, on the rocks, laced with Rohypnol.

I poured two glasses out of his sight, making sure I was extra careful remembering which one was his. I added cranberry juice to mine, so I could easily identify it.

Mitch sat down, slapped my ass as I leaned over to serve him. Before he took a single bite, he downed his drink. "Pour me another, babe."

Fuck. I was scared. I had administered a strong dose, but Mitch was a huge man. What if he realized I'd drugged him? He could kill me. I'd considered using GHB instead, but I couldn't risk killing him. He deserved to die, but I didn't want both Cruz children jailed for murder.

I slowly poured another glass of vodka, my premixed liquid doubling his dose. He downed that drink, too.

He pointed at the food. "What did my woman make for me?"

"Pelmeni, it is Russian dumpling, and golubtsi, it is the stuffed cabbage. I hope you like it."

His head shook a bit, as if he was trying to focus. "Looks great. My wife never cooked." He dug his fork into the plate and began his feast.

I picked at my food, for once not even caring that I was eating animal flesh. I remembered the night I'd been drugged. I'd been having such a good time with my girls, drinking, dancing, and goofing around. I remember my stomach churned and I felt like the room was spinning. I went to rest in a spare bedroom, and that was the last thing I remember, until I awoke to a man on top of me, my panties by my feet. I never saw his face, but I'd marked him forever.

But tonight, I had turned the tables.

"You're a really good cook. I haven't had a home-cooked meal in a while. I could get used to this."

Not happening, buddy.

We made small talk for about twenty minutes, the entire time I was staring at him for any symptoms. Maybe Mitch had tiger blood and was immune.

A lone sweat bead appeared on his forehead and his skin tinged red.

"Man, it's getting hot in here. Do you have air?"

Bingo. I walked over to air conditioning unit and turned it on.

"Thanks, babe. What did you the put in the food? You're not trying to poison me, are you?

Fuck. Was he kidding? "Funny. Is my cooking very bad?"

He clasped his stomach. "Nah, babe. I'm just not feeling that well. Can I use your bathroom?"

"Sure. It is right over there."

He stood up, his legs wobbly, and he entered the bathroom.

My heart beat rapidly. Did he know I'd drugged him? Did he remember doing it to me that night? Or to Tiffany? It had to be him, just had to be.

I paced around the kitchen, biting my nails. I considered calling Grant to help me, just in case Mitch figured out what I had done, but that was an even dumber idea than drugging a Navy SEAL.

I heard a loud thump in the bathroom.

"Mitch, are you okay?"

He didn't respond. This could be a trap. I said a silent prayer and opened the door to find Mitch slumped over the toilet.

First stage of my plan had worked! Pride beamed through my body. But the hard work wasn't done yet.

I couldn't exactly drag a 250-pound Navy SEAL to my bedroom. I scanned the bathroom, searching for something I could handcuff Mitch to. The hand railing for my old roommate was the best option. No doubt a fully conscious Mitch could pull that thing out of the wall, but he would wake before he regained full mobility.

I retrieved all my equipment and made myself comfortable on the bathroom floor. The hours were torturous, planning what I would say, what I would do.

A few hours later, he began to stir, first a twitch in his leg, then a blink of his eye. I cocked back the Glock that Grant had taught me to shoot years ago, and pointed it at his head.

After a few more minutes, he focused on my face. His eyes bulged out of his head and I could see the vein in his neck pop.

"What the fuck are you doing? I'm gonna kill you, you fucking bitch. Lay down the weapon, Ksenya!"

I wasn't scared, I'd dreamt of this moment so many times, but for years I could never picture the face of my victim. I pressed the gun to his forehead and dropped my accent. "My name isn't Ksenya, asshole. It's Mia. Mia Cruz."

39

MITCH

What the fuck did that psychotic bitch just say? "No fucking way you're Mia. Are you insane? Put down the goddam gun."

"No, jackass. You don't get to make demands. I'm in control, now. You're going to pay for what you fucking did to me! I know it was you, you motherfucker; I stabbed you with my fucking heel—I saw the scar the other night. I was helpless; I was your Teammate's woman, your other Teammate's sister. You ruined my fucking life!"

Oh fuck. Memories of that night flooded back into my already hazy brain. She must've drugged me tonight, and now I was handcuffed to a railing with a gun pointed at my head. But I wasn't scared; nothing fucking scared me. In fact, I was impressed.

I stared at this woman, who looked nothing like the Mia I'd lusted after. This chick in front of me had fake titties, puffy lips, and a too-tight face. Mia had been gorgeous, but there had been nothing fake about her. Naturally beautiful, not like the rest of the women in San Diego. Every guy on the Team wanted to bone her, but Grant scooped her up first. On deployments, I would steal a few pictures she had sent Grant, use them for my spank shots.

Had she transformed herself to trap me? What a fucking waste. In my life, I'd done so many shitty things—I'd cheated on my wife, I'd killed a few men, but I'd never violated a woman.

"Babe, please put down the gun." I had to change my tone, smooth talk her, or she could kill me. In an unaltered state, I could rip the railing out of the wall and take her down, but I was too fucked up to move.

She finally lowered the gun. Her shoulders caved, and she collapsed in the corner, tears streaming down her face.

Her chest heaved. I'd get her to calm down first, then figure out what the fuck was going on. "Listen to me. I swear to God I didn't touch you."

"You're fucking lying to me. I remember. I remember you on top of me."

I put my toe on her leg, the only part of her body I could reach since my wrists were still restrained. She flinched back. "No, you don't. You remember waking up with me there. I was checking to see if you were okay. I was looking for April that night, and the guy saw me and bolted. I didn't rape you, I fucking saved you. I may be an asshole, but I'm a goddamn Navy SEAL—I would never hurt you. I swear on my Budweiser." As a SEAL sister and former girlfriend, she should know we didn't fuck around when talking about our trident, our code.

"No, no. It was you, it had to be you. You raped me, you got me pregnant, you ruined my life."

Pregnant? When did she have a baby? Neither Grant nor Joaquín ever mentioned that she had a kid. "Where's the baby? Do a fucking DNA test—swab my goddam cheek or test the glass of vodka you just poisoned me with."

She didn't answer me, tears welled in her eyes.

"Look, I opened the fucking door. The room was dark and smelled like weed and vomit. Everything was hazy, and I couldn't see anyone at first, but then I saw some jerk with a hoodie jump off the bed and sprint past me. I was going to run after the guy and fuck him up, but I wanted to make sure the girl was okay. I didn't even have a clue it was you until I saw your face. I was about to call 911—I sure as hell wasn't going to leave you there drugged up so someone else could attack you. But then you fucking stuck your heel into my groin so I got the fuck out of there so I wouldn't get arrested."

She shook her head repeatedly. "Why the fuck were you at the party? You were all supposed to be deployed."

"We were in country. They always fly us in to an undisclosed location to detox after a mission before we're allowed to see family. It's called third location decompression."

"So Grant was in town? Joaquín too?"

"We were all in Arizona, Grant was being transferred to the hospital here. April and I got into a huge fight, she'd told me she was going out to that party with you. I was so fucking pissed off, I drove straight to San Diego. But when I got there, I couldn't find her. I went door to door, and that's when I found you. I would never rape you, or any woman. I'm not that man."

She exhaled, her lip trembling.

"Try to remember, Mia. You just drugged me, right? I'm fucked up but I know what's true. What do you remember about that night?"

"I—I…I remember pain. Hand around my throat, my panties ripped off, blood between my legs, then I remember you."

I locked her eyes. "When I entered the room, he was pulling up his pants. You have to believe me. Look at me! I'm not lying to you."

She remained silent. Well, that was better than her pointing a gun at my head.

"Uncuff me."

She cautiously grabbed the key from her pocket and freed my wrists.

I immediately reached for the Glock and emptied the chamber. My strength was coming back, and I could handle her. I wanted to be pissed off at her, for drugging me, for pointing a gun to my head, but I just pitied her.

I wrapped my arms around her, inhaled her scent, and pretended for a moment that she was my girl. But I knew that her heart would forever belong to Grant.

"What's going on, babe? You can tell me. What did you do to yourself? You said you were pregnant? Where's your baby?"

She turned around and curled into my chest. It felt so good to have a woman who needed me, even if it was only for tonight.

"I lost the baby two years ago. I…I did this for Joaquín. He's innocent, Mitch. I know it. He's all I have. I don't have anyone anymore. My parents died, Grant despises me. I had this crazy idea that I could free Joaquín. I got plastic surgery, learned Russian. I thought if I could go undercover I could figure out who killed Tiffany. But all I've done is fuck everything up. Joaquín knows what I've done, and he's talking all crazy in jail. And his lawyer does, too. Grant still doesn't have a clue I'm Mia, but he will kill me when he finds out I lied to him. I hate myself."

I brushed her hair out of her face, resisting the urge to kiss her, fuck her until I made her mine, until she forgot about Grant forever. "You're fucking crazy, do you know that? But you're my kind of crazy. Look, I know you love Grant, but you're right, once he finds out you're Mia, he'll cut you out forever. Forget about him. Be my girl, as Ksenya. We can start a new life together. I won't ever hurt you. When I saw that guy in that room with you, it took every bit of self-control I had not to murder the motherfucker. I'll die for you, Mia."

She looked up at me and then kissed me. Not one of our fuck-me kisses, but a real kiss, like she cared about me, like she loved me. It had been so long since I'd felt that passion from anyone.

"I'm sorry, Mitch. I believe you. I was wrong. I don't even know what is real these days. Thank you for saving me that night. But I didn't change to seek revenge on you, or to get back together with Grant. I did this for my brother. And I'm going to see it through. Will you help me?"

My heart sank. Years of lusting after Mia, watching her with Grant, the way she loved him, the way she looked at him like he was the only man in the world. She never flirted with any of the other Team guys. She was loyal and loving. April always tried to make me jealous, and I'd reacted imma- turely. But she didn't love me the way Mia loved Grant. I'd never felt the devotion I could see they had between them.

"I'll do anything for you. Tell me what you need from me."

40

MIA

My skin broke into chill bumps, and my stomach lurched. I'd drugged Mitch, but I was the one who felt high.

Mitch was still fucked up, so I helped him to my bed so he could sleep it off. I'd been so fucking sure I was right, but his story made sense. I didn't remember who raped me—I remembered pain, blood between my legs, tightness around my throat, and a man on top of me. The man I'd scarred was Mitch, but his story could easily be true.

I'd just lied to him again, though. I told him I believed him, and I did about raping me. But he wasn't off the hook yet for Tiffany's murder. And I still needed to figure out who the fuck was this Rafael guy he was texting. Mitch didn't have a clue I was tracking his phone.

I covered Mitch with a blanket and watched him drift off to sleep. Maybe Mitch was right—maybe I should just forget about Grant. Grant deserved to be with a better woman. Mitch and I were so incredibly fucked up we almost made sense. We could move to Virginia Beach and he could try for one of the East Coast Teams. I could start over and create a new life.

But I could never leave Joaquín. And despite how hard I tried to get over Grant, as long as he was alive, he would own my heart.

41

GRANT

I checked my phone again, waiting for the results of the DNA test. But when I entered my case number, the screen flashed "pending."

Joaquín had mentioned the name Julián, claiming he was another man in Mia's life. Complete bullshit. I would've known if she'd had a serious boyfriend.

So what did Joaquín know? He clearly knew about the boy, and wanted both of us to find out. But why? Was Julián Joaquín's child, hidden away by Tiffany, and he found out and murdered her? Or was Julián my child, Mia and her brother keeping him from me for some fucking reason? Until I received the DNA results, I could do nothing but drive myself crazy speculating.

But I could never forgive Mia.

I needed to accept she was no longer the innocent woman I'd loved. I had no doubt Mia was capable of hiding aspects of her life from me; she clearly was unstable and had hidden a pregnancy and a baby from me.

I had a plan. I had to fucking figure out if Julián was mine, and if not, what had happened to Mia's baby. I had to seduce Mia. I called to ask her out, and she eagerly accepted.

I was pulling out all the stops. Buying roses, dressing up…fuck, I even shaved.

I picked her up after her shift at the Pickled Frog. Kyle made some comment alluding to the fact he thought I'd broken up with Ksenya. I laughed, that girl couldn't wait to tell the world we were through. She'd probably already moved on to one of my friends, most likely Mitch. He hadn't partied with the rest of the guys last night, and Mia had also not bothered me. It didn't matter—my emotions toward her were turned off. She was nothing more than a mission to me now.

As angry as I was, seeing her at the Pickled Frog still made my heart race. She'd changed out of her work clothes and wore a tight red wrap dress that hugged her curves. Fuck, I didn't care anymore about my feelings. I'd been acting like a bitch. Tonight, I would fuck her to gain her trust. Nothing would stop me.

"You look beautiful, Ksenya."

She blushed and I was shocked to see how easy it was for her to fake her emotions. She didn't love me. She used me. Fine, I'd use her too.

First stop, dinner. I chose a romantic Italian restaurant in Coronado, just a few blocks from the BUD/S compound. Her eyes widened as we walked up the steps. She clutched my arm, and I winked at her.

The hostess sat us at a table overlooking the ocean. Mia bit her lip and nervously sipped her water.

"Ksenya, I need to apologize. I'm sorry about kicking you out of my place that night that we hooked up. It had nothing to do with you," I lied. It had everything to do with her, her scar, her deceit. Enough, focus. "I was fucking mad after seeing you with Mitch, and I didn't want to fuck you when I was filled with rage."

She let out a sigh, surely buying my crappy excuse. "It is okay. I am sorry too, about Mitch. I do not like him the way I like you. But I have confession to give to you."

She continued to speak with her thick accent. I doubted she would break out as full-on Mia right now. "Shoot."

The waiter picked this moment to tell us the specials. I ordered the osso buco, and Mia ordered pesto fettuccine sans meat.

Once we were alone again, Mia started her story. "After you made me quit Panthers, I got scared about the money. At party with your friends, I asked to Mitch about job, and he told to me about club. That is only reason I talked to him."

Lying again. She probably suspected Mitch of having something to do with Tiffany's murder. Not a crazy assumption, but she didn't know Mitch like I knew him. He was a classic hard-partying Team guy— loved hard liquor, harder drugs, and loose women. After BUD/S and two long deployments with the asshole, I knew for a fact he was actually compassionate. He cared about people, his kids, his Teammates, even his ex-wife and their dog. He had many vices, but he was not a murderer. "Go on."

She twirled her hair. "That night you kick me out, I went again to Diamond. I was afraid you did not want me no more. Mitch, he try to get me in the bed, but I told it to him, no. And I cook for him dinner last night, but I told him that I am not interested in being together with him. You must believe me, I am sorry."

The hair stood on my arms. Mitch, the fucking jackass. But I couldn't be too mad at him. He didn't know Ksenya was Mia, and I sure as hell wasn't going to tell him. As fucked up as it was, our Team guy code didn't apply to strippers.

"I believe you. Let's not talk about it. But you can't work at Diamond. Call me an asshole, but I don't want other men seeing your body." At this point, she and Mitch could star in a sex tape and I wouldn't care—but I needed to keep her close to me until I could figure out what was going on with her kid.

She didn't hesitate. "Deal."

We spent the next hour enjoying the view, the wonderful food, and a bottle of wine. Her body posture mirrored mine. She lied and told me stories about growing up in the Ukraine, I told her stories about my buddies in Chicago.

There was a lull in the conversation, and I knew it was time. She had had enough alcohol, and I couldn't be fake to her any longer. I needed answers.

I swirled the wine in my glass, took her hand across the table. "Ksenya, I need to ask you something. I noticed your scar—I'm a corpsman, a medic. Are you a mother?"

She bit her lip and said nothing.

I wasn't going to give up that easily. "You can trust me, baby."

The color drained from her face and she gulped. "I had baby boy, two years ago," she said. Her voice was weak and soft, and even her accent seemed to vanish.

A boy. I was more certain than ever that Julián had to be our son though I didn't have any proof yet, just circumstantial evidence. Despite her lies up until this point, her body language made me think she believed what she was saying.

"Where is he?"

She clutched her wineglass and downed it, her hand shaking. "He is sweet angel and I love him. But he is sick, so he die. And I die inside."

Died? He was dead? How the fuck did he die?

My body heat rose, as if I was suffocating in this suit.

No, it couldn't be. If her baby was dead, who the fuck was Julián? He had to be our kid. Or maybe he really was Joaquín's.

Was she lying about the baby being dead, knowing she hid him somewhere? Or if Julián was our son, maybe Mia didn't even know he was alive.

This nonstop uncertainty, lies, and deception made me feel like I was living in a nightmare.

I wanted to reach across the table and shake Mia until she told me the truth, about everything. Inject her with a truth serum.

The knowledge that Mia had a baby, possibly my son, alone, and that baby was now gone, sent wrath seeping through my pores. I steadied my breath, as if I was holding it underwater during a mission. "I'm sorry. What happened?"

Mia looked me dead in my eyes, a stone-cold stare. Like the day she dumped me. Blank, no emotion, vacant.

"I go to party. My boyfriend, he was out of town. I love him very, very much. He is good to me, good man. I drink many drink, and I think it was no good. I go to lie down, and I do not remember what happen next. When I wake up, a man he is there, my clothes down on my feet. I attack the man but it is too late. My boyfriend, he come home, but I did not tell to him. I find out after I am with baby and because I do not know who is father, I am scared and I leave. Nine months after, I have baby."

What in the fucking hell? My eye twitched and my ears pounded. I resisted the urge to grab a plate and hurl it through the bay window of the restaurant. Every word, every moment we had shared flashed before my eyes, like a fucking movie show.

Who'd fucking attacked her?

"Who attacked you? Did you file a report? Did you do a rape kit? Did you call the fucking police?"

"No, I am very scared. And I am ashamed that I drink so much. I only want the man to go away."

So this motherfucker was still out there? And she'd never fucking told me?

Was her baby my son or the attacker's? I'd slept with Mia when I'd come back from deployment, so it was possible, especially because we hadn't used a condom. She'd been on the pill before we deployed so I never asked, but how the fuck did I know if she was still taking it while I was gone. Why hadn't Mia ever told me? She had done nothing wrong; she was a victim. How could she not trust me enough to tell me the truth? Instead, she ghosted me—ran away like a fucking coward.

I would've done anything for her, anything. I would've taken care of her through her pregnancy, married her even if the kid wasn't mine, supported her no matter what the decision. How could she not trust me with the truth?

I squeezed her hand tightly. "I'm sorry, baby. But I give you my word, as long as you're with me, I'll make sure nothing happens to you again."

She shrugged her shoulders and stared out at the ocean. Tears welled in her eyes, and I didn't think her story was another lie. This was real, she had finally told me the truth. And she believed our baby was dead.

"It does not matter. Nothing matters. I can never bring him back. I have no family. I have nothing."

And like that, this sense of protectiveness trumped all the hatred I'd built up for her inside me. "You're wrong, baby—you have me."

42

KSENYA

The night seemed clearer, the stars brighter than I'd seen them in years. After keeping the most painful secret buried deep inside, I'd finally told someone my truth about Elías. And not just anyone, I'd told Grant.

Well, not the whole truth. I didn't mention how I prayed that he was the father. But once I held Elías in my arms, his paternity didn't matter. All that mattered was that he was my son—a part of me, a part of Joaquín, a part of my parents. He had the most beautiful brown eyes and big mop of black hair. The happiest time in my life was spent with my baby boy.

But then he was taken away from me.

Grant pulled me into his arms, his lips pressing into mine, the heat of his body making my core ache for him. I didn't want to wait anymore. I'd never felt closer to him as I had in this moment. I needed to express my love, I needed his skin against mine.

"I want to go to home together with you."

A devilish smile graced his face and we headed back to his bike. The salty breeze blew my worries away. I briefly contemplated abandoning my mission to save Joaquín. I could embrace life as Ksenya, and try to make a new life with Grant. But just like the roots of my hair showing, I was certain the cracks in my story would expose me to Grant sooner than later. Too many people knew now, it was only a matter of time.

The ride back to his place was torture, feeling the vibration of the bike between my legs, aching to feel his hard cock inside of me. Deciding I couldn't wait, I reached around his waist and rubbed his thighs in small circles, purposely running my thumb over the tip of his arousal that now bulged in his pants. He leaned back into me and groaned. I'd been such a fucking tease with him, but this time, I wasn't leading him on.

Grant pushed open the door to his place. The gentleman was gone, replaced with a primal beast. Before we'd even taken a few steps inside, he'd shoved me up against the wall, kissing me hard. Gripping my ass, he pulled me up and down against his cock. He breathed hard against my neck as he picked me up and turned us toward the coffee table.

Setting me down on the table, he undid my wrap dress, the fabric pooling on the floor. He paused for a moment, and I could feel the intensity of his gaze fall on my body. He shooed Hero outside and then turned his attention back to me. Grant nibbled on my neck, burying his head into my cleavage and kissed my skin. He unhooked my red lace bra, and lavished attention on my nipples, making circles over my flesh.

My pussy pulsed, and my entire body was on fire, relishing his touch. When his hand dropped down between my legs, I moaned.

He kissed his way slowly down my belly, and I couldn't wait one more second for him to give me what I craved.

He pulled my panties off, kissing between my thighs down to my toes.

His fingers rubbed my clit, and the pressure made me gasp. "Tell me what you want."

"I—I want your tongue."

He growled then held my legs apart and buried his face deep in my pussy. He licked me like it was his mission to make me come, his free hand tugging on my nipples. I moaned and pulled his head tightly against my body, rocking on his face, his nose rubbing against my clit. My reaction seemed to excite him even more. He pushed my knees up until my thighs were against my chest.

I didn't know how long I could last, it had been so long and he felt so amazing. Years of love, loss, lust, hatred, and longing added to the intensity of this moment.

"Oh, please. Make me come."

Grant sucked on my clit as he pressed two fingers deep inside. I squeezed my legs tightly around his head and arched my back, coming all over his face. My body trembled and I let out a giggle, pure bliss taking over my body and mind.

He sat back and looked at me with a satisfied grin. Setting my legs down, he pulled me up. He lifted me bridal style and carried me to his bedroom.

There was no turning back. Grant was about to fuck Ksenya. And Mia couldn't wait another second.

I'd been fantasizing about this moment since the day I'd left him. And now, even though my body looked different, my soul danced in anticipation of being reunited with its mate.

He sat me on the corner of his bed and stood over me and pulled off his shirt. His tan skin showed off every line of definition, and his tattoos made him look like even more of a badass.

His jeans and boxers dropped next, releasing him.

"Suck my cock."

Yes, Instructor Carrion. I loved him ordering me around, like I was one of his recruits. I grasped his cock with my hand, rubbing over the length, and he tangled his hand in my hair, pressing my mouth down on him.

He tasted delicious, masculine and earthy. I licked over the head, playfully rubbing my lips over the tip.

"Stop being a tease. Suck me."

I took him deep, as he fucked the back of my mouth. I sucked deeper, harder, I couldn't get enough. The fire grew in my pussy, and he pulled me up by my hair and threw me back down on the bed.

I spread my legs. "I need you. Fuck me, please."

He climbed over me, taking a moment to stare at my body. I kissed his neck, my hands tracing his shoulders, his scar. He took one hand and held his cock, rubbing the tip along my opening, and over my clit. Bending down, he took a nipple between his teeth and flicked it with his tongue.

Should I ask for a condom? I was on the pill, and Grant and I had never used condoms since we'd been each other's firsts. I knew he had been fucking strippers since our breakup, but I also knew the Navy tested their SEALs every month. Call me stupid, but I trusted him.

But why would he sleep with *me* without a condom? He thought I was a stripper. He must have believed my good girl act or have been really careless.

Fuck it, I didn't care.

He thrust deep in me, and I gasped. My pussy clamped down, never wanting him to pull out. He squeezed my ass and pressed my hips flat and pushed until he was deep inside me. I wrapped my legs around him, my nails digging into his back. I'd waited for this moment for so long and it was even more incredible than I had imagined.

I savored every stroke, every push, relishing every second our bodies were connected as one. It had been too long since I'd felt him deep inside of me, where he belonged.

He slid out and then pounded my pussy, deep and hard. His rhythm quickened and I was lost in the sensation. His body slapped against mine. I never wanted him to stop fucking me.

He growled. "Come baby. Come all over my cock."

I couldn't hold back anymore, I wanted this release, I wanted this connection. I wanted my man back.

My body quivered, pleasure ripping through my body. He rocked me through my orgasm. I came so hard I was unable to hold back my words.

"I love you, Grant." I looked deep in his eyes, our souls connected. Even with this mask I wore, I was finally one with my love.

His body tensed, he grunted and jerked, releasing inside me. We collapsed together on the bed, and he held me in his arms.

He cupped my face, the way he had the night he'd first told me that he loved me. Then his hand squeezed my chin, so hard it stung.

"Stop fucking lying to me, Mia."

PART IV

CARNAL

SE7EN DEADLY SEALS EPISODE 4

"LUST'S PASSION
WILL BE SERVED;
IT DEMANDS, IT MILITATES,
IT TYRANNIZES."

— MARQUIS DE SADE

43

MIA

M ia? Did he just call me *Mia*?

Oh, fuck.

I trembled but remained speechless in Grant's grasp. His fingers tightened around my jaw, bringing the realization into sharp clarity that I was naked and in bed with a very angry SEAL who knew how to kill me three hundred different ways.

He finally released me, and I let out a gasp. His brow scrunched, his face flushed red, and a vein bulged in his neck. The look on his face was pure disgust.

What the hell was I going to do now?

"Say something, dammit. And don't you fucking lie to me again."

I bit my lip. "How did you know?"

His eyes bugged out. "How did I know? That's all you ask me? You're fucking unbelievable. How about 'I'm sorry I lied to you, Grant. I'm sorry I've been fucking with your mind. I'm sorry that you fell in love with a psychopath.'"

Yup. I was dead. Like actually dead. No one would ever find my body, and technically, I didn't exist. Mia Cruz had vanished, and he could erase Ksenya Pavlova in an instant. I had to do something, and the only weapon I had was my body.

I attempted to touch him, but he shoved my hand away.

"Don't fucking touch me, Mia." Hearing him openly call me Mia was jarring. "Listen, I'm only going to say this once. You're going to start answering my questions now. If you lie to me again, I'll punish you. From now on, I'm in charge. Do you fucking hear me?"

I hopped off the bed, stood at attention, and saluted him, knowing full well that I was buck ass naked. "Yes, Instructor Carrion." Of course he was pissed and had every right to be, but he was still being a jackass.

He flashed his teeth at me like a rabid dog. "Stop being a smartass. What the fuck were you thinking? Did you think you could fool me?"

I hesitated. I honestly thought I could. I wouldn't have gone through everything I did if I didn't think it would work, but I didn't want to insult him any more than I already had. "No, of course not," I lied. He gave me a disbelieving glare, so I explained, "Not forever. I mean, I hoped I could go undercover at the strip club and find out more about Tiffany and free Joaquín. But I knew that you would figure it out eventually."

"And you just decided to use me in the process?"

"Come on, Grant. You were using me just as much."

"No, I was using a stripper who threw herself at me."

Ouch. That hurt more than I would admit, but I shook it off.

"Yeah? Is that what you're telling yourself? How long have you known that I was me and not Ksenya?" He just glared at me, and I backpedaled. "When Joaquín was first arrested, I came to you and begged for help, but you shut me out. Then one of the strippers told me that *you* were the one who had invited the girls to the party. So, yeah, I wanted to find out what you knew and if you were hiding anything from me. I wanted to get closer to the rest of the SEALs to learn more about that night. I suspected Mitch and Paul, but not you. Never you."

"Whatever."

He pulled on his boxers, and I took his cue and hastily put on my panties and one of his T-shirts. This was not how I wanted to spend the time after the most amazing sex of my life, but it was better than him offing me and disposing of my body, so I rolled with it.

"What kind of surgery did you get? Where did you get the money?"

I felt like I was a teenager confessing my dirty thoughts to my priest as I pointed to each part as I listed them. "Breast implants, a nose job, a chin implant, lip and cheek fillers, lasers for my freckles, and Botox for my eyebrows. As for the money, I used what Joaquín left me before he was arrested."

"You were beautiful, perfect. Why did you ruin your face? You're insane, you realize that, right? This goes beyond you trying to free Joaquín."

"No, I'm not insane. I love Joaquín. I would do anything to free him. He's all I have."

He paused for a second, and I hoped that maybe he would tell me what he told me earlier this evening. *"You're wrong, baby—you have me."*

One look in his eyes as he sat down on the bed and I knew the truth. He'd only said that to get between my legs.

And I'd fallen for it.

"What if he gets convicted? Then you did this for nothing. You will definitely have no one—not even yourself."

"I guess I won't." I wiped away a tear. We fell into a silence, each of us lost in our own thoughts. When I couldn't take it anymore, I turned to him. "You never told me when you figured it out."

"I suspected the first night you came home with me. The way Hero reacted to you first set me off. I thought I was crazy at first, but then I paid attention and it was all the little things that gave you away. The way you bite your lip when you lie, the way you taste, the way you smell, the way you touch me."

My heart ached. "I touch you like that because I love you. Can't you see that?"

"What you think you feel for me isn't love. It's something darker. What you have for Joaquín is love." He stood and turned to face me. "Now, tell me about your baby. Were you lying to me earlier tonight? Where is he? Is he mine?"

A lump grew in my throat. The truth. He deserved the truth. At least on this.

"He's dead. I told you the truth. He was in the NICU and passed away, but I got an infection from my C-section, so I was in ICU when he died. I never even got to say goodbye. And honest to God, I don't know if he was yours. I prayed he was, and I loved him even though I didn't know for sure."

"If he lived were you going to tell me?"

"Yes, of course. I was going to do a DNA test and if he was yours, I would've told me. I would never keep my son away from his father—well, if he was yours and not the rapist's."

He swallowed and bit his lower lip, as if he were physically stopping himself from saying what he wanted to say. After a moment, he just shook his head and closed the small distance separating us.

He cupped my face in his hands and forced me to stare at him. "You were fucking raped and didn't tell me?"

"I couldn't tell you! You were deployed! And next I heard you were in the hospital."

"You should have told me. Why didn't you?"

"God, Grant." I moved to pull away, but he held me in place, demanding answers with his eyes. "I don't know. I'd been so stressed with you and Joaquín both deployed, and I just wanted one night to let loose and relax. So, I went to that stupid party with April and Dara and got so wasted. I still don't know exactly what happened, but I think I was drugged. I woke up sore with my panties around my feet. I didn't know what to do. Then I found out you were home. You were injured, but you were home, and suddenly what happened to me didn't really matter. A month later when I found out I was pregnant, I was so damn ashamed I couldn't tell you and left instead."

Maybe he didn't believe me. As part of his SEAL training, he had perfected a poker face. I had no idea what he was thinking.

"How could you have not told me? I would've done anything for you. I was about to propose. I would've raised your baby no matter who his father was. Didn't you know how much I loved you?"

I hadn't been ready for this. I had practiced answers in my head for questions about my identity a thousand times. I'd spent the past two years burying my emotions deep in a place I couldn't reach, a place where the memories of my parents lived.

"No, I didn't. I knew you loved me but, no matter what you say now, you would've been livid that I'd been raped. It would've driven you insane. You would've hunted down the guy who did it and tortured him. I couldn't let you ruin your life over what happened to me. I just wanted to forget it ever happened, and then I couldn't."

He sat back down and placed his head in his hands. "But if I hadn't deployed, that wouldn't have happened to you."

"That's ridiculous. It could've happened to me walking Hero or on my way to my car. A girl was attacked the other week at the dog park. What happened to me wasn't your fault. It wasn't anyone's fault but the person who did it. Unfortunately, I don't know who that person is."

He shook his head, and I placed my hand on his face, attempting to force him to look at me and really see me. Mia, the girl he once loved.

The girl maybe one day he could love again.

"I'm sorry, and I love you. I never meant to hurt you—not then, not now. I hope you find it in your heart to forgive me."

He pushed my hand off his face. "I will never forgive you for what you did." He ground his teeth together and took a deep breath. I knew that he was shutting himself down. He got the answers he wanted and now it was back to the cold shoulder I'd gotten when I showed up here begging for his help. Something inside me died a bit but I refused to let it show on the outside. I was stronger than that. "Now, it's your turn to listen to me. I'm in control now. I call the shots. You're going to do exactly what I say you're going to do, or I'll cut your access off to the Team. I'm going to stay with you until Joaquín is either convicted or released. But once his trial is over, I'm done with you. Do you hear me? I'm through. In fact, I never want to see you again. Are we clear?"

I gulped, my heart literally breaking inside my chest. "Crystal." I fidgeted on the bed as anxiety pulsed through me. I couldn't help staring at his naked chest. "I have one more question."

"What?"

"What just happened between us? The incredible sex? That's over? You don't want me?"

He let out a growl. "No, baby. I'm going to fuck you every night, all night, in all the ways I always wanted to. But it will only be fucking, because I'll never love you again."

He left the bedroom and slammed the bathroom door.

I should have expected that. I knew he hated me, I knew he wouldn't just forgive me because of one night of amazing sex. I had crushed him when I left and, even though he would never admit it, he was crushed because of the baby and that I'd lied to him. He had every right to be, too. In his eyes, I was a horrible person.

I could change that, though.

I could make him love me again the way I had always loved him. I would help clear Joaquín's name and I could win back Grant.

44

GRANT

I scrubbed her scent from my chest, and my heart pounded, threatening to burst with rage. *"How did you know?"* What the fuck kind of response was that? It wasn't a response. It was resignation. It was acceptance. It was her forfeit. She said she didn't think she would be able to hide what she was doing from me, but there was that look in her eyes. Mia was always like a damn open book to me, and I knew ... knew by that look she thought I would never find out.

It was probably the reason she let me fuck her the way I had. It was raw, passionate, and uninhibited, which was exactly how I'd always wanted to fuck her. It was incredible, best I'd ever had.

And I couldn't get enough.

But Mia was an actress, apparently an excellent one. When we were together, I hadn't attended a single one of her plays.

Ever.

I regretted now not taking the time to fully encourage her to pursue her dreams. She'd supported mine.

Mia had taken care of me every night after BUD/S, dressing my wounds, rubbing my feet, and cooking me dinner.

I'd had my reasons. I was always training; too focused on my goal of becoming a SEAL. Looking back now, the young and stupid version of me was a selfish ass.

It was too late now.

The water beaded down my chest and a memory flooded my head. Of the last night she had been mine.

Mia stood in the hospital door. My palms were sweating, nervously clutching the small black velvet box in my hand. I had worked up the strength to finally leave my bed, kneel before her, and ask her to be mine forever.

Her long brown hair shone in the bright lights, and her sundress clung to her body. She looked different. Her breasts seemed fuller, her face rounder, her skin brighter.

She was glowing.

"Come here, babe."

She gave me a halfhearted smile, and her teeth clamped down on her lip. Why was she acting nervous? My excitement turned to worry. "I ... Grant, I-I need to tell you something."

My gut clenched, but I forced the word out. "What?"

"I've decided to transfer to San Francisco State. They have a better theater program, and I can do shows with A.C.T." Her voice cracked with emotion. She couldn't even look me in the eyes.

She was breaking up with me.

My hand released that stupid box, a box that contained a ring that was worth three months of my salary including hazard pay that I earned while being shot at by the Taliban.

"What the fuck? Are you serious right now? You're breaking up with me?"

She bit her lip, and I knew she was about to lie to me. "No. Of course not. We can still see each other when I'm in town and you can come visit me."

Fucking bitch. My face, neck, and ears burned. "You want a long-distance relationship? Wasn't Afghanistan far enough?"

Her hair hung over her face like a curtain, shielding her from making eye contact. "I don't know what to say."

"Say what you mean, goddammit. That you're breaking up with me. Tell me fucking why? Tell me why you think that breaking up with me while I'm in a fucking hospital bed is a great idea, Mia? Fucking look at me!"

She turned her head and gazed out the hospital window. "Don't make this harder than it is. I love you; you know that." Her voice cracked and she rubbed her nose. "Every night during your last deployment, I was a worried wreck about you and Joaquín. I constantly lived in fear that you would be killed. You're injured. You could've died. My parents died, and it broke me. I can't bear to have my boyfriend be killed also. And I've never been on my own. I moved here when I was seventeen to live with Joaquín and then I became your girlfriend. I just need some space to find out who I am."

"'Space'? So you are breaking up with me. You've had nine months of space! You've had nine months of long distance." Rage consumed me. How could I have been so wrong about her? I'd never been surer about anything in my life. Why was she doing this to me?

"It's for the best." Her words were a whisper, but I heard them as loudly as if she has screamed them at me.

I used my strength to get out of bed, grab her by the arms, and stare into her eyes. "What is it, Mia? You're not telling me something. You would never dump me to transfer schools or because you needed space. You love me, and I love you. We're meant to be together. You're mine, fucking mine. I see it in your eyes when we make love. I hear it in your voice when you call me. I fucking know you. Why are you doing this? Please just be honest with me."

She stepped toward the door with tears staining her face and paused, one hand clutching her belly. "No, Grant, you're wrong. I'm not hiding anything. I just don't want to be with you anymore."

And before I could hobble after her, she gave me a final glance and walked away.

I took the ring box and threw it across the room.

Fuck that bitch. I was about to propose. She'd been with me every night for the past month taking care of me, making love to me. Why now? Had I really become that much of a burden?

I vowed at that moment to never let her, or anyone else, in again.

I would never be that pathetic boy again, consumed by his girlfriend. I was a man now, and I refused to rely on any woman, especially Mia.

I did believe that she had been raped, and I could sort of understand why she ran away. She was right—the knowledge that some motherfucker violated her would've driven me mad.

The cruel irony of being a Navy SEAL was that while we were out on missions protecting America, our loved ones were back at home completely vulnerable. She said it wasn't my fault and that it could have happened anywhere or anyone. But it happened to her while I wasn't home.

I took a deep breath and loosened my fingers, which had been balled into fists. It happened years ago. She made the choice not to tell me, *she* took that away. I didn't know her anymore and couldn't trust her. For all I knew, she was probably still lying to me about something.

As nuts as I thought she was, I didn't think she was lying that she believed her son had died. There was no way even the Mia I thought I knew back then would give her son to a stripper to raise and then lie about it. No. In my heart of hearts, I couldn't believe that, and I never would. If she went this far for Joaquín, I was sure she would do anything for her own child.

I only had one goal: figure out if Julián was my son, *our* son. She had given me two more clues tonight. The child she had was a boy, and she believed he had died.

She had told me her truth. If she was telling the truth, what did that mean? Was he kidnapped? Switched at birth? What the fuck was going on?

I wouldn't rest until I figured out what happened to her son.

I emerged from the shower. Time to lay out some rules.

Mia was sitting on my bed with her shoulders slumped as she bit her nails.

"I'm not done with the questions. What happened to you the other night when I picked you up in El Cajon?"

She hesitated. "Well, actually I was kidnapped by Daniel Reed, Joaquín's lawyer. That's my own dumb-ass fault. I was the one who showed Joaquín my bracelet when you took me to the jail the first time, and then he told Daniel that I was Mia. Daniel decided to have his buddy run me off the road so he and I could have a little chat."

I had been right about the bracelet. I put on my boxer briefs and shook my head.

"A chat about what? What the fuck did he want from you?"

"Oh. Just to confirm Joaquín's suspicions."

I narrowed my eyes. "He could've just asked you. Why did he run you off the road?"

"To get me alone. Probably didn't want to raise suspicion with you or any of the other SEALs at The Pickled Frog. But either way, I think Daniel is shady."

So did I. But I kept my suspicions to myself. "How could you have been so careless? You went through thousands of dollars of plastic surgery and then you go around waving your wrist? Who else knows?"

She crinkled her lip. "No one."

"Dammit, Mia!" I took a step toward her. "I told you to stop lying."

Her gaze focused distantly above my head. "Just Mitch."

I clenched my fist. Why the fuck would she tell him and not me? "Mitch? You fucking told Mitch?"

"Well, not just straight out. I drugged him first."

"Jesus. He could've killed you." The hits kept coming. "I'd almost give you a high-five for pulling that off, though. Why did you drug him? When?"

Her lip curled, but she stopped herself from biting it. She was about to lie to me. Again.

"Last night. I thought he killed Tiffany."

I never once thought Mitch killed Tiffany, and I didn't really care about her thoughts on the subject. "And you don't now?"

"I'm not sure anymore. It doesn't fit."

That was all she was going to give me.

"You will move out of that place you've been staying at. You can keep your job at The Pickled Frog for now, but you will not work at Diamond. And you are to have no contact with Mitch. I'll tell him we're back together. Do you understand me?"

"Yes."

I stared at the girl I once loved. For years, I had imagined what it would be like to fuck her again. There was never a single scenario where it happened like this.

"No arguing? You're going to agree, just like that?"

"Yes. Just like that. Listen, Joaquín's innocent, and even I know there is only so much I can do. His lawyer won't help him, and no one else on the Team will help either. So, if agreeing with you means that you'll help me, then I'll agree."

"Fine, I'll help," I said reluctantly. I had my doubts about Joaquín's innocence, especially since I found out about Julián, whoever he was. Joaquín now had a motive for murder. If he had a one-night stand with Tiffany years ago and found out she had his kid, he could've snapped and killed her. Or alternatively, if he found out that Tiffany was involved in kidnapping Mia's kid, he could've also lost it and murdered her. Either way, I would do anything I could to find out what really happened so I could learn more about Julián. "But no games. You have to do exactly as I say. You don't go anywhere or do anything without my permission. Once Joaquín's trial is over, we're done, and I don't ever want to see you again. I'm doing this for him, not you. Got it?"

"Yup."

Mia's eyes brightened, and she stood up and kissed my cheek gently. "I promise I'll obey you if you help me free Joaquín. Is there anything else you want me to do?" Her voice was breathy.

This beautiful woman, the only woman I'd ever loved, was standing right before me. I wasn't going to waste this opportunity.

"Yeah, one more thing."

Her eyes widened in anticipation.

"Get on your knees and suck my cock."

45

MIA

"My pleasure."

Mia had never given Grant a blow job, no matter how much he hinted that he wanted one. Ksenya was happy to be his sex kitten. But now I would prove to Grant that I wanted him. I loved him. As me. As Mia.

I turned off Ksenya's act. She would no longer control my actions.

I knelt before him, pushing him back so he was sitting on his bed, and releasing his cock from his boxers. "You know how many times I fantasized about this? How much I wanted you? How many nights since I left you that I dreamt of this?"

He caressed my face, urging me toward him. "Yeah, baby? Tell me."

I kissed his thighs as I grasped his base with my hand.

"I always knew you wanted me to, but I thought I would be bad at it."

For a moment, he looked at me with not just lust but love. I savored that look in his eyes. "Nah, baby. You were never bad at anything. I loved you so fucking much I would've thought it was perfect. You were perfect. You are still perfect."

Damn, I was the one getting turned on. He had told me tonight that he didn't love me. And I knew in his heart he believed that, but I prayed that deep in his soul, someday, once my brother was exonerated, Grant would forgive me. Grant would love me again.

"Come on, baby. Don't tease me. Show me how much you want me."

I inhaled a deep breath and wrapped my lips around the head his beautiful cock. He gasped as my tongue licked up and down his shaft.

"More." He twisted his fingers in my hair and pressed me deeper.

I glanced up at him, and there was a self-satisfied smirk on his face. All those years we were together, I had always been curious about his fantasies, but we never shared them with each other. That smirk told me that this was only a very small fraction of whatever fantasies played out in his head. Would I be with him long enough to discover his deepest desires?

"Deeper, baby."

I obeyed, taking him as deep as I could and gliding my lips up and down his cock.

But then everything shifted. His fingers tightened and his hips started to thrust. With each pass of my lips and tongue over him, his façade of calm fell away and the badass SEAL took over.

I inhaled through my nose and did my best to keep from gagging, making sure not to scrape him with my teeth. He thrust harder, and the tip of his cock hit the back of my throat.

"You like that, Mia? Taking my cock in your greedy little mouth? Are you my dirty girl?"

I hummed yes and nodded, taking him deeper into my throat.

His rhythm sped up, and I held my breath steady. He was so big, this was so fucking hot and demanding that I fully yielded, letting him take control of my movements.

"God, baby. I'm going to come all over your sweet lips."

Yes, please. I was dying to taste him.

I sucked as hard as I could, grabbing his hips, and urging him into my mouth. Two more deep thrusts and he let out a final groan, his hot cum hitting the back of my throat and filling my mouth. He tasted incredible—salty, manly, virile.

His body jerked, and he released me.

I swallowed and then lapped up the remaining cum from his cock.

Grant's eyes looked dazed as he pulled me up to my feet and clutched me to his chest.

He stroked my hair. "That was so hot, babe."

I savored the feel of his arms around me, and if I closed my eyes, I could imagine that, if only for this moment, I was his again.

He'd just shown me who he really was—raw, primal, nasty. I'd never seen those sides of him. He'd never let me. Back when we'd been together, I'd been the inexperienced virgin, too worried that I would never be enough for him. I finally knew that I could fully satisfy him, and I would for as long as he let me.

And there was never any doubt in my mind that he could satisfy me.

46

GRANT

We spent all night fucking, each time more intense than the last. I'd never been so gratified in my life, and I didn't have a clue how I would break my addiction to her. I woke before dawn and rolled out of bed, careful not to disturb Mia. I watched her sleep for a few minutes and attempted to push the bittersweet emotions out of my head. I felt vindicated. I had been right—Ksenya was Mia, but my heart was full of sadness. This entire situation was so incredibly fucked up. Joaquín was still in jail, Mia had fucked up her looks and her life, and Julián had no parents.

Though I hoped he was my son.

I hurriedly dressed and scribbled Mia a note, letting her know I was going to work and that she was not to leave. The notes I used to leave her were always much nicer, but I wasn't that guy anymore, and she wasn't that girl. I didn't want to be nice and sweet. I wanted her to stay the fuck in this house until I got back.

I climbed into my truck and headed into Coronado, taking a moment to appreciate the duality of the place. Coronado was beautiful on the surface but hid a dark side: murders, excessive wealth, and drugs.

Drugs.

There had to be a connection. I tried to remember the details of every Team party where my brothers had been high. Never me, though. I'd gone through too much to become a SEAL, I wasn't going to throw away my hard work and sacrifices for a fleeting high. Plus, we were drug tested randomly. That would be like playing Russian roulette, and I had known more than one guy who had received a dishonorable discharge for popping positive.

Many of my Team brothers loved to live on the edge.

We all had our vices, but mine was lust, not drugs.

Sex was the ultimate high for me, especially sex with Mia.

I rolled up on base and flashed my ID to the guard, who waved me through.

I had to find Mitch.

I parked and headed into our compound. The morning was eerily quiet, which wasn't unusual since half the place was deployed, but there were a handful of guys in the common area.

I was about to shoot a text to Mitch when the devil himself walked through the door, wearing a cocky smirk and dark sunglasses to shield his eyes.

"Hey. What's up?"

I looked around the room at the few guys who were lingering around and tilted my chin to the door.

"Let's go PT."

He nodded, probably sensing that I wanted to talk to him alone. I wasn't as close to Mitch as I was to Joaquín, but even so, Mitch was my brother. We'd been to war together, and I trusted him with my life.

Just not with my woman.

We changed into our PT shorts and ran along the beach. It wasn't until we were out of sight of the buildings that I slowed my pace a bit and let him catch up.

"I know you know about Mia."

He didn't reply at first. Instead, he just gave me a side-glance and we ran in silence for a bit before he answered. "Yeah, I assumed you'd already figured it out. She's fucking crazy."

"Batshit." I was certifiable too because I was helping her and jealous of the fact that Mitch had spent time with her. I had no intention of staying with her once this was over, but that didn't mean I wanted Mitch anywhere near her. "Did you fuck her?"

"Nah, man. But that bitch drugged me and put a gun to my head."

"What the fuck?" I stopped running, and the sand from Mitch's shoes flew into my face. She told me that she had drugged him, but she held him up at gunpoint? She had really gone mad.

Mitch finally stopped, turned, and jogged back to where I was standing. "Look, she's lost it, but she loves Joaquín. She'd do anything for him, clearly. They have no family but each other. Not many women are that loyal to anyone. You have to admire that."

"She's only loyal to Joaquín, not me. Why the fuck did she drug you? Did she think you had something to do with Tiffany's murder?" I lifted up my sunglasses and stared right at him. "Did you?"

Mitch laughed at me. "No, not at all. You got it all wrong. I don't think she suspected me in that, but maybe she did. I don't know." He paused, his eyes scanning my face.

"Spill it, Mitch."

He looked toward the ocean. "My scar."

I gritted my teeth. I'd seen the scar on Mitch's crotch a thousand times, it wasn't like our occupation offered much in the way of personal privacy. "Yeah. What about it? I thought you didn't fuck her? How did she see it?"

"Relax, asshole. I already told you I didn't. I pulled my dick out at the club and she freaked. She thought I raped her years ago."

What the— "At that party? Why would she think that? We were in Yuma."

"Because." He raked his hands through his hair and took a deep breath. I wanted to wrap my hands around his throat and squeeze the information out of him. "I was there that night. I was the one who found her. Sorry, man, I never told you."

My blood incinerated through my veins. "You fucking knew she was raped and never told me? Start talking, Mitch, start talking right fucking now." I didn't know when I had closed the distance between us, or when I had twisted my fist into the front of his shirt, but I had, and he smacked my hand away.

"You were being transferred to the hospital. April and I were fighting, which wasn't anything out of the normal, and she was taunting me about some guy who wanted her at the party. I was so fucking pissed about her partying with some guy while our kids were with a sitter that I drove out there and went into the frat house to find her. When I opened one of the doors, I saw this girl passed out with some guy standing over her. He saw me and bolted, but I didn't get a look at anything other than his freaking hood. I was going to run after his ass, but I wanted to make sure the girl was okay. That was when I realized it was Mia."

I pointed my finger in his face. "Then why the fuck did she think you raped her? I swear to God if you touched her, I'm going to stuff your balls down your throat."

"I swear to God I never touched her. When she woke up, I was the only one there. It was dark, I don't think she could even see my face. She plunged her fucking heel into my groin."

My hands shook. "Are you fucking kidding me? We're brothers! How could you keep something like that from me?"

His voice cracked. "I never said nothing because you were all fucked up and recovering, and then you guys broke up anyway. So, I figured it didn't matter."

"Didn't matter? It completely fucking mattered. Did you know that was why she left me? That she was pregnant and didn't know who the father was? Did you fucking know?" I shouted at him.

"No, I didn't know. Grant, if I had known, I would have helped you track her down myself. Come on, you know that."

I did know that. Mitch might be a dick most of the time, but he followed the damn code. I took a deep breath and tried to focus past my anger. "You don't remember anything about the guy? Height, weight, build, anything?"

"Nah, man. I mean he was a bit taller than me, ran out fast as fuck covering his face. Probably an athlete. It was a fucking frat house."

Who else was at the party? April? Dara? Someone had to have seen him. "Did you find April? Did she see anything?"

"No, that's the thing. She wasn't there. She was home by the time I stumbled in after I had Shane clean me up back on base and give me stitches. She said some guy gave her a ride. I bet. Fucking Jody."

Jody. Our name for men who fucked our women while we were deployed. "Some friend. She just left Mia there that night? Drugged? Did you even tell her what happened to Mia?"

"No, of course not. April and I were barely speaking, and I didn't want her to think I'd raped Mia. It was just so fucked up. I wanted to tell you, but you would've killed me. I told Joaquín, and he agreed with me that I shouldn't tell you."

Joaquín knew? A raw, gnawing feeling grew in my throat. Who else knew? "You fucking told Joaquín and not me? I was her man."

"Yeah, her man who was laid up in a damn hospital bed almost dead. He is her brother; I figured he would take care of her while you couldn't. Like I said, by the time I figured you should know, she was gone. I didn't feel like shoving more salt in the wound."

"You're a fucking cocksucker." I turned around and started my jog back toward base. I knew he had a point, but I couldn't see past myself right now. I had to find April and Dara. Talk to them and find out who else was at the party. Maybe they saw someone and just didn't tell Mitch.

Mitch caught up to me, refusing to shut the fuck up. "This is exactly why I didn't tell you. It wasn't my story to tell, and I didn't know she was pregnant until the other night. I just thought she left you. Joaquín said—"

"Fuck Joaquín. This wasn't about him. She's his sister not his woman. She was mine! You saw me drinking myself into oblivion at The Pickled Frog night after night."

"I'm not a damn mind reader, Grant. I did what I thought was best. How was I supposed to know it wasn't the same old song and dance, huh? There is a reason SEALs have a ninety percent divorce rate. I finally accepted that and let April go. I'll never see my kids. Some other man will raise them, and there is nothing I can fucking do about it. It fucking kills me. The Teams own us. We're deployed nine months out of the year, and even when we're home, we're training. You were stupid enough back then to think you could have a wife and kids while on the Team, but that was never going to happen … it never happens."

"Fuck you, man." It was another fucking thing he was right about. Either Mitch was turning into the rational one of the group or I needed to pull my head out of my ass. After Mia had left me in the hospital, she cut off all contact with me. If I had known what happened … If she had told me the truth back then, I would have gone after her. I would have found out she was pregnant and married her, regardless of whether that baby was mine. But what then? Would we have ended up just like Mitch and April or any one of the other countless couples that the SEALs drove apart? Maybe. In a twisted way, I understood why Mitch never told me. Joaquín should have said something, though, and that was unforgivable.

"What are you going to do about Mia?" Mitch asked, daring to break the pregnant silence between us. "I mean, I know we've stayed out of Joaquín's case on orders of the command, but we owe it to her to at least try to figure out what the fuck happened to Tiffany."

"I'm going to do what I can to find out what happened, but fuck Mia. She's been using me and fucking around with you. Once this is all said and done, I'm done with her too." I said the words, but I wasn't sure I believed them. I still hadn't considered what the fuck was going on with Julián or what she knew about him. If she didn't know her son could possibly be alive, and if that little boy was mine ... the possibilities were endless.

"I don't understand what she expects us to do. It's not as if we're cops. We can't just go walking into the station and demand to see the case files."

"You're right. We can't. I've been over it a hundred times, and all I can come up with is there were drugs at the party that night and no one said shit to the cops about them. So that's where we should start. Who's your dealer? Is there any connection there? To Tiffany?"

Mitch was silent for a beat. "I don't think so. I'll check it out."

"No. Don't fucking 'I'll check it out' to me. Tell me."

There was another beat of silence, and I stopped to turn to him.

"Mitch."

"Fine. His name is Rafael, he's actually one of Joaquín's buddies. I've never had a problem with him and seriously doubt he was involved."

"Joaquín introduced you? I thought he never got high." Where did Joaquín meet this guy? I'd known that motherfucker for years, and I'd never heard the name Rafael.

Mitch laughed. "No, he was just smart enough never to get high around you because he thought you'd tell his sister. Joaquín used harder than I do."

Joaquín did drugs? Fuck. I guess I never knew him at all. There'd been a rumor going around a few years back that Joaquín was caught up in some drug smuggling, but he used to laugh when I brought it up, and I never believed it because I never saw him use drugs. I hadn't really thought about it until the other night when Autumn mentioned that Tiffany said Julián's dad was a drug dealer. I'd racked my brain trying to think of any other connection between Joaquín and Tiffany, but the only thing I could think of was that Tiffany had brought the drugs to the party. It was thin, but it was all I had right now.

"Yeah? Real smart. He just ended up in jail for murder instead of drugs. How did the two of you never get caught?"

"I hook Paul up. He hooks me up."

Oh, Jesus. Paul was in on this too? Paul was the polar opposite of Mitch. He wasn't a bad boy, a womanizer, or an asshole. Granted he was cocky as hell, but he had every right to be. Paul was a ring knocker, an Annapolis graduate, and a second-generation SEAL officer. As the commander of the squad, if something shady was going on, he had to know about it.

Plus, the party had been at his in-laws' house.

No wonder they always pissed clean.

"When can I meet Rafael?"

"I'll invite him to The Pickled Frog tonight. I doubt he'll talk to you, though. Maybe he'll hit on *Ksenya*."

Great. Just what I needed. Another shady motherfucker sniffing around her.

"Fine. I'll make sure she shows up to work tonight, but she doesn't need to know who he is. With our luck, she'll try to drug him and interrogate him at gunpoint, too. She wants answers, but I don't want her anywhere near this. In fact, I don't want you calling her, either."

He laughed. "I thought you wanted to be done with her? I mean, fuck it, man, she's fucking hot. Always has been, but now, she's perfection. I know we aren't supposed to take a Team guy's girl, but if you want nothing to do with her, I'll gladly take her off your hands. Technically, she's a new woman now, and she's just my type. Hot, dangerous, and crazy as fuck."

Fuck this dude. I got up in his face and stared him down. "Stay the fuck away from her or I'll kill you. It'll be over when I say it's over. I fucking hate her right now, but she'll always be my girl."

I left him in the sand and ran past him, letting the rhythm of the waves guide me. I had hoped that confronting Mia would help resolve this mess, but talking to Mitch made me realize I had just begun to scratch the surface of all the secrets and lies that surrounded my Team.

47

MIA

I woke the next morning and, for a few minutes, thought that last night had been an incredible dream. It only lasted a second before the haunting realization that last night was no dream settled into my stomach. It wasn't a wonderful dream; it was the beginning of a nightmare.

At least I didn't need to pretend to Grant anymore. I fought the urge to dash out to the drug store and buy hair dye but that was out of the question. I needed to remain Ksenya for a while in order to gleam more information from the other SEALs. Going back to my natural color or ripping out my hair extensions would not bring back the real me. One glance at my surgically enhanced figure was all the reminder I needed for how I had permanently and irrevocably changed my body. I would be able to drop the act, but the old physical me was gone forever.

"Grant?" I slid out of bed and listened for any noise in the house, but there was only Hero, who was barking at the door.

"So, you're the one who gave me up, buddy?" I rubbed the scruff of his neck and then let him outside. Grant had made coffee, and next to the pot was a folded piece of paper. Scribbled in all-too-familiar handwriting was his dictate for me to stay in the house. He hadn't even signed it. I sighed and dropped it back on the counter. It had been fewer than twelve hours since he found out, so I'd play by the rules.

For now.

I had so much to do. I needed to see Joaquín, alone, and I needed to pick up a new phone in case Daniel was tracking mine. I needed to check if my former Russian teacher, Roman, had received the second set of DNA results comparing my hair to Julián's. I needed to get back on track. I felt like I'd lost my focus, narrowing in on Mitch and pursuing him because I thought he raped me.

The last night I had gone to The Pickled Frog as Mia, Kyle told me that he, Pat, Vic, and Joe left the party before the strippers arrived, which was what was in the police reports. That didn't mean they were being honest, though. There were a number of reasons they would have lied to the police, not the least of which was because there was a dead stripper. I had taken their words as truth, but maybe I should verify it. Autumn would know. Or, hell, so would Grant.

I still needed to look into Paul. The party had been at his in-laws' place. Did they still live there? Had they sold it? His father was a SEAL. Maybe he had pulled some strings and covered up for his son?

Hero finished his business, so I opened the door for him and made myself coffee. I was supposed to work the night shift at The Pickled Frog.

My mind raced with anxiety. This constant agony and stress was taking a toll on me. I had to take a much-needed break. I turned on the television and settled for some old sitcom.

I needed to laugh.

Two shows and three coffees later, my phone rang.

"You're not mad at me?" Autumn said in lieu of a greeting, and I forced myself to switch to Ksenya's accent.

"No, I am not mad with you. Why it is you think that?"

"Oh. It's silly really. I just hadn't heard from you since we went to Tiff's mom's house, and I didn't see you at Diamond, so I thought you were mad at me because I had coffee with Grant. I wasn't trying to hook up with him, I swear."

When the fuck did she have coffee with Grant? "I have not worked at Diamond yet. I do not know if I am going to. It is no big deal about Grant. He told to me." The lie was bitter on my tongue.

"Oh, thank God. I didn't think you were, but I wanted to make sure. You're so nice to me and all."

God, I hated myself. She was way too nice to be wrapped up in this mess. I wanted to drop the accent and come out to her, but I couldn't. Yet.

"I am friends together with you. I work tonight at The Pickled Frog. You can meet me, and I buy for you drink if you like?" I would also get to see her interact with the other SEALs. Maybe I could learn something.

"Oh, that sounds fun. I'm off tonight. Maybe Grant can introduce me to one of his fine ass friends."

"The bar will be full of the SEALs."

"Okay, great. I'll come by at eight. Did you guys find out anything about Julián? When I showed Grant a picture of him, he said he looked like he could be Joaquín's kid."

Oh my God. What the fuck!

"No, I do not know nothing yet. Did Tiffany ever mention his father?"

"Barely. Just that he was a drug dealer."

I gulped and a hint of sadness hit my core. I would have known if Joaquín ever used drugs. Roman had already told me that the DNA didn't match Joaquín and that running them against mine wasn't likely to give us different results. I had to accept that I was grasping at straws, hoping to find a connection when there wasn't one. At least I wasn't the only one who had been suspicious about who Julián's father was. Grant obviously considered it too. We were probably both just trying to eliminate Joaquín as a suspect. Even I could understand that if Joaquín found out she had hidden his kid from him, he could've snapped.

"That is very bad. I see you tonight, yes?"

"Yes. I'm excited. Bye."

"Bye."

I hung up the phone with a dozen different emotions twisted inside me. As usual, I had more questions than answers, but until I heard back from Roman, I would hold out the faint hope that the little boy who had eyes that looked like my father's could somehow be related to me and could fill the hole in my heart that had been ripped open when my own son died.

48

GRANT

I checked my phone again to see if the DNA results of my hair against Julián's straw had come in—nothing. I still couldn't believe I had even submitted the damn DNA test, but there were too many coincidences for me to ignore. Julián was probably conceived around the time I was in the hospital, Mia gave birth to a son she thought was dead, and the kid looked just like us. But it made more sense that he was Joaquín and Tiffany's son. That would have meant Joaquín met her around the time we came back from deployment, which was within the realm of possibilities. The rational part of my brain knew that there were hundreds of kids born a day, and the odds that Tiffany's son was really my and Mia's son were astronomically slim. I felt like a fool for even considering it. But astronomically slim didn't mean nonexistent, and as long as there was a small chance, then I would keep asking questions. It absolutely slayed me that I could have a living child out there and not know about it.

I left the base and headed back to my apartment, finding Mia still there sitting on my sofa. She was wearing nothing but one of my old T-shirts and was watching some trashy television show. For a second, it almost seemed normal—like a flashback to another time when Grant and Mia were solid, unbreakable. But one glance at her implants, her platinum hair, and her trout pout shattered that image.

"Hey." She brightened when she saw me.

"So, I talked to Mitch. Seems you omitted parts from your story about why you told him who you were. You pointed a gun at his head? You thought he raped you?"

She cast a downward glance. "Yeah, it wasn't a big deal. I don't think he raped me anymore. I kind of ... lost it."

Understatement of the year. "No shit. Do you know how betrayed I feel? You not only didn't tell me you were raped, but my friends knew and didn't tell me either? Joaquín knew?"

Her jaw dropped. "What are you talking about? Joaquín doesn't know. I never told him. I swear!"

"Yeah, but Mitch told him. I'm just trying to figure out why Joaquín never told me."

She shook her head rapidly. "No, you must be wrong. Joaquín doesn't know. He couldn't have. If he knew, he would've asked me about it. He would have fucking killed the guy."

"Why are you so shocked? Do you really think there were never secrets between you two? You didn't tell him you were raped—that was a secret. You didn't tell him you were pregnant—that was another. It makes me wonder how many more secrets and lies you're hiding."

Her voice grew shaky and her bottom lip trembled as she spoke. "How could I possibly tell you that I'd been raped when you were recovering in the hospital? You almost died, Grant."

I took a deep breath and sat next to her, caressed her hair, and inhaled her scent. I wanted to hold her and tell her that being raped wasn't her fault and it didn't change the way I felt about her. "That's the thing. It was never your problem; it was *our* problem. You were mine."

I leaned in and kissed her like I used to. Her lips were sweet and soft, and I could almost taste her love for me in them. Emotion flooded my body, and I had to break the kiss before I lost my resolve to stay away from her. Sex was one thing. But loving kisses with Mia were too intimate, too painful.

I wasn't her boyfriend anymore. I refused to comfort her or allow her to soothe me. She'd lost that right. I stood up and put some distance between us.

"We're meeting Mitch at The Pickled Frog tonight."

Her brow furrowed, and she let out a deep sigh, obviously upset that I had closed the door on whatever was almost happening between us. "Okay. Does Mitch have any leads about Tiffany's murder?"

"Maybe." I paused, refusing to tell her that he was bringing Joaquín's dealer. She was such a loose cannon at this point that she would probably blab to Joaquín. And Mia wasn't aware that Joaquín did drugs. Hell, I wasn't aware until tonight.

"Maybe?" She stood up and walked over to me. "What are you keeping from me? I'm trying to free him. I ruined my life to help him. What do you know?"

"I know that Mitch is meeting us at Pickled Frog tonight, and that's all you need to know. Now, go take a shower and get the fuck out of my clothes."

I leashed up Hero and left Mia standing alone in my apartment. It had only been fifteen minutes since the last time I checked my phone, but I did again for the DNA results. Where were they? I wanted answers so I could make a plan.

A plan to get back the boy I thought was my son.

49

MIA

Grant drove me to my place so I could get the rest of my clothes and move out. The lady I was living with was out of town, so I wrote her a letter giving my thirty-day notice, and Grant left her cash for another thirty days of rent. I was almost sad leaving my private apartment of secrets behind for my new prison with Grant as my personal guard, but I didn't say anything, and I didn't look back when I left.

I was too consumed by Grant's confession that Joaquín had known this whole time that I had been raped. I couldn't think of a single reason why he wouldn't say anything to me. Had he been waiting for me to open up to him? Was that what set us down the path of keeping things from each other?

I got ready for my shift at The Pickled Frog in a fog of indecision and what-ifs. I pulled on a tight T-shirt over my head and slipped my jean skirt over my hips, making sure Grant watched me. I might be lost in my own head, but I didn't ever forget he was there . . . watching me. I could feel how much he wanted me and how hard he was trying to deny it to himself.

I climbed on the back of his bike and he drove on the freeway to the bar. I wondered how many more nights Grant would allow me to work here. Mitch and Grant both knew my secret, so it was only a matter of time before one of them outed me to the entire SEAL Team. I should probably resign before that, just to ensure my cover and all the hard work I put into it weren't blown sky high.

We arrived at the bar, and I dismounted Grant's bike. He put his arm around me and grabbed my ass.

"As far as my Team is concerned, you are my woman. Don't start acting all crazy in there and interrogating people. I'm doing some investigating on my own. Your job tonight is to be Ksenya the bartender. That's it. Last time you worked here, you were followed and then run off the road. I'm here to protect you."

"Seriously, Grant. I get that you need to be in control, and I'll give you that. But don't talk to me like I'm five and stupid."

His lips pressed into a tight line, but he didn't say anything else as I re-centered myself back into Ksenya's world.

The bar was packed, even for a Friday night, but there was no sign of Autumn yet or even Mitch.

After an hour or so, Autumn showed up dressed in a turquoise miniskirt and tight white tank top. All eyes in the room zeroed in on her, and she seemed to take in every single one of them before claiming the last open seat at the bar.

"Hey, girl! Oh my God! This place is amazeballs. I can't believe I've never been here before. There are so many smoking hot guys here. Tell me! Who's single?"

"Most of men here are not with only one woman. What it is you want to drink?"

"I'll have a beer. Whatever you have on tap."

I poured her the beer as she scanned the room, her smile widening as Mitch walked in with Paul and a man I'd never seen before. He was dark skinned, around forty, built, and covered in tattoos. Mitch made a beeline straight for me, and I felt Grant's gaze focused on us.

Mitch eye fucked me and sat next to Autumn. "Hey, Ksenya. This is Rafael, a friend of mine."

Rafael! The number in Mitch's phone? "It is pleasure to meet together with you. What it is I can get for you to drink?" I tried not to let my eyes stray from Rafael as Paul slid into the seat next to him.

Rafael ordered tequila on the rocks and then turned his focus to Autumn. "I'd like to buy a drink for this pretty lady, as well."

Autumn's smile widened into an animated arch of lips, but if she were SEAL hunting, she was way off the mark—this guy didn't even look like a former Team guy.

It was only after I served Rafael and Autumn that I turned to Paul. He looked wrecked, worse than I'd seen him before. Even when he had a mission go wrong, Paul hadn't looked so distraught.

I leaned over the table and touched Paul's hand. "Why it is you look so sad?"

Paul sighed. "Nothing. Just a long week. I'll take a draft." Just that like, I had been dismissed, which was fine for now. I made myself scarce but kept my eyes on the trio, noting the way Paul kept glancing at Autumn. The looks weren't in an "I want you" way. They were more knowing glances, like an unspoken communication that you only ever really see in couples or coworkers. Both had been at the party the night Tiffany died, but neither Mitch nor Grant had ever said anything about Paul hooking up with anyone. Well, Paul was married, but that ring didn't mean much to these guys. The only piece of metal that bound these men was those damn tridents that were literally stapled to their chests.

Mitch made his way over to Grant and whispered something in his ear. Grant nodded and then glanced back at me.

I returned to Paul, Rafael, and Autumn. Paul didn't say a word to either of them, and Rafael and Autumn were in deep conversation. Autumn was batting her eyelashes, laughing at his jokes, and had even put her hand on his thigh. He whispered something into her ear, and a flush crept across her cheeks.

Something inside me twisted. Again, that feeling that something was off. Autumn had told me time and time again she wanted a Team guy. This guy didn't look like one at all, especially with the tattoo of a barbed wire on his neck. What the hell was he doing hanging out with a bunch of SEALs? Maybe he and Mitch were just old friends. It was still strange.

I caught Autumn's eyes, which was quite the feat, and glanced pointedly to the restrooms.

She turned to Rafael. "I've got to run to the ladies' room. I'll be right back." She hopped off her stool, grabbed my hand, and took me into the bathroom. "What's up?" she asked, pressing her back against the closed door.

"Nothing. Do you want to meet one of Grant's friend? Rafael, I do not think he is the SEAL."

"Oh, he's not. He told me that he's an entrepreneur. That's sexy. I'm sick of SEALs, you know? I mean, I'm a stripper. I see them all the time, and they're all cheaters. Maybe Rafael is the change I need."

I bit my lip to stop myself from telling her she was right. *I* wanted to be alone with Rafael, try to figure who he was, why he was texting Mitch, and if he knew my brother. I couldn't do that if she was hanging on him. "Okay. I understand. He looks like the bad news to me."

"I like him! He's very mature. He even owns a summer home in Lake Tahoe. How cool is that?"

"Very cool." I internally rolled my eyes. There was slim to no chance that guy was an "entrepreneur."

We used the bathroom, reapplied makeup, she spritzed some of that nasty body spray that was on a tray on the counter, and we went back to the bar.

The rest of my shift was a blur. Autumn left with Rafael without saying goodbye to me, Mitch went home with one of the resident frog hogs, Grant pretty much ignored me, Paul didn't speak a word, and my feet were tired from running up and down the bar all night. What a bust.

Kyle left early with his girlfriend and tossed his keys to Grant, telling him to close up with me. Once the customers cleared out, Grant and I counted the money in silence.

Just as we finished, Grant walked over the to the doors and locked them.

"What are you doing? Aren't we going to leave?"

"No, baby. I've been watching you all night, counting down the minutes until I could fuck you."

Grant slammed me against the wall and pressed his hard cock against me, proving just how much his watching me had turned him on.

Guess tonight hadn't been a bust after all.

50

GRANT

My hands grasped Mia's wrists as my lips covered hers. I couldn't believe how fucking sexy she looked. I had watched her flirt, flaunt, and strut all damn night and it almost broke me. The only thing that kept me from taking her in front of a room full of SEALs was that deep down I knew the show was entirely for me.

And I loved it.

My lips made their way down her chest and settled in on her cleavage. I buried my face in her tits and undid her bra with my free hand. She didn't try to stop me when I reached for the hem of her shirt and pulled it off her. I had to break contact with her skin for only a moment, but then I sucked one of her nipples between my lips, and she let out a sweet little moan.

"Oh, baby. Just like that. It feels so good."

Mia never used to talk during sex. I loved how confident she was now, only wishing she had been that secure before.

"You like that?" Her skin tasted tart yet sweet. Just like her.

I threw her over my shoulder and carried her to the bar, where I placed her on her back with her legs spread wide.

I took a moment to appreciate her beauty, but I hitched at the sight of her eyes. She was still wearing Ksenya's dark brown contacts, but even so, I saw something more in them. Something that I'd never seen. Pain, loss, longing lingering in her soul.

I would flush out the agony and replace it with ecstasy. At least for a moment, she could escape with me to paradise.

I forced myself to pull away from her and move around the bar. I grabbed a bottle of tequila, some salt, and a lime before settling back between her thighs.

Mia's mouth widened into a smile. Neither of us had ever had the fun young college experiences full of frats and parties. I'd enlisted in the Navy at eighteen, and though Mia had attended SDSU, she lived with Joaquín and spent all her free time with me. Since our split, I'd learned a few things and was more than willing to give her a glimpse.

"Open your mouth."

She licked her lips and parted them. I placed the rind of the lime in her mouth so its flesh pointed toward me, sprinkled salt on her chest, and then poured the tequila in her belly button.

She wiggled, causing a drop to spill out and down her side, but I bent and licked it off before taking the small shot from her belly button. I kept my eyes on her hooded ones as I licked the salt off her tits in long, slow movements and smiled when her breaths became a little erratic. I was still smiling when I took the lime from between her lips.

She giggled and arched her back, which made her knees pull up a bit.

I climbed up onto the bar, tore her panties off, and gave myself an even sweeter taste.

Her.

She ran her fingers through my hair as I devoured her, her scent making me high. After all these years, she still tasted the same, the one taste that I was addicted to. I loved eating her pussy, watching her react to my tongue and knowing how much she loved it, making her feel good.

Her legs tightened around my face, and I licked her for all I was worth.

"Oh, oh my God, oh, baby."

A final gasp, and her legs tensed and she came all over my face. I didn't give her time to come down from her high before I was turning her over. I took a moment to admire her incredible ass as I pushed her skirt up over her hips. I spanked her and then with quick, borderline frantic movements, dropped my pants, took myself in my hand, and pressed my cock to her slit.

She melted against me, throwing her head back and gripping the bar top. "Yes, baby. Fuck me."

I growled and entered her slowly, inch by inch, wanting to take her, but I also wanted to savor this moment, the taste of her pussy on my lips, the bliss of being inside her, fucking the only woman I'd ever loved.

I increased my pace, rubbing her clit, wanting her to come again, come with me, share the pleasure she was giving me. I could feel her pussy clamp around my cock, pushing me closer to my own orgasm.

"Grant, yes!"

I couldn't hold back anymore. I slammed into her over and over again. I needed her, needed this moment.

I could feel her orgasm approaching, and I drove into her harder, not caring if I was leaving bruises. My own pleasure was exhilarating, and every nerve inside me was completely euphoric.

"Mia, fuck!"

I came so fucking hard, and for a moment, I was lost inside her. When I released her, reality came crashing down beside us. No matter how much I wanted her, this could never work.

I could never trust her.

But how was I ever going to let her go?

51

MIA

The next morning, I woke draped over Grant. Despite his declarations that he was through with me, I felt more connected to him than ever. When I opened my eyes, he was still next to me, which almost never happened. He had always been an early riser.

I slipped out of bed and let Hero outside before making some coffee. Then I made the only vegan breakfast Grant actually enjoyed: avocado toast with pink Himalayan sea salt and cherry tomatoes. It was a San Diego classic.

I must've been too loud, because when I looked up, Grant was standing in the kitchen staring at me, a suspicious look on his face.

"Morning."

He sat down, and I served him toast and coffee. After eating for a few minutes in silence, I broke and set down my coffee mug.

"What? Why are you looking at me like that?"

"No reason."

"Grant, I know when you're lying to me. What do you want from me? I've been one hundred percent honest with you since you found out who I was. Every time you look at me, you have this suspicious scowl on your face. If you have any questions, just ask me. I have nothing to hide anymore."

He sipped his coffee, his poker face in full effect. "Your son, did you ever take a picture of him?"

I swallowed, trying to stop the tears from starting. "Yes, of course. I have one."

"Show me."

I'd never shown anyone the worn picture I kept hidden in the back of my wallet. For the first year after I lost him, I looked at that picture every day. Then, one day, I stopped. Looking at my handsome little boy was unbearable. Wondering who he would be today or how different my life would be, broke my soul.

I stood up, grabbed my wallet from my purse, and shoved it at Grant, refusing to look at it myself.

"It's in the wide slot."

Grant retrieved the photo, and I kept my gaze on his face, knowing what he was looking for. He wanted to see if the boy was his.

He examined the picture, and his eyes blinked rapidly. He lost the battle with the emotions I knew were raging through him, and for the first time since I had met him, Grant shed a tear.

"He has a cleft in his chin like mine. He's mine."

I swallowed and choked back tears. Deep down, I knew he was Grant's. They had the same face shape and that telltale cleft. But I never saw my attacker's face, so how did I know he didn't share the same traits? The loss of my son was hard enough, but I couldn't bring myself to think about losing Grant's son. It was unbearable.

"I hoped he was. But I never wanted to know. If he wasn't yours and his dad was the guy who raped me, I didn't want to love him any less. Please forgive me."

"Did you bury him?"

I centered myself and spoke rapidly. "No. He died while I was recovering from my C-section. I had an infection, almost died, and was in and out of consciousness. By the time I was awake, he'd been taken to the morgue. I signed a form for him to be cremated and took his ashes to Mt. Tam."

He nodded, almost emotionless. What the hell? He had a look that I would almost describe as hopeful. What the fuck was wrong with him?

"And you never told Joaquín? We now know from Mitch that your brother knew you were raped."

"No, you all were deployed most of my pregnancy. I never told him, and he never met Elías."

"Elías? You named him after your dad?"

"Yes."

Grant nodded and then reached over and held my hand. "Let's go see him today."

"You want to go to San Francisco to see where I scattered his ashes?"

"No. I want to go see Joaquín. But you have to trust me on this. Don't go telling him anything about Mitch, Elías, or that we know that he knew you were raped. Promise that you will follow my lead."

"Of course," I agreed, not willing to fuck up my shot at seeing my brother again.

I excused myself from breakfast and went into the bathroom to get ready. When I walked out fifteen minutes later, I found Grant already dressed and the breakfast table cleared. The picture of my son was nowhere to be seen.

***

After a longer than usual wait, Joaquín was pushed through the door by a guard.

As he stumbled to the blue plastic chair, I wanted to cry. He looked exhausted, beaten down, and defeated. There was a brand new tattoo on his neck. The skin was so red and blotchy I couldn't tell what it was at first, but when he finally situated himself in the seat and turned to the phone, I got a good look. It was a thinly drawn barbed wire.

Just like the one Rafael was sporting the other night.

A pit grew in my stomach.

I finally had a realization that even if Joaquín was exonerated, his life would be ruined forever from this experience. There was no coming back. My brother, the former SEAL, now sported what I believed to be a gang tattoo on his neck.

He picked up the phone. "Hey."

"Hey." I dropped my accent. "Grant knows. I guess he knew last time we visited."

Joaquín smirked. "Damn, sis. You're fucking crazy. I told you to stay away from me, but you didn't listen. You did this all for me? Man, you look hot! First time you showed up here looking like a porn star, I wanted to fuck you."

Grant gave him a disgusted look.

"Funny. I'm still your bratty kid sister. Yeah. I have to get you out of here. What's with your new tattoo?"

He gave me a stone-cold stare. "I'm in jail, Mia. We're Mexican. I do what I have to do to survive. No more questions. What have you turned up on your investigation?"

I opened my mouth to answer and was about to tell him that Tiffany had a child and that I thought the little boy was his, but Grant stole the phone from me.

"Nothing yet, bro. We're following some leads. I'm going to keep your sister out of trouble until you get out. Do you need anything?"

"A woman. And I appreciate you watching over Mia for me. I know she can be a handful."

"She can be, but we both already knew that."

Joaquín laughed, but it was a hollow sound. And he kept staring at me. It must've been hard for him to see his beloved sister as a new woman.

Grant and Joaquín made some more small talk about the Team until our time was up. The guard led Joaquín away, and for the first time since this nightmare started, I was happy to see him go. I hadn't realized how hurt I was that he knew I'd been raped and he hadn't comforted me. It was silly for me to feel that way. Something like that wasn't easy for anyone to talk about, and it was likely that he had been waiting for me to talk to him about it first. It didn't stop the irrationality that was swirling around my mind and fogging my thoughts.

"I hate to say it, Mia, but he could be guilty," Grant said when we were safely away from anyone who could overhear us.

"Why would you say something like that? How could you doubt him?"

"I mean . . . fuck, what was with his tattoo? The Joaquín I knew would never have agreed to get tagged like that. He can never go back to the Teams with that shit."

"Have you heard of lasers? He's doing what he has to do to survive in there. I don't see how my brother getting a tattoo equals him killing some-one, Grant. You know Joaquín! How can you stand there and say he could have done something like that?"

"I'm just wondering if either of us really knew your bother, that's all. People do things sometimes that they wouldn't normally do. I want to help, I do, but what do you think we are going to find that the cops haven't already looked at? If he didn't do it, why isn't he being more forthcoming with information? He just sat there and gave us nothing! All he cares about is getting laid. And call me jealous, but did you see how he was looking at you? You're his fucking sister."

"You're paranoid, and again, what part of any of that points to him being guilty? He wasn't looking at me like anything—I can't believe you would think that. I'm his sister for crying out loud! He's scared of something, don't tell me you didn't see it. Why else would he agree to get that tattoo? There has to be something we are missing. Some information that will free him."

"And what if there isn't? What then? Huh?" He was getting agitated, but so was I.

"I have to believe there is something. Otherwise, I did all of this for nothing!" I screamed, reaching up to rip out one of the stupid hair extensions. It hurt, and I was sure my scalp was bleeding, but I didn't care. The pain in my skin was nothing compared to what was ripping apart my heart right now. "Don't you see? I have to get him out of there. He didn't do it, and I will move heaven and earth to fucking prove it."

"And what if he did do it, Mia?"

Grant's voice was so low and so soothing that it finally broke through the anger, releasing a flood of sorrow I had been holding back. My lip trembled and tears fell from my eyes. "He didn't," I sobbed.

52

GRANT

"I'm going to take Hero for a walk," I told Mia, who was busy in the bedroom getting changed. She had been quiet the whole way home, and I hadn't known what to say. I didn't know if I had said those things to upset her or because I truly thought them, but it didn't matter anymore. Everything else in my life stopped mattering the second I pulled up my email account on my phone and saw the message waiting for me. I hadn't opened it yet. I didn't want to risk Mia either seeing it or asking about it. I also couldn't guarantee my reaction to whatever I found inside.

"Want some company?"

"No. I want to be alone."

She poked her head through the doorway and gave me a strange look before she shrugged.

I left, letting Hero lead me down the sidewalk and around the bend. When my apartment was out of sight, I stopped, pulled out my phone, took a deep breath, and opened the email.

And there it was in black and white.

Percentage of Paternity: **99.9998%**

I gasped for breath.

Julián was my son.

I was a father.

Mia was a mother.

Emotions twisted inside me. What the fuck did this mean? Did Mia really think he was dead? I knew her, and I knew she hadn't been lying. Not even she could have faked the emotions I saw in her eyes when she talked about him. She really thought her son had died. So how had our son ended up with a stripper?

Had he been kidnapped?

Switched?

It was impossible. Hospitals had ID bracelets, buzzers, and security procedures. Even if she had been knocked out cold because of some infection, why would the hospital lie to her and say her son died? Who would be capable of switching an infant? Was it a coincidence that my and Mia's son ended up with Tiffany, who ended up murdered at a Team party? What the fuck was going on?

I had to talk to her. I had to tell her that her son was alive ... that Julián was Elías.

But I couldn't risk that slight possibility that she knew that he was alive.

I sent Mia a quick text telling her I had a work emergency, and then Hero and I jumped into my truck, and I raced up to Temecula.

I was going to get my son.

53

MIA

G rant left hours ago, and I'd been hovering somewhere between pissed that he doubted Joaquín's innocence and embarrassed that I'd cried in front of him.

When my phone buzzed around three o'clock, I figured it was him calling to demand I don't go to work, but it wasn't Grant, it was Mitch.

Mitch: *I'm outside Grant's place. I'm taking you somewhere. It's for Joaquín.*

I didn't even bother to text back. I grabbed my phone and purse, locked the door, and climbed into Mitch's truck. Grant had forbidden me from leaving his place but he didn't believe me, he didn't care, and he wasn't going to help. I didn't entirely trust Mitch, but I couldn't just sit here all day and do nothing.

Mitch grinned when he saw me, leaned over, and gave me a kiss, his stubble grazing on my neck. And for once, I didn't even pull back.

"Where are we going?"

"To see your brother's dealer."

Wait, what?

"His dealer? What the fuck are you talking about?"

He laughed. "Grant didn't tell you? Rafael from the other night? Joaquín introduced him to me."

I flinched as if I'd just been punched in the stomach. "What? No, he didn't. You're wrong. Joaquín never touched drugs. He hated them. Did you ever seen him get high?"

Mitch placed his hand on my shoulder. "Listen, Mia, there's a lot of stuff you don't know about your big brother. Trust me, he's no saint. Joaquín got high every chance he got. It's not a big deal. Paul warned us when we were going to have piss tests.

Why would Paul would warn Mitch and my brother about piss tests? Didn't seem like Paul—he was a hard ass officer.

And why hadn't Grant told me Joaquín used?

"Did Grant know Joaquín got high?"

Mitch shook his head. "No. We never used around your goodie two-shoes boyfriend because he would've told you, and Joaquín didn't want you to know—obviously. We would just distract Grant with some big titty stripper until he got lost in her pussy and left us the fuck alone."

I gave Mitch a death glare. I didn't *not* want to picture Grant balls deep in some woman. I forced my jealousy down to a dark place within my soul. A place filled with guilt and regret. Because I knew that I had been the one to leave Grant.

Instead I focused my energy pondering the new piece of evidence Mitch had just provided me about Paul. What did Paul have to hide?

Mitch attempted to comfort me. "Don't worry. Your beloved man never cheated on you. This was after you dumped his ass. Anyway, I told Rafael you were my new fuck buddy and we were looking to score."

"Why am I just now hearing about this?"

"Really? I was supposed to tell some no-name stripper about him?"

"You could have told me once I told you who I was."

"Yeah? After you drugged me, pointed a gun at my head and accused me of rape? That would have gone over well, right?"

"Why now? Why tell me now? What that fuck is going on?"

"Because I still believe in your brother, even if Grant doesn't."

Mitch parked, and my head buzzed. There was a pit bull in the yard, which was surrounded by a chain link fence. The drug dealer's house was so stereotypical it might as well have had a damn sign and blinking arrow pointing to it. Mitch put his arm around me, grabbed my ass, and led me into the house.

Rafael emerged from the kitchen, and all I could do was focus on the tattoo on his neck. "Hey, bro."

"Hey. You remember Ksenya?"

"Yeah sure," he said with barely a glance in my direction. "Autumn's friend. Man, what a bitch. Fucking cock tease. All over me that night, but then she bounced without saying goodbye."

Bounced? I could've sworn she went home with him.

In contrast to the run-down exterior of the home, the interior was clean and sleek. The walls were painted gray, the furniture looked taken care of, and the floors were glossy black hardwood.

This guy had money. Serious money. Well, of course he did, he was a drug dealer.

Mitch sat on the sofa, and I cuddled up next to him. Though I hated the act I was putting on, it was something I knew I had to do.

"So, what you want?"

"Just an eight ball." Mitch didn't even twitch. He was clearly used to buying from Rafael.

Rafael's gaze focused on me. He pulled out a bag of what I assumed was cocaine. Mitch reached for it, but Rafael stopped him.

"No. Let your girl try it."

Fuck. I understood. Of course, I had to try it. Joaquín and I used to love that old movie *Rush*. Jason Patric was so hot. I remembered when he had to use to prove he wasn't a cop, which he was, but he did it anyway.

I pursed my lips as Mitch cut my line. Rafael handed me a dollar bill and for the second time in my life, and I snorted some cocaine.

This time, it was different. I wasn't scared anymore. I was on the verge of losing everything. A week ago, I had more hope. I believed I had a chance to free Joaquín, and I still had my true identity hidden.

This time, my world looked different. Grant was in control, he doubted Joaquín's innocence, and he doubted me. Despite our incredible lovemaking, I couldn't shake the sense that Grant would stay true to his word and leave me soon.

I wanted to lose myself in this drug, make my pain go away, get so fucking high that I could forget my misery.

Like a dog, Mitch must've sensed my weakness. His mouth covered mine, and I kissed him back, transferring our pain between us.

I wanted him to make me feel good and do whatever it took for me to forget about my fucked-up life.

Because I knew no matter how much I loved Grant, he would never love me again.

Rafael's voice broke our kiss. "Feel free to fuck. I can set up a camera. Better yet, I'll join in."

¡Ay dios mío¡ Hell no. His words brought me back. "I am sorry about Autumn. I do not know why it is that she tease to you. I have other friends." Complete lie, but I was sure I could scrounge up a stripper for Rafael.

"It's fine. Sick of stripping bitches."

Stripping bitches. Maybe…he meant Tiffany. Her mom said her ex was a real loser, the one she thought was Julián's father. It was a stretch, though. And Autumn mentioned that Tiffany said he was a drug dealer, which wasn't really a very specific description of someone.

"I am sorry you had bad experience with stripper. I am stripper, too. We are not all the bad girl. I do it for the money."

He didn't answer me, but he didn't need to. My eyes scoured this home. Trying to soak up every detail, memorize it. Praying to find a sign of Joaquín but there was nothing.

I squeezed Mitch's hand, and he looked at me as if he understood what I wanted.

"Thanks, man. I needed this shit. Joaquín is probably going to plea."

Nice job, Mitch.

Rafael's eyebrow rose. "Yeah? Don't beat yourself up about it. There's nothing you can do for him."

I wanted to smack Rafael and question him about Joaquín, Julián, and Tiffany. He sounded almost confident that Joaquín was guilty. I wanted to know how he knew Joaquín, and if he had been at the party. I wanted to verify everything Mitch had told me on the way over, and I wanted to find out what the fuck he meant by "There's nothing you can do for him."

Before I could say anything, Mitch gripped my hand so hard I almost squeaked and Rafael stood, holding out the baggie for me to take. I stuffed it in my purse. Mitch handed him a wad of cash, and we walked out.

Once safely inside Mitch's truck, I glared at him. "Thanks for taking me there. And for bringing up Joaquín. Did he know Tiffany? What did Rafael mean by saying there's nothing you can do for him?"

"Don't mention it. He didn't tell us anything we didn't already know. Yeah, he knew Tiffany. She brought the drugs to the party and got them from him. I still don't know her connection to Joaquín, if there was any. And I don't have a clue what he meant by that."

I debated telling Mitch that there was a possibility that Joaquín and Tiffany had a kid together, but decided to wait until I knew for sure. Maybe Julián was Rafael and Tiffany's son. That would make much more sense. Either way, I should get the new results from Roman any day.

"Fine." I held the baggie out to Mitch, but he waved his hand at it.

"Keep that. I have a feeling you need it more than I do."

"No. I don't want it."

"I can't do any. We have a piss test coming up. I'm sick of it, anyway. I want to start clean. With you, Mia."

A metallic taste filled my mouth. "I appreciate everything you're doing for me and Joaquín. But you know I love Grant. That will never go away."

"Grant's never going to love you again. He's a good man, a better one than I am. I was telling you the truth the other night. And I know you feel alone in this whole thing, like you have no one. But you have me. I've always wanted you, babe. I promise I can make you happy. Happier than Grant ever could. You're so not like him. I know you love him, but just think about it. If he's not going to love you, I will."

I couldn't believe he was serious. Mitch was fucking gorgeous, no doubt, but I loved Grant. Even so, it was nice to hear that someone cared about me. Mitch's loneliness filled the truck, and I stuffed the bag in my purse, not even understanding why. "I will, Mitch. I will."

54

GRANT

I finally arrived at the street and made a sharp right turn. Fuck the twenty-five miles per hour speed limit. My son was being held hostage in this house.

I spent the drive trying to formulate a plan, but nothing satisfied me. I could bust down the front door and take my son by gunpoint, an act that would surely land me in jail for kidnapping. I also didn't want to threaten a poor old lady if she had no idea that she was part of some elaborate scheme.

And I still didn't understand the connection between Joaquín and Tiffany and my and Mia's son, but there had to be something. There had to be. Joaquín had said that Mia had a boyfriend named Julián, which had to have been code. I couldn't analyze why he needed to talk to me in code, but I knew... I just knew that he was telling me to come find this kid and it would lead me to my answers. All it told me was that Joaquín knew about my son being here. It made me think that he killed Tiffany because he found out she was involved in kidnapping his nephew and he wanted me to find him. I just didn't know why he never said anything to me or Mia about it.

Then there was Autumn. She randomly took Mia to meet Julián and then showed me a picture of him and gave me the address where he was at. I was grateful that she had, but it just seemed to be too big of a coincidence. What did she know? Was she involved in any part of this mess? She was a stripper with Tiffany. They had been at the party together. Hell, I think they came together. What the fuck was going on?

I parked next to the curb and immediately my stomach dropped. A few newspapers cluttered the porch and a delivery notice was stuck to the door.

I grabbed my gun from the glove compartment, tucked it in the back of my jeans, and slid out of my truck, Hero by my side. The grass looked a bit long, and the absence of a car in the driveway chilled me. I opened the mailbox, but it was empty. One look inside the window at the vacant house and my worst fears were confirmed.

They were gone.

My son was gone.

Fuck.

I hopped the side gate and jimmied open a window with my Gerber tool. One jump and I was inside, leaving Hero to guard the yard.

The house was empty except for a few cardboard boxes. The floors were filthy and there was an egg carton on the counter, as if someone left in a hurry.

I walked slowly through the house, looking in closets and opening doors, but they were all empty. No furniture, no toys, and no clothes. I stepped foot into a small blue room, which must have been where my boy slept. The only thing left inside was a ripped Spider-Man poster on the wall. Then, for the second time that day, I cried.

Fuck.

I sat in the middle of the room, completely lost and disorientated. I didn't even know where to start.

The silence was broken by a slight sound coming from the closet. I jumped to my feet and flung the flimsy folding door open.

A small orange-and-white tabby stared back at me.

I didn't like cats, but if there was even the smallest chance that it was my son's pet, I wanted her. I scooped her up and held her close to my chest. The thing was so small, it could fit in my pocket. With one last look at the torn poster, I walked out of the room, down the stairs, and to the front door. I collected the papers sitting there, the oldest of which was delivered three days ago. I'd been here four days ago.

She knew.

She took one look at me and knew I was Julián's father.

So she bolted.

I punched the wall with my hand.

Where the fuck was my son? The next time I saw Mia, there was no holding back. This was all her fault. All of it. If she had never left me and had told me the truth about being raped I would have been with her every step of the way. I would've been with her at the hospital. And no one, no one would've taken my son.

I would not rest until I was reunited with my son. I would take leave, do anything to get custody of him.

But first I had to find him.

55

MIA

Once back at Grant's place, I considered flushing the drugs down the toilet. I sure as hell didn't need them. Instead I stashed them in a secret pocket in my luggage. Maybe they could be used for some type of evidence.

I sat on Grant's bed, attempting to quiet my mind. He'd left in such a hurry, I wondered what he was up to. He'd told me he was going to the compound, but I didn't believe him for a second.

My phone lit up, and Roman's name flashed across the screen. Finally, I would have at least some of the answers to this puzzle.

"Privet."

"I have results. Are you sitting down?" Roman's voice sounded stern, serious.

I took a deep breath. "Yes. Am I right? Is Julián my nephew?"

He paused, and for a second I thought I'd lost the call. "Hello? Roman? Are you there?"

"I am here. He is not your nephew."

My heart sank. "Are you sure, I mean—"

"Listen. *Ksyushen'ka, zaika,* Julián is not the son of Joaquín. There is no match with him. I've run the test several times with different samples you have give to me. I have question for you. Have you ever had a child? A boy?"

What kind of question was that? How was that any of his business? "Why are you asking me that?"

"Just answer it to me."

"Yes, I did. What does this have to do with Julián?"

"The child ... he is your son."

What the fuck? A wave of nausea hit me. "No, no, you must be wrong! Did the lab mix up my sample with Joaquín's?"

Roman spoke with an urgent tone. "There was no mistake. Listen to me. I know nothing about you, not even your real name. You ask of me to help. I do not know what you are involved with or who you are involved together with, but the boy, he is your child. Your son. Where is the boy now?"

"He's dead!" My breaths became labored, and I started to panic. No. It couldn't be. My chest tightened. Elías was dead. The doctors told me they had done everything they could but were unable to revive him. It had all happened so fast, I was still recovering from my C-section and drugged up, and they had come in the room shoving forms in my face and telling me my son had died.

"You gave me sample of his hair. Where did you find him?"

God, I couldn't breathe. "No. No, you don't understand. My son died!"

"No, *Ksyenka*. He is very much alive."

"You must be mistaken. He couldn't be. He can't be my son!"

"He is."

My hand shook so violently the phone slipped, and I almost dropped it. How? How was my son still alive? This couldn't even be possible. There had to be another explanation.

Unless he was taken from the hospital.

No! That was impossible. He was given a bracelet with my social security number! I had a matching one. That was what they told me. They'd given me his bracelet ... hadn't they? I couldn't think. I tried to remember, but it was all a fog. Just flashes of sound, of papers, of that woman...the nurse. I couldn't remember her name. She told me my son was gone. I remember her face, it was cold and uncaring, as if she were shutting herself away from the pain any woman would feel for a new mom who had lost her baby. My mind latched on to that. She was cold. Uncaring. I didn't know her name.

She hadn't given me a bracelet ... she had taken mine.

Was she a nurse?

¡Ay, dios mío!

Julián was Elías? My son was alive. I had to go get him. I had to tell Grant.

In my haze, another question popped in my head. "But this doesn't make sense. Joaquín is my biological brother, my flesh and blood. How can he have no DNA match to Julián? His sample must've been wrong."

"The sample is fine, it is accurate. This is second test. *Ksyushen'ka*. I tested the hair from the brush and from an envelope he sent you. You left it here. Both of the samples of his had the same DNA but neither of them matched the boy's. I wanted to be certain, so I compared his DNA against yours. DNA does not lie. It can only mean one truth."

He continued to speak, but I did not comprehend his words. My mind raced through the millions of images of Joaquín and me as kids. Every memory I had from childhood had Joaquín in it.

But it didn't matter.

After a few seconds, the realization hit me.

Roman was right. There was no other explanation.

If Julián was my son, then Joaquín was not my brother.

Then who the fuck was he?

PART V

CRAVE

SE7EN DEADLY SEALS EPISODE 5

"IT IS *GREED*
TO DO ALL THE TALKING
BUT NOT TO WANT TO
LISTEN AT ALL."

— DEMOCRITUS

56

MIA

I threw my phone across the room and let out a piercing scream. What the fuck was happening to me? Was I cursed? How could my life fall apart any more than it already had?

How could Joaquín not be my brother?

Heat flooded my body, and my brain burned. How much more heartbreak could I endure? I'd known nothing but pain since the night my parents had died. I'd been raped, my boyfriend had almost been killed by a bomb in the Middle East, my baby had died, and then my brother had been arrested. I didn't know if I could take one more curve ball being thrown at me.

I forced myself to take some calming breaths as I left Grant's bedroom and went into his office. On his desk was a picture of my brother. I studied his face. Dark skin, deep set eyes, long eyelashes, strong chin. I searched the image, trying to match any of our features.

But there weren't any.

Sure, we looked similar, but it was in a cultural way and not a brother-sister way. But he was a spitting image of my mom, and I was the spitting image of my dad.

What the fuck did that mean?

He had to be adopted. Or maybe I was.

We were raised together, I knew that for sure. He was my brother, same DNA or not. But why wouldn't my parents have said something?

My lips pressed together as I came to my decision. It didn't matter. A DNA test wouldn't change the way I felt about him. I loved him, always and forever.

Joaquín wasn't some stranger. I knew him. I trusted him. Hell, I'd ruined my life to try to exonerate him. If that wasn't love, then I wasn't sure what was.

Whatever the reason was, it didn't change anything. What had changed was ten minutes ago, my son was dead.

And now, my son was alive.

Alive.

Julián. The name someone had given him.

Elías. The name I had given him. My father's name.

The sickening wave of adrenaline, excitement, and anticipation hit me so hard my hands started to shake. Holy fuck, he was alive. I should be ecstatic, but the emotions were too much—too sudden, and they made my stomach twist and tears spring to my eyes.

How many nights had I cried myself to sleep, wishing he were alive so I could hold him in my arms, kiss him, and never let him go?

My dreams for him, for me, could finally come true.

I just needed to get him. The thought threw every fiber in my body into panic, and I raked my hands through my hair, pulling at it until my scalp burned. He had been kidnapped, stolen from a hospital right under the noses of nurses and security and . . . me. I didn't know Tiffany, but something in my gut told me she wasn't the one who had taken him. She had somehow ended up with him and pawned him off on her mother to raise.

So who took him?

I didn't know. What I knew was that Tiffany was dead and her mother had custody of him. Tiffany's mother wouldn't just hand him over to me. She loved the kid and when she'd met me, I'd been pretending to be some Ukrainian stripper with huge boobs. She would be more likely to call the cops than give me my son. I would need to figure out a way to prove he was mine.

But I wanted to just grab him.

Fuck.

My head was buzzing.

I needed to calm down. Think rationally. Get a hold of myself, which was hard to do, especially since I'd snorted a line of coke an hour ago.

I left Grant's office, went to the kitchen and boiled some water. After a few minutes, the tea kettle whistled. I poured myself a mug and stared at the color of the water as I bobbed the tea bag. As the scent of cinnamon and cloves tickled my nostrils, my mind began to slow down. A few sips of the warm liquid, and my thoughts cleared.

Grant was still not home, and I had no idea where he'd gone. I reached for my phone, which was sitting on the counter, but stilled my hand. I was about to call him and tell him the truth. I curled my fingers. Grant would help me. I knew he would, especially since there was a chance that he was Julián's father.

That was what stopped me. I didn't know if Grant was actually Julián's father. I believed in my heart he was, but I wasn't certain. I'd always wanted to know the answer to that question but had been afraid to find out the truth. Too afraid of the possibility that my son wasn't Grant's and instead was the child of my rapist.

If Grant was his father, he would want to be part of our lives. I wasn't naïve enough to believe this would change things entirely between Grant and me. We wouldn't go rushing off into the sunset as a family. No. Grant despised me too much for that. I had lied to him. I had run away from him. I had broken his heart. But maybe, just maybe, this new beginning could help us heal a bit.

What was my plan? Show up at Tiffany's mother's house and demand to get my son? Show some DNA test done by Roman's friend? Kidnap my boy back?

The rational Mia knew that I should take a deep breath, call Grant, contact the police, and file a case.

But Mia had been missing for six months.

Ksenya was anything but rational.

I could call Grant, but he would realize I was high—a conversation I did not want to have with him. I couldn't possibly drive. No matter how desperate I was, I refused to drive intoxicated. My parents had been killed by a drunk driver. I would not risk innocent lives.

I could call an Uber or call Autumn to take me up there? Neither of those options sounded appealing. Especially since I had no idea what Julián's grandmother would say when I confronted her. That was likely to end with her calling the cops and having me, the crazy woman trying to take her grandson away, put in jail.

There was only one other option.

I texted Mitch.

Mia: Can you take me somewhere?

Only a few seconds passed before I saw the text bubble.

Mitch: On my way.

I finished my tea and went outside to wait. Twenty minutes later, Mitch showed up, a satisfied grin on his face. I hopped in the truck and gave him a kiss on the cheek.

"Thanks for coming."

"I was surprised to hear from you so soon. Where to?"

"Temecula."

"Why?"

I considered telling him but paused. It wasn't fair to tell him before Grant. I wasn't adding my blabbing the news to everyone else before him to my long, long list of indiscretions.

"I need to visit Tiffany's grandmother. Get some more information to free Joaquín."

He glared at me. It was never a good idea to lie to a SEAL. They could always tell. "Why isn't Grant taking you?"

This time, I'd tell the truth. "Because I don't have a clue where he is. He left this morning and hasn't answered my texts. Besides, he seems to think Joaquín is guilty, which is why you're here, big guy."

"Fine. But I'm going in with you."

"Okay."

We drove up to Temecula in comfortable silence. I appreciated Mitch helping me, even if it was just because he wanted me. Maybe I'd misjudged him. He might be a misogynist jerk, but he was loyal and protective.

We turned onto the street, and I let out a gasp when I saw a truck parked in front of the grandmother's house.

Grant's truck.

Oh, fuck.

"What's Grant doing here? I thought you said you didn't know where he was?" Mitch asked, slowing.

"I didn't." I turned to Mitch. "Please, just drop me off. He can't see us together. He will freak."

"No way." He turned the truck down an adjacent street and parked. He pulled me toward him, his piercing stare penetrating me. "Mia, tell me what the fuck is going on."

I burst into tears, unable to stay strong any longer. I told him everything. When I finished, my tears had slowed and Mitch looked mildly shocked. I expected him to ask a million questions, but he didn't. He waited until I got myself under control and looked right at me. "How'd you find out?"

"Autumn took me to meet Tiffany's mother last week. I thought the boy was Joaquín's, so I plucked a hair from his little head. I had it tested, and he's my son."

"And Grant knows? He found him first? Is this why Joaquín killed Tiffany?"

"I don't know. Maybe Grant took him from the hospital. I don't know anything anymore."

"Get a hold of yourself." His strong hands gripped my shoulders. "Listen, Grant didn't kidnap him. No way. He would never do that." He kissed my forehead. "I'm going to drop you off at the bottom of the street. You tell Grant you took an Uber. I'll stay around the area in case you need me. Text me to let me know you're okay."

"Thank you, Mitch. You've been really great to me. You're a good guy."

"You make me a good man."

I gave him a kiss on the cheek and jumped out of the truck. Anticipation and fear twisted inside me as I headed toward the house.

Toward Grant.

Toward my son.

57

GRANT

I spent two hours alone in my son's house, painstakingly examining every wall, opening every drawer, and scouring every square inch of the floor trying to find some clues as to where that lady took my kid. I wasn't even sure what I hoped to find. I doubted she was dumb enough to leave her forwarding address. Even so, she must have had some help to pack.

I went to the back yard and saw a man in his thirties taking out his trash. I headed in his direction.

"Hey, buddy. My mom hadn't heard from her friend in a few weeks so she asked me to come check on her, but she's clearly gone. She left her cat here, too. Did she happen to tell you where she went?"

The guy eyed me suspiciously. "Lorraine didn't have any friends."

Lorraine. Hearing her name sent a chill through me. I didn't know anything about the woman who was raising my son.

"They hadn't seen each other in years." I needed to give this guy a reason to trust me, so I reached into my back pocket and pulled out my wallet, flashing the guy my military ID. "I'm a Navy SEAL and wanted to make sure she was okay."

He scowled at me. "Did you know that guy who murdered her daughter?"

Well, fuck. I knew I looked upset by the question but hoped the guy would just think I was disturbed about Tiffany's death. "Yeah, I did. Guy's a lying piece of shit." And that was true. No matter if Joaquín was guilty or innocent, and I was leaning toward him being guilty, I would never forgive Joaquín for knowing that Mia had been raped and not telling me.

"Well, Tiffany was fucked up. What kind of woman never visits her son? That little boy of hers was better off without her. Great kid."

I smiled. Hearing him say that my son was a great boy warmed my soul. I yearned to get to know him.

"Anyway, I don't know where they went. A moving truck packed them up in the middle of the night, and by morning, they were long gone. She never told me goodbye."

Fuck. I had been right. Middle of the night, packed up their stuff, and vanished. And I didn't have a clue where they were or who this Lorraine woman was. "Thanks, man."

I went back inside the house. I needed to call Kyle and have him run some intel. We could find property records, birth certificates, arrest records, something, anything that could lead me to my son.

I walked upstairs to get the cat. I wasn't going to leave him here to die.

But then I heard a noise.

I grabbed my weapon and peered downstairs, prepared to find the grandmother, my son, or an armed intruder.

Instead, the barrel of a gun pointed right back at me.

And the person holding the gun . . . was Mia.

58

MIA

"Put down the fucking gun, Mia."

I clutched the gun and kept it pointed at him. Seeing Grant inside this empty house enraged me. Well, really, it was more the empty house that enraged me, and I was taking it out on him. Still, I wanted to know what the hell he was doing here.

"What are you doing here? How did you know my son was here? Where is he?" I could barely breathe. The place was empty. Just boxes and dust remained.

"The neighbor says they packed up in the middle of the night. I've scoured every inch of this fucking place for clues but found nothing. Put down the fucking gun!"

I slowly lowered the gun, desperate to shoot something, shoot myself, end this pain and suffering. Gone, my son was gone. A tight fist squeezed around my heart.

Grant descended the stairs and disarmed me faster than I could blink. "What the fuck? You better start talking now. You told me our son died. Yet, here you are, fucking looking for him. So, which is it, Mia? I swear to God that if you lie to me, I will kill you myself."

My lip trembled. "*Our* son? What makes you sure he's yours? You know I was raped."

"He's mine, Mia. I didn't actually know Julián was mine until this afternoon. About a week ago, Autumn showed me a picture of him, and I knew I had to see him with my own eyes, so I drove up here and met him. I took his empty juice box and ran his DNA. He's my son. Our son."

I gasped and my knees threatened to give out. There it was. Everything I had been desperate to hear. Julián was his son, our son. Not that had Julián been the son of my rapist I would have loved him less. But still, knowing that Julián was the result of our love was the only light in this incredibly fucked-up situation.

But my joy was soon replaced by anger. Grant had known there was a possibility that our son was alive and hadn't told me. What I had done was different—I'd thought he was Joaquín's boy, but not mine. Never mine.

"You did all that, and you never told me? This morning I didn't even know he was alive, and you . . . you have known—" Suddenly, it was too hard to breathe and spots danced across my vision. My hand blindly reached out, bracing against the wall so I didn't fall over. Grant, to my surprise, wrapped his strong arm around my waist and helped lower me to the ground.

"Slow. Slow breaths." He rubbed my back as I leaned forward, trying to force my heart to slow and my lungs to expand. Finally, after what felt like a lifetime, I sat up and let my head fall back against the wall.

"I just found out today also, and no I didn't fucking tell you." Grant said, clearly still pissed despite his small show of support. "You don't tell me anything. I can't trust you, Mia. Did you give up our son? Answer me, goddammit!"

I whipped my head in his direction and narrowed my eyes. "No, of course I didn't. I thought my son was dead. I thought Julián was Joaquín's child, but never, never did I think he was mine. I believed with my whole heart that he was dead! I did a DNA test on him to see if he was my nephew. Do you really think I would do that, Grant? I have spent the last two years mourning my son. You have no idea what that was like."

I wanted to tell him how horrible it was and how, more often than not, I would cry myself to sleep. How I couldn't even look at the scar on my stomach and not break down. I attempted to finish my thoughts, but tears overtook my voice.

"How can I believe you, Mia? You're full of secrets. You've hidden every aspect of your life from me. Everything. Your rape, why you broke up with me, that you were pregnant. That I could be his father."

I closed my eyes, hiding my shame. He was right. I'd fucked up everything. If only he could understand me, he'd realize I never meant to hurt him. I had been trying to protect him. He didn't need to go through the pain and fear and heartache that I had. I was trying to save him.

"I have nothing to say for myself. This is all my fault. Had I told you I was pregnant, I would've never had the baby in San Francisco. I don't know what to say. But I'm not lying, I swear to God I thought he was dead." I took a deep breath and opened my eyes.

Indecision crept across his face. I knew deep down he probably wanted to believe me, but I'd done something that was probably unforgivable.

He looked away from me and cracked his knuckles. "Why would someone take our son? Tiffany was young. She could probably have her own kids someday. Plus she gave him away to her mom. Clearly she had no interest in being a mother. Think, Mia. Is there anything else you haven't told me? Anything?"

I hesitated to tell him my latest secret, but I was too emotionally spent to keep anything else inside. "Joaquín isn't my biological brother."

His nostrils flared, and his voice was so quiet I almost didn't hear him. "What?"

"Yeah. I tested Julián against Joaquín first. No match. I figured it was because the sample of Joaquín's hair was old, so I sent in a sample of my own hair, hoping to prove that Julián was my nephew. Turned out there was no genetic similarities between them. None."

"Was the sample of Joaquín compromised?"

"No, he tested two separate samples. Besides, it doesn't matter, does it? So what if he isn't my biological brother? Maybe he was adopted. Or I was. He's still my brother. Every memory I have of my childhood was with him."

Grant's mouth slackened. "Don't you see, Mia? Everything matters. We learn in the Teams that there is no such thing as a coincidence. Let's focus on the facts. We know our son was kidnapped after you gave birth. Somehow, Tiffany got our son and gave him away to her mother to raise. Joaquín knew about you being raped and he is now sitting in jail, accused of murdering Tiffany. He knows more than he's telling us. He's connected too closely to all of this—"

"Don't even go there. Are you fucking kidding me?" I stood and put distance between us, rage consuming my every step. I knew what he didn't want to say. He thought Joaquín was involved with the kidnapping, which was something I refused to entertain. "The only logical explanation is that

Joaquín found out that Tiffany kidnapped my son, so he murdered her. That means he lied to me about killing her, and I ruined my life for his lie, but he did it to protect our son, his nephew. He's my hero if that's true. But me transforming into Ksenya led us to our son."

"If that were the case, why didn't he tell you about him? If he were willing to go to such extremes to protect our son, why hide it? Besides, he had no idea you would do all this."

"Maybe he thought telling me would put me in danger. Or put Julián in more danger."

"Because keeping it from you kept you so safe, right? Did you forget his attorney attacked you?"

Dammit, he was right that something didn't add up, but not about Joaquín being involved. "There is something we are missing." I turned to the window and bit my bottom lip. Then, after a second of indecision, I knew what we had to do. "We just need to go ask him what he knows about Julián."

Grant closed the distance between us and clutched my wrist. "Over my dead fucking body. And even if what you think is true, he won't or can't tell us. He's about to go on trial for a murder he probably committed. Our son is missing. We have no idea who kidnapped him from that hospital, why they did it, or where he is. Until we figure that out, we aren't telling Joaquín about him. Keep your goddamn mouth shut. Do you fucking understand me?"

He released his grip on me, but I stayed in his space, forcing him to look at me. "Don't you dare tell me what to do and what to say! Even though Joaquín and I aren't blood related, he's still my fucking brother!"

Grant didn't back down. I'd never seen him this pissed. He bared his teeth at me. "I'm not fucking playing with you anymore. You robbed me the chance of ever getting to know Elías when you had him. If I'd known you were pregnant, I would've never let you out of my fucking sight. If I'd been at the hospital, I'd have been right next to you, taking care of our son. You owe me this. Let me fucking handle it."

I gulped hard. He was right . . . again. Even so, he was being a complete jackass.

"Elías is my son! I carried him for nine months, and I have spent every minute of every day for the last two years missing him. You only found out you had a son today. I have every fucking right in the world to find out what happened, so stop acting like this is all about you!"

His face was red, and his brows were furrowed. I exhaled, forcing myself to calm down. He was furious. I was furious. Yelling at each other wasn't helping anything.

"No matter how much you hate me right now, we are in this together," I said, trying to keep my voice as calm as possible. "He's our child. I would never have kept him away from you had I known the truth. I had intended to test his DNA, and if he was yours, I was going to immediately tell you, beg your forgiveness for leaving you, and pray you would take me back. They told me he died, Grant. How could I put that heartbreak on you? Tell me. How?"

He looked at me, maybe for the first time since I walked back into his life as Ksenya, and let my question hang heavy in the air between us. "Fine," he relented, as his shoulders dropped, and he finally lowered his voice. "We can go see your brother. Is there anything else you haven't told me?"

Well, today Mitch took me to Rafael's where I snorted cocaine and Mitch kissed me. Then he drove me here.

I shook my head, a knot of guilt building in my stomach, but I couldn't speak. It wasn't relevant really—none of that had anything to do with finding our son.

"Promise me, Mia. Say the words."

Before they had the chance to choke me, I spit the words out. "I promise."

"Good. Listen, I'm going to ask Kyle to hire some former Team guys to trace Tiffany's mother. Her name is Lorraine. I just hope to God she hasn't harmed him, but she seemed to love him. Clearly my judgment sucks. I fell in love with you."

Just like that, all my guilt for holding back information fell away, and a spark of anger flickered.

"Real mature, Grant."

He looked out the window. "Where's your car?"

Fuck. "Oh, I took an Uber."

He cocked his head and lifted a single eyebrow. "Why?"

I forced myself not to bite my lip. "I was so overwhelmed finding out that Julián was my son, I didn't want to drive." That seemed reasonable when I said it.

Grant shook his head and went upstairs while I stayed planted where I was. Numb. I sent a quick text to Mitch to tell him that I was okay and that he could head home. Then I deleted my texts to him.

After a few minutes, Grant came downstairs, holding a tiny kitten. She was orange and white and fluffy.

"The only thing I found in this place is this fucking cat."

I grabbed her from his arms. She let out a tiny meow, and I stroked her until she purred. "Can we take her?"

"Of course. She'll die here if we don't. Plus, she was probably our son's."

59

GRANT

The ride home was torturous. Hero wouldn't stop sniffing the cat. I wished she had driven her car—that way I wouldn't have been forced to listen to Mia's apologies or that damn cat's meow. I didn't believe her Uber story for a minute, but I didn't press.

I drove to a pet store where we bought the requisite cat supplies: litter box, scratching post, cat food, and those stupid feather things. A fucking cat. Hero would probably treat her like a chew toy, and I would have to protect the ball of fluff. But that stupid cat was the only connection I had to my son so I'd deal with it.

We arrived at my place and quickly corralled the cat into my small office.

Mia sat in a chair, holding the fluffy orange thing. "What are we naming her?"

"I don't care. You choose."

"Okay. How about Curry?"

"Sure, whatever. I'm going to make some calls." I left them inside my office and shut the door.

Hero pawed at the door. "Sorry, buddy." I gave him a treat and grabbed my phone to call Kyle. He picked up on the first ring.

"Hey, man, what's up?"

"I need a favor. Can you call that PI you know to help me find someone?

Tiffany's mother? Her name is Lorraine, but I don't have a last name for her." I rattled off all the other details I could remember: her address, what kind of car I saw in the driveway when I met my son, what the neighbor had said about her leaving. "She pulled up stakes sometime last week, and I need to find her."

Kyle paused. "Sure thing. I'm on it. Man, how's Joaquín? Have you heard from his sister? I feel bad that we never helped her out."

I stared at Mia, who had just emerged from my office. She poured herself a glass of water and curled up in a ball on my sofa while Hero lay at her feet.

This wasn't the time to tell Kyle about Mia. I changed the subject. "Gotta run. Let me know when you hear anything."

"Will do. Later."

I hung up and grabbed a beer from the fridge, lingering in the kitchen as I took the first sip from the bottle.

I believed Mia that she didn't know that her son was alive, but ultimately, her decisions caused us to lose our son. Could I put myself in her shoes? I thought about that question as I strode into the living room and took a seat on the opposite end from her.

She had been raped when I had been injured. I understood why she hadn't told me about that. I would've been livid but helpless to do anything. Then she'd found out that she was pregnant and didn't know who the father was, which must have been terrifying. So she left, went through the pregnancy alone, had a rough delivery where she became very ill, and then she was told her son had died.

She could've died, alone. I would've never recovered from her death. I wished I could've been there for her.

I took another sip.

Mia had always been proud. Always tried to be independent. Strong. Knowing her, she probably really thought she had been saving me from some kind of burden or stress.

But I would've done anything for her.

I still would do anything for her.

I thought the drive to protect her had left me when she walked out of my hospital room, but clearly it hadn't. I'd slept with her. I'd agreed to help her. Sure, I pretended there weren't any emotions involved and it was just fucking.

That was a lie.

Something inside me was unwilling to let me actually cut my ties with her, and that made me think that maybe . . . one day, I would be able to move past all the fucking hurt that woman caused me. After all, we were now in this together. We were Julián's parents. If there was any hope I could learn to trust Mia again, I had to try.

For Julián.

Mia moved closer and looked up at me, eyes pleading. "What are we going to do?"

"Kyle's going to try to find Tiffany's mom. We'll find him, I promise."

She gulped and leaned into me.

I put my arm around her. "What do you think about Autumn? She was the one who led us both to Julián. Do you think she knew he was our kid?"

Her face crinkled. "Autumn? You suspect Autumn? No, I don't think she knew. She's a naïve stripper—she seems too nice to hide something like that. She doesn't even know I'm Mia."

"She knows who I am, though. Thinking back on that night Tiffany died, I almost feel like Autumn targeted me. Just the way you did at Panthers."

She lightly punched me in the gut. "I didn't target you at Panthers, buddy. You zeroed in on me the second you walked into the door."

I tickled her until she laughed. "Yeah? Because you're irresistible." I kissed her and she climbed onto my lap. I enjoyed our chemistry and brief levity in this incredibly fucked up situation.

I pushed her hair out of her face. "But seriously, maybe Autumn wanted to tell me she thought he was my son and then chickened out. She maybe took you because she knew we were seeing each other so she hoped you would tell me."

"I think you're crazy. No way did she know Julián was your kid. It was just a coincidence that she told us both. She likes you," she teased.

I didn't even respond to that comment, because what was I going to say? Autumn did like me, and she'd been all over me the night of Tiffany's murder. We didn't fuck, but there had been flirting and drinking and laughing. It hadn't bothered me that when we went to a room she shot down my advances. I'd never been one to get pissed about not getting laid, especially when the girl was actually fun. Looking back on everything Autumn and I had talked about that night, something hit me that I hadn't realized until now. Autumn was much smarter than she pretended to be.

So smart, I remembered asking her why she had chosen to be a stripper. She'd never really given me an answer.

Mia interrupted my thoughts. "What are you going to say to Joaquín? Can I ask him about not being my brother?"

"Yes, I want to hear what he says. Maybe you're right, and he was adopted. But don't breathe a word about Julián. Joaquín told us both at the jail that you had an ex name Julián. Do you?"

"No, of course not."

A chill ran through me. "Exactly."

"What does that mean?"

"That means that he knows about Julián and didn't tell us. There's a possibility your brother killed Tiffany after finding out that she had stashed our son at her mom's." I pounded the rest of my beer. "Or, there's a possibility that he's involved in something else."

She rolled her eyes at me. Damn, she still couldn't believe that Joaquín could be capable of anything shady.

"So why visit him?"

"Because I want to see how he reacts when you tell him about the DNA test. Maybe it will trigger something with him—maybe he will suspect we found out about Julián and let something slip. Just trust me."

"I do trust you." Mia looked up at me. "I'm so sorry, Grant. Sorry about everything. Sorry for leaving you, lying to you, getting this stupid plastic surgery."

I stared deeply into her eyes and inhaled her familiar citrusy scent. If I closed my eyes and just breathed her in, I could still sense Mia. My Mia. Who she was. How much she'd loved me. How much I'd loved her. How she always knew how to calm me down no matter how shitty of a day I'd had, how she'd always believed in me.

I needed to believe in her.

"It's okay, babe. I'm not going to lie and say I understand what you did, but I know you didn't mean to hurt me."

"I didn't." She pressed her palms to her eyes. "I need you to believe me that I didn't know he was alive. I would never, ever give my son away or keep him from you."

I placed a few kisses on her head and then embraced her as she sobbed into my arms.

And then I finally said the words she needed me to say.

"Baby, I believe you."

And was surprised to find that I meant them.

A struggle built in my chest. I wanted to forgive her, maybe even fall in love with her again, but I could never allow myself to become that dependent on anyone. Right then wasn't the time to figure it out, so I said nothing. I kissed her face, her neck, tasted her salty tears and then I scooped my girl up and carried her into the bedroom.

60

MIA

G rant placed me down on his bed, gently, with no urgency. Every time we'd had sex recently, it had only been fucking. Amazing fucking. He'd fucked me so fast, so hard, so deep it made my head spin in pleasure.

But this time, everything seemed different. His face softened when he looked at me. No more angry scowl or lustful hunger. It was almost as if I was in a time warp back to how we used to be.

He brushed a lock of hair away from my face as he lowered to kiss me. A sweet kiss. Soft, loving. His hand made its way down my body, slowly, oh so slowly, stopping only to caress my breast before moving to trace the outline of my waist and eventually settling on my thigh.

His beard scraped the palm of my hand as I cupped his face. I stopped and considered his eyes, which were just a little more trusting and loving than they had been since I'd came back.

I seized that moment, taking advantage of this opportunity that he seemed to be truly open to me. "I love you. I love you so much, baby. I'm so happy that Julián is your son."

He pressed his finger to my lips, bidding my silence. With his free hand, he peeled off his shirt. A smile graced my face as he moved his fingers to let his shirt fall to the floor. I would never tire of staring at his chest, ever. He motioned for me to lift my arms, and I did as he slipped my T-shirt over my head, taking my bra with it, and flung them off the bed.

His attention turned to my breasts. He thumbed my left nipple and sucked on my right one. I let out a moan as he lightly nibbled my bud.

His mouth detached from my sensitive skin. "You're so beautiful, babe. You were always beautiful."

I arched my back as his mouth made its way down my body, pausing over my hipbone and showering my belly in kisses as he pulled my jeans off. His hands pulled down my panties and then he cupped my ass as I gripped his hair.

His tongue gave a long, slow lick down my center, drawing a low, throaty moan from my throat. He teased me, tasting me without focusing where I needed him and making me squirm. When his tongue found my clit, my body arched off the bed, and I felt him smile against me.

After I was throbbing for him, he knelt in front of me, taking his cock in his hand. He pulled me onto his lap, sat back against the headboard, and guided me onto his cock. Gripping my hips, he slowly urged me to lower onto him, until he was fully inside me.

"Oh, Grant, baby."

His mouth went to work on my nipples as I rode him, rubbing my clit on his crotch, feeling his huge cock filling me. It wasn't long before we were both covered in a light sheen of sweat, our breaths short pants of lust and need. Then, right before the tight coil low in my belly threatened to ignite, Grant lifted my chin and stared into my eyes, never losing my gaze. I loved him so much, in every way, mind, body, and soul. He thrust me down one more time, pushing me deep as I came, with him falling over the edge right after I had.

This time, he didn't throw me off him. He paused, stroked my hair, and buried his head in my chest.

"Mia, I don't think I can ever let you go."

61

GRANT

"Then don't. We can make this work. You know how much I love you."

I pulled her against my chest. My head was still buzzing from our incredible sex. This time, my orgasm brought me a surprise.

I hadn't just been fucking her or using her to get off. I cared more about her pleasure than my own.

I wanted to find my way back to the guy I had been when I was in love with her. I wanted the girl she had been when she was in love with me. I craved her. But I could never be with her if I couldn't trust her. And I was balls deep inside her, I had just made love to her, and yet my anger over her lying to me wouldn't quit. I might believe that she didn't know our son was alive, but she had still made all those choices without me.

"Tell me everything. How was your pregnancy?"

"You really want to know?"

"Yeah." There was a slice of cool air over me as she slid off my lap and curled against my side.

"It was great, actually. I was sick at first but felt better after the second trimester. He was growing perfectly, and I was really excited to be a mommy."

I rubbed her arm. "When's his birthday? Where was he born? What was his legal birth name?" I had so many questions I unloaded them like rapid fire.

She gave me a small smile. "September 6. San Francisco General. Elías Joaquín Cruz."

I flinched. She'd given him her brother's name as our son's middle name. It pissed me off, but I wasn't going to make a big deal about it.

"Do you have any records from the hospital?"

"Yeah. But not with me. They're all in storage up in Marin."

Note to self—time to go to Marin. "How did you support yourself?"

"It was tough doing it all alone. After I left you, I knew I couldn't go to school full time once I had Elías, and I didn't want to ask Joaquín for help since he didn't know I was pregnant, so I moved to a small apartment in Marin. Got a job at Nordstrom's as a makeup artist because they had medical benefits immediately after training."

My chest constricted. "I have the best medical insurance."

"I know. So many times I picked up the phone to call you. I was going to show up at your place with my small bump, beg you for forgiveness. But I wasn't sure the baby was yours. I didn't know if you would believe me about being raped, or if you would've thought I'd cheated on you. I didn't know what to do, so I didn't do anything. You don't know how much I missed you. I was so alone, Grant, just like I am now. But I never stopped loving you."

"I know." I pulled her tighter into my arms and kissed her tears away. And in that moment, all my hatred for her washed away. I believed her. I finally pulled my head out of my ass and, for the first time, could see things through the veil of my own anger. She only had me and Joaquín, but she had shut us both out. She had been raped. She was pregnant. I was injured—she felt she had no choice. What must it have been like to go through that alone? The pregnancy, childbirth, getting sick and then losing him. And how could Joaquín abandon her knowing she had been raped? Had he known she was also pregnant?

I cupped her face with my hands. "I want to try to make our relationship work. I can't promise you more than that right now. But I need you to be completely honest with me from here on out."

She rapidly blinked. "Babe, really? I know we can find our way back to what we had. Maybe find something even better. If we can get through this, we can get through anything. I just need to know you forgive me."

"I forgive you. You're a strong woman. I know you were doing what you thought was best and didn't want to burden me because I was in the hospital. Do I like it? No. I hate it with every fiber of my being, but I understand why you thought it was your only choice. I need you to promise me that if we do this, we do it together. No more lies or keeping stuff to yourself because you think it's for the best."

Her face brightened, and she nodded before pulling herself on top of me. We kissed like we were teenagers on a first date. A new beginning for us. Her eyes sparkled. I enjoyed making her happy.

We both got ready for bed and within a few minutes, Mia was fast asleep. But the sandman refused to pay me a visit. Curry's tiny meow beckoned me to the office. When I opened the door, I found her pacing around the room, probably desperate for some affection.

Curry rubbed my leg, so I picked her up and pet her until she purred. I prayed that my son was somewhere safe and that I would be able to find and protect him.

I'd always loved animals, dogs more than cats, but it was still nice to imagine that my son shared my love for animals. I wondered what else we had in common. Was he competitive like me? Stubborn like his mom? Did he like being outside? I couldn't wait to get to know my son.

I looked around my office and saw a picture of Mia and me kissing at BUD/S graduation with Joaquín in the background. I remembered that day so clearly. Mia was wearing her sun dress and beaming with pride. My chest was bloody from when my commanding officer pounded my trident into my flesh, a scar I wore proudly. Best day of my life. I'd achieved my goal, was about to embark on my dream career, and had the love of my life by my side.

But after studying the picture, a wave of nausea hit me. Something had set me off. The way Joaquín was looking at Mia. His lips were pressed flat and his face wore a pinched expression. He looked angry on what should've been the happiest day of his life. I couldn't be certain, and I was probably reading something into it, but it almost looked as if he was jealous of us. Maybe he had just been jealous that he didn't have a steady girlfriend who loved him the way Mia loved me.

He and Mia had always been strangely close, but I figured it wasn't my place to judge. I didn't have a sister. But Joaquín and Mia's relationship just seemed unnatural, like that stupid *Friends* episode where that guy Rachel was dating was bathing with his sister. A few times, I caught Joaquín watching Mia too long—too intently. Fuck, I didn't even know what I was thinking. I was probably a sick fuck for even thinking something was off. Either way, had he been any other man, I would've punched him for looking at Mia like that.

We were going to go see him tomorrow, and I was worried that I wouldn't be able to speak clearly. But the facts were clear in my brain.

Joaquín and Mia were not biologically related. Did that matter? Did he know? And if so, when did he find out?

Joaquín knew she had been raped yet never told me or comforted her. Why? He and I could've banded together to try to figure out who had done it. Gone to where the party was held, interviewed people, gone to the police. And even if we hadn't been able to find out anything, we could've been there for Mia. I was certain that if I'd been told about what happened, I would have convinced Mia it wasn't her fault and she would've come back to me. I would've taken care of her and married her and raised her son no matter if I was the father or not.

Also, Joaquín was accused of killing Tiffany, the woman who gave my son to her mom to raise. That could not be a coincidence. He either knew all along that she had our son and killed her to ensure her silence. That possibility was so horrifying that I didn't even want to think about it. Or he found out she was involved in kidnapping our son and killed her in a rage, which would make him a good guy—a hero who killed to protect our child.

That still didn't explain why he never told me or Mia about the child, so I had my doubts.

I rummaged through my desk to find the number of my vet. I needed to get Curry her shots and get her spayed. But my hand landed on something else.

A box containing the engagement ring I had bought for Mia.

I'd chucked that stupid ring across my hospital room the day she'd left me. I'd considered pawning it, swallowing it with some tequila, or even incinerating it. But something made me hold on to the ring, maybe a small hope that, one day, Mia and I would get back together again.

I opened the box and stared at the small oval diamond ring. It had a thin, rose-gold band, which I had thought would look perfect on Mia's finger.

I snapped the box shut and shoved it to the bottom of my seabag. Too many what-ifs and unknowns. I felt like I was living in my own choose-your-own-adventure book. Somehow, I doubted that I could change this saga into a happy ending.

62

MIA

The next morning my head buzzed like I had a hangover, which was probably from all the crying I'd done last night. Grant didn't make any smartass remarks to me, though. He greeted me with a loving kiss, freshly brewed coffee, and slow-cooked oatmeal. For the first time since this nightmare started, I wasn't scared of what he would say next or what my next lie would have to be.

I pressed the coffee mug to my lips. "How'd you sleep?"

"Not good. Curry kept me up all night meowing." He stared at my hair. "You going to stay blonde?"

"Not forever. I do need to touch up my roots. I thought you liked blondes?"

He smirked. "I like your natural color." He took my hand across the breakfast table. "Finish up. We need to go see your brother."

I shoveled down my oatmeal, hopped into the shower, quickly dressed, and we left.

We sat in silence in the truck as we made our now familiar route to the jail. My nerves were raw, and I kept glancing at Grant, wondering what he was thinking.

Before we exited the truck, Grant turned to me. "Remember what we talked about. Only tell him about the DNA. That's it. Not about finding out that Julián is our son, not about Joaquín knowing you were raped, none of that. Promise me."

"I promise."

He leaned over to my side of the truck and gave me a kiss.

We walked into the jail and followed the same procedure, but it was faster this time. Apparently, we were becoming regulars here and the guards were starting to recognize us. I wasn't sure how I felt about that, so I just gave them a tight smile as I passed.

As I waited for Joaquín to turn up into the room, I realized I felt uneasy about seeing him. Everything had changed when I found out my son was alive. Nothing made sense to me anymore.

But I couldn't allow my mind to doubt him, and I wouldn't give up on him when I'd been through so much to help him. I had to believe in him until I had irrefutable evidence that he was guilty. If I didn't, who would?

Joaquín grinned when he saw us. He picked up the phone, and I clutched the other end. "Damn, I can't even miss you two. You're allowed to go on living your lives." I glanced at Grant, who just gave me a small shrug. "I'm playing. What's up?"

I turned back to my brother and gave him a pursed smile, debating how to handle this awkward conversation. I didn't know the best way to ask, so I just let the words come. "Did you know we aren't biological siblings?"

His face turned white, and his brow furrowed. "What the fuck are you talking about, sis?"

I'd rehearsed this answer in my head, remembering the lie I'd created about why I would've needed his DNA. "I'm working with a private investigator to help you get out of here. He asked for your DNA sample to check for other evidence. I didn't have one of yours, so I sent mine since we're siblings, then later I found your hairbrush and sent hairs from it in. The lab said there is no biological relationship between us."

His fist clenched. "I don't know what the fuck you're talking about, Mia. You're my sister. Maybe your guy fucked up?"

Fuck, he didn't know.

I glanced at Grant again, but this time, his gaze was locked on Joaquín.

"No, it isn't a mistake. I had it retested with a letter you sent me—he took the DNA from the envelope seal. I don't know what to say. Maybe Mama and Papa adopted you? Or me?"

"Fuck if I know. So, what the fuck are you saying? Because of some piece of paper, you're no longer my sister? We grew up together. You're everything to me." His voice dripped with desperation.

"No, no, it isn't that at all. I swear. I just wanted to know if you knew."

"No, I didn't fucking know. Papa and Mama's secrets died with them. Not that it matters. You are my sister, Mia. Mine. No matter what that fucking test says. No piece of paper is going to change the way I feel about you. I love you. Is this why you came here today? To destroy the only thing good left in my life?"

"God, no. I just thought you should know."

His vein visibly throbbed. "Fuck you, both. I'm stuck in here, and you're running DNA and shit? What the fuck does that have to do with the case?"

"The PI wanted to run your DNA against other evidence at the crime scene. If we can find someone else's DNA in the room, it could prove someone else was in that room other than you and Tiffany. I had no idea I would find this out."

He exhaled and clutched the phone. "Well, that didn't solve shit. Maybe you need to look closer to home." His gave Grant an intense, fevered stare.

What the fuck? Was he insinuating that Grant had killed Tiffany?

I glared at Grant. His arms were crossed, and his teeth were clenched. Grant stood and walked out of the room.

Fuck. My thoughts froze. I looked up at the wall, as if it would give me some answers.

Finally, the cloud evaporated from my mind, and I forced myself to speak again, softly. "What the fuck does that mean?"

"It means what it means." He blew out a deep breath and narrowed his eyes on me. "Never mind. Go run after your boyfriend who treats you like shit. Do you know how many women he fucked after you left him? He doesn't love you, Mia. Not like I do. I'm done."

Joaquín dropped the phone and signaled to the guard to open the door back out of the waiting room.

I gathered my purse and exited the visitor room. Grant was waiting for me by the door.

"Dammit. That didn't go well."

Grant stood and grabbed my wrist, tugging me toward the door. "No. It went perfectly. Don't you see?"

"See what? What are you talking about? He's destroyed, and I just basically told him that the only family he has left isn't really his family at all. Of course he'd be upset."

"Yeah. And he reacted by accusing me of killing Tiffany."

"No, he didn't. He didn't say that."

"He didn't have to. He was looking right at me when he said it."

Grant was right. Joaquín had seemed to imply that Grant was involved. But I would never believe that, either. They were both innocent. They had to be.

Grant led me out of the jail. Once safely inside his truck, he snapped.

"Wake the fuck up. Joaquín is hiding something from you. I'm not sure what. But he *knew* about Julián. Now he's freaking out about a DNA test. Don't you get it? He either killed Tiffany or he's involved somehow in the kidnapping of our son."

"No! How could you say that? He clearly name-dropped Julián to alert us to his presence. He obviously knew that he had been kidnapped but was trying to protect him."

Grant sped down the freeway. "How the fuck would he even know Julián wasn't Tiffany's kid? What? He just saw a picture of the boy and thought to himself, 'Wow, that kid looks like my sister's baby that I didn't know she had! I should keep this a secret but also drop ambiguous clues. That's a great idea!' Seriously? Wake. The. Fuck. Up. You're so fucking blinded by your love for him, you aren't seeing what is right in front of you."

I had absolutely no response for that. I didn't have the answers and I refused to follow his logic or reasoning.

"He's not who you think he is—he hasn't been for years," Grant rambled on. "I protected you, but it's time for you to learn the truth. Joaquín wasn't a saint—we now know he used drugs. He also fucked a bunch of women and always treated them like shit; he always had secrets. We all have secrets. It wasn't my place to tell you, but now we need to examine the facts."

"So he partied hard, who cares? You're no saint, either. He just told me you fucked a bunch of women too while we were broken up. Emma at the strip club told me the same thing."

"Who gives a flying fuck how many women I slept with when we were broken up? You left me and we weren't together, that's what breaking up means. And I never treated them like shit. They were meaningless hookups I had trying to get over you."

Whatever. He was right but that wasn't the point. "He didn't kidnap our son! And he's not a murderer."

Grant reached across my lap and turned my face toward him, gripping my chin in his hand.

"No, Mia. That's where you're wrong. We're SEALs, that's what we do. Joaquín is a killer, and so am I."

63

GRANT

We didn't talk for the entire ride back to my place. When we arrived, Mia retreated to the office, slamming the door shut behind her. The whole afternoon was a mess. I hadn't meant to yell at her. She was just so thick-headed sometimes, and I didn't understand why she just couldn't see what was so clear to me.

I looked at the door she was hiding behind and heaved a deep breath. If I went in after her, we would just end up fighting more. She needed space. Hell, I needed space, too, so I grabbed my keys off the table and headed to Liberty Public Market.

I walked into the market and inhaled the scent of freshly brewed coffee and slow-roasted carnitas. I loved Liberty Station. It was a former Naval base that had been turned into a gathering for artisan foods, craft beers, entertainment, and shopping.

A tall white bin of sunflowers caught my eye, so I gathered a bunch and purchased them.

When Mia had left me, I'd become a changed man. I had been romantic and loving but turned hard and cynical that day. Though I could never go back to who I was before, a part of the old me remained.

I decided to plan something special for Mia. I bought a New York strip steak for me, a vegan smoked apple and sage sausage for Mia, a salad, and a nice bottle of wine.

It was a small offering of peace, but I hoped it would be enough.

When I returned to my place, she opened the door, and I handed her flowers.

"Thank you. These are beautiful." She gave me a kiss as if the fight had been forgiven already, and placed them in a pitcher of water that she used for a vase.

"You are beautiful." I started cooking our dinner as she leaned against the counter, watching me.

"So tell me, where did you learn to dance like that?"

A blush spread on her cheeks. "Well, I always danced growing up, you knew that. Ballet and jazz. Cumbia with my mom. But I took pole dancing lessons in San Francisco. It was really fun actually—the dancing, not the taking my clothes off part. It's hard too and like the best workout for my arms."

I laughed. I completely admired that she had fully thrown herself into this psychotic charade. "Well, from now on, I'm happy to be your audience. Your only audience. I'll even install a pole in the bedroom. Maybe for your next challenge, you can train to be the first female SEAL."

She raised the glass to her lips. "I would, but I don't want to make you look bad. I run very fast and per my small arms instructor, I have a ninety-five percent shooting accuracy. I'd smoke you."

Smartass. "Oh, you think so?" I grabbed her, carried her to the sofa, and pinned her down as she giggled. I kissed her, and she kissed me back, us both laughing. And for a few brief moments, we just enjoyed being with each other. We were perfectly in the moment, no stress about the past or future.

"I think the food is burning," she mumbled between kisses. I jumped up and strode to the kitchen. My steak was a bit too dark, but her meal was okay.

"It's still good." I smiled over my shoulder at her before plating everything and carrying it to the table. "So, when we get our son back, what is our plan?"

She bit her lip as she poured us both wine. "If we get him back."

"We're going to get him back. Are you going to move in here and take care of him while I work? I have a deployment coming up soon."

Her eyes brightened and she gave me a hopeful smile. "I know. Yes, of course I'd love that. I probably can finish my last few courses at SDSU and transfer the credits for my degree." Her smile vanished, and her brow furrowed. "This will be so hard on him. He doesn't even know us. He will probably need therapy."

We'll all need therapy after this. "Yeah, well, we're his parents. We'll get through this. We can move to a house on base and give him a normal life." I paused, not wanting her to clue into my plan. Thankfully, she seemed to miss the implication of my words.

"We can work out the details once we get custody of him. Do you want to watch a movie?"

"Sure. My choice, though."

After dinner, she sat on the sofa, and I popped in a DVD. Her jaw dropped when it started.

"We're watching my old play? Seriously? You never wanted to watch it. You never even saw me act."

"I know. I'm sorry. I was such a selfish asshole. But clearly you're a great actress. I'm sorry I never supported your dreams like you supported mine."

"It's okay. I understood. But thanks, this means a lot." She relaxed in my arms as I watched her perform Portia in *The Merchant of Venice*. By her first soliloquy, I was blown away by her talent. She completely transformed into her character.

Just like she had transformed into Ksenya.

And as happy as I was with her, I questioned if I really had any idea who Mia really was. Or if she was putting on a play, with me as her captive audience.

The next morning, I slipped out before Mia woke and drove straight to Kyle's pad in Mission Beach. Dude had more money than I would ever see in my lifetime, and the dumbass gave up that lifestyle to go hunt terrorists. I loved what I did, and I knew he loved it, too, but it didn't stop me from thinking he was out of his mind for becoming a SEAL. He was, however, exceptional at what he did, and if anyone could find this woman, it would be Kyle. He was whip smart, and even former Team guys had mad respect for him.

I rang the doorbell, hoping I wasn't waking anyone. Kyle answered and stepped aside so I could come in. His girlfriend Sara, one of the cheerleaders who had been kidnapped on a USO tour, was relaxing on his sofa—another SEAL falling in love with the girl he saved. It was like none of us could ever be in a normal relationship.

Kyle put his hand on my shoulder. "What's up, my man?"

"Can we talk?"

Kyle gave me the same look he gave me when I was smarting off at work before nodding to the back hallway that led to his office.

I waved to Sara as we passed and she smiled as she returned the gesture. She'd completely recovered from being held hostage in Afghanistan, but every time I saw her, my mind flashed to how she looked when we'd found her. Blood on her neck, dirt covering her body. Cowering in a cave in her bra and panties. Finding her alive had been one of the best moments of my life. One of the moments that I realized all the pain and sacrifices I'd made to become a SEAL had been worth it. We'd saved her.

I stepped into his office and Kyle shut the door behind us.

"This is about the boy, isn't it? The guys I have on it think that he could be Joaquín's son. Is that why he did it? Because Tiffany had his kid and he never knew?"

My heart pounded. I had no intention of lying to Kyle. "The boy isn't Joaquín's son. He's mine."

Kyle's eyes widened, and he leaned forward, bracing his elbows on his desk. "Say what? Are you serious, man?"

"Yup. Turns out Mia was pregnant. I never knew—just found out. She left me and had the baby in San Francisco. But she was told our baby died in the hospital, which obviously wasn't the case since he's alive and well. We have no idea how Tiffany ended up with him."

His mouth slackened, and he rubbed his jaw. "Are you sure?"

"Positive."

"So, Mia's back in town? I thought you hadn't heard from her. I've been worried about her. You were such a dick to her when she came to The Pickled Frog asking for help."

"Yeah, she's back. Actually . . . she's Ksenya."

Kyle let out a laugh and smirked. "Are you serious, man? You're not going to believe me, but I had my suspicious. I chalked them up to too many concussions. She looks so different—what did she do? She had plastic surgery to fool us?"

"Something like that."

"Wow. You're blowing my mind."

"Yeah, well, it gets worse. I don't think Joaquín is innocent. There are just too many questions, ya know?"

He nodded. "Joaquín was always a bit off, but murder? I'm not sure. Don't get me wrong, lots of guys snap for no real reason, but just because you have questions doesn't mean he's a murderer. But do you remember what happened in Afghanistan? Before Sara was taken?"

That deployment was a haze. War was always a mind fuck. "No, what?"

"Joaquín had snuck off one night on that deployment with some village elders. When I asked him about it, he looked me dead in the eye and said he wanted to have tea with them, learn about their culture. He technically hadn't done anything wrong, so I didn't write him up, but why the fuck would he do that?"

My mouth became dry. "I never knew about that." Maybe he had been smuggling drugs. I remembered that he had been buddies with another Team guy who had smuggled drugs from Aruba but I'd never thought anything about it. That dude had been kicked out. "Did you ever catch Joaquín doing drugs?"

Kyle glared at me. "No, did you?"

"No." I paused, careful not to rat out Mitch. "But I heard rumors that Joaquín had been using and had a local dealer."

"Yeah, well he pissed clean. I'll look into the drugs, too. But for now," he said, waving away that whole line of thought, "back to your son. We haven't located him or the woman yet. We did find the company they rented the U-Haul from and traced the truck to San Rafael."

San Rafael was in Marin County across the Golden Gate Bridge. It was also where Joaquín and Mia were from. "Anything else?"

"We traced the grandma's family to an area called the Canal. Staked out her sister's house, but we haven't found anything. But my guy asked around, and someone said he thought he saw the grandma and the kid at the bus stop, but we couldn't verify it."

"I need to check it out." I had to go up there. With Mia. See if we could find something . . . visit the hospital . . . get her medical records.

"Hold up. No, man. Let me handle it. I'm not doubting that you could find them, but if they know you are on to them, they could spook and disappear. You can't risk that. If you go up there, I'd steer clear of the area. I have men on it."

"Fine. Okay. Can you get someone to investigate SF General. Our son was born there. September sixth, two years ago. His birth name was Elías Joaquín Cruz."

Kyle picked up a pen and wrote the information on a note pad. "I'm on it. What's your plan when we find them? Kidnap him back?" He smirked, apparently knowing me too well.

"I mean, what can I do? If I do that, it will look like I had a motive for Tiffany's killing. My psycho SEAL instinct is to find him and take him by gunpoint, but I realize that's insane."

"Insane and illegal. The law doesn't give a shit about reasons. Kidnapping is still a felony."

"Right." I nodded, not really caring if it was a felony. I just didn't want Kyle to pull the plug on the manhunt. "Plus, I don't want to traumatize the boy. I mean, he doesn't know me, the woman he knows as his mom is dead, and he only has his grandma. I need to keep my emotions out of it, and just come up with a plan that keeps him protected as much as possible."

"True that. Once we find him, we can work with law enforcement to take him from his grandmother. You need official DNA tests, statements from you and Mia, and a good lawyer. Joaquín is using Daniel, but I'll be honest, I don't trust that motherfucker. If I were you, I wouldn't breathe a word of this to anyone on the Team, either. I'll let you know the second I hear anything about your boy. We have a good group on this case. And don't worry about the cost. We will find him."

"Thanks, man. I feel like you're the only person I can trust."

"I got your six." Kyle gave me some business cards for lawyers. "Need anything else?"

I hesitated to ask, but I was desperate. "Is there any way I can get some unofficial leave? Just a few days. I want to go up to Marin and check out some stuff. I promise I'll steer clear of my kid. I can work doubles on base when I get back."

Kyle stood and placed his hand on my shoulder. "Consider it done. Just don't get into any trouble. That's an order."

"Yes, sir. I appreciate it." I shook his outstretched hand and left his place. I made some more phone calls on the way home, securing a flight to

Marin and booking a hotel and rental car. As I planned, another idea settled in my mind, and as much as I tried to reason my way around it, I couldn't. My head and heart were at war with each other, and by the time I pulled into my parking spot, rationality was lying on the ground, bleeding and broken.

It lost.

64

MIA

Ever since Elías died, it had felt as if a part of my soul were missing. The urge to be with him and mother him had only become stronger since I learned he was alive. When I added Grant into the mix, it made me yearn for something more. I wanted to belong to someone. Create a new family to replace the one I had lost. Elías bound Grant and I together forever.

I jumped in the shower and heard Hero bark a greeting to Grant when he came back from wherever he had been. When I emerged, clean and wrapped in a big fluffy towel, I saw him packing his seabag.

"Where are we going? Oh my God. Did you find Julián?"

"No, not yet. But there was a sighting in San Rafael. Kyle doesn't want us intervening, but I figured we could go up there anyway and go through those medical records you said you'd kept."

"Can you get off work?"

"Kyle's covering for me. Come on, our plane leaves in an hour."

"Plane? I don't want to go to the airport. I mean, my Ksenya documents may be good, but they're fake. And I don't look like my old IDs."

"My buddy's taking us. He's a Blue Angel."

"Wow, really? That's nice of him." Damn. I loved Blue Angels. When Joaquín and I were kids, my father would drive us to the top of a hill in Tiburon to watch them fly. After I told Grant about the trips, he made it a point to take me to see them every time they did their airshows at Miramar.

We dropped Hero and Curry off with friends and headed to Carlsbad Airport to meet Beckett, who would be flying us in a small airplane. I had to admit I was disappointed by the news. I'd secretly hoped that I'd be able to hitch a ride in one of those glorious blue-and-yellow Hornets. Still, it was cool that we were getting a ride in a private plane.

We walked over to the hangar, and Grant strode toward the gorgeous man in a green flight suit who was waiting for us. He was tall, had dark hair, and wore black aviators.

"Hey, man, this is my girlfriend, Mia."

I smiled and tried to play it cool even though my stomach exploded in butterflies when Grant called me his girlfriend. We were finally back together.

"Nice to meet you. I'm Beck."

"Nice to meet you, too," I said. "Thanks for taking us."

"No problem. Works out fine. I was headed up to the wine country for the night anyway."

We climbed into the tiny plane, and I wanted to laugh. I might love to watch the Blue Angels doing their stunts, but I hated flying. "How do you know him?" I whispered to Grant.

"He deployed with us a year ago. He was our pilot, and then he got selected to be an Angel for the upcoming season. I'm happy for him. It's harder to become an Angel than a Navy SEAL."

Grant and Joaquín were always bragging about how impossible it was to graduate from BUD/S so it was nice to hear that Grant could acknowledge that Beck was as badass as he was. I gave Grant a beaming smile and tried to stuff my nerves down as deep as I could. Still, I spent the entirety of the two-hour flight white-knuckling the side of my seat, and Grant laughed at me more than once.

We landed at the Sonoma airport, and I was the first person off the plane. I wanted to puke, but Grant just rubbed my back and led me to the rental car he had waiting for us.

"Are you sure we can't go look for Elías?" I asked when I regained my composure.

"Kyle doesn't want us seen around the area just in case we get spotted and they get spooked."

I gritted my teeth. "So we're really just here for medical records?"

"Well, those and anything else you want to bring home with you. You said it was in storage, let's go get it."

I took a deep breath and let my shoulders slump a bit. We really weren't here to find our son. Grant was here to find some intel about Joaquín. "Yeah, we have a Grange box in San Rafael. There's not much in there. Joaquín and I threw out most of it. We pretty much kept pictures. What are you looking for?"

"Nothing. Anything. Something."

Great answer. I directed him to the row of storage boxes behind on the side of the freeway. I hadn't been back since after Elías died. I didn't even have a key. I was about to suggest calling a locksmith, but Grant just pulled into a parking spot and cut the engine.

"Which number is it?"

"Three-oh-four, but I don't have a key."

He just turned and gave me a wry smile and waited. It took me a minute, but then it clicked. He was a SEAL, and SEALs didn't need keys.

"Right. Let's go then."

Grant grabbed a Gerber tool out of his pocket and picked open the lock as if it were nothing more than a damn bow holding the door closed. In my mind, I always knew what he was capable of, but I had to admit it totally turned me on to see his ninja skills in person.

Grant rolled up the steel door, revealing all the dust and spiders. My first step was toward a small box I'd shoved in the back of the locker just in case Joaquín visited the unit. I trusted Joaquín, of course, but I hadn't wanted him to go through that box. I'd never told him I'd been pregnant and didn't want him to find out that way. I opened the box and found the manila envelope where I'd kept all my pregnancy records.

Grant sat beside me, and we looked at blood tests, ultrasounds, and invoices. He gazed longingly at the final ultrasound, and I had to close my eyes to stop the tears from welling up. I remembered what it felt like to have my son in my belly, the joy of counting his kicks, the thrill of seeing him on the doctor's screen. Hopefully, I would replace those memories with better ones.

When I reached the bottom of the pile, I expected to find another stack of paperwork, but there was nothing.

"That's weird. I swore I put the hospital papers in this envelope."

Grant grabbed the pile and rapidly thumbed through the papers. "They're not here. Did you put them in another file?"

"No. This was the only one I brought that day. I must've misplaced it— my memory is so hazy. I was a wreck after he died."

Grant clenched his jaw. "Or . . . Joaquín could've taken them."

"What? Please don't start with me again. Why on earth would Joaquín take my paperwork? He didn't even know I was pregnant. Maybe I left them at my old apartment."

But I remembered bringing them here. I had sat in alm*ost this exact spot and read th*e words: infant not compatible with life. I didn't read them once or twice. No. I read them a thousand times through my tear-blurred eyes, clutching my belly, trying to convince myself to keep living a life without my son.

"Maybe whoever kidnapped my baby followed me here and took them? You picked the lock. If someone can kidnap a newborn, they would probably be capable of picking a lock, too."

"You know who taught me to pick locks? Your brother." Grant shook his head and grabbed another box. I was too spent to argue with him. But I was sick of him blaming Joaquín for every bad thing that had ever happened to me.

I quickly migrated to the old photo albums, losing myself in memories. Joaquín and me at the park, Joaquín and me holding hands on my first day of school, Joaquín and me posing near the Christmas tree. But then I focused on some older pictures. Pictures of my parents. I found one of my mom when she was pregnant with Joaquín and another of my father holding me as an infant. I couldn't find any of my mom pregnant with me. Nor could I find any of my father holding Joaquín as a baby.

I grabbed an album and turned to Grant, who was knee deep in some old papers. "I can't do this right now, I need a break. I'm going to run and get some coffee."

He threw me the keys. "Okay. I'll be here when you get back."

I didn't even kiss him goodbye. I jumped in the car and drove away from my past. I hoped Grant found whatever he was looking for. All I knew was that who I was looking for, our son, was nowhere in that storage unit full of memories.

65

GRANT

I didn't believe for a second that Mia had misplaced her hospital records. I agreed with her that they were stolen, just not by whom. Joaquín had taken leave after the murder, and I would put money on the idea that he went to the storage unit for something and found the papers.

I didn't have any proof of that. Maybe I could find an old security camera. I'd put Kyle on it.

I was starting to get discouraged going through this junk: old tax returns, a few pieces of furniture, boxes of old toys. But I wasn't going to give up until I scoured this place.

Thirty minutes passed, and Mia still wasn't back, which was fine by me. I didn't want her around in case I found something. I opened the last box and cringed. Their parents' will, a funeral program, and a newspaper clipping about their accident were the first things I picked up.

I skimmed the article. Their parents had been driving home after visiting family in San Jose. A suspected drunk driver hit her parents' car dead on when they were a few miles from home. The driver had never been caught, though witnesses saw two Hispanic men fleeing in a truck, which had later been reported stolen. The truck had been registered to a Rafael Hernandez, but he had denied any involvement and had an alibi at the time of the crash.

Rafael? Joaquín's drug dealer?

My mouth went dry as I pulled out my phone and unlocked the screen.

I googled "Rafael Hernandez, San Rafael." But before my slow ass phone could load the page, the rental car came to stop outside the door.

Come on, dammit.

Mia walked toward the box as a photo finally loaded.

Holy shit.

I closed the window on my phone, my mind buzzing.

"Did you find anything?"

I stood. "Nah, babe. Just some old receipts. Let's get out of here. I want to take you somewhere."

I had to protect Mia from Joaquín. He knew the man accused of killing her parents. He was probably involved in kidnapping our son. She blindly trusted and loved her brother. She was in way over her head.

Hell, I was pretty sure I was in over my head, too.

66

GRANT

P ushing every single thought about that picture out of my head, I drove toward Mt. Tam. Mia had brought me here once when we first started dating. I remembered hiking to the summit, finding a secluded place, and telling her for the first time that I loved her. That night we'd made love under the stars. For the first time in my life, I'd allowed myself to truly become lost in her.

She figured out where I was headed the second I exited in Mill Valley. "Ah, you remembered." She squeezed my thigh.

"Of course. Do you know how many times I thought about that night while I was deployed? I remembered every second of our time together. Wanting to come back here again with you was the reason I survived after the roadside bomb." That was true. Every night I pushed through my pain, willing myself not to give up so I could see her again, kiss her again, make love to her again.

We drove up the mountain, and I was overtaken by the view. Being out in nature, appreciating the landscape meant the world to me. I'd been around the globe so many times and I never took for granted the freedom to explore the outdoors without the threat of being caught up in mountain warfare.

After we reached our destination, I grabbed a few things from my seabag, took Mia's hand, and led her to the top of the mountain.

We passed some hikers on the path but eventually veered off the trail.

The scent of oak trees and sage intoxicated me. This spot was as breath-taking as I had remembered it. Shrouded by the towering redwoods, I took a deep breath, determined in the decision I was about to make.

I threw down two blankets and then knelt to the ground. Mia was about to crouch down beside me, but I stopped her, grabbed the small box out of my jacket, and took her hand.

"Angelita Mia Cruz. You're the craziest woman I've ever met. But no matter how hard I try to deny it, I love you. After all these years, I still love you. I'll never love another woman. Will you marry me?"

I expected her jaw to drop or maybe for her to let out a scream, but instead, her eyes welled with tears. "Are you sure? I thought you would never forgive me."

"I'm sure. We have a son together, and we need to try to make our relationship work for him. But this isn't just about him. I love you, and I'll love you until the day I die. I think about you every minute of every day, no matter how many times I try to stop myself. Marry me, Mia."

She wrapped her arms around my neck. "Yes, yes!"

I placed the ring on her finger, and she showered me with kisses.

I returned her kisses, and this time, I didn't hold myself back. My hands cupped her face as I claimed her for mine. For forever. My mouth took hers, and I could feel her come alive, her hands exploring my body, finally letting down her own guard.

I threw her on the blanket and pressed my chest on top of her, pulling the other blanket over us. We were isolated, but I wasn't stupid enough to think we were completely alone on the mountain. No one would ever see what was mine ever again. No one other than me.

I pushed her jeans off her hips and kicked them to the ground, the soft earth melting under her body. I pulled my own pants off. I kissed her neck, rubbed her nipples until she moaned. She was writhing underneath me as I pulled down her panties, my fingers lingering on her slit for only a second before she was pulling me to her. I didn't hesitate. I sank into her heat, feeling at home inside her.

I couldn't control myself—not just my cock but my emotions as well. I pounded into her over and over as I kissed her. She met me move for move, rocking against each of my thrusts until her breath started to come in puffs and her whole body tightened around me.

"I love you, Mia. I fucking love you so much."

She dug her fingers into my back. "I love you, too."

The pressure built in my balls, and I exploded inside her as she gasped with her own release.

Afterward, we lay in silence. She cuddled on my chest, and I stroked her hair.

I did love her.

I would do anything to protect her.

67

MIA

I stared down at my ring. It was perfect—an oval diamond set on a rose-gold band. I was engaged. I couldn't even believe it. Only a few weeks ago, Grant would barely speak to me. It was a strange turn of events, but I embraced the joy of it all.

"Are we camping up here? Did you bring any equipment?"

"No, I have a reservation in Tiburon. I just wanted to propose here. It's always where I wanted to propose. Beats the hospital."

Ouch. I wished I had never broken up with him that day and let him propose to me. Our lives would be so different now. "I agree. This was the best proposal. Super romantic and meant even more to me because this is where you first told me you loved me. It was perfect. We should get married up here, too. But I want to wait until Joaquín gets exonerated so he can be here."

He gave me a halfhearted smile and clenched his teeth. I was too happy to fight with him.

"Let's get going." Grant was already on his feet and grabbing blankets to fold them. I stood to help, and when everything was stashed back in his bag, we headed to the rental car and drove to the hotel. Grant didn't let go of my hand once.

He treated me to a romantic dinner, before we retired to the room, made love, and fell asleep in each other's arms.

Hours later, I woke to the sound of my phone beeping.

Mitch: We need to talk.

Fuck. Mitch? Grant still didn't know that I had gone with Mitch to Rafael's or that we had done drugs there. Or that Mitch had kissed me and I'd kissed him back. Or that he'd been the one who had driven me to Temecula to find Julián. Oh my God, Grant would freak. I never planned to keep it from him forever. I just hadn't found the right time to drop that bomb on him. Seeing Mitch recently was different from seeing him at the club. I'd gone behind Grant's back after Grant had found out who I really was.

Me: Stop texting me. If it's important, you can tell Grant.

Mitch: This is urgent, Mia. Please call me. It's about Joaquín.

I deleted his texts, my heart beating rapidly against my ribs. I would tell Grant tomorrow about going to Rafael's with Mitch, and about Mitch driving me to Temecula. Then, after I had begged for his forgiveness for lying to him . . . yet again, we would find out what Mitch needed to tell me. And we would do it together.

68

GRANT

I 'd slept better than I had in years holding Mia. My fiancée. I would do anything to make this work. For her, for me, for our son.

We had an early morning breakfast in Tiburon before we met up with Beck, and he flew us home.

After we picked up Hero and Curry, we went back to my place. It was still early afternoon, so I texted Kyle letting him know that I needed to talk to him when he had a second. I wanted him to find out everything he could about Mia's parents and Rafael.

My phone rang, but it wasn't Kyle, it was Paul.

"I need to see you right away. Meet me at the NCIS office downtown. And wear your dress whites."

What the fuck? "May I ask why, sir?"

His voice switched from formal to angry. "No, Carrion, just get the fuck down here."

Fuck. I tossed my phone on my bed and grabbed my uniform from the closet and quickly pressed it. I hated this fucking outfit. The bib, the bell bottoms, the neckerchief—I looked like I belonged on a fucking Cracker Jack box.

As I was polishing my boots, Mia walked into the bedroom.

"What's happening, sailor? Your ass looks amazing in those bells."

"Not now, woman. Paul called me down to NCIS." I gave her a quick kiss on the lips.

Her face twisted. "Is this about Joaquín?"

"I don't know. Got to go." I left her standing there with her mouth open as I dashed out the door and jumped into my truck.

As I sped down the freeway, I convinced myself this had to be about Joaquín. I'd never been called in for anything. My record had always been stellar. And, God willing, it would remain so.

I arrived at the building, flashed my ID, and checked in at the front desk. An older lady led me to a room where I found Paul sitting in a chair.

"What's this regarding, sir?"

Before he could answer me, a woman entered in a tight black suit, her bob grazing her shoulders. Her makeup was natural, her body was perfect, but one look at her face, and my breath stopped.

It was Autumn.

"Petty Officer Carrion, thank you for joining us today," she said, sliding past me to take a seat at the table.

What the fuck? Gone was the stripper makeup and clothes. I'd seen her dancing in a thong with gold pasties on her tits.

"I'm Special Agent Ashley Pierce. I can assume you know who I am, correct?"

Stunned I looked to Paul, but he didn't offer an explanation.

"Yes, ma'am."

"Good. I've been undercover as Autumn while I've been investigating drug smuggling within the SEAL teams. Joaquín Cruz is currently being investigated for his suspected involvement with the Ramirez cartel. We need your help. In return, I will put all our resources toward getting your son back."

Holy shit! What the fuck was Joaquín involved in? A gang was bad enough, but he was working with a cartel?

My mind replayed every encounter I'd ever had with Autumn. First at Paul's party. How she had targeted me, teased the fuck out of me but never let things go too far. I'd next seen her at the first party I took Ksenya to. She'd cornered me there, offering to help me free Joaquín, and she'd told me that Tiffany had been involved in something shady. And Autumn had been the one who had shown me a picture of my son.

She was as great an actress as Mia was.

Agent Pierce. It made perfect sense. How had I not suspected she was an agent?

I attempted to regain my composure. "Of course. I'll do anything."

"You are not to mention any part of this conversation to Mia Cruz. We believe she may be involved also."

My mouth dropped open, and she gave me a small smile.

"Yes, we know who she is."

"Mia is not involved. And I think you should know that we're engaged now. So you can stop yourself there. I've known her for years. Yes, she underwent this extreme makeover, but she did that because she loves Joaquín, not because they are in cahoots together."

"Are you sure about that? How much do you trust her?"

If she had asked me that a month ago, I would have laughed in her face and said that I didn't trust Mia at all. That had changed, though. I did trust Mia.

When Agent Pierce reached into a manila envelope and pulled out three black-and-white pictures, my eyes narrowed. My stomach lurched when they came into focus. One was Mia doing cocaine with Rafael. The next one was Mitch and Mia kissing as Rafael looked on, Mitch's hand gripping her thigh. My throat burned, and I cringed at the sight of her straddled on his lap. And the last picture was of them sitting in Mitch's truck—location tagged in Temecula. He had been the one who had given her a ride to Julián's house. The pictures were date stamped three days ago. The day I'd found out that Julián was mine.

"While we were at the bar with Rafael, I had another agent set up surveillance at Rafael's house. These pictures were taken the next day."

Mia had gone behind my back even after she knew I knew who she really was. After we'd fucked. After we'd agreed that she would let me control the investigation. She'd done drugs . . . with Mitch. She'd kissed him.

Pathetically, I told myself that maybe she was still trying to get information about Joaquín, justifying her actions. But it didn't matter. None of it did. She had promised that she wasn't hiding anything else from me, yet irrefutable proof of her lies were spread out on the tabletop.

"You have my word." My jaw clenched and I struggled with my anger.

I was going to fucking kill Mitch.

PART VI

CONSUME

SEVEN DEADLY SEALS EPISODE 6

"THE FLESH ENDURES
THE STORMS OF THE
PRESENT ALONE; THE MIND,
THOSE OF THE PAST
AND FUTURE
AS WELL AS THE PRESENT.
GLUTTONY
IS A LUST OF THE MIND."

— THOMAS HOBBES

69

GRANT

N CIS Special Agent Ashley Pierce's eyes narrowed in on me. "Your son is in grave danger. Our time is limited, and we must have your complete cooperation." Her gaze was icy—a look that told me that she felt there was a good chance I would never see my son again.

My blood ran cold. I wasn't afraid of terrorists in a firefight, bombs injuring me again, or guns pointed at my face. My only fear was being unable to save my son. If something happened to my boy, a kid I didn't even know and had only met once, it would destroy me. "Of course. I'll do anything. Please tell me everything you know."

My eyes were locked on Autumn AKA Ashley. I'd suspected her of being involved in this case but not as law enforcement. I'd been with her the night of Paul's party, and I'd realized now that it hadn't been a coincidence.

I attempted to make eye contact with my commanding officer, Paul Thompson, but his gaze remained locked on his feet. His white summer dress uniform blended into the barren walls, as did his skin, which seemed paler than normal. I felt his pain. This claustrophobic space wasn't doing anything to ease my anxiety.

"Lt. Commander Thompson, you are free to leave. I would like to speak with Petty Officer Carrion in private."

Paul didn't even reply. He stood, nodded to both of us, and made a quick exit. I watched him until the door closed again. Mitch had told me that he would hook Paul up, and in exchange Paul would tip him off about drug tests. And Ashley had Mitch's dealer, Rafael, under surveillance. Man, depending on what she had discovered, Paul's career could be over. But there was no guarantee that Ashley had unearthed any of our secrets. SEALs covered for each other. That had never been more apparent to me than when this whole ordeal started.

And although my priority was locating my son, I would not rat out my brothers. I had to tread carefully.

"Special Agent Pierce—"

Her turquoise eyes brightened with a twinkle of amusement. "Grant, I think you've earned the right to call me by my first name."

My mind flashed to our drunken makeout session the night Tiffany had been murdered. Autumn's mouth had been hot and wet, her tight little body had pressed against mine. I had tried to drown my longing for Mia in Autumn's embrace. And for a moment in time, it had worked.

"Fine, *Ashley*. Where is my son?"

She pushed out a deep breath before saying, "We don't know. What we do know is that Joaquín has gang connections and we believe he was involved in kidnapping your son from Mia in the hospital."

I almost felt relieved to hear her say that because it validated my theories, which Mia had dismissed. "When did you find out he was mine?"

"Well, officially we don't actually know he's yours. We would need a court-ordered DNA test for that. But when I brought Mia to meet the boy, I had hoped to be able to trip her up, that she would've known about her nephew. But then when I saw her reaction to the boy, I started to connect the dots. He looks like you, by the way. I found records that showed that Mia had given birth to a baby boy in San Francisco two years ago."

I was immediately suspicious of her. She had found records that had vanished from Mia's storage unit. The ones I believed Joaquín had taken. Maybe he had given them to her. How did I know she wasn't a crooked agent? And she had approached me at the SEAL party I took Ksenya to, offering to help me free Joaquín. I couldn't trust her at all. "How could you have possibly made that jump from him resembling me to him being my son? Seriously. It's a big one."

"It was just a hunch, and I'll admit it was a weak one. Grant, I'm trained to hunt down leads and test all the angles, so I did. Plus, I couldn't shake the feeling that he was Mia's kid. Since you were the only guy she'd dated, it was logical that you were the child's father. That was why I met you at the coffee house and showed you a picture of Julián so you would investigate on your own."

I tempered my anger and forced myself to acknowledge her impressive detective work. "If it weren't for you, I wouldn't have known I had a son. Thank you."

Her lips pressed into a satisfied smile. "Don't thank me until we find him. We have eyes on Joaquín's known gang and cartel connections. But so far, we have been unable to locate your boy."

"Tiffany's mom was last seen in Marin." I gave her the only piece of information I had, hoping that she could find something we couldn't.

"We know. After you gave Kyle the DNA results, he called in an inquiry to a former SEAL turned PI, who tipped us off."

Damn, NCIS had eyes and ears everywhere. "Does Kyle know who you are?"

Ashley shook her head. "No, Kyle doesn't have a clue about my involvement or my identity. Only Paul knows for now, and I'd like to keep it that way."

I wasn't going to praise her for her correct assumptions. I was more pissed that she was following me. But I wasn't going to call her out—my son's life was on the line. "You said Julián is in grave danger. Why? Isn't he with the grandmother? Is she involved? Who is she?"

"Her name is Lorraine Reynolds, and we don't think she would hurt him. But we believe that the Ramirez Cartel is holding your son as leverage to keep Joaquín in line."

She was blowing my mind. "Cartel? So what does Joaquín know about Julián? He mentioned his name to us at the jail. Mia's theory is that he did that so we could find our son. I think he did it to frame me for Tiffany's murder. Because if I had thought she had kidnapped my son, I'd have a motive to kill her. Hell, I probably would've killed her."

She eased over to me and sat so close I could inhale her floral perfume. "You shouldn't repeat that. And remember, I was with you the night of the murder. I know for certain that you didn't murder Tiffany. And for you, Grant, I would blow my cover and risk my career to ensure you were never charged." She cast a downward glance. "As for Joaquín's name drop, I have a different theory."

I hated that she was making me ask exactly what she thought, but I did it anyway. "Would you care to share?"

"No, I wouldn't. And I don't want to speculate until I have proof. We need to stick to the facts."

I exhaled, knowing that she had been running most of this investigation on her gut instinct with little facts to back her theories up.

"And the facts are that your son is missing, Joaquín has been involved with a cartel, and we aren't sure of Mia's involvement."

"This doesn't point to her being involved. It is consistent with her obsession with freeing Joaquín. As for your pictures of her and Mitch at Rafael's . . ." I closed my eyes and tried to push the thoughts of Mitch's hand riding up her thigh, her lips covering his mouth, his cock pressed against her as she straddled his lap, "they don't prove that Mia or Mitch are involved with a cartel. I know Mitch. He's a jackass, but he probably brought her there so she could scan Rafael's place. Hell, he even told me that he thought *Ksenya* could make Rafael open up."

"You knew Joaquín well also. Did you know he was involved with a cartel?"

I sneered at her.

"That's what I thought. Whatever Mia's motives are, she's lying to you. About how much, we aren't sure."

Ashley sat on her desk and crossed her legs. I scanned the room and made a mental note of the lack of personal effects in her office. There was a steel name plate, and a framed picture of a little girl. But the picture seemed dated, from the nineties by the clothes the girl was wearing. There were no other pictures on her desk.

At the party I met her at, she'd told me she'd been a screw up in school, dated some abusive guy, and didn't talk to her parents. I realized now that her story was probably a pack of lies as part of her cover, but the way she'd told me made me think there'd been an ounce of truth in her lies.

She noticed me looking around the room and hopped off the desk.

"I thought we were dealing with facts now, Ashley. What kind of proof do you have that she's still lying?"

"She's crazy, Grant. She has gone too far and done some incredibly outlandish things to free her brother. Why is she doing this? Yes, she loves him, but it isn't normal for a sister to do this for her brother. Their relationship is atypical. Maybe . . . Never mind."

"Say it, dammit. Maybe what?"

"Maybe she gave your child to Tiffany. After all, she hid the pregnancy from you, the baby's father. Have you considered that she's plotting something with Joaquín?"

I let out a bark of laughter. "No, I haven't considered that. If you believe that, you're crazier than she is. She loves her son and would never have considered giving him away." I knew she had lied to me, but I also knew why she lied. I could feel her love for me. She loved people so deeply that she was blinded by her devotion. To me, to Joaquín, and to our son. "You don't have a fucking clue about what happened to Mia. She left me because she had been raped, and then she almost died in the hospital after giving birth. Mia is elated that her son is alive. Do you have any other theories?"

Ashley's eyes bugged. "I had no idea she had been raped. I'm sorry to hear that. Did she press charges?"

"No. She doesn't know who did it."

"You just need to consider everything. You're a good man, Grant. Better than most of the SEALs I've met. I can't find anything negative in your background. You deserve better than her."

I shot a look at her. "Like you? You targeted me from day one and haven't given me a single reason to think Mia is lying about anything she knows. You were at the party when Tiffany got killed. All over me, but you were just using me. You came with Tiffany! Why were you there, damn it?"

"Because we were investigating Joaquín's connection to the cartel. Tiffany had been arrested for prostitution with a SEAL and in order to get the charges dropped, she traded us information."

"Which SEAL?"

Ashley shook her head. "I'm not going to divulge his name, but he has been disciplined and is cooperative. It isn't relevant to finding your son."

The hell it wasn't. It wasn't a secret that SEALs frequented hookers. But if the SEAL was with Tiffany, maybe that SEAL was involved with Joaquín's shady deals. Maybe that SEAL was Paul. "And you didn't know she had a kid?"

"At the time we made the deal with her, we were unaware that she had given a boy to her mother to raise. If we had known, we would have investigated that before we allowed her to go undercover for us. She tipped us off that Rafael dealt to some SEALs who also smuggled drugs. We believe Joaquín pirated drugs in Aruba and Afghanistan."

I believed that, too. Kyle had mentioned that Joaquín had snuck off one night in Afghanistan. It made perfect sense. I kept my thoughts to myself and let Ashley finish.

"That night Tiffany was supposed to just wear a wire and try to get him to talk. We think Joaquín saw the wire and killed her. Unfortunately, she's dead and Joaquín's a psychopath so we'll never know why he killed her."

"And you didn't get any of it on recording?"

"No." Her lips pursed, and I shook my head. "We believe Joaquín disabled it."

Of course he had. We had both been trained on how to deactivate bombs and disable wires. Joaquín was smart. NCIS was stupid if they thought a highly trained SEAL wouldn't notice a wire.

"If you have all this evidence against Rafael, why aren't you arresting him?"

"Because we aren't after him. We're working with the DEA, and he'll be dealt with later. I'm NCIS. My concern is drug smuggling in the Teams."

My blood chilled, remembering the picture of a young Rafael Hernandez, the man whose truck had killed Mia's parents. But maybe Rafael wasn't the mastermind; maybe Joaquín was. There were still some clues to the puzzle that both Ashley and I were missing.

"So what's the plan? What can we do now?"

She sighed and sat behind the desk. "We're working with the DA to build the case against Joaquín. Maybe if they offer him a plea deal, probation, and time served, it will be enough incentive for him to give us some information about the cartel. And he would have to reveal the location of your son."

My throat constricted. That was the stupidest idea I'd ever heard. Joaquín would never admit to anything. He would rather hang himself in jail than give up his secrets. We were SEALs. We were taught how to resist interrogation. How to lie. Not even the promise of his freedom would make him confess, and I told her as much.

"Well, we think it's the best shot we have of finding your son. The murder charge won't stick in court, and we're still building our case against the cartel. We have enough to get him on the smuggling charges, and we do believe he murdered her, but our goal is to find your child and get intel on the drug operations."

For months, I had dreamed of the day that Joaquín would be freed, that

I'd have my best friend back. But now, everything had changed. I'd learned too many of Joaquín's secrets. I didn't trust him anymore. My best friend was dead to me forever. In my heart, I knew he had killed Tiffany, and I believed that he had been involved in kidnapping my son. I wanted him to rot in jail. If he was freed, I would kill him myself.

"When will this plea happen?"

She pursed her lips. "I'm not at liberty to say. But soon enough."

Soon enough didn't cut it. This could take months, and by then who knew where my kid would be. How the fuck did they expect me to trust them to find my son when they had lost him once?

I didn't trust them. I only trusted myself.

"And when you free him, Mia will be in danger."

"Yes, she will. But we can protect her."

I laughed, not caring if it was rude. The only person who could protect Mia was me. I was still pissed as fuck about her pictures with Mitch, but she was still my girl.

I made up my mind that I'd tell Ashley what she wanted to hear, but I would plan a counter attack to ensure that neither Mia nor my son was hurt and that they would both be safe. To ensure that Joaquín wouldn't harm them, I'd assemble my own Team.

"Well, I'm yours. Whatever you need from me, I'll do."

"I need you not to mention this conversation to Mia or let Joaquín know that you suspect him of anything. The reason I called you in here today was to ask you to try to get Mia to stop her investigation into Joaquín. And you also need to stop trying to locate your son. You are hurting the case, not helping it. I need you to trust me. We have good agents on this."

I inhaled and let out a calming breath. "I won't say a word." But I purposely didn't promise her to stop doing my own intel. Luckily, she didn't call me out on my omission.

Ashley might have fooled me about her identity, but a NCIS agent wasn't any match for a SEAL. And Ashley was a fool if she thought she could outsmart Joaquín. He may be a drug smuggler, but he was still one of the best operators I'd ever met. A lethal weapon. A deadly SEAL.

I stood, locked down my anger, and forced myself to pretend to be grateful to her. She had, after all, shown me the picture of Julián that day at the coffee house. Without that photo, I might never have learned the truth.

She stood and held her hand out to me. "I'm sorry you're wrapped up with these people. I promise I will do everything to return your son. We will be in touch."

I left the room and went to my truck, already making a mental checklist of everything I needed to do.

Mia definitely had some explaining to do. I didn't believe Ashley that Mia had been involved with Joaquín's criminal activities, but Mia had still been lying to me. I had to find a way, without divulging what Ashley told me, to get Mia to tell me the truth and to get her to abandon this need to save her brother.

I needed her for once in her life to choose me over him.

70

GRANT

F irst mission—get rid of any mobile tracking devices. I drove my truck to the mechanic most of the Team guys used. It was across the street from Panthers. The neon lights seemed gaudy in the daylight, and I cringed as I imagined Mia dancing on stage, praying that I would show up, knowing that I haunted that joint.

Only two weeks ago, I had met her again as Ksenya. At least twenty girls were in that club that night, but I'd been hopelessly drawn to her. Yes, she had transformed her body into my exact physical type, but it ran deeper than that. One look at her, even under the bright lights with her eyes covered by colored contacts, and my soul recognized her as my mate.

I pulled open the door to the shop, and Carlos greeted me. "Need an oil change?"

"Hey, man. Nah, I can do that myself. Can you sweep my truck for tracking devices? I think someone is following me."

Carlos nodded, not even fazed by my request. He was used to dealing with paranoid SEALs. "Sure thing." He looked at my mileage. "I'll do a service for you, too. It will take a day or so. Do you need a loaner?"

Man must've read my mind. "That would be great."

He led me over to a line of parked vehicles. I pointed at an older model truck.

"Keys are in the ignition. I'll call you tomorrow and let you know when your truck will be ready."

"Thanks, man. I'm going to bring my fiancée's car in soon, too, but not for a few days. We're headed out of town."

His brow wrinkled, and he wiped the sweat off his forehead with his sleeve. "Yeah? Where you headed?"

"Vegas. I'm getting married tomorrow." And I was. Even though I hadn't yet asked . . .

"Congrats. Your truck will be clean and ready by the time you come back."

I thanked him and climbed into my loaner truck. It smelled a bit musty, but as long as it wasn't bugged, it was fine by me.

I stopped at the Fashion Valley Mall and purchased two new phones but transferred our old numbers. I also made sure to activate the "find my phone" app on Mia's phone so I could locate her if I needed to. Then I went next door to the jeweler and picked out wedding bands. For myself I picked a black titanium band, which was the best option for a man in my line of work.

For my beloved, I chose a rose gold band with beveled diamonds.

"Can you engrave it?"

"Sure. We can do it while you wait. What do you want it to say?"

"*Worth fighting for.*" She was. And I'd fight for her until my dying breath.

Then the jeweler made me an offer. "Do you want me to add a fidelity tracking device on the ring? Behind the diamonds. It's new technology."

My immediate thought was fuck, no. I didn't want to start my marriage by betraying Mia. And I wasn't that kind of paranoid asshole. Any guy who would install a hidden tracking device on his wife's wedding ring was a piece of shit. Why bother to get married if you didn't trust your wife?

But on second thought, the SEAL in me thought that this may be a good idea. Not to make sure she was faithful, but as a way to find her if Joaquín ever escaped and held her hostage.

I pointed at another band. Nothing fancy, just simple and gold with one diamond. "Engrave the diamond rose gold ring, no tracker. But I'll take this ring also, with a tracker." When the time was right, I'd present her both rings, explain why I wished her to wear the tracking one, and if we could ever put this mess behind us, we could burn that ring.

By the time I'd arrived back home, Mia was standing outside waiting for me.

Even though her roots were showing and her brow was furrowed, she still looked beautiful. "Where were you? I was worried sick. I called you and texted you but then my phone stopped working. What happened? Where's your truck?"

I was paranoid and assumed there was a camera or audio surveillance in my house. I placed my hand over her lips and went inside to change out of my uniform. Once I was in my civilian clothes, I grabbed Hero's leash, removed her old phone from her hands, tossed it on the sofa, and then led them both outside.

"Dammit, Grant, what the fuck are you doing?" she asked, dragging her heels as I tried to urge her along.

Once we were far enough away from my home, I turned to her. "I need you to listen to me and for once, not argue. I can't tell you any details, in fact I'm not supposed to tell you anything that was said at NCIS. Do you understand?"

She blinked back tears. "I do. I'm so sorry, I—"

I interrupted. "I believe we are under surveillance even now. The truck is a loaner. I think mine is being tracked. Yours too. I'm going to bring your car in to get swept. Until then, you aren't to drive it. Okay?"

She nodded.

"First, is there anything you need to tell me?"

She bit her lip but then exhaled. "Yes, there is. Mitch. He came by the day you went to find Julián. He took me to Rafael's place, hoping to get a lead to free Joaquín. Rafael forced me to do a line of coke, probably thinking I was a narc. I was so fucked up that when Mitch kissed me, I didn't stop him. Well, I couldn't've stopped him—Rafael thought we were together. I should have told you. I was *going* to tell you but then I found out that Julián was alive and I was too overwhelmed. I didn't mean to hide it from you."

I stared into her hazel eyes as my brain battled my heart. I forced myself to lock down my anger. "Anything else?"

She nodded. "Yes. Mitch dropped me off at your place, but then I found out from the DNA that Julián was Elías. I was still coming down from the coke so I asked Mitch to drive me to Temecula. I'm sorry I lied to you. It won't happen again."

I kissed her forehead. Relief swept over me. She had told me the truth.

She had told me everything that Ashley had shown me in the pictures. Mia was being honest with me. I had to believe in her. I did believe in her.

"I forgive you. But you need to be honest with me. There's nothing you can't tell me. Nothing. I love every part of you. Look, there's so much going on, and I can't tell you any of it. Do you understand?"

She nodded.

"I've thought it over, and I think we should get married. Tomorrow. We can drive to Vegas tonight. What do you say?"

Her eyes brightened and then narrowed a bit. "What's the rush? I mean of course I want to marry you. But I wanted to wait until everything calms down. I want Joaquín to be there, and of course, our son."

I refused to acknowledge her wish to have Joaquín present. "I want our son there, too, but I think we need to be practical. We can have a big ceremony later."

Her face wrinkled. "Practical? That's romantic. Can't we at least wait until after the trial?"

She wasn't getting it. I had to spell it out for her. "We need to get married to get on the list for housing."

"What's wrong with your place? I love being walking distance to Liberty Market. And there are so many great parks here I can take Julián to."

"My hours are so long it would be better if we could live in base housing in Coronado. That way, I could come home for lunch or even when I just have a break. I loved living here, but I was single. Also, when I deploy it might be easier for you to be around some other Team wives with kids the same age as Julián. Pat and Annie live on base and that way, if you need to go to school or even take a break, you would have someone nearby who could help."

She sighed and her shoulders slumped. "Yeah. It would probably be better to be married to prepare to file for custody of Julián. We can't give the courts any reason to deny us."

"That, too." Everything I said was true, but the real reason I wanted to marry Mia as soon as possible was to protect her from her brother.

A flush of reluctance swept across her face. "Okay, you're right. Let's do it. We can have a big ceremony later for everyone."

"That's my girl." I pulled her in for a kiss. I was shocked she didn't press me about my conversation with NCIS, but she'd been around Joaquín and me long enough to know that we weren't allowed to talk business. "Thank you for this. I can't wait to marry you."

We returned to my place and she packed our bags as I loaded our pets into the truck. Hero and Curry, who were becoming fast friends even though Curry did use Hero's tail as her own personal scratching post, were again dropped off at our friends' house and we headed to Las Vegas. After all these years, after all we'd been through, Mia was finally going to be my wife.

And I couldn't wait.

71

MIA

I stared out the window at the barren desert as Grant drove toward Las Vegas. Something was seriously off with him, and I was certain his meeting with NCIS involved new information about Joaquín. But Grant wasn't telling me what had been said. I understood that he couldn't confide in me even if he wanted to. But it wasn't just the meeting that bothered me. Something he found out today made him seriously believe we were under surveillance, which made my palms sweat. I'd spent most of the ride going over every place I'd driven to and every phone call I'd taken and every text I'd sent.

And why was Grant so insistent on marrying me as soon as possible? Just a week ago he despised me. Sure, his reasons were logical, but I couldn't shake the feeling that he had an ulterior motive.

Maybe it really was about spousal privilege. If he married me and the feds tried to get him to talk about my crazy antics, he wouldn't be forced to tell them anything. Not that anything I had done was bad enough to throw me in jail, but it could mean he was worried about my safety.

Or maybe he wanted to marry me because he was about to do something illegal. And he wanted to save me from having to testify.

Grant could sense my uneasiness. "You okay?" His green eyes glinted in the sunset, and he looked so handsome that for a moment, I forgot why my gut was wrenched.

"Yeah, I'm fine. I just always dreamed about my wedding, my father walking me down the aisle. Once he died, I always imagined that Joaquín would give me away. I never thought I'd abscond into the night and elope to Vegas."

He placed his hand on my thigh. "I think it's kind of romantic."

"Anything with you is romantic." I leaned over and kissed him. "So, how long will it take to get housing?"

"A few months. Once we locate our son we need to see a lawyer to begin the process of getting custody. I want to show the court that we can provide a stable home. There are some parenting classes on base we should take, too. I don't know anything about raising kids."

A wave of nausea hit. Julián was almost two. I knew nothing about kids and even less about two-year-olds. He didn't know me. I'd be raising him mostly alone since Grant would always be deployed. Joaquín could help, once he was exonerated. "Yeah, I don't know much either. But we'll figure it out."

We pulled over at the gas station, and I stared at my new phone. At least it had the same number and the contacts had transferred over. Even so, I felt completely isolated from the world and from all my hard work. At the moment, I was completely dependent on Grant, and I didn't like it at all. I loved Grant with all my heart, and I had no doubt that I wanted to marry him and be with him for the rest of my life, but my love for Grant didn't replace my love for my brother. Without Joaquín, I wouldn't have met Grant. Without Joaquín being arrested, Grant and I wouldn't be back together.

Our three lives were bound together.

I could not be happy when Joaquín had no freedom. This quest was to free him, not to get Grant back. I would not allow him to dissuade me from my original purpose—freeing my brother.

Grant purchased a cola and a beef jerky and I threw in some sunflower seeds. A county corrections bus pulled in the gas station. The passengers were surely on their way to some prison in the middle of nowhere. A lump grew in my chest, and I blinked back tears. Was this Joaquín's future? To be carted along like some animal? He could never live like that. A horrible thought crossed through my head—Joaquín would rather be dead.

Grant pulled me into his arms and gave me a soft kiss when he saw me staring at the muted blue bus. "I love you. I can't wait to spend the rest of our lives together. Let me make you happy."

And I was happy. Wrapped in his embrace, I allowed my negative thoughts to dissipate. This was just the next step in our journey. Ultimately, I would be happy again. I believed that in my soul.

My nerves calmed as we headed toward the bright lights and gaudy billboards. I'd never been to Vegas, though Grant and Joaquín had often gone. I willed myself to be happy—I was marrying the love of my life.

So why did my heart feel like something was very wrong.

72

GRANT

A fter getting into Vegas late last night, we crashed and woke up early to go to the county clerk office to get our marriage license. Then I took her to the shops at Bellagio so she could pick out a dress. She didn't want me to see her in her dress before the wedding, which I thought was adorable, and she wanted to get her hair done, so we agreed to meet in a few hours at the altar.

Mia had shot down my idea of getting married by Elvis, but she had agreed to have a simple, romantic ceremony. It wasn't the huge wedding she wanted, but she seemed to be happy that our vows would be something that we would share only with each other.

While she got ready, I headed over to the nearest bar and ordered a whiskey on the rocks.

My phone rang—Mitch. I refused to ruin my wedding day talking to that asshole. I was still fucking pissed off at him for kissing Mia, even if he had been just trying to help her get information to free Joaquín. No matter the reason, next time I saw him, I was going to fuck him up.

The blinding, fluorescent lights of Vegas rattled me. Last time I'd visited I'd been on a bender with Joaquín and Mitch. Those assholes had dragged me out here, probably sick of me moping around about Mia leaving me. Joaquín and Mitch had taken me to Crazy Horse, where I'd gotten drunk on lap dances and liquor.

At the time, I'd thought they were such great friends, that Joaquín's friendship had held strong even after his sister had broken my heart.

It had been a lie.

He'd known that she had been raped. He should've told me. It was almost as if he'd been happy that we'd broken up.

"Want another?" the scantily clad bartender asked.

"Nope. I'm getting married tonight—I want to remember everything."

"Oh, wow. Congrats. She's a lucky gal. But you aren't married yet . . ." She gave me a wink and a playful tickle of my beard. I didn't even react. I only had Mia on my mind.

After people-watching for a bit, I'd had enough of this scene. I stopped by the flower shop and returned to my room to get ready.

I ordered a romantic feast for later, changed into my suit, and placed my trident in my lapel. A final glance in the mirror and I was ready to see my bride.

I entered the chapel, paid the fees, and waited for Mia.

And waited.

And waited.

Where the fuck was she? I texted her phone, but she didn't answer. I was tempted to use the find-my-phone app, but I'd vowed I was only going to use that if I believed she was in danger. I refused to stalk my wife.

Maybe she'd changed her mind. Maybe she didn't want to marry me.

I stood up to leave when the doors opened and I saw my bride.

My heart skipped. Her hair was now dark, close to her natural color, and she looked more like the woman I'd fallen in love with years ago. The woman I had wanted to marry, the woman I had conceived a child with. She took my breath away. She wore a low-cut white slip dress, which draped over her curves, and I couldn't believe how lucky I was.

She smiled when her eyes met mine, and I took her hand. "You look beautiful." I leaned down to kiss her, but the officiant stopped me.

"You can kiss her after the wedding."

As he performed the ceremony, Mia's eyes were locked with mine.

"Have you written your own vows?" the officiant asked.

I took Mia's hand. "Mia, I have loved you for what feels like my whole life. I humbly give you my hand and my heart as I pledge my faith and love to you. Just as this ring I give you today is a circle without end, my love for you is eternal. Just as it is made of incorruptible substance, my commitment to you will never fail. We will not fail."

Mia choked up as I placed the ring on her finger. "Grant, I promise to love and care for you, and I will try in every way to be worthy of your love. I will always be honest with you, kind, patient, and forgiving. But most of all, I promise to be a true and loyal friend to you. I love you."

"Do you, Grant Joseph Carrion take Angelita Mia Cruz to be your lawfully wedded wife?"

"I do."

"Do you, Angelita Mia Cruz take Grant Joseph Carrion to be your lawfully wedded husband?"

"I do."

"By the power vested in me by the state of Nevada, I now pronounce you husband and wife. You may now kiss your bride."

I grabbed Mia and kissed her passionately. She was mine, forever. No one, not even Joaquín, could ever tear us apart.

73

MIA

M y husband threw me over his shoulder like his seabag and raced up the stairs to the hotel room, too impatient to wait for the elevator. My husband. Grant's new title seemed so foreign to my tongue. He'd been my boyfriend, my ex, my target, and just briefly, my fiancé. And now, he was mine, until death do us part.

Grant flashed the key card over the door sensor and carried me over the threshold. I gasped when I saw the room. Rose petals strewn in a heart on the bedspread, champagne on ice, and chocolate-covered strawberries on a shiny silver platter.

After my heartfelt vows to Grant, I silently made another vow to myself. Tonight I would celebrate our love, our marriage, and our future. I would put aside my reservations about how rushed this wedding had been, about all my doubts and uncertainties. Because no matter what thoughts culled in my head, I knew that I loved Grant unconditionally. And I was thrilled to be his forever.

Grant tossed me on the bed, which sent up a waft of rose-scented air, and he climbed on top of me.

"You're mine now, Mrs. Carrion. Mine until the day I die. I'd do anything for you." His hand tugged at my hair, and he pulled me into a kiss. As his beard scraped my face, his tongue penetrated my mouth, aggressively tasting me, giving me a preview of what was to come.

He'd kissed me thousands of times before, but never like this. Savage, raw, unbridled. It was as if now that I was his forever, he was holding nothing back with these kisses. There was no more uncertainty about how much we loved each other.

I savored this kiss, but he wasn't the only one with surprises. I pushed him off me, grabbed his tie, and pulled him to sit in a chair.

His lips upturned in a smile, and his deep green eyes danced with fire.

"I just realized that you didn't get a bachelor party."

He licked his lips. "You're all I need, baby."

Damn straight. I wiggled my hips and slowly peeled off my dress, revealing a white corset, garters, thong, and stockings.

Grants pupils dilated as I prepared to give him a private dance, but unlike last time I'd danced for him, this time he could touch me. I grabbed my phone and played a song. Once the haunting beat began, I lowered myself onto him.

I slowly unbuttoned his shirt and took a moment to appreciate the beauty of my husband. His broad shoulders, his intricate ink, the bulge of his biceps, his hard cock pressing through his pants.

He licked his lips. "I should've booked a room with a pole."

I switched into my best Ksenya accent to have some fun. "I want it to be pleasing to you."

He let out a laugh. "Come here, baby."

His strong hands stroked my curves, settling on my hips, as I ground on his lap. His fingers kneaded my ass as I nibbled on his ear lobe. His scent intoxicated me, so masculine, so virile.

I twisted, giving him my back, and his lips kissed my neck as his hands cupped my breasts, rubbing my nipples until I moaned. Our bodies moved in rhythm to the music, and I got off on teasing him.

Finally I turned and knelt in front of him, unbuckled his belt, and took his cock into my mouth.

"Yeah, baby."

He placed his hand on the back of my head, and I licked up his length before taking my husband deep in my throat. I grasped my hand around the base of his cock and glided my lips up and down.

He let out a growl as my pace increased. Tasting him, sucking him, stroking him with my hot mouth.

I didn't want to stop, but he took control back and pulled me off him.

"My turn."

He flipped me around and sat me on his lap, slowly unclasping one hook after another down the back of my corset. Then shifted so I was sitting on the chair with him between my knees as he peeled the fabric from my body. My nipples puckered under his gaze. I was so wet, so fucking turned on, so blissfully happy. Cupping my breasts in his hands, he bit my lower lip and sucked on my nipple, the heat between my legs begging for relief.

"That's it, baby, I want to watch you come."

"Make me," I challenged.

He unclipped my garter from my stockings and removed my thong. As he pressed his hand between my legs to spread them wide, he lowered his head between my thighs and licked my pussy.

"Oh, Grant."

His hand was still working my nipples, and his tongue felt like heaven. When he pressed his fingers deep inside me, I thought I was going to explode, but he pulled back, forcing the heat to simmer inside me.

"Look at me, baby."

His thumb rubbed my clit as he gave me a long lap of his tongue and pleasure pulsed through me.

But he wasn't done.

He pressed his finger inside me again, slowly penetrating me as he sucked on my clit. My thighs squeezed around his face as I came undone.

I was still breathless as he licked up my body again to my nipples. He lifted me up and carried me to the sofa, where he lowered me on top of him.

It was too soon—I didn't think I could possible come again but the urge grew as I rode him, his mouth sucking on my breasts. My head fell back in pleasure, and I took a moment to acknowledge the incredible beauty of our lovemaking. Grant was my first lover, my only lover, and my last lover.

Grant worked my hips, and I could feel his huge cock pressing against my G-spot. My hunger for him, for this pleasure, built again until I was desperate to come again, come with him. My body tensed, and I was right on the edge, and Grant angled me and kissed me as we came together.

Our bodies remained intertwined for blissful minutes until he finally lifted me off of him. We climbed on the bed and he kissed me on the head, whispering, "You are my everything," before we fell into a sated sleep.

74

GRANT

Mia was still fast asleep on the bed. I crawled out, careful not to disturb her, and sat on the sofa.

I clutched my phone, and my heart raced when I saw that I had six missed calls from Mitch. I knew whatever was so important wasn't a work emergency because I didn't have a single call from Kyle or Pat.

I didn't want to call him back, but I needed to know what the fuck he wanted.

Our room had one of the rare balconies in Vegas, so I stepped outside and dialed Mitch's number.

He picked up on the first ring.

"Dude, where the fuck have you been?"

"I'm in Vegas, asshole. I just married Mia. By the way, she told me you kissed her. I'm gonna fuck you up."

"Congrats, man. And forget about the kiss. I was just trying to help her with Joaquín. Nothing happened."

"Better not have. You touch her again, and I'll beat the living shit out of you. Understand?"

"Yeah, yeah," he mumbled dismissively. "Look, I'm the least of your problems. When are you getting back?"

"Tomorrow. Seriously, why are you blowing up my phone?"

Mitch paused, and his breath seemed labored. "April flew out so I could see the kids. Anyway, I finally admitted to her that I was there the night of the party when Mia had been raped."

"And? Did she see who went to the room with Mia?"

"No. She said she and Dara searched around for Mia but couldn't find her so they left. But when they were leaving, they saw Joaquín drive up, park, and run into the party. They figured Mia had called him to take her home."

"Is she sure?" I shook with fury. One horrible scenario popped in my head. A possibility so horrendous that my mind refused to verbalize it. I forced myself to ask Mitch more questions before I exploded. "Joaquín was at the party? You didn't see him? He was with you that night in Yuma, right?"

"Yeah. I told him I was going to go get April and she, Dara, and Mia were at the SDSU Phi Delt party. He must've left after me, but maybe he beat me. You know how fast that motherfucker drives. I had no clue—I never saw him there. But, man, now that I think back, the guy I saw in her room—he was Joaquín's height and build. It was dark so I couldn't see much, but I think it could've been him."

I pounded my fist into the wall. Holy shit. Joaquín was the one who raped Mia. It all made sense. He must've kidnapped her child . . . because he thought the boy was his son. Proof of his rape. Proof of his crime.

But the boy was mine.

Mitch was still talking, but my brain couldn't comprehend what he was saying.

Rage poisoned my veins. Mia didn't have a clue that her beloved brother was a psychopath.

I had to make her hear me. Make her listen to me. Make her believe me.

But I knew she wouldn't believe me. Couldn't believe me. It would take more than April's sighting, more than Mitch's guess, more than me begging for Mia to see the light.

She wouldn't believe Joaquín raped her until he told her himself.

But that didn't mean I wasn't going to try.

75

MIA

I'd been hoping for a repeat of last night or maybe breakfast in bed, but when I woke, Grant had a scowl on his face. And our bags were already packed.

"Morning, hubby. Do we have to leave so soon? I was hoping we could stay in bed all day."

"I have to get back to work." He came over to me, put his finger under my chin, and gave me a kiss. "I love you. Once everything gets settled, I'll give you a big wedding, and we'll go on a honeymoon. But for now, we need to get back home."

I understood, even though I was disappointed. I hopped in the shower, dressed quickly, and we checked out, and headed back to San Diego.

Grant blasted the music for the first hour of the drive, and the air between us made me nervous. He'd been so warm and loving last night. What had changed?

I touched his thigh. "Any word from Kyle on Julián?"

"Nope."

I pursed my lips. "Okay. Well next time we see Joaquín, I think—"

"There isn't going to be a next time. That's it, Mia. You're not going to see him again. It's final."

Anger flushed through me. "You may be my husband, but you're not going to tell me what I can do and who I'm going to see. Joaquín is my brother, my family."

"I'm your family now! I don't want you to see him. Do you hear me? He's not even your real brother!"

"Fuck you! He is too my brother. Biology doesn't matter. How can you say that?"

"I'm trying to protect you, goddamn it."

"Protect me? From Joaquín? Joaquín would never harm me. How dare you say that."

Grant turned and faced me, daggers shooting from his eyes. "Damn it, Mia. How can you not see it? Joaquín is a psychopath. You have to trust me, you have to believe me. I love you so fucking much. Please, for once, I need you to believe in me."

"You have nothing to prove that he's a psychopath. Just your crazy theories. You won't tell me anything, anything about the meeting, any—"

"He raped you!"

My whole world stopped and then tilted so sharply I saw spots dance in my eyes.

When Grant spoke again, his voice was a stark contrast to the sudden chaos inside me. "I talked to Mitch. April told him that she saw Joaquín at the party that night, and Mitch said the guy who ran out of your room was around Joaquín's height. I always thought he wanted you, but I thought I was a sick fuck for even thinking about that."

I let out a scream. What the fuck? "How dare you say something like that to me," I seethed through clenched teeth. "To use what happened to me as a way to keep me from my brother . . . I can't believe you. My brother would never hurt me. Never. Especially not that way."

"It's the only possible explanation. He's obsessed with you. He never wanted us to start dating. And the reason I never asked you to move in back then was because Joaquín was against it."

"No," I said through sobs. "You're wrong."

Grant's tone dropped and he attempted to grab my hand but I swatted it away. "Baby, please. I know you don't believe me. But it's what they saw. I would never, ever lie to you and they have no reason to lie to me. It explains why he never told me you were raped after Mitch told him. And why he never told you he knew you were raped."

"I don't know. But I'm sure he had a reason. Probably because he didn't want to upset me. Or he didn't know how to approach it. And he didn't tell you because we'd broken up. Just stop talking!"

"No. He was hiding his guilt."

I really, really didn't want to hear anything else he had to say, but I *knew* more was coming.

"Listen to me. I think Joaquín was the one who took Julián. Remember the missing papers in your storage? He took them. He was the only one who could have. Joaquín took him, because . . . he thought Julián was his son."

"Be quiet!" I covered my ears like a child but could still hear Grant.

"And did you ever look into your parents' death? Did you know the truck that hit them was registered to Rafael? That is not a coincidence. I'm so sorry, baby. It's true."

"No!" I screamed so loud, the single word burned my throat. "No. Shut the fuck up. You are wrong. I'll prove it, I'll show you!"

"I'll stop and give you a chance to try to absorb this. But I love you, Mia. You're my wife now. The mother of my child. I'll lay down my life to protect you. But somewhere, deep in your heart, you know what I'm saying is true."

After an excruciating four-hour drive in silence and a pit stop to pick up our pets, we were back home in Point Loma. Despite my anger, Grant still lifted me and carried me over the threshold into our home.

I began to unpack and found the drugs from Rafael still stashed in my suitcase. I had to get rid of these before Grant saw them. I hid them underneath my wedding gown.

I would flush them down the toilet next time Grant left the house.

I emerged from the bedroom and found Grant just staring at the television, which was off.

"Can you get dinner? We have nothing."

"Yup."

Grant kissed me, walked out the door, and left me alone. What a horrible way to start our new marriage. I did not want to spend the rest of my life having to choose between my brother and my husband.

My phone rang, and I ran to retrieve it from my purse.

"Hello?"

A woman's voice played on a recording. "You are receiving a call from—"

"Joaquín Cruz," my brother's voice said.

"—an inmate at the San Diego County Jail. Press one to accept this call and two to decline."

I pressed one as fast as I could. "Joaquín? Are you there?"

"Hey, sis. I needed to hear your voice."

An ache twisted in my chest. *Nothing has changed. Grant has no proof. This is your brother.* "Me, too. I miss you. How are you?"

He exhaled. "Been better. Just sick of this shit, you know? Any progress getting me out of here?"

"I'm working on it. Hey, when we were at the jail, you mentioned to Grant that I had an ex named Julián. Why?" I made sure not to ask how he knew about Julián or who he thought Julián was.

His voice dropped. "Because I wanted you to find him."

"And by him, you meant the little boy, right?"

"Did you find him?" His voice was strange, hopeful and scared at the same time. Maybe I had been right, but it didn't stop me from wondering why exactly Joaquín had wanted me to find him.

"I did, but he's gone. Do you know where he is now?"

"I'll take you to him if you get me out of here."

My mouth became dry, and I talked rapidly. "Please, I need to find him. Tell me where he is."

"Then you know what you have to do. Later, sis." And with that, the phone went dead.

Did he really just leverage my son for his freedom? What the fuck? Why wouldn't he tell me where Julián was? My brain raged against the truth that was right in front of me, scrambling for an answer that fit with what I needed to believe. He had done it to protect Julián. My brother was in jail, the phones were recorded. I had to get him out of there fast.

Grant was wrong about him. So was Mitch.

So was April. She couldn't have seen Joaquín because he hadn't been there that night. And Mitch himself had told me that he didn't see the guy— it had been dark in that room—there was no way he could have seen my attacker's face, and lots of people had the same build as my brother.

I hadn't known that the truck that hit my parents was registered to Rafael. But even if that was true, it didn't prove anything. Maybe Rafael targeted my father, and when my father was gone, he targeted Joaquín. Blackmailing him. For what? I had no idea, but criminals rarely needed rational reasons for anything. Rafael had probably kidnapped my son to get something from my brother, and once Joaquín found out, he killed Tiffany in a moment of rage. Yes, that made sense if I ignored the fact that there was no way that Rafael or my brother should have known I was even pregnant.

On it went with my thinking in tiny circles and dismissing one idea after another and explaining actions away time and time again. I sat and thought until my head throbbed and my eyelids grew heavy.

76

GRANT

I didn't want to leave Mia alone, but I knew she needed space, so I texted Ashley to meet me at Point Loma Seafood in twenty minutes.

When she got there, I was already seated. She was out of her NCIS business suit and back in her Autumn summer casual clothes. I ordered us some fish tacos, and we sat and gazed at the pelicans and seals playing in the harbor.

Ashley's eyes narrowed in on my hand. "Please tell me you didn't marry her."

I flashed my band at her. "Best decision I've ever made. You know where I stand. You're wrong about her."

She shook her head. "Grant, look, I hope you are right, for your sake, and your son's, but something isn't adding up."

"Look, I need your help getting my son back. You said you're working on it, but honestly, that's not good enough. Joaquín is a psychopath. I've learned some new information, which is so fucked up I won't repeat it."

"Come on, spill."

"Nope. It's not about drugs or the Teams, so none of your business. Do you have a date for offering the plea?"

"Sometime in the next month. We're still negotiating the offer with his lawyer. He does have a pretrial hearing tomorrow, so I think everyone is waiting to see what happens with it."

A month? My son could be dead in a month. No way. "That's not acceptable. I need to find my son now."

"I'm well aware, Grant. I need you to trust that we are doing our best. We can't jeopardize the investigation. You have no legal claim over the child at the moment. Third-party testing isn't admissible."

Fuck this shit. I stood. "What's the time of the hearing?"

"Nine in the morning, but I won't be there." Her eyes narrowed, and she added, "If I hear that you try to interfere with the proceedings, I'll have you arrested."

"On what charges?"

"Obstruction of justice."

"Do what you got to do."

I walked away from her and got in my borrowed truck. I stopped at Liberty Market and picked up a vegan tofu bowl for Mia and some flowers.

When I showed back up at our place, she greeted me with a sleepy kiss and an apology.

"I'm sorry. I know you're just trying to protect me. I still think you're wrong. By the way, Joaquín called while you were gone."

I ground my teeth. "Yeah. What did he want?"

"Just to talk. I asked him why he name-dropped Julián. He said it was because he wanted me to find him. Don't you see? He told us about him so we could discover him. I'm more certain than ever. I think that maybe Rafael kidnapped him, and Tiffany told Joaquín that she had his nephew and he lost it."

I understood how Mia thought that. But she didn't know that Tiffany was working for NCIS. And I wasn't at liberty to say. "Did he say anything else?"

"I asked him to tell me where Julián was, but he refused. Said he would take me to him if he was free. I think that's the only way we are going to see Julián again. We have to get Joaquín out of jail."

And for once, I agreed with her.

"I already ate. I'm going to take Hero on a run. I'll be back in a bit."

I leashed up Hero and left again. I made several calls and put my plan into action. No longer would I be the pawn in Joaquín's game.

I was done letting everyone else make the decisions.

77

MIA

Grant came home an hour later, but we didn't talk any more about Joaquín, which was fine. At least he wasn't pushing any more of his theories down my throat.

At bedtime, he pulled me to him. "I need you tonight. This may be the last time for a while."

"What? Why?"

"I may be going away for a bit."

I didn't question him. He'd taken so much time off work that I knew he had to pick up the slack. His lips reached mine, and we kissed for what seemed like a blissful eternity. It always amazed me how such a strong, masculine man could kiss me so softly. I loved his contrasts. He held me in his arms, and we made love, so tender, so beautiful.

The next morning, Grant woke at seven and pressed his uniform.

"You going to work?"

"No. We're going to court. Joaquín has a hearing today."

I stuttered. "Wh-why didn't you tell me? He didn't mention it to me yesterday. How did you find out? What's the hearing about?"

He shot me a cold stare. "It's a pretrial hearing. Get dressed."

He didn't need to tell me twice. I hurriedly put on my most conservative outfit. Maybe today would be the day that this nightmare ended. Joaquín would be freed. Without the bars that separated us, he would be able to explain everything. What he knows about Julián. How he met Rafael. How he found out that Tiffany had my child. Why he never told Grant that I had been raped.

And even worse, why he had never told me that he knew.

Grant tossed me my keys. "We're taking your car."

I squinted at him. "Why? You told me I wasn't allowed to drive it because you thought it was tracked."

"I changed my mind."

"You don't want to drive that truck you borrowed?"

"Nope."

Okay. That was incredibly odd. Grant always wanted to drive, everywhere. I didn't question him about his reasons as he squeezed into the passenger side of my car.

As I drove to the courthouse, a knot built in my stomach. I felt like after all this time I was finally on the cusp of getting the answers that I needed in this puzzle.

We parked in the parking garage. I opened the door to get out but Grant reached over me and pulled it shut.

"What?"

He clutched my shoulders. "Mia, I need you to listen to me. I want you to know that I love you. I've always loved you, no matter how hard I tried to deny it. I'm not going to be around for a while to protect you after today."

"What? What are you talking about? Why are you saying this?"

"Just listen to me. I've left you all the passwords to my bank accounts in my nightstand." He shoved three hundred dollars into my hand and then handed me a gold band. "I want you to wear this. It has a tracking device on it."

"What? Why?"

"Just do it. Please. When I come back, you can chuck the thing."

"Okay." His pupils were dilated, but he remained calm. Too bad I wasn't. I removed my wedding band from my finger, and for the first time noticed that it had been engraved with the words *worth fighting for*.

I gulped and put the band in a zippered pocket in my purse before sliding the tracking band on my right hand instead of my left. I didn't want Joaquín to see it and find out that way that Grant and I were married.

"I want you to know that I've never killed anyone outside of combat. I need you to tell me that you believe me."

My hands shook. "Yes, of course I know that. Grant, I need you tell me what is going on right now."

He didn't answer me and just cupped my face and kissed me. His lips crashed on mine in an urgent kiss. He'd only kissed me like this once before, the day he and Joaquín had left before their first deployment. A kiss to last me through the nights without him.

As if it could possibly be the last time he ever kissed me.

We exited the car and walked up the court steps, Grant holding my hand. The metal detector didn't beep when Grant passed through, and my nerves calmed a bit. He didn't have a gun or a knife on him. But he was a SEAL—he could kill a man in three hundred different ways. He didn't need a weapon. He was one.

Daniel Reed, Joaquín's lawyer, sat at a table but there was no sign of Joaquín. After an agonizingly long hour, Joaquín walked in. He was wearing a suit, his face was cleanly shaved, and his neck tattoo peeked out from his collar. He smiled when he saw me, and I gave him a wide smile back. For a moment, I could pretend he wasn't imprisoned. He was just my handsome brother. He was not behind bars, not in handcuffs. He was momentarily free.

But then I noticed the *way* he was looking at me. Studying my body. Giving me a slow eye fuck. I had dismissed Grant's theory, but maybe I had been wrong. Did my brother covet me?

A female judge walked into the court and began the proceedings.

"For the hearing of The People vs. Joaquín Elías Cruz. Would the prosecution like to begin?"

The DA stood and then Grant stood as well. I attempted to pull him back to his seat, afraid he was going to lunge at Joaquín, but he remained at attention.

The judge did not look amused. "Excuse me, Sailor. Please sit down, or I'll find you in contempt of court."

"Your honor, I'd like to address the court. My name is Grant Joseph Carrion. I was at the party the night of Tiffany's murder. I was the one who killed her."

What the fuck? It was all I could think as the court erupted into chaos. The judge pounded her gavel.

Daniel stood. "Your honor, with the new information I'd like to motion for my client be released immediately."

"What have you done? Take it back. It's not true." I tugged on Grant, pleading him to retract the lies he'd just told, but he wouldn't even look at me.

I caught a glimpse of Joaquín's face. I knew my brother better than anyone. But the look on his face wasn't one of relief—it was one of shock.

Holy fuck. Joaquín was shocked by Grant's confession, because Joaquín knew Grant was lying.

The judge finally spoke. "Bailiff. Take Mr. Carrion in for questioning immediately. Council, please see me in chambers in five minutes."

The bailiff walked over toward Grant, who pulled me into an embrace.

"Grant, why are you doing this?" My voice cracked over the words as tears stung the backs of my eyes.

"Don't be scared," he whispered. "This is the only way we can find our son. You can do this. I believe in you. You are strong and brilliant. I love you. Mitch will follow you to make sure you're safe. Promise me you won't lose him, Mia. And wear that ring."

"Yes. Yes. I promise. I love you. You didn't have to do this."

"Yes, I did."

One final kiss, and he was taken away.

Daniel and the DA exited the courtroom to go to the judge's chambers.

I leaned over to Joaquín, not knowing what to say.

He turned to me, a devilish smirk on his face. "Good job, sis. When you pick me up, I'll take you to meet our son."

Wait, what the fuck did he just say?

Before I could react, the bailiff led him away, leaving me to stare after him with a slack jaw.

Our son? Did he say our son?

Which meant . . . It could only mean one thing.

I stood in the empty courtroom, tears welling in my eyes. I knew these two men. Grant had just lied and confessed to a murder he didn't commit. A murder my brother had likely committed.

Grant had been right.

Joaquín raped me.

And he thought Julián was his son.

PART VII

COVET

SE7EN DEADLY SEALS EPISODE 7

"DO NOT OVERRATE
WHAT YOU HAVE RECEIVED,
NOR ENVY OTHERS.
HE WHO ENVIES OTHERS
DOES NOT OBTAIN
PEACE OF MIND."

— BUDDHA

78

MIA

I drove back to Grant's place in a daze, trying not to completely break down. I didn't have a clue what was going to happen. Would Grant go to jail? I was his wife, I needed to get him a lawyer. I prayed that my phone would ring soon.

I arrived home, let Hero out, and just lost it on the sofa. My chest heaved, my breath came in short spurts, and I wanted to collapse into the sofa and die.

The words *our son* rang in my head. Our son . . . our son. I couldn't get Joaquín's voice out of my head. My brother had raped me. He had just promised to take me to meet *our son*. He knew where he was because he had been the one to kidnap him.

Holy fuck.

Grant had been right. And I'd been so stubborn that I refused to believe him. I doubted the only man who truly ever loved me, who had always had my back. Not only had I refused to entertain his logical conclusions but also I had accused him of trying to keep me from my brother.

I was a horrible person. I didn't deserve Grant.

I'd ruined my life to protect my brother. A man who was a killer. A rapist. A kidnapper.

In my darkness, I realized a truth. I could've never imagined how determined I would become to free Joaquín when he had been arrested. But witnessing Grant being taken away in handcuffs was worse.

I loved Grant more than I loved Joaquín.

I stared at my phone. Should I call a lawyer to get him out? No, I would wait until I heard from Grant. He was calling the shots and he had sacrificed his freedom so I could find our son. I was desperate to hear his voice. But at the same time, I was dreading getting a call from Joaquín, knowing he could be set free. I knew this was my path—the only way to find my son, but I was terrified of being alone with my brother. As the minutes turned into hours, I fell deeper into the self-hate that had been sparked the moment I realized I had been so very, very wrong.

I walked into the bedroom and caught a glimpse of my wedding gown covering my suitcase. I clutched it and could still smell Grant's woodsy scent. I cradled that dress as if I were cradling him. I'd put him through so much that if I ever got a chance to have a real life with him, I would do anything to make him happy.

I rummaged in my suitcase to find my jeans but instead, my hand fell on the cocaine. My fingers kneaded the bag of white powder.

One line. One line to make me feel better. Replace this low with a high. Forget this day. Forget this life. Joaquín wouldn't be released until tomorrow. I needed a fix to take the edge off my pain.

Using a credit card, I cut a line of coke on Grant's nightstand, and then I took a dollar bill from my purse and rolled it up. Before I could talk myself out of it, I snorted it.

And then I snorted another.

And then another.

The high pulsed through my body, leaving my insides numb and humming with euphoria. My vision sharpened and wobbled as I bent to snort another, but I didn't stop.

My heart raced faster and my hand shook so hard the makeshift straw fell from my fingertips. My chest constricted, and I knew something was wrong. I reached for my phone and called the only person I could think of—Mitch. But before I could scream for help, my world went black.

79

GRANT

I was led to a holding cell and refused to talk to the detective without an attorney. But instead of calling a lawyer or my wife, I made my one call to Ashley.

After an hour, Ashley showed up in a business suit. Her identification allowed her immediate access to me.

"Dammit, Grant. What were you thinking? A false confession? I was with you the night of the party. All night. You did *not* kill Tiffany."

"No shit, Sherlock. But this is the only way I will find my son. Joaquín will be released as they investigate me. And he will take Mia to Julián."

"What makes you think he will do that?"

"Because he told her he would. And as twisted as it is, he loves her."

She shook her head. "I hope you are right. This stunt will ruin your career."

"No, it won't. I'll get a slap on the wrist. And honestly, I don't give two shits about my career if I can't find my son. I need you to make sure that when they release Joaquín, you have someone tail him. Mitch is on it, too. Promise me."

She reached for my hand, and I didn't pull it back. "I promise. We'll have every man on it. He will be released tomorrow at eleven." She paused. "I admire you and your loyalty to Mia. I thought I could break you, but I was wrong. She doesn't deserve you."

"No, you're wrong there. I don't deserve her. And Mia's as loyal to me as I am to her. That's what true love is, Ashley. Willing to die for someone you love."

Ashley released a heavy sigh and flashed a longing gaze at me. "I'm going to go to the DA and give a statement about how I was with you the night of the murder. But per your request, I'll delay my statement until Joaquín is released. I hope you're right about this plan. And I promise I'll follow Joaquín and find your son."

"Thank you. I appreciate it." I squeezed her hand and felt a tinge of compassion for her. Being a female NCIS agent investigating secretive SEALs was by no means an easy task. She had thrown herself fully into this operation by transforming into Autumn the same way Mia had transformed into Ksenya. Mia's motivation was clear—to free her brother. I wondered what motivated Ashley.

Ashley left the conference room, and I was led back to my cell. NCIS and Mitch would be following Joaquín, who would hopefully honor his promise to Mia and lead her to our son. If this operation went according to plan, I would have Joaquín back behind bars and my family reunited within a few days. What could go wrong?

80

MIA

C old water drenched me, making me gasp for breath. My first vision as I began to regain consciousness was a man cradling me in the bathtub. Mitch's face came into focus as he screamed my name.

"Mia, are you okay?"

As my vision improved, I wiped the blood from my nose. God, I was so stupid. What the fuck had I been thinking? Especially when I was this close to finding my child.

"I'm fine. I-I just . . ." I couldn't admit to my own stupidity so I waved at my bloody nose.

Mitch carried me to the bedroom, undressed me, and put me in some new clothes. His hands grasped my wrist as he checked my pulse.

"Your heart rate is elevated"—his hand moved to lift my eyelid—"and your pupils are dilated. How do you feel?"

Like a fool. "Like I can't feel my face and I'm going to throw up."

"It should pass. How much did you take?"

"I wasn't trying to overdose. I just wanted to take the edge off." I knew he wanted to question that but he didn't.

"I'm going to monitor your breathing. I can't let something bad happen to Grant's wife."

I felt the urge to curl up in a ball and shoo him away from me, but instead I allowed Mitch to take care of me. He placed me on the bed. After twenty minutes of him watching me breathe, he finally gave me a thumbs up. "You're good."

I sat up and exhaled. "Thanks, Mitch. You saved my life."

"Don't mention it."

I turned to him. "Did you know Grant was going to confess?"

"Yeah, he told me his plan yesterday. But he didn't kill her. I was there that night. He was with Autumn the entire time. And your brother was with Tiffany." As much as I hated imagining Grant hooking up with Autumn that night, I knew that her alibi would be the key to getting him out of jail. But was she a reliable witness? What if the court didn't believe her because she was a stripper who had a fling with Grant? What if Grant wasn't released?

"Hey." Mitch paused and reached for my hand. "Grant told me he told you what April saw."

I swallowed. "He did." It was all I could manage.

"I'm so sorry."

Yesterday, I would've screamed at Mitch for even suggesting Joaquín had raped me. But now everything was making sense. Mitch had told me the night I'd drugged him that the guy he'd found me with had sprinted past him. Joaquín would be out soon, and then I would finally get some answers.

"So, what's the plan? Are you going to pick up Joaquín?"

"Yup. And I'm not supposed to let him out of my sight. He'll probably want to be dropped off here, and I'll be following you two. Grant will join me when, or if, he gets released. Joaquín won't have a car, so I'll put a tracking device on yours so we don't get separated. I'm also going to monitor you on your phone."

"That sounds intense. Grant thinks my car already has a tracking device on it." I pursed my lips. "I'll be honest, Mitch. I'm scared. I'm not sure I can pull this off."

"You can. You fooled Grant and me. And I have your six." His brow cocked. "Listen, Mia, I need you to keep your guard up around Joaquín. You have a gun, hell you pointed it at me. Don't be afraid to use it if you need to protect yourself."

I gulped. He didn't need to elaborate. I knew he was telling me that I might have to kill my brother. "Okay. I'll be cautious."

He took my hand. "I'm going to spend the night here, on the sofa. Grant wants me to stay with you until I get Joaquín."

I nodded. "Okay. That's fine. I'm going to crash."

He kissed my forehead. "Night, Mia."

"Night."

As I fell into a deep slumber, I dreamt for the first time in a while. But my dream quickly turned into a nightmare. I was back at the frat house the night I had been raped, and I could hear the words "Mia, Mia, are you okay?" But they weren't spoken by Mitch.

They were spoken by my brother.

81

MIA

When I woke the next morning, Mitch was sitting on the sofa staring at his phone

"Good, you're up. Daniel called me a few hours ago. Joaquín will be released at eleven."

I glanced at the clock. It was nine thirty. I would see my brother soon. But I didn't care about seeing him. All I wanted to do was see my husband. "Any word from Grant?"

"No. Kyle is trying to get access to him. Kyle's pissed, by the way—I hope he doesn't throw Grant in the brig. I'm going to head over to the jail to get your brother." Mitch walked over and knelt in front of me, forcing me to stare at him. "Stay here until I drop Joaquín off. And if he hurts you, make sure you protect yourself. Promise me."

"I promise."

"Okay. I'll give you a call when I have him. Don't open the door to this apartment until you hear from me."

"Okay, okay. I get it. I'll behave. Thanks, Mitch." I hugged him, needing to feel safe and protected before I embarked on this journey.

Mitch left and closed the door behind him. I locked it and jumped in the shower, trying to wash yesterday out of my mind. Within an hour, my brother would be free.

I tried to take my mind off of Grant being locked up and what I would do when I saw my brother, but it was useless. There was only so long I could stare at my phone, so I eventually turned on the television.

After twenty minutes, I heard the lock click and all my attention focused on the knob. When the door pushed open, my whole body froze.

"Hey, sis."

Joaquín stood in front of me, and his mouth widened in a devilish smile. His chest was even more massive than when he'd been a SEAL. He'd developed some new lines on his face and his dark eyelashes shaded his haunting eyes.

A lump grew in my throat. "Oh my God! Joaquín! What are you doing here? Did Mitch give you the key?" I instinctively rubbed my ring on my finger, as if I expected it to shoot a message to Mitch, alerting him that the plan had been altered.

He laughed. "No, I picked the lock."

Grant's words echoed in my head. *"You know who taught me to pick locks? Your brother."*

I tried to move, say something, do something, but I remained frozen on the sofa.

"Aren't you going to give me a hug?"

"Of course. I'm so sorry. I'm shocked, that's all." I stood and ran into his arms. He lifted me, his strong grasp holding me tight, and I fought the urge to be sick.

I pulled back as soon as I could without looking suspicious, but before I could start talking to him, he grasped my face and pulled me in for a kiss.

But it wasn't a kiss the way a brother kisses a sister. It was a kiss the way lovers kiss.

My skin crawled.

I pulled away, my jaw dropped, and my eyes bulged.

He didn't let go of me as he walked me backward into the apartment and kicked the door closed. Then he grabbed my jaw and turned my face back toward him. "Listen to me. I know this will be a little weird for you at first, but you know the truth now. I lied to you in jail—I did know that we weren't biological siblings."

"What? How?"

"On my sixteenth birthday, I went to get my license, and when I read my birth certificate there was another man's name on it. I thought it was a mistake, but Papa told me the truth. It crushed me. I'm Mama's son and you're Papa's daughter. They married when we were young. After I flipped out, they got a fake birth certificate for you so you would never know and they made me promise not to tell you. I fucking hated them for making me think I was crazy. I hated them so much . . ."

He didn't finish that sentence, but the hair on the back of my neck stood up.

"Why didn't you ever tell me? It's been years since they passed away!"

"I couldn't. It would have crushed you, and I couldn't stomach the thought of having you look at me the way Papa did. Mia. I've always fought it, hated myself for thinking these unnatural thoughts. I knew you didn't know how I felt about you, how I *still* feel about you. But I wasn't sure you felt the same. I tried to be happy and move on when you were with Grant. I thought I had. But what you did for me in jail—now I know you feel it, too. I see the devotion in your eyes. There's nothing wrong with it. We are meant to be together."

My gut wrenched in horror. He was my brother. I had never, not a single time, thought about him in that way.

I took a slow step backward, nausea rolling in my stomach as the realization that I was facing my rapist hit me. I wanted to vomit at the thought of him forcing himself on me.

Then as quickly as the sick feeling hit, anger boiled right over it. He had lied to me and raped me—all for some twisted fantasy about me. I loved Joaquín, no doubt, but as a sister. Nothing more. Never, ever. I only saw him as a brother.

Anger consumed me. I was angry at the drunk driver who had killed my parents. Angry at the man who raped me. Angry at whoever stole my son. Angry at whoever killed Tiffany.

And I realized at that moment that one person committed all of these crimes. And that person was my brother.

Utter panic took hold of my body. But a moment of clarity passed through my brain. Grant's words rang in my head. *"Don't be scared. This is the only way we can find our son. You can do this. I believe in you. You are strong and brilliant. I love you."*

I had to go along with this. Getting this psychopath to believe that I was in love with him was the only way I had a chance to get my son back. If not, he could kill me, or kill my child.

I thought my biggest act had been making sure Ksenya could trick Grant, but I had been wrong. That had been nothing but a dress rehearsal. My greatest performance was now.

And it was showtime.

I turned back to him, my hands rubbing his hair, as I forced the bile back down my throat. I disconnected my mind and pretended Joaquín was Grant.

Acting, I was acting. This was a love scene, a fake kiss, nothing more.

I leaned up to him and kissed him on the lips. "You know I love you too. I did all this for you. I can't live without you."

He seized the moment, his hands rubbing down my body and his mouth raped mine. "I've dreamed of this, baby."

Hearing him call me "baby" was like hearing nails on a chalkboard.

"Me, too," I forced myself to reply.

A grin swept across his face. "I can't wait to make love to you again."

82

MIA

M*ake love?* He saw forcing himself on me when I was passed out as making love?

There was no mistake.

My brother had raped me.

My silence was deafening.

Oh God, I don't think I can pull this off. Say something damn it.

I tried my best to hold my emotions in, but I was unable to and let a tear escape down my cheek.

"Hey, hey, it's okay." Joaquín broke the hush and reached his arm out to comfort me.

"What happened that night?"

His eyes darted around the room, and then he gazed out the window. "We need to get out of here. We can talk on the road."

I swallowed and grabbed my purse. I was relieved when it felt heavy. My gun was tucked inside a secure pocket. I'd purchased that gun to protect myself, but I never thought I would need to defend myself from my brother.

Joaquín opened the door and led me outside. I had no choice but to go with him.

"Do you want to take my car?"

"Nope. Daniel lent me his truck. Get in."

I climbed in the truck, a truck that was not tracked, and forced my body not to shake. I'd dreamed of this very moment for the past seven months. Reuniting with my brother, seeing him walk free as the reward for all my hard work.

I wish I'd never fought for his release.

Though this mission had led me to my son. And back to Grant. I centered myself with a few calming breaths. This was my path. Everything happened for a reason.

I couldn't even fathom how Joaquín had thought this would go. Maybe he thought he would just tell me he was in love with me, he raped me, and we had a son together, and I would just be like okay, I love you, too.

"Give me your phone," he said as he secured his seat belt.

"What? Why?"

"Just do it."

I didn't protest. I couldn't protest. I handed my phone to my brother, who tossed it out the window in front of the truck and then proceeded to run it over.

My phone. I had no way to communicate with the world. My fingers stroked my ring. At least Grant could track me.

Before Joaquín said another word, he whipped out of the lot and headed north. I was alone with him in a steel trap. I didn't have a clue where Mitch was, and Grant was still in jail. I hadn't even had a chance to leave a note or some kind of indication that I hadn't just up and left.

But I could do this. I had to do this. And there was no chance for error.

I exhaled and placed my hand on Joaquín's thigh. He smiled and squeezed my hand.

"I'm going to try not to get upset, but I have to know. Tell me what happened. Please, the truth."

Joaquín stared straight ahead at the road, swallowed once, and then started talking. "Grant had been hurt in the roadside bombing. The military wasn't going to tell you before they told his family because you weren't his next of kin. He was still in a hospital overseas, but the rest of us had just been transported Stateside to Yuma to decompress. I was about to call you, but Mitch called April, who was at a party with you. He sped off after her, and I figured I'd go and tell you about Grant in person. I didn't want you to be alone when you found out about him."

He glanced at me, but I didn't have anything to say. I wanted to know how his good intention of coming to tell me that Grant had been hurt turned into my brother forcing himself on me.

"Go on."

"I drove straight without stopping. I didn't tell anyone I'd left, not even Mitch. When I arrived at the party, I couldn't find you anywhere. I went room to room, searching. I finally found you passed out in a dark room, some other motherfucker standing over you. He must've drugged you, but when he saw me walk in, he took off. I was going to go after him, but I couldn't leave you there alone. I didn't know if you had been drugged or raped or whatever."

"Someone gave me a drink, and I felt dizzy. I went to the room to lie down."

"I-I saw you on a bed. And I tried to wake you, honestly I did. But you spoke to me. You recognized me. You said, 'Joaquín, Joaquín.' I leaned in to hug you, and I just couldn't stop myself. I'd been deployed for nine months, and all the years of denying what I felt, how much I loved you, how much I lusted after you, I lost control."

My skin was crawling. He was seriously trying to downplay what he had done as nothing more than a lack of control. "I don't understand." I took a slow, deep breath and reminded myself that I was playing along. I couldn't scream at him like I wanted to. "Joaquín, how would you feel if someone else had done what you did to me? You tell me that you love me, but . . ."

"I know. I know. I fucking hate myself. I love you, Mia. I tried to stop, but I couldn't. You just felt so good—" He stopped himself, his voice shaky. "After . . . I couldn't stand the thought of what I'd done. I was there, waiting for you to wake, but then the door opened, and I bolted."

"And that's why you never told Grant you knew I'd been raped. Because you were the one who raped me."

"It wasn't rape. It didn't feel like rape to me. I love you. I made love to you. And yes, that was why I didn't tell him. I was so happy you dumped him. I drove to San Francisco one night to tell you how I felt, hoping you felt the same. I saw you at Nordstrom's and you had a small baby bump. I knew the baby wasn't Grant's because he'd been gone and then was in the hospital. I figured you left him because you knew you were pregnant and the child wasn't his."

A flaw in his logic. A fatal flaw. Julián *was* Grant's son, not Joaquín's.

I'd visited Grant every day in the hospital. We'd made love. But Joaquín thought Julián was his. He must not have run a paternity test on Julián.

We drove up the freeway, and I forced myself to continue this charade. "You're right. That was why I left him. I found out I was pregnant and dumped him."

He grinned, a smug, satisfied look. I wanted to slap it off his face. "I kept tabs on your pregnancy, you know."

"If you kept tabs on me, do you know who took our son?"

He stared ahead at the traffic, still unable to face me. "I arranged to have our son taken. Don't ask how, because I don't want you to know. I made a deal with some bad people, and I've been holding my end up of the bargain ever since."

I couldn't hold my tongue any longer. "Why? Why not just never tell me the truth? Why put me through hell thinking I'd lost him? I loved him before he was even born."

"I couldn't bring myself to tell you we had made love. I knew you wouldn't see it the same way I did, and I didn't want you to hate me. You never would have gotten over it. You always would have wondered who his father was, and every time you looked at him you would have been reminded. I've loved you my whole life, and I couldn't put you through that kind of pain. I also couldn't stand the thought of you hating me for what I did."

"So you took him from me?"

"I did. He's my son, too. I'm his father and I did what I thought was best. As much as I couldn't stand the thought of you mourning him, I also couldn't stand the thought of him growing up wondering why his mom hated him so much."

"I never would have hated him," I told him again, knowing that even if things were different and that little boy wasn't Grant's son, I never would have held it against him.

"I thought I was helping you both."

I believed that he believed that. I took a deep breath and forced myself to calm down. My son's life depended on it. "Why did you kill Tiffany?"

"She was working with NCIS. She was going to tell them that Julián was my kid. She wouldn't shut the fuck up about it, so I killed her. I'm sorry I lied to you about that."

He was sorry he lied to me about murdering a woman who was involved in hiding my son from me, but he wasn't sorry he raped me or kidnapped my son? "Now what? I do love you, more than anyone." I paused, forcing myself not to bite my lip as I lied. "Even more than Grant. But you just admitted that you raped me and kidnapped my son. How am I supposed to get over that?"

His foot pressed on the gas pedal, and we accelerated. He was swerving so fast and crazy it made my chest ache. "I fucked up, but I did all of this because I love you. I fucking love you, Mia. Can't you see that?"

My hands became clammy, and I prayed for the strength to get through this scene. "I love you, too. I've always felt that there was something special between us, a bond stronger than normal brothers and sisters. But it's going to take some time for me. The rape ruined my life. I didn't feel like anything could hurt so much, but then I lost my baby. I've been through so much."

His foot lifted and he finally glanced at me. There was something close to remorse in his eyes, and I knew he believed what I was saying.

I mustered up the strength to continue. "I can't promise anything, but I'm going to try to forgive you. Will you give me that time? See if I can get there?"

He let out a growl. "What about Grant?"

Grant. My husband. The love of my life. I reminded myself not to bite my lip. "It's over between Grant and me. He's a controlling asshole. And you were right. He treats me like shit and will never love me the way you do. I only used him to free you."

His shoulders relaxed. "I'd do absolutely anything for you. I'll give you all the time you need, just give me a chance to make you happy. I promise I can make you happier than Grant ever could."

He was delusional. It was the only explanation.

"Thank you."

Silence fell between us, and I turned to the window. How had I missed the signs? I had always thought we were exceptionally close, but clearly our connection was abnormal. We had always been affectionate. I had never seen it as wrong.

I threw him another olive branch. "I can't imagine how hard it must've been for you to feel like you couldn't talk to me about how conflicted you felt. I had no idea."

"It was so damn hard. Mama and Papa told me they would either kick me out of the house or they would sign their consent so I could join the

Navy at seventeen. I just wanted to make you proud of me. You're the only one who has ever loved me."

I grabbed his hand, and again, the tears came—both for real and for fake. I cried for me, I cried for my parents, I cried for my son, I cried for Grant, and then, I even cried for Joaquín. I hated myself for feeling sympathy for this mad man who'd destroyed my life, but I still saw him as my brother and I couldn't help myself.

83

GRANT

I spent a restless night in jail. It was almost like being on deployment, completely cut off from the world. At least I slept on a cot in here, which beat being in a dirt hole with gunfire overhead.

I was waiting for someone to escort me to the interview room so I could talk to the detective, but that didn't happen. The door swung open and the bored-looking guard muttered. "Carrion, you're free."

"What?"

He didn't answer, just handed me the paper bag that held all my belongings and led me out to a waiting Ashley and a stern-looking Kyle.

"That was quick."

"Yeah, well, you cost us a year on this investigation. I was so close to breaking this smuggling case, Grant. With Joaquín free we've lost our leverage." She rubbed her eyes and her mascara smeared. On closer examination, I could tell that her eyelids were puffy. I felt guilty that my actions jeopardized her hard work.

"I'm sorry. But I did this to find my son. You understand that."

She sighed. "I do. Anyway, luckily for you, your brass didn't want to make a scandal of a second SEAL being charged for murder. And the courtroom was closed, so your stunt wasn't released to the media. I gave my statement that I was with you at the party and convinced the judge not to hold you on obstruction charges. You owe me."

"Thank you, Ashley." I gave her a hug, and she leaned into my arms.

I released her and turned to Kyle, who was up to date on the NCIS involvement.

"May I have a moment alone with Petty Officer Carrion?"

Ashley stepped away, and Kyle handed me my ass. "Start talking, Carrion. I've been covering for you, but I've had enough. What the fuck were you thinking?"

"I'm sorry, sir. Joaquín told Mia he would only lead her to our son if he was released. Mitch is following them. This was the only way I could ensure that we would find our son. I'm ready to accept my punishment."

Kyle gave me a quizzical look. "But Joaquín was released a few hours ago. Mitch didn't pick him up. Daniel met him and he took off in Daniel's truck."

What the fuck?

I stormed over to Ashley.

"Where's Joaquín?"

She didn't respond as she increased her pace and walked ahead of me.

"Ashley, where is Joaquín?"

"He was released a few hours ago."

"Mitch didn't pick him up? You have guys trailing them, right?"

She pulled me and Kyle into a stairwell. "No. I'm sorry. There was . . . a mix-up. He was released two hours earlier than schedule."

My ears pounded, and I clenched my fist. "Are you fucking kidding me? Where is he now?"

"I don't know. We're working on it. We have every—"

I grabbed her by the wrist. "You are completely incompetent. I asked you to do one thing for me, and you fucked it up. Where is Mia? Do you even know that?"

Kyle stepped in between us. "Cool it, Carrion. This isn't her fault."

Ashley scowled at me. "We believe she's with him. We had a camera set up, focused on your door, and it captured a picture of them leaving. They got into a truck registered to Daniel, and he kissed her. He kissed her, Grant. It didn't seem as if she was resis—"

My throat burned. That sick motherfucker. I couldn't wait to put a bullet in his head.

"Don't you fucking say it. He raped her, goddamn it. He fucking raped her, and due to your fuckup, he also kidnapped her. He's a psychopath. She's a fucking actress—she's acting. If she looked like she went willingly, she was playing along to save herself. And our son."

"Oh, this is all my fault? It was your dumbass idea to make a false confession to secure his release. Had you not done that, he would still be behind bars."

"All you had to do was make sure you watched him when he was released. If I left this up to you, by the time he got out of jail, my son could be dead! Who knows where he is now." I ran down the stairs. "I'll find them. Get the fuck away from me. You've caused enough problems."

Her hand reached to grab me as her heels clicked behind me. "You aren't going anywhere. You are released to my custody, and you have a hearing at Captain's Mass for your stunt. If you're going after Joaquín and Mia, I'm going with you. Otherwise, I'm happy to escort you back to the Naval Amphibious Base, where you will be placed in a holding cell."

I turned to Kyle, my eyes pleading, knowing I didn't have a leg to stand on. "Please, sir. Please let me go after my wife. You can lock me in the brig forever once I get my family."

Kyle shook his head. "Sorry, Carrion. The only way I'll let you go is if you take Special Agent Pierce with you."

Fuck, she had me by the balls. "Thank you, sir."

"And when you're back, you report straight to me. Is that clear?"

"Crystal."

"Good luck, brother." Kyle left the building, and we followed behind him.

I turned to Ashley. "We need to stop at my place and get my gun. And I'm going to find out where Mitch is so he can go with us."

I didn't have my truck, so I climbed into Ashley's car and grabbed my phone out of the paper bag to call Mitch. He picked up on the first ring.

"Hey, man. What the fuck happened?"

"I went to pick up Joaquín, but he'd already been released. I bolted back to your place, but Mia was gone. Her purse was missing and her phone was shattered on the ground, but the rest of her stuff was there."

Fuck. But then a realization hit me. Her ring. I had opted for the tracking device. All I had to do was activate it.

I used my phone to log into the site the jeweler had given me and traced her ring. When a map popped up, I breathed a sigh of relief.

"Dude, she's about two hundred miles up the coast. They just passed Carpinteria."

"How the fuck do you know?"

"I installed a tracker on her ring."

"Nice, bro. Hey, I'm in Carlsbad. I'll hop in my truck and keep driving north until you catch up."

"Good. We're on our way."

"We?"

I glanced over at Ashley. "Yeah, we. Autumn's coming with me."

Mitch didn't even bother to ask why. Maybe he knew who she was. I didn't care at this point. I just needed to get to Mia before Joaquín tried to touch her, again.

We made a quick pit stop at my place to get my gun. As we drove up the coast, I considered what Ashley had said—that this was my fault for pulling that stunt. Well, if she hadn't lost sight of my son in the first place, I wouldn't have had to do it. It didn't matter who was to blame. I was going to fix it.

84

MIA

It took all my inner strength not to jump out of the truck when we stopped for gas in Santa Barbara. Pretending to like Grant as Ksenya had been easy. I was in love with Grant; I'd just been pretending to be another woman. But pretending to have amorous feelings for my brother was completely different—I had to pretend he was another man.

"Where's Julián? How do you know where he is? You've been in jail."

"He's safe. That's all you need to know. I always told them to go to a certain place if Grant came knocking around."

Damn it. I'd hoped that in an effort to seduce me, Joaquín would be more open with me. But he was controlling every aspect of our road trip.

"Okay. Where are we going?"

"To unwind, relax. I've been locked up for seven months. I want to be alone with you."

Fuck. I would not sleep with him; I would kill him first. But luckily, he'd promised to give me time. But . . . my son. Where was he? This was my only hope to find him.

Joaquín leaned over the truck as he pumped gas, and I noticed the outline of a gun in his pants. Of course he was armed. It would be more shocking if he wasn't carrying. His lawyer must've hooked him up.

But I was armed, too. The gun was in my purse. But who was I kidding?

Despite my training, I was no match for Joaquín. Grant and Mitch could take him, but not me.

Mitch was supposed to be following us, but Joaquín being released early had fucked up Grant's entire plan. Joaquín had destroyed my phone and brought me in a vehicle they weren't tracking.

Mitch won't have a clue where I was, until Grant is released. Grant had given me this ring, and when he's free, the ring will lead him to me.

Joaquín climbed back into the seat, and we headed up the coast. I'd imagined this reunion so many times, but it had never ever been like this. I didn't know what to say; anything that came to my mind seemed wrong. So, I kept my mouth shut and stared at the ocean.

After a few hours of listening to music, Joaquín exited toward Carmel-by-the-Sea, and my stomach twisted a bit. Mama and Papa would always bring us here in the summers, and Joaquín and I would spend our days rolling in the sand dunes and our nights gazing at the stars. We'd raced our remote-control cars up and down the sidewalks and had spent hours at the Monterey Aquarium. It had been one of our happy places.

How would he ruin this memory?

When Joaquín turned toward a cottage on the beach, my heart raced. "Where are we staying?"

"Daniel has a place he's letting me borrow. I need to clear my mind. The only good thing about being in jail is that I wasn't force-fed all that media bullshit. I spent so much time alone, wrestling with my feelings and figuring shit out. It gave me time to realize what would make me happy. It's not being a SEAL or having money or getting high. It's you. You're all I need, Mia. I'm gonna show you how much I fucking love you."

I had to separate who I thought he once was from who he actually was. He'd been different for years, but I had been blinded to his dark side. My soul ached. How could I feel compassion for this monster? He'd raped me, kidnapped my son, and murdered a woman. And possibly my parents. There was something wrong with him. He needed to get help. I just wished he had received the therapy he had needed before his life spun out of control.

I couldn't say these things. My son's life depended on my compliance.

Instead, I took his hand in mine. "Let's get dinner at the Mexican restaurant that Mama and Papa loved. And then we can get ice cream and stop by my favorite gallery. Just like old times."

He pulled in front of the house and grasped my face, kissing me again. "I fucking love you. You're so incredible. I'll love you until the day I die, until I take my last breath. Listen, Grant will love another woman. But I won't, Mia. You're the only woman for me."

His words were choked with emotion, and for the third time today, I burst into tears. What had happened to him? It couldn't have just been my parents' lies that drove him to this madness—there had to have been something else that had triggered him. He'd been such a great brother to me, he'd been such a happy boy, when did he crack?

Lies. Lies destroyed everything. For the first time I saw that. My lies destroyed Grant, Joaquín's lies destroyed me and my son, and my parents' deception destroyed Joaquín.

A crushing feeling enveloped my chest. I knew in my soul that this would be the last time I would ever be with my brother. This would not end well. One or both of us would end up dead once he realized that I had no feelings of romantic love for him.

But for this moment, for tonight, I would hold on to him and our childhood dreams as I bid my long goodbye to my brother.

85

GRANT

That ring tracker had traced Mia and Joaquín up the California coast. Mitch was closing in on them, but I was still speeding to try to catch up.

The phone rang, and I picked up. "Yeah, where are they?"

"In Carmel. Parked in some driveway near the beach."

"Okay. I'm a couple hours away. Keep watch on them."

"I am, but man, hey. They were just kissing in the truck. How far are we going to let this get before we take him out? He'll probably rape her again."

Dammit, why had I taken this call on Bluetooth? Ashley glared at me with a look that screamed, "She's fooling you." Fuck her.

"Mia has a gun. She won't let that happen. I'll be there soon. Just keep your eyes on them."

"Okay, man. Let me know when you're close. I'm texting you the address now."

Ashley opened her mouth "Grant—"

"Stop. I don't want to hear it."

But she didn't stop. "No. Listen to me. She's playing you."

Fuck this bitch. "No, I fucking told you. Joaquín is a psychopath, and Mia is doing what she has to do to make sure he doesn't fucking kill her. Or our son. Joaquín is crazy and has nothing to lose. Nothing. What the fuck do you expect her to do? Tell him off? He kidnapped her."

A few hours later, I pulled up to the address Mitch had given me. I quickly located Mitch and hopped into his truck, unfortunately with Ashley in tow.

I slammed the truck door, and Ashley climbed in the back.

Mitch did a full eye fuck on Ashley. "Why's she here exactly?"

Apparently he didn't know she was NCIS. "She bailed me out of jail." That wasn't actually a lie.

He turned to Ashley. "You clean up nice. Though I prefer your rhinestone thong and thigh highs."

She smiled and batted her eyelashes at him. "Maybe I'll give you a private show later."

Damn, Autumn was back.

Mitch licked his lips. "I'd like that, baby doll."

I ignored them and pointed at the house. "Have they been here all this time?"

"No. They went downtown. Grabbed some food, stopped at a touristy store and then did some window shopping. Even shared an ice cream cone." Mitch's voice dripped with sarcasm.

Ashley touched Mitch's shoulder. "What flavor, big boy?"

Mitch's brow cocked. "Mint chocolate chip. Want me to buy you some? I'd love to lick it off your pussy."

Ashley laughed, and there wasn't a hint of her previous disdain for him in it.

"Hey, if you two want to go fuck, that's fine. I prefer to operate alone."

"Whatever, dude. See for yourself." Mitch handed me some binoculars. We were four houses down, but with Mitch's optic equipment, I might as well have been sitting inside the house with Joaquín and Mia. Good thing I wasn't because I would've strangled him.

Once the lens focused, I saw exactly what I didn't want to see. Joaquín and Mia cuddled on the sofa, watching something on television. He had his arm around her shoulders and was stroking her hair, and she was snuggled into his chest.

My mouth filled with a bitter tang, and I closed my eyes, praying to erase the image of them together. Like a fucking rubbernecker, I couldn't help myself from opening my eyes and taking another peek.

And there it was. Joaquín was kissing my wife, his sister. His hand touched the top of her breast, and it took every inch of my self-control not to reach into my holster and put a bullet through his head. I could've made the shot from a mile away.

I handed the binoculars back to Mitch, who willingly gave them to Ashley.

Ashley squinted. "She seems into it to me. She just touched his face."

"Just fucking watch them and stop speculating. This isn't some fucking reality show you're viewing—this is my life."

Was I wrong? Was Mia some sort of psycho in love with her brother?

She hadn't been convinced of his guilt when I last saw her.

Could Ashley be right?

Mia was snuggling on the sofa and appeared very intimate with Joaquín.

No. No. I knew my wife. She was a warrior, strong, and capable. She was willing to do anything for her family. And I knew that she was risking her life to save our son.

86

MIA

Tequila. I needed Tequila.

I decided that getting Joaquín drunk was the best option. After we walked around town, I stopped at the liquor store and bought a bottle of Don Julio Blanco. He'd been jailed for seven months; he'd definitely want to cut loose and get wasted.

I tried to pretend that Joaquín loved me only as a sister and that we had been reunited after a long deployment. It worked for the most part. We ate enchiladas suizas from our favorite cantina, indulged in ice cream, hit up a store to get a change of clothes and toiletries, and then strolled through the galleries.

Back at the cottage, Joaquín started a fire. Even though it was the middle of summer, the thick Carmel fog made the night air chilly. We watched television on the sofa, where he gave me a few kisses. I was completely grossed out but kept telling myself this was just like a love scene.

He stood and placed blankets in front of the hearth. "Come here, babe."

Babe? Fuck. I walked over to him and lay beside him, staring at the embers. "It's so beautiful here. I just wish we could go back to the way we were. With Mama and Papa. We were so happy."

Joaquín turned toward me, his eyes radiating anger. "Fuck them, Mia. They lied to us. They fucked me up. Dad beat me within an inch of my life when he caught me staring at you and then kicked me out of the house. I had no choice but to join the Navy. I was only seventeen."

I remembered the night Joaquín had left, his face bloody, his nose broken. Papa had told me that Joaquín was involved in a fight, but he wouldn't let me go see if my brother was okay. The next day, he was gone. I never even got to tell him goodbye.

"I never knew he was the one who hit you. I had no idea why you were in such a rush to join the Navy. They told me some guy was bullying you and you just wanted to leave so you took the GED and joined. I was hurt that you didn't tell me yourself."

"I couldn't. They wouldn't let me. I was just a teen, and they tried to deprogram me. The mind doesn't work like that. You can't tell someone to stop thinking about someone, or to stop lusting after someone. No matter how hard I tried, I couldn't deny it. They deserved everything they got."

My blood chilled. "Joaquín, did you have anything to do with their deaths? I need you to tell me."

He looked at the fire. "I wished them dead. Out loud. And someone made my wish come true."

My breath hitched, and he must have heard it because his eyes turned back to me. I was playing a part. I had to calm down. Plus, he wouldn't have brought me all the way here just to kill me.

I took one of my yoga breaths and said a sil*ent prayer. Please keep my son safe from thi*s monster.

Joaquín kissed my hand. "I did it for you, Mia. I did it for us. Without them, nothing stood in the way of us being together."

I held back my tears, refusing to let him see me cry. How could I have never seen how disturbed he was?

He didn't press me any further, and before I knew it, the warmth of the fire overtook him and he drifted to sleep. I considered taking the keys and running away from him, but then I would never find my son.

***

I woke the next morning and found Joaquín sitting on the deck staring at the ocean. I sat next to him. "Hey. Will you take me to see our son? I just need to hug him. Please?"

"Sure. But we can't take him with us. I'm only on bail; I could be re*charged anytime."*

*Especially si*nce you are guilty.

I kept that thought to myself. "Where is he?"

"Get ready, and we'll go."

I brushed my teeth and pulled my hair into a ponytail. With my hair back to my natural color, I looked more like myself, which was a small comfort in all this chaos. I wasn't the same person I was a year ago, though. I was stronger, relentless. I wouldn't give up.

When I emerged from the bathroom, Joaquín was staring at me. He pulled me against him. "If I take you to see him, you need to do something for me."

He didn't need to say what he wanted from me. His hand on my ass told me everything I needed to know. I ran my fingers through his hair. "I'll do whatever you ask if you take me to see him."

He released me and went to get ready himself. I went to the front porch and saw a truck a few houses down.

Mitch's truck. Luckily, Mitch had purchased this truck after his divorce so Joaquín wouldn't recognize it. There were three people inside, and I didn't need to see their faces to know one of them was Grant.

I wanted to run to him, but I didn't dare. Instead, I raised my hand just a bit and waited. The driver flashed the lights just as Joaquín came out, and I was forced to turn away. Acting casual, I followed Joaquín to his truck, knowing Grant would follow.

Three hours later we were back in my hometown of Marin and pulling in to a small apartment complex in the Canal.

Joaquín opened the truck door. "Wait here."

I nodded, and he went to an apartment and came back in a few minutes with an older Mexican man. Joaquín got back into the truck. "Julián is at the neighbor's apartment for a playdate so you won't have to worry about the grandma recognizing you. Tomás will take you over to meet him."

"You're not going to come?" Not that I wanted him to.

"Nope. Look, we can have other kids. But it's best if we forget about Julián. His existence gives me a motive to have killed Tiffany. I'm going *to let you say goodbye to him.*"

Fuck you. The only person I'm going to say goodbye to is you.

"I understand. He doesn't even know us."

I scanned the parking lot, looking for Mitch's truck, but it wasn't there.

And no other vehicle entered the parking lot. After ten minutes, Tomás opened my door, and I followed him to a third-floor apartment, which was apparently his since he just walked right in. Tomás greeted the woman standing in the kitchen with a kiss. He motioned me over to the sofa.

Again I nodded, but before I could sit down, Julián ran out of the other room dressed as a superhero. He was holding a little girl's hand.

All I saw in his perfect face was Grant. The strong cleft in his chin, the devilish grin. How had I not seen it before? Had Joaquín ignored this strong resemblance? Well, he clearly hadn't seen him in a while and Julián's features must've become more developed. I shuddered. If Joaquín looked at my boy now, it would be clear that Julián was Grant's son, not his. I wanted to scoop my boy up and run away. But I couldn't, I had to wait. I knew that if I could buy myself enough time, Grant would be here.

Tomás handed me a bag of weed. This fake drug deal was a cover for my being in this apartment. My son was being babysat by a drug dealer.

My hand grasped the outline of the gun in my purse. I could grab my son and run, but where would I go? Julián ran into another room, and I forced myself to thank Tomás as he ushered me out almost as quickly as I came in.

Fuck.

He escorted me back to my brother. I sat next to him, and he locked the door and drove away.

Tears welled in my eyes as the distance betwee*n my son and me grew greater an*d greater.

Please, Grant, please find him.

87

GRANT

Joaquín and Mia sped away from the complex as we pulled in from across that street. I had the target, the tall guy who'd walked Mia out of the complex. I prayed the second that we drove into Marin that Joaquín was taking Mia to meet Julián and for once luck was on my side.

My son was somewhere in that building, and I wasn't leaving without him.

Ashley grabbed my arm. "No, Grant. Let's wait. I'll call the FBI. Once we get a warrant—"

Mitch's head whipped around. "Warrant? Who the fuck do you think you are?" he yelled at her.

She spat at him. "I'm NCIS Special Agent Ashley Pierce."

Mitch's eyes bugged. "Holy shit."

"It's true, man." I narrowed my eyes at Ashley. "But fuck you, Ashley. My son is being held hostage by some thugs. I'm not waiting for the feds. You want to arrest me? Go right ahead. I'll be back in three minutes with my kid. Be prepared to drive or get the fuck out of the vehicle if you don't want to be involved. Mitch, let's roll."

Mitch parked, and he and I exited the vehicle. Ashley stayed behind, which was fine by me.

The guy was walking up the stairs, and Mitch and I followed him. When the man approached a door, Mitch slammed his ass to the ground, kicked him once in the ribs and then once in the jaw, knocking him out cold. I busted open the door, my gun surveying the space.

A lady screamed, but I wasn't here for her. I scanned the room and saw my little boy, dressed as a superhero, standing in the corner screaming. I scooped him into my arms and was out the door as quickly as I'd entered.

Mitch and I dashed down the stairs, piled into the truck, and Ashley stepped on the gas.

I secured my weapon and hugged my screaming son. "Hey, hey buddy. I'm your daddy. It's okay. I'm a good guy."

I didn't have a clue if he understood me. He continued to wail, but Mitch and I attempted to calm him down. After a few minutes, my son wrapped his arms around my neck, and I held him tighter than I'd ever held anyone.

Ashley drove straight to the police station and didn't bother finding a parking spot before cutting the engine.

By this time, Julián's screams had turned into sobs. Yet when Ashley tried to take him from my arms, he clung tighter.

"There, there it's okay. You're going to be fine. We've been looking for you." She turned to me. "I need to take him inside and call the FBI, my office, and Child Protective Services." She placed her hand on my shoulder. "You go find your wife. I hope you're right about her, but if not, do what you have to do."

I knelt in front of my boy, Mia's eyes staring back at me. "I'm your daddy. I love you. I'm not sure if you understand me, but I need you to be brave like a superhero until I come back. Can you do that for me?"

He nodded as his tears continued to track down his face.

"This is Ashley. She's going to take care of you. I'm going to get your mommy." I gave him a final kiss and hugged him.

And with that, she carried my son into the police station. I didn't want to let him out of my sight, but I didn't have a choice. I needed to go save my wife.

Mitch stared at his phone. "Any idea where he would take her? The tracking shows up somewhere near Mill Valley?"

I smiled. I was this close to ending this nightmare, once and for all. "Mt. Tam. Let's roll."

88

MIA

I knew exactly where we were going as I turned to face Joaquín for the first time since leaving the complex.

"Did you know that the day I found the key was the first day in months I had hope to free you," I offered.

Joaquín grinned. "I didn't leave you the money so you could help me. I left it so I could take care of you."

"I know, but you had to have known I would do anything I could to get you out of jail."

"Well, I never thought you would go quite as far as you did. When Grant brought you to see me in jail, I thought you were smoking hot, but I had no idea it was you. Once you flashed the bracelet, you blew my mind. I couldn't believe you had done all of this for me. That was when I realized how much you loved me, and that I wasn't crazy. That what we have is real and that you felt it, too."

It was real. Our love was real, but it wasn't romantic love. I was smart enough not to point out that distinction, though.

We drove up the winding hill. I knew where we were headed, but I had no idea why he would bring me up here. He'd agreed to give me space, but he'd also asked me for something in return for seeing my son. I had no way to know for sure, so I kept my purse close to me when he finally pulled into the parking area.

My hands shook as we exited the truck. Joaquín put his arm around me and led me to the dirt patch. The same patch where we'd buried our time treasure years ago. The same patch where Grant had made love to me under the stars after telling me for the first time he loved me. The same patch where Joaquín had hid the safe deposit key. The same patch where Grant had proposed to me just last week.

This one spot held all my secrets, all my bliss, all my pain.

Joaquín stood next to me as we took in the view of the mountains. We were on top of the world, but still, I could feel him looking at me. Waiting.

"I need you to show me how much you love me," he whispered after what felt like a lifetime of silence. "I've given up everything for you. Sacrificed my career, my life. We have no one but each other. But I need to know that you feel the same way I feel about you. Prove to me how much you love me, *Angelita Mia*."

"I've never asked you to give up anything for me." I closed my eyes and tried to pull myself together. I had snapped at him, and even though he wasn't touching me, I could feel his anger spike. I forced myself to turn to him and lay a hand flat on his chest before turning my eyes to his. "You said you'd give me time."

And then his eyes narrowed as he focused on my right hand. "What's that on your finger?"

Fuck. My ring.

"Nothing, just a promise ring Grant gave me."

"A promise ring. What? Are you twelve? Show it to me."

I pulled it off, and he grabbed it from my hands.

"This is a fucking wedding ring. Did you marry him?"

"No," I lied.

His hand fisted around my ring. "You're lying to me. It isn't an engagement ring, either. I saw the one he bought for you years ago. This is a wedding band. You married him."

My chin quivered. "Yes. I did. The other day."

His teeth clenched. "You told me you loved me. That you didn't love him. How could you lie to me? You're playing me now. Does he know you're here?"

"Of course not. You've been with me the entire time. He's in jail."

"Show me, Mia. I don't believe you anymore. Show me that you love me." He held my eyes as he reached into his pants. Vomit raced its way up my throat, and I forced it down. If he pulled his dick out, I didn't know what I was going to do. When his hand rose again, I almost wished it held his dick instead of the gun he pointed at my temple. "Or we end it here. I don't believe you want me. If I can't have you, no one can. Take off your clothes."

"So, you would do that to me again? You would rape me? That isn't something you do to someone you love."

He didn't flinch. Fuck. He was crazy. Completely unhinged. The weight of my gun in my purse beckoned me, but by the time I reached for it, he would kill me.

He'd raped me once. I'd rather die than have him rape me again. At least that time, I had been passed out. I would never be able to get over this trauma.

"Now."

I slipped my T-shirt off my head and pushed my jeans down over my hips. I felt the burn of tears behind my eyes as humiliation, anger, and shame stormed through me.

He motioned toward my bra, and as I went to unhook it, Joaquín spun, pointing the gun at the two men who just stepped into the clearing.

At Grant and Mitch.

Thank fuck.

Grant approached us, his gun steady on Joaquín. "Put the gun down, Cruz."

I didn't give my brother a chance to choose his fate. I reached into my purse, grabbed my gun, aimed at my brother, and before I could talk myself out of it, pulled the trigger, aiming directly at his shoulder.

It was the perfect shot. Joaquín collapsed to the ground, dropping his own weapon, which Mitch quickly retrieved.

Grant ran over to Joaquín and pointed the barrel of his own gun at my brother's head.

"No!" I screamed. "No!"

I ran over to my brother, bleeding into the earth, and put myself between him and Grant. "Please, Grant. Please. Help him."

"Are you fucking kidding me? He just tried to kill me! And you! You just shot him. He raped you and kidnapped our kid."

"I know. . . I know." I sobbed. "But he's my brother. I love him."

"Dammit, Mia." Grant ripped off his own shirt and tied it around Joaquín's shoulder to stop the bleeding. "Call 911," he barked at Mitch.

Joaquín looked up at me. "I'm sorry, Mia. I love you. I just—"

"Shh. You're sick. You need help, not another bullet."

89

GRANT

I kept Joaquín from bleeding out until the paramedics and cops came. I wanted to canoe the motherfucker, but Mia had been through enough pain in her life. Mia, Mitch, and I gave statements to the police. Joaquín was placed under arrest for attempted murder, rape, and kidnapping. He was transported to a hospital and would be arraigned when he recovered.

I took Mia back to Mitch's truck.

"Are you okay? Did he hurt you?"

She shook her head. "No, he didn't."

I had to ask. "I saw you in Carmel. I saw you kiss him."

"Yeah, nothing more than that happened. I had to—I had to convince him I loved him. To find our son. Did you find him?"

"Yeah, he's at the police station." I didn't mention Ashley because I was still under strict orders not to reveal her identity to Mia.

"Now what?" Her body shook, and I wrapped her in my arms.

"Now we file for custody. I'm sure they're going to place Julián in a foster home until we have a hearing, but we will get him back soon. Let's check into a hotel and call a lawyer."

She nodded, and we didn't say a word as Mitch drove us down the mountain.

We checked into the Tiburon Lodge. Once we were alone, I needed to ask her a question. "Why didn't you kill him? Or let me?"

She gave a faraway glance. "Because he's sick. I know what he did was wrong, but he needs help. He'd been fighting his feelings for me for years and thought he was disgusting for feeling the way he did. I know it doesn't even come close to excusing his actions, or even remotely making them okay, but he needs help, Grant. He'll go to jail for the things he's done; he doesn't need to die. Enough people have been hurt in all of this."

I held Mia. I would never understand her devotion to Joaquín. But it didn't matter. We were safe. Joaquín would be locked away for years. And for the first time since she'd left me in the hospital years ago, I knew that she was finally mine forever and I would never lose her again.

90

MIA

TWO MONTHS LATER . . .

G rant clutched my hand outside the courthouse in Marin County. After official DNA tests, intensive therapy for Julián and me, parenting classes, and visits from social workers, we'd been awarded custody of our son. Turns out, Lorraine had known all along that Julián wasn't her grandson and had been receiving payments for years from Rafael, who had been involved in arranging his kidnapping. I wanted to beg the DA not to press charges against her, but I knew it would be no use. She had knowingly harbored a kidnapped victim, which made her an accessory to a crime.

But all I cared about now was that I was finally going to have my son. I was as excited as I was scared. As far as he knew, Tiffany was his mother, so how would he react to suddenly having a new mommy?

Grant sensed my fear. "You got this. You're going to be the best mother."

The social worker led us to a room, and after an excruciating ten minutes, she brought our little boy into the room. He was holding a teddy bear. I tried to speak but was overcome with emotion.

Grant knelt in front of him. "What's your bear's name?"

"Oso."

Grant talked through Oso in a deep bear voice. "Hi, Julián. Meet my friends. This is your daddy and your mommy. They love you very much."

Julián smiled and reached his arms out for a hug. I ran over to him and fell to my knees before gathering my son into my arms. Never in my wildest dreams did I think I would have my son and Grant back in my life, but here we were.

Against all odds.

One happy family.

I exhaled and then inhaled the smell of my son for the first time, letting it settle into my heart. When I had started this journey, I'd thought that the purpose of my transformation was to save Joaquín. But it wasn't. My road led me to save my son and save myself.

"Let's go home, buddy."

Grant and I walked out of the courthouse and drove back to San Diego.

Together.

To start the next chapter of our life.

EPILOGUE

On a beautiful winter day, Grant and I drove into the gates of San Quentin Prison. I had to beg Grant to let me visit Joaquín. Grant wanted us to move on, put this nightmare behind us, heal as a family. But no matter how awful Joaquín's crimes had been, he was still my brother.

As I gazed at the gorgeous Bay, I marveled at the irony that Joaquín would spend the rest of his days locked up in our hometown with some of the most notorious inmates in history.

After Joaquín had recovered from me shooting him, he'd been charged with kidnapping, rape, and second-degree murder. This time, he didn't even try to fight the charges. He had pled guilty, which was a huge relief because I didn't want to live through a trial.

"Are you sure you want to see him?"

"Yes."

Grant shook his head but didn't fight with me. We'd settled into our new life easier than I had imagined. Luckily, Grant hadn't deployed and was still on BUD/S instructor duty. I loved being a stay-at-home mommy for now. I finished my final course at SDSU and received my diploma and had started my masters in criminal justice. When Julián started preschool, I was thinking maybe one day I could work for NCIS.

Julián was thriving. We spent our days at the beach and at playdates with some of the other SEALs' kids. He loved going to work with his daddy. Grant was an amazing father. So kind and patient. I was truly blessed.

The guards opened the gates and led me to the sitting area to await my brother. Grant sat by my side, refusing to let me come here alone.

Joaquín shuffled out in his orange prison jumpsuit, obviously having adapted better to prison life than I thought he would. Grant and I were both certain he was part of a gang, and after Grant told me about the drug- smuggling investigation, I didn't question him. Neither of us knew if NCIS dropped their investigation or not, or if there were still some nefarious crimes haunting his SEAL Team.

Joaquín smiled when he saw me and even acknowledged Grant's existence with a nod.

"What's up, sis?"

"Not much. How are you?"

"Surviving." His eyes were heavy. My heart ached, feeling his loneliness. "I miss you."

"I miss you, too." And I did. I missed who he had been to me.

"Look, I need to apologize to you. For everything. For raping you—I see now that it was rape. And for arranging for Julián to be taken. I've been in therapy and I realize now how fucked up I was. I hope one day you can forgive me."

A big lump grew in my throat. Why hadn't he sought out therapy earlier, before it was too late? My parents should've forced him to go.

"You don't have to wait. I forgive you. I'm glad you're getting help. I wish, I just wish—" I rocked back and forth and Grant reached out and held my hand.

"I'm really sorry, Mia. If I could take it back I would."

I wanted to scream and break down. If only I could turn back time and help him. "Do you talk to anyone? On the outside?"

"I have some pen pals. This one chick is begging me to marry her."

What the fuck? "Seriously? Who?"

"Her name is Larissa. She started writing me when I was first arraigned. She's hot, but obviously crazy if she's in love with me. California is only one of four states to allow fuck visits, so maybe I should marry her."

Grant let out a laugh. "Do it, dude."

Damn. Well, women always loved Joaquín. "Well, I don't know. Maybe you should. I'm happy for you. I'm glad you have someone, someone you can talk to. I just wish . . . you could've found someone else earlier. Maybe everything would be different."

He smirked. "I'll always regret what I did, but I'll never regret loving you."

I bit my lip and choked back tears. I pressed my palm to the plexiglass and he pressed his hand back. "I'm not sure when I'm going to be able to come back. I'm in school and Grant's deploying. I need to be with Julián."

"It's okay. It means the world to me that you're still willing to visit me. I want you to know that I never wanted to hurt you."

"I know. Bye, Joaquín."

"Bye, Mia."

I watched him walk away and wept for the sweet boy he had been, the brother I had loved, and the man he could've been.

I never understood the saying "there is a thin line between love and hate" until the moment I held a wounded Joaquín in my arms. You can't turn love off. At least I couldn't. I remember listening to an interview of a woman whose son had murdered people in a mass shooting. She wept, and I couldn't imagine how she still loved her son.

But now, I knew.

I hated every bad thing Joaquín had ever done. He took everything from me and caused me unbearable pain, but sometimes, in my dreams, I remembered the little boy who had protected me from bullies, had held me when I feared the dark, had read me my favorite story over and over again.

Forgiveness is more powerful than love and hate. I made a decision not to live the rest of my life in a cog of what-ifs and regrets.

I took Grant's hand. "Let's get out of here."

I led him through the halls and out the prison's gates, promising to leave my past behind me and live for the future in front of us.

And I couldn't wait to live it.

THE END

SE7EN DEADLY SEALS SEASON 2

ASHLEY

"Pierce. There's been a shooting. Get down here immediately." My boss didn't waste time on pleasantries, not even when he called on my day off.

I hopped out of bed and threw on the first clean work clothes I could find. Where were my fucking heels? I dug for them under my bed, hobbled over to the coffee pot, and poured myself a stale mug of joe before nuking it.

I swiped through my phone and there it was.

"Navy SEAL dead."

Holy shit. I'd been avoiding SEALs since the Joaquín Cruz case. What a mind fuck that had been. The investigation into the drug smuggling was still ongoing, but I had recused myself from the case. I had gotten too close to crossing a line with Mitch, and I wasn't willing to put my career on the line for anyone.

I raced down to the location my superior had texted me. The BUD/S compound. After weaving between tourists on the bridge trying to catch the Coronado sunrise, I finally arrived.

After I flashed my badge at the gate and drove onto base, dread started to sink into my stomach. SEALs were the worst. Their codes of silence were impossible to break. And they would choose the brig before they flipped on another SEAL.

I joined the swarm of officers hovering outside and saddled up to the first familiar face I saw.

"Who was it?" I asked a fellow agent.

"The SEAL was Paul Thompson." Oh my God. He was Grant's superior officer. I scanned the men. No sign of Grant. But Mitch's face registered a look of amusement when he saw me.

His eyes undressed me as he approached. I might not put my career on the line for the guy, but it didn't stop me from eye fucking him right back. I couldn't help but stare at his massive arms and ripped chest underneath his dark blue instructor shirt.

"Good to see you again, *Autumn*. You going to crack this case, too?"

Son of a bitch. That cocky motherfucker. He represented everything I hated about SEALs.

"You bet. Who discovered him?"

He smirked. "I did." Then he whispered in my ear, "You might as well give up now, because I'm not going to tell you anything."

I exhaled. "Telling me nothing will only get you arrested on obstruction, Mitch. Paul was a fellow SEAL, I would think you would want his murderer brought to justice. Plus, I never take no for an answer."

He brushed my hair, and I slapped his hand away. "Then you and I have something in common, sweetheart. Neither do I."

Stay tuned for season two of Se7en Deadly SEALs
Releasing Early 2018

AUTHOR'S NOTE

Thank you for reading my book.
If you liked it, would you please consider leaving a review for *Se7en Deadly SEALs?*
For the latest updates, release, and giveaways, subscribe to *Alana's newsletter*.
For all her available books, check out Alana's *website* or *Facebook page.*

Follow me on *Bookbub*.

ALSO BY ALANA ALBERTSON

Want more romance?

Love Navy SEALS?

Meet Erik! I'm a Navy SEAL, a Triton, a god of the sea.

And she will never be part of my world. *Triton*

Meet Pat! I had one chance to put on the cape and be her hero. *Invincible*

Meet Kyle! I'll never win MVP, never get a championship ring, but some heroes don't play games. *Invaluable*

Meet Grant! She wants to get wild? I will fulfill her every fantasy. *Conceit, Chronic, Crazed, Carnal, Crave, Consume, Covet*

Meet Shane! I'm America's cockiest badass. *Badass* (co-written with *Linda Barlow*)

Love Marines?

Meet Grady! With tattooed arms sculpted from carrying M-16s, this bad boy has girls begging from sea to shining sea to get a piece of his action. *Beast*

Meet Bret! He was a real man—muscles sculpted from carrying weapons, not from practicing pilates. *Love Waltzes In*

Love Immortals?

My mad wish may cost me my soul. *The Picture of Dulce Garcia*

Who's haunting America's favorite ballet? *Snow Queen*

ABOUT THE AUTHOR

ALANA ALBERTSON IS the former President of RWA's Contemporary Romance Chapter. She holds a M.Ed. from Harvard and a BA in English from Stanford. A recovering professional ballroom dancer, she lives in San Diego, California, with her husband, two young sons, and five dogs. When she's not saving dogs from high kill shelters through her rescue Pugs N Roses, she can be found watching episodes of 48 Hours Mystery, Younger, or Dallas Cowboys Cheerleaders: Making the Team.

For more information:
www.authoralanaalbertson.com
alana@alanaalbertson.com

ACKNOWLEDGMENTS

¡Ay, Dios Mío! I can't believe I finally finished this series. I wanted to thank everyone who made it possible.

To Nicole Blanchard to listening to me whine about this series. Thanks for putting up with me.

Deb Nemeth—for always fitting Grant and Mia in and reading me the riot act when I wanted to nix their HEA.

Ashley Williams—Thank you for helping out Mia and Grant in their hours of need.

To my fabulous cover designer, Regina Wamba for these incredible covers.

Julie Titus—for your beautiful formatting, your warmth, and for always fitting me in.

To my audio team at Brick Shop: Jason Clarke & Jennifer O'Donnell for bringing Grant and Mia to life. To Rob Granniss for doing an excellent job producing the book.

To my husband Roger—for loving me in sickness and in health. Even when I'm writing all day in my fuzzy pajamas. For watching the boys while I write. For being my HEA.

To my two beautiful sons, Connor and Caleb. You are my world. I love you more than anything. To my two unborn daughters who I lost while writing this series and will never meet, I love you both and wanted you so much.

To my betas:

Jen Negron—you are the bomb. I adore you. Thank you for believing in my writing. I can't wait to read these books in Spanish.

Storm Bayraktar—thank you for your kind words and reading Carnal. #teamjoaquín!

To all the wonderful bloggers who review my books.

To all the fans that have written me about this series.